GIVE ME YOUR ANSWER TRUE

SUANNE LAQUEUR

CATHEDRAL ROCK PRESS

NEW YORK

2015

Suanne Laqueur/Cathedral Rock Press

Somers, New York

www.suannelaqueurwrites.com

Publisher's Note: This is a work of fiction. Names, characters, places, and incidents are a product of the author's imagination. Locales and public names are sometimes used for atmospheric purposes. Any resemblance to actual people, living or dead, or to businesses, companies, events, institutions, or locales is completely coincidental.

Book Interior Design & Typesetting © 2015 Write Dream Repeat Book Design

Give Me Your Answer True/ Suanne Laqueur. -- 1st ed.

ISBN 978-1508985211

For Julie,
who always thanks me for dinner.

"A human being with no daemon was like someone without a face, or with their ribs laid open and their heart torn out: something unnatural and uncanny that belonged to the world of nightghasts, not the waking world of sense."

—Philip Pullman, *The Golden Compass*

"We come back from war changed."

—Joseph Bianco

IN BROAD DAYLIGHT

THE DAY DAWNED BORED and looking for trouble, and Daisy woke up needing to get high.

Not a breath of air came in through the screened window of her room. The sunlight splashing across her bed was hot and sullen. Against her face, her boyfriend's back was cool and damp. Erik ran like an engine through the night. His sleep generated a dry thrumming heat that broke like a fever when he awoke. The hair at the back of his head divided into small, wet sections.

"What time is it?" he asked, his voice a croak.

Eyeballs clanging in her head, Daisy twisted back to look at the clock on her bedside table. "Ten after seven."

They both kicked the twisted, crumpled sheets away from their legs. Turned pillows to the cool side, rolled and rearranged and fell back asleep.

When Daisy awoke again, she knew the morning had slipped away and afternoon now closed around her room like an angry fist. Erik's shoulders pushed back against her belly and chest. His skin had dried. His hand ran along her thigh.

"What time is it?" he asked.

She looked. "Almost twelve-thirty."

"I need to turn that paper in by two."

Daisy set the back of her hand on her forehead, trying to think what she had to do in these last days of her college career. A couple of exams later in the week. Today, though, she needed...

I need to get high.

"God, I feel hungover," Erik said. He wasn't. Neither was she. They hadn't gotten high in a week. No coke, no pot, no ecstasy. And since sex went hand-in-hand with substance, they hadn't made love in the same amount of time.

Daisy was ambivalent to the loss of physical intimacy. Her brain, however, was a howling dog, craving a fix.

Erik crawled over her to get up. Daisy's eyes slid along his body with a tired appreciation. He still worked out every day, but he wasn't eating much lately. Wasn't feeding the muscle. His chest and arms were defined but his ribs showed.

He bent over, trawling the floor for his clothes. From the gold chain around his neck swung four small charms. A saint's medal. A fish. A boat with his surname, Fiskare, engraved on its flat bottom. And a tiny pair of scissors. The necklace was an heirloom he was never without.

He yawned as he dressed, tucking things in his pockets. He tugged on a shirt, ran hands through his dark blond hair. Then he sat on the edge of the bed and pulled Daisy to sit up so he could fold her in his arms.

"You feel all right?" he asked.

"I'm good," she said, lying.

They compared schedules to see where they overlapped but neither seemed to know what was going on. They left it with a vague reassurance they'd meet up at some point. Erik took her head in his hands and kissed her. Forehead. Each eyelid. Right cheek. Left. Then her mouth. Daisy curled her fingers around his left wrist, her thumb running along the daisy tattooed beneath the heel of his hand.

The fog lifted and she saw the golden beauty in his face, tasted the blend of tenderness and ferocity in his love. Her hand slid up the nape of his neck and she drew his forehead down on her shoulder.

"I love you," she said.

"I love us." He turned his head and breathed in deep against her neck. Then he left.

Daisy lay in bed, listening to Erik's footsteps thump down the stairs, followed by the slam of the screen door. She didn't move.

She'd missed ballet class this morning but she didn't care. She didn't care about anything anymore. She was defeated before she began. The day was a yawning chasm of danger and the only bridge across was getting high.

When the need threatened to split her apart, she got up, dressed and pulled her hair back. She walked out into the hot May afternoon with a fistful of twenties, leaving her little apartment on Jay Street and walking around the corner to David Alto's place.

She went looking for it.

Drugs, she insisted later. *I went looking to get juiced. I didn't go looking for sex.*

David was awake, wet-haired and wearing nothing but shorts. He used to be slightly chunky with bulky muscles. Now he seemed more whittled away than Erik. Not skin and bones but a slimness that came from stress and a drug-quelled appetite.

It wasn't unattractive.

He didn't seem surprised to see her. Squinting his bloodshot eyes against a ribbon of cigarette smoke, he batted her money away. "Wish I'd known you were coming, Marge. I already cut in."

"I want to roll anyway," she said, irritated by the nickname, David's version of her real name, Marguerite.

"In broad daylight?" he said, grinning. "I thought you only got ecstatic at night."

"I need it now," she said.

"I know, I know." His voice turned gentle and soothing. "It's hard."

He searched a couple pairs of shorts and a jacket before he found his magic box, in this case an old Advil bottle with the label half-scrubbed away. Daisy's palms started to sweat as he shook it like a maraca.

She hated it.

"Open your mouth and close your eyes," he said. "And you will get a big surprise."

She stared at him.

I hate you.

Her eyes closed and her lips parted. The seconds squeezed by. His mouth pressed hers. A dart of his tongue, depositing an ecstasy pill behind her bottom teeth.

She planted her hand in his chest and pushed him away. "You're an asshole," she said, and swallowed.

"Gotcha," he said, still grinning.

He sat on the couch, cutting the last bit of cocaine into a tiny line. Daisy sat a cushion away and put a foot on the coffee table. As she listened to the crisp sound of the razor's edge on glass, the high began to roll over her scalp and trickle down the back of her neck. She closed her eyes, wondering who was the first person to refer to an ecstasy high as rolling.

She opened her eyes. Her eyelids were thick. Numb tongue. Numb lips. The euphoria slid around her body like tectonic plates, locking her into place. Confidence across her shoulders, security bolstering her stomach, self-assuredness like a cape. Warm wonderful in her head. She was all right now.

David sat back, sniffing and shivering.

"God," he said. "I love it and it hates me."

He laced his hands behind his head and shut his eyes a moment. Then he turned his head toward Daisy and his fingers moved in slow motion through the air. They touched the scars on her calf. Two raised vertical lines running from knee to ankle on both sides.

"Do they hurt?" he asked.

"Bits of them. This part here is numb. You could put a cigarette out on it. This part here is really sensitive, especially to hot and cold."

She had rolled all the way over. She was flying now, transfixed by her own voice.

David's fingers walked along her scar. "I dreamed about you last night."

"Oh?"

He touched one of the sensitive parts and her skin twitched. Her long-sleeved T-shirt was too hot on her back and chest while the fan blew too cool on her legs.

"Nothing special," David said. "Just you lying in a pool of blood on the stage. Crying for me to make it stop. Make it stop, David, please make it stop."

He smiled at her startled expression. "That's the only way I dream about you now. Doesn't that suck, Marge? I can't even dream about you. It's like I'm not allowed anything good anymore."

She nodded, allowing him to touch her leg. He caressed the gunshot wound, a starburst pucker of skin above her left knee. She swallowed. Her throat was dry but her mouth was watering.

"It's almost over," David said. "Nobody can wait to get the fuck out of here. Graduate and blow this joint. I feel like I want to go home, but I have nowhere to go. Only a few more weeks and everybody will scatter."

"We'll stay in touch." The high was crystallizing. Daisy's thoughts were like ice.

"No we won't." His palm pressed her scar, sliding up her thigh. The ice was getting sticky. "If Fish has any sense, he'll get you as far away from here as he can."

Fish was Erik. His last name, Fiskare, meant fisherman in Swedish.

"You mean far away from you," Daisy said. Sticky ice in her head. Strong hands on her legs. Nipples growing hard in her bra. A damp aching pulse beneath her skirt.

It felt good.

"I'd like to see anyone keep me away from you…"

I should go.

I'll go.

I'll just feel it a little bit and I'll go.

Just a taste.

"Just a taste," David whispered. Her eyes flew open as her thoughts became sound. He pushed her skirt up. No doubt he could smell her. He'd found her out.

"David, don't."

"We'll all scatter. You won't see me again. Just give me my dreams back." His fingers slid beneath the leg holes of her underwear. He was touching her. In places belonging only to Erik. This couldn't happen. She was private property.

She was so high.

She was so hot. So aware of the heat and the cold.

And numb.

"I'm going," she said, pressing her eyes shut and then open again. Sticky eyes. Trying to break out of her own skull.

"Stay," he said. "For a minute. You're so soft. You're the only soft, pretty thing I know anymore."

"I'll leave you the cash," she said through a thick, damp mouth.

"I don't want your money."

"I don't have anything else to give."

He touched where she was wet. "You have everything I want."

Just a little taste.

"I want it so bad..."

His finger hooked the leg of her underwear and pulled it aside. The fan blew cool. She could smell his wet hair as his head dipped. His cheek brushed the inside of her thigh where the blood raced through her grafted artery. His tongue. Velvet. Soft. Wet. He was tasting her. That should be enough. She needed to go.

She couldn't move. Desire paralyzed her. His tongue. Oh, his tongue. Her pores screamed out for it. Her hands wanted to grab his head and push his mouth deeper. Harder. Feel his teeth. He'd be rough with her. He'd do anything for her. She only had to ask.

I don't care.

It's all going to scatter.

David on his knees between her calves. The fingers of one hand sliding deep inside her. The fingers of the other reaching into the baggie on the coffee table and pinching a bit of sticky snow. Holding it to her nose. She breathed in sharp and quick.

"I hate you," she said.

"I know." His fingers reached deeper. "Everyone hates me."

Hate was good. Pain was good. Erik wouldn't fuck her hard anymore and lovemaking made them sick and afraid. She'd been numb since the last time. Now she was alive and on fire and wet and high. So high and sticky and bad. She didn't care.

"I hate what I am," she said. The truth was delicious in her mouth. Her shoulders relaxed in liberated relief. Sitting on David's ratty old couch, her skirt hiked up and her thighs open, high and slovenly with her scars on display and her true colors exposed. The stupid maw between her legs that had one job to do and blew it. A useless black vein of ugliness. Like the nothingness of the nightmares that had been haunting her since she was shot last year.

Maybe her nightmares were her truth.

I hate what's dark in me.

"Make it stop, David," she whispered.

His eyes flared wide. "Oh, honey," he said, pulling her up in his arms. "I'd do anything."

The breeze from the ceiling fan blew on her face. She could taste herself in David's mouth. See her ugly pain reflected in his eyes. She could let it out, let it spill and she didn't care what he thought. Didn't care if she pleased him or made him proud. He wasn't hers to keep safe. Not hers to save. She hated him. His coke and his nastiness and sarcasm. David showing her how to roll high and come to pieces. Making her need it so bad, she'd fuck him to get it.

They were up in his room now, a small tight room redolent with cigarette smoke, dirty laundry and an unmade bed. Not Erik's oasis of neat, clean order. It was a hole. It smelled.

"You're gross," she said.

He kissed her but he tasted of her juice and cigarettes and she turned her mouth away. She took her own clothes off. If he thought he was getting the hot dancer's body of his dreams, he was dead wrong. She was twenty-one years old and looked like a bony old woman. Scraped and bruised.

An ugly, cowardly mess.

He could have it.

She pushed dirty clothes aside and lay down, waiting with an almost bored passion as he put a condom on.

Take it. Take all this dark away.

And if you can't, then make it darker.

Later, when she could bear to think about it, she recalled his smile. She remembered the lift of his cheekbones and the flash of his teeth in the dim light. David's face in her hands while he was on top of her and inside her.

"Oh, God," he said. "Daisy..."

She didn't recognize her name. Didn't recognize herself under this boy. *David of all people. Strange.*

"You feel so good," he said, his voice strangled with pleasure.

She did? She couldn't feel him at all.

"Come on top of me," he whispered. "I always wanted to see you up over me."

He hooked an arm around her waist and rolled down to his back, pulling her along. Her hair got caught under his shoulder. A cry of annoyance as she tugged it free. David laughed.

"You're such an asshole," she said, spitting hair out of her face and tossing it back from her shoulders.

And then she saw Erik standing in the doorway.

WHAT I FEEL HAS NO NAME

IN THE MIDDLE

"WHY DON'T YOU start from the beginning?"

Daisy stared at the woman sitting across from her. "Because I like starting in the middle."

She felt foolish as soon as the words left her mouth. She was twenty-four years old. Snotting back like a sullen teenager served no purpose.

"Sorry," she said. "I'm so tired. And I don't have much of a filter lately."

The woman tilted her chin, her smile was understanding. She had a head of salt-and-pepper curls, parted on the extreme side and anchored behind her ears. Her glasses looked expensive and trendy but the rest of her looked second-hand thrift. Despite it being January, her feet were bare in worn, scuffed Birkenstocks. The orange toenail polish was chipped.

Her name was Rita Temple. She was Daisy's third therapist in five weeks.

"What happened with the previous two?"

"I couldn't connect," Daisy said. "The first one... He was at the hospital. Maybe it was because he was a man. I don't know. But I walked into his office the first time and it felt horrible. The air in the room was so oppressive. And it had such a clinical smell. It was an office, like this, but it reeked of alcohol and disinfectant. I felt like I was in a gown on the exam table, waiting to get a shot." She shrugged, embarrassment uncomfortably warm along her cheekbones. "I had an instinctive reaction to both the space and him. I gave it a second chance but the same thing happened."

"People have instincts for a reason," Rita said.

"The second therapist, Dr. Reilly, she was nice. I saw her a few times."

"This was also at the hospital?"

"Yeah, but she came to my room. Not that my room was all that great a space, but at least I had some of my things around me. I still felt like I couldn't connect. She was so quiet. And I know…" She held up her hand to stop any verbal traffic. "I know I'm supposed to talk and you're supposed to listen. I think I'm looking for a therapist with a streak of big sister. Someone a little tough."

"Why tough?"

Daisy looked down at her take-out coffee cup. "I don't know." But a little entity within her turned from its prim wooden chair facing the corner, lifted its woebegone face and whispered, *I've been such a bad girl.*

"Sounds like you want to be told off," Rita said. "Or punished."

Daisy rolled her lips in and blinked back the threat of tears. "I fucked up," she said. "I've fucked up my life so bad."

She sniffed hard, scraped her fingernail against a stain on her pant leg then looked around the room. The walls were painted a soft grey, silvery and warm, like sable. She had a weird impulse to run her hand along the surface, sure it would have a nap.

The knick-knacks adorning the end table looked personal and significant. A bowl of sea glass and several small, corked bottles containing sand and labeled with names of beaches. Books lined the shelves like multi-colored bricks, most battered and creased, obviously read and consulted many times.

"See anything you like?" Rita said.

"A lot of children's books stuffed between the professional ones." Daisy pointed. "The *Betsy-Tacy* series. And what looks like every Maurice Sendak book ever written."

"I'm a huge fan."

"And something smells like lemon, and lavender."

"The bowl on the table has both. Does it remind you of something?"

"Home."

"Where is home?"

"My parents' house in Pennsylvania. They have a little farm and orchard. My mother grows herbs. In summer she'll have bunches of lavender hanging all over to dry, lemon verbena and mint. Her family was all perfumers. Except her, she was a dancer. Like me."

"Where do you dance?"

"With the Metropolitan Opera Ballet. I've been on leave since December. When I went into the hospital..."

The silence pulled tight. Daisy reached to the bowl, crushed lavender buds between her fingers and wished for a cigarette.

"While I was out, one of the tenors died," she said. "Richard Versalle. Right onstage in *The Makropulos Case.* He was climbing a ladder, singing the opening aria... Had a heart attack and fell twenty feet to the stage. Dead." She shook her head. "I don't know what any of that has to do with my little breakdown."

"Here's a tip, and this will apply to any therapist you may choose to work with: don't worry about relevance. The first few months of therapy are about spilling your guts. Good, bad, ugly and incoherent. Because you won't know what's relevant or isn't until it's all in front of you."

"More is more," Daisy murmured, not sure how she felt about *months.*

"Exactly. The plan is you spill and I sort. If you decide to stay, that is."

Mulling over the plan, Daisy thought about taking her shoes off and pulling her feet under her. No sooner did she think it when Rita kicked off one of her own sandals and drew that foot up beneath her knee.

"Try to find a beginning," Rita said. "Or just start somewhere. We can go backward or forward, it doesn't matter." She had a marble composition notebook in her lap. She opened it now, clicked the end of her pen.

"I love that sound," Daisy said. "When the spine of a new book cracks."

Rita smiled. "So do I."

"So," Daisy said. "It could start six weeks ago when I started cutting myself."

She paused for a reaction, but Rita only kept writing.

"Or," Daisy said, puzzled, "I could start two weeks prior when a broken window triggered some kind of flashback."

"A flashback to?"

"To when I got shot."

Now she waited for Rita to show a startled expression. To gasp or say "Oh my goodness."

Silence except for the scratch of pen on paper.

"Or maybe I should start the day of the shooting," Daisy said, now throwing whatever she could think of in a careless volley. "Or when I cheated on my boyfriend and destroyed my life. Or when I started doing drugs, because I was high when I cheated on him. But the drugs started after the shooting so it really goes back to then. I guess it has to start with the shooting. But really it starts with Erik."

"Erik was your boyfriend?"

Daisy nodded. "He was my life. My life started with him. And I fucked up and he left and I deserved it. But I can't leave. I can't leave it and it won't leave me and I don't know what to do anymore."

She exhaled and took a sip of coffee. Then sat up choking as hot liquid dribbled over her chin.

"Dammit."

Through the monologue Rita had been taking notes. Her eyebrows went up and down. She gave short, brief nods, sometimes with a twist of her bottom lip. A terse sound of agreement in her throat, or a more lyrical "Hmmm." Now she looked up, pen still poised over the pages.

"This is good," she said.

Daisy's own eyebrows rose. A first. She'd expected more non-verbal invitations, not praise for the mess she had made of her life.

"Glad you like it," she said, smiling as she ran her singed tongue along the roof of her mouth.

"Basically, you've given me a story in reverse," Rita said. Her smile was broad as she turned her notebook upside-down and squinted at it. "Now how about we turn it around?"

Tears sprang to Daisy's eyes. She could feel her heart press against the inside wall of her chest in a terrible longing to be free. The little penitent gazed hopefully from its chair in the corner.

Please turn it around.

The unexpected simplicity of it stole her breath. The cup trembled in her hands. "I want to turn it around," she said. "I hurt so much and I can't... I've tried everything."

Rita put the end of her pen between her teeth. Behind her glasses, her eyes were kind. But something was mischievous in her expression. "You haven't tried me."

Daisy pressed the back of her hand into one damp eye, then the other. Something in her reached across the expanse of carpet and plugged into Rita Temple's socket. A small current began to thrum in her chest.

"When did you graduate college?" Rita asked.

"Nineteen ninety-three." Nearly three years ago. It felt like two decades.

"From?"

"It was a fine arts school outside Philadelphia." Why was she being coy? Was this the final test to decide if she'd come back again?

Rita intertwined her fingers and set them down on her notebook. "Were you at Lancaster?"

Daisy put her cup down, heeled off her shoes and pulled both feet up. She drew one of the throw pillows into her lap, hugging the chocolate-brown chenille to her stomach.

"Yes," she said.

PARTNER BOTH SIDES

PROFESSOR MARIE DEL'AMICI headed the ballet department at Lancaster University. Although 1989 marked her fifteenth year in America, she still spoke a mix of broken English and technical French, overlaid with a thick Italian accent that teetered on the verge of unintelligible. She had little memory for names, lumping most of the student body under "darling" or "caro." If fond of you, she would recall your name but either butcher it or convert it to the nearest Italian equivalent.

"Margarita, darling," she said now, snapping her fingers and beckoning to Marguerite Bianco, one of the freshmen students. "Vieni qui. I want to see you dance with Wheel. Wheel, caro, come."

Wheel was Will Kaeger, a Canadian sophomore. Marguerite hadn't any personal interaction with him yet. Only observed his astonishing skills in class and heard him speaking fluent French around the student lounge. She also overheard him claiming Native American blood on his mother's side. He looked like a warrior: six feet two inches tall, straight-spined and proud, with tattooed arms and dark hair falling to his broad shoulders.

Shoulders back and spine straight, Marguerite walked closer to him on the hard blocks of her pointe shoes. A lifetime of ballet training made acting confident second nature. Still, her stomach did a slow, wary somersault. Will Kaeger was gorgeous, with a magnificent and uncompromising presence. A pressing-essence, she thought, as they shook hands. It leaned against her in a way that made her feet feel too big.

"Daisy," Will said, around a rubber band held tight in his teeth. His hands scraped his hair back into a thick tail. "Right? I hear your friends call you that."

"Yes."

"Daisy, short for Marguerite," he said. "I get it. Is your family French?"

"My parents. I was born here."

"Tu parles français?"

"Oui." Hands on her hips, she went up on her pointes. Shifting her weight from foot to foot, she stretched first one arm, then the other across her body.

"Bon." Will's hair was secure now and he reached a hand to her. "Viens danser."

Come dance.

Keeping up a patter of conversational French, he engaged her in a few simple movements and she followed where he led. Taking and releasing each other's weight, getting a feel for one another's balance and center. And although neither knew it yet, laying a foundation of trust, the bedrock of their partnership for the next three years.

Most of Daisy's previous experience with partner work involved uncertain boys holding her too hard or not hard enough. A lot of grabbing, falling, fumbling and misunderstanding. A lot of hard work, the end result never satisfying, never looking how she expected a pas de deux to look.

But within a minute of dancing with Will, Daisy knew he was different. Although he dwarfed her in height, their bodies were proportioned the same. When he proffered his palm, it was exactly where she needed it to be. Excitement began to pulse along her veins. He was not only confident, but competent. His hands were strong but they didn't grab. They felt like an extra pair of her own hands.

She went into arabesque—on one leg with the other straight behind—and he took her waist, moved her back and forth over her supporting leg, experimenting with her center of gravity.

"Here?" he said, squinting in the mirror. "No. More here, this is your axis."

"Right there," she said, perfectly balanced, pulling up out of her waist and letting her arms float free. Not knowing where she stopped and he began was a thrilling sensation. Their reflection made the pretty picture she'd always imagined. She smiled, feeling all the years of training coalesce and click. *This* was ballet.

She brought her pointes together, feet crossed tight. Will moved her like a metronome from side to side, catching her lightly in one elbow then the other. Letting her fall further with each pendulum swing, holding off on catching her until the last second. She closed her eyes, trusting him.

"You're easy," he said.

"Don't tell my father."

He laughed and let her fall low, arching back in his arms this time, her head nearly to the floor. The blood rushed to her face. His hand, spread wide between her shoulder blades, was strong. He brought her upright and her arm slid across his broad shoulders. She felt power without bulk. Everything about him was long and lean. The strength of his muscles lay vertically.

"I think we're going to be friends," Will said to the mirror as they practice supported pirouettes.

"Bet you say that to all the freshmen," she said. The color was high up in her face. Exertion made a film of sweat creep up from the neckline of her leotard and bloom in two splotches on her rib cage.

"I do and they all believe me. Especially the boys."

Daisy kept her eyes on her reflection but her antennae perked up. Will was a rare bird: a straight man in the ranks of male ballet dancers. According to conservatory gossip, he was straight with a slight bend. Daisy found this fascinating. Growing up in the world of dance, she had no shortage of gay friends. Someone openly bisexual, however, was a novelty.

"Sorry, I've never partnered a left turner," he said, catching her as she teetered off balance. "That was my fault. Try again."

It took several tries to work out the mechanics. His instinct was to support her with his left hand, which only got in her way as she turned counter-clockwise. She kept smashing into him.

Marie came over. "Wheel, what are you doing to the little flower? You're going to break her." She grabbed his left wrist and held it captive in the small of his back. "I'm surprised at you. I thought you partner both sides."

Will's head whipped back over his shoulder and Daisy burst into laughter. The professor blinked innocent eyes and patted Will's cheek. "Keep practicing, caro."

"Damn," Will said, watching her walk away. "You see what she did there?"

Hands braced on knees, Daisy nodded.

"Come on," he said, holding out a hand. "I need to fix this or my reputation won't precede me."

In a few more tries, his right hand had the knack of providing discreet support for the double spin Daisy could accomplish on her own. The left came in at the last minute and coaxed the momentum into a third turn.

"Definitely friends," he said.

"On both sides."

They would be extraordinary partners and close friends within a month. And turning counter-clockwise would work to their advantage in another three years, when a boy called James Dow shot the fingers off Will's left hand and set the name Lancaster forever into memory.

A CRIME OF PASSION

IT WENT FROM A geographical location to an event. A singular proper noun loaded with context and definition. Like Verdun. Omaha Beach. Dealey Plaza. Kent State.

Lancaster once carried the same cachet as Juilliard or Tisch. Now it was a battlefield.

"I was at Lancaster that day," Daisy said to Rita Temple.

April 19, 1992 was a Sunday afternoon. In the theater of Mallory Hall, Lancaster's performing arts complex, the first tech rehearsal for the spring dance concert was in full swing. Daisy was onstage when James Dow came out of the wings with a gun. He'd already shot and killed five students backstage.

James was a ruthless killer and a crack shot in the wings. But stepping into the spotlights and setting the Glock pistol's sights on his former lover, Will, turned him inept.

"Or he wasn't shooting to kill," Rita said.

"What do you mean?"

"From what you've told me so far, Will seems to have been the primary target. He and James had a relationship but Will broke it off."

"Yes."

"It was a crime of passion."

"That's the consensus. Will was the target."

"But when James went to fire, you were in the way. In the wrong place at the wrong time. My gut reaction—and I wasn't there—but when you described how he fired, my immediate thought was James was trying to shoot Will without shooting you."

Daisy stared at her feet.

"Or do you think you were a target as well?"

"He killed all those kids backstage," Daisy said. "He shot both Will and I. Then he jumped off the stage to keep shooting. I guess you can look at it a hundred different ways but nobody will ever know his plan or intentions. He's dead. My friends and my teacher are dead. And the rest of us... We died in different ways."

Will took one bullet straight through his left side. Another blew his left hand to a pulp. The impact of the shots made him buck and rear, throwing Daisy off his shoulder where she had been perched. James's third shot hit her while she was still up in the air. Through the left thigh, nearly severing a branch of her femoral artery.

"Do you remember it?" Rita asked.

"No," Daisy said. Invisible fingers had reached into her mind that day, found the flame of memory and pinched it out. What she told of April 19 was what she had been told.

"You were awake," people said. "The EMTs asked you things and you answered. I heard you talk. Oh yeah, you were moaning in pain. You screamed at one point. I remember."

It was strange to be told of an event she participated in, even played a starring role. Surreal to hear what happened after she was shot and before the police and the EMTs got into the theater and to remember none of it.

As Daisy and Will lay bleeding out, James jumped off the stage into the orchestra seats. He fired right and left, filling the theater with chaos as students fled or hid. Marie Del'Amici was fatally wounded, shot in the chest and head. James then started up the aisle toward the rear of the house, heading toward the lighting booth where Daisy's boyfriend, Erik Fiskare, was trapped.

"Until a couple weeks ago, I had no memory of the shooting," Daisy said. "None. The last thing I remembered was walking down the aisle toward the stage, going up to rehearse with Will. Then I woke up in the hospital."

She leaned forward and rolled up the left leg of her sweatpants. Two long scars down either side of her calf, from knee to ankle. Further up past her knee, a starburst of puckered flesh on her inner thigh.

"This is the actual gunshot wound," she said. "It got the artery. They repaired it with a graft but I developed something called compartment syndrome. Your limb rejects the oxygen coming back to it and pressure starts to build up." Her fingers ran down the sides of her shin, along the ridges of flesh. "They had to make these cuts to relieve the pressure."

"Fasciotomy," Rita said.

"This is what I woke up to." She rolled her pant leg back down.

"It must have been horrible."

"I didn't know what happened. It made no sense to me, even when they explained it."

"The injury or that it was James?"

"Both. I remembered nothing and understood nothing."

"But some weeks ago, a memory came back. You said a window broke?"

Daisy nodded. "The sound of the breaking glass and all at once, I remembered."

"Remembered what, specifically?"

"When James shot out the windows of the lighting booth."

"Where your boyfriend was."

"Yes."

"You actually watched him shoot the windows."

"Yes, from where I was lying on the stage, I saw them all break."

"And when you started cutting yourself... What did you use?"

"Glass."

POMPATUS OF LOVE

AFTER THEIR SECOND partnering class, Will offered to buy Daisy lunch.

"You're one of our Brighton Scholarships," he said, when they were ensconced in a booth at the campus center.

"As were you," Daisy said, winding the string of her tea bag tight around the pouch and squeezing.

The Brighton was Lancaster Conservatory's top scholarship and awarded full tuition to two incoming freshman.

He unwrapped a turkey sandwich. "What else do you hear?" He bit off a third of the corner.

She rolled her lips in, thinking. "You went to private school in Montreal so I assume you're from Quebec. You were in the junior company of Les Grand Ballets Canadiens. Arturo Castellano and Andre Mejia were your teachers. You're part Native American—"

"How'd you know that?" Will asked, shielding his full mouth against the back of one fist.

"I heard you telling someone. Your dad's name is Maurice, which I also overheard."

"And my mom is the pompatus of love," Will said.

"I see what you did there."

She liked him. She didn't feel a physical attraction, good-looking and charismatic as he was, but in his company she felt *on*. As if they were dancing verbally, partnering each other through conversation. Which was exhilarating in its own way.

"Kaeger, though," she said, "sounds German to me. I heard you mention sisters the other day in class so at least two but I don't know if older or younger. You study martial arts. That's no secret. You were offered a corps position at Ballets Canadiens but instead you took the scholarship here."

Will wiped his mouth and sat back from the table, eyeing her. "You don't seem the spying type. I think you're one of those rare people who shut up and listen. And those crazy eyes of yours probably don't miss a thing."

Daisy smiled into her tea. She was used to comments about her intense, blue-green eyes.

"Kaeger is German," Will said. "Mom is the native Canuck. Saint Brunswick. Not Quebec. Two sisters—one older, one younger. And I came here because my old man wouldn't let me take the corps contract without having at least two years of college. He's the intellectual in the family."

Daisy nodded and bit into her own sandwich.

"Now you," Will said, and held up a finger. "First of all, you're a baby."

Stung, Daisy flicked her eyes up to him. She chewed methodically and stared, waiting for clarification.

"I hear you're only seventeen. Did you skip a grade?"

She shook her head. "Just born late in the year. I'll be eighteen in December."

Another finger went up. "Outside of dance, the two words I hear associated with you are rich and virgin."

She nearly choked. "What?"

"You know David Alto?"

"Who?"

"Huh. I thought he would've made a move by now."

"What are you talking about?"

"So David's a rat."

"A rat?"

"Technical theater guy. Leo Graham's army. You rarely see them in Mallory, they usually roam around down in the basement shops and then emerge for production. Like rats."

"I see."

"David roams above ground, though. He's got a thing for dancers and he loves the observation windows above studio B. Anyway. He's got the hots for you."

Daisy raised her eyebrows. "You know this? You guys are friends then?"

"Friends?" Will rolled his eyes. "We have some overlapping edges. Theater arts and we both speak French. I like him in small doses. Anyway, I've been getting an earful from him about you. He's definitely the spying type, hence the words rich and virgin."

Daisy put up her own finger. "I'm not rich."

"Gladwyne isn't the slums."

Daisy brought her teeth together and exhaled carefully. "Fair enough, but I was born in Philly. I grew up in Fairmount. We didn't move to Gladwyne until I was fourteen. Certainly I'm not poor but my father worked his ass off to make a good life."

Will reached and pushed her finger back down into her fist. "What does he do?"

Daisy sat back smiling, her arms crossed. "Are you asking or spying?"

Will smiled back, his bottom lip disappearing under a side tooth. "Asking," he said quietly.

"He's a plumber. Or was. He sold the business last spring and he and my mom bought a place out in Lancaster County."

"What kind of place?"

"A little farm, mostly orchards and they want to put in a vineyard someday. It's their dream."

"Is it yours?"

"I love it there," she said, laughing a little. "Funny thing about me—I like to be dancing or I like to be at home. And my mom is one of those people who make a beautiful home wherever they go."

Will took a long sip of his soda. "And what about virgin?"

"What do you think?" She smiled at him over the rim of her cup and their eyes held.

"Pure but not stupid," he said under his breath.

Her eyes itched but she didn't blink. "Are those your own words for me?"

He looked away, laughing. Victorious, she let her eyelids close.

"Anyway, about David," Will said.

"I wouldn't know him if I passed him on the street," she said. "So I don't know how he would know I'm a virgin. Unless it was a lucky guess."

Will dug into his shirt pocket for his pack of cigarettes and thumped them on the table. "Or talking to the right people."

"Why are you telling me this?" she asked.

He exhaled a plume of smoke and ran a hand along the back of his neck. His eyes flicked over her shoulder then his face twisted in a look of chagrin. "Look, don't kill me."

"What?"

"He's coming this way."

"Who? David?"

"Don't turn around."

Her mouth hung open. "Did you buy me lunch as a setup?"

"I bought you lunch because I wanted to buy you lunch, but..." Will looked around miserably. "I also owed Dave a favor."

"Jesus Christ."

A voice behind her. "Speaking."

"Monsieur Alto." Will flicked his middle finger against his thumb and sent the pack of cigarettes spinning toward Daisy. She took one, glaring at him, then turned a placid face up to the newcomer.

Her first impression was he looked like a bear. A sturdy, well-fed bear with a long torso and short limbs. His hair was brown, curly and rumpled, with longish sideburns. He was cute. And he slid into the booth next to Daisy with a little too much confidence. She practically felt his ego sit in her lap.

"Hi, I'm David," he said.

"Of course you are," she said.

"This is Daisy," Will said, flicking his Zippo lighter. Beneath the table, he slid his foot close by Daisy's, tapping a soft, supporting Morse code on the toe of her sneaker. She pressed her ankle bone hard against his, stilling him. She didn't like to be tapped or patted.

"How are you?" David said.

She leaned the cigarette into the flame, took a drag. "At what?"

She exhaled smoke in David's direction. He waved it away, his dark brown eyes hungry. She worried it was a good comeback, but the wrong answer.

POSITIVE I'M DYING

"I WAS YOUNG," Daisy said.

Rita continued to sit quietly as Daisy tried to put her thoughts in order. The silence pressed her to hurry up.

"That must sound ridiculous to you," she said. "I mean, I'm only twenty-four. But I feel so old…"

She ached with weariness. The skin stretching over her bones hurt.

"Seventeen when I started college," she said. "It was a lot to get used to. The dance program and the academics and the social life, too. All these new people. New rules."

Rita nodded with a small smile that seemed nostalgic.

"I had boyfriends in high school. I wasn't ignorant of physical relationships. I just hadn't gone all the way yet. And David Alto was…"

A wave of heat swept over her. A prickling anxiety at the back of her neck, creeping down her arms.

"Are you all right, Daisy?"

She drew in a breath. "It's hard to talk about him."

"Do you feel anxious?"

"I feel like shit." She lifted her trembling hands from her lap. "This is how I go around feeling. Sick and scared. I hate it."

The panic swelled in her, threatening to blow her limb from limb.

I hate everything. I hate what I did. I hate who I am.

"I swear I'm dying," she whispered. A bitter laugh spilled up out of her throat. "At least once a day I feel like some kind of shit and at least once a week I'm positive I'm dying."

Her fingers clenched open and shut. She felt herself poised on the edge of a secret. And like a bad dance partner, the anxiety was grabbing at her. Upsetting her balance and knocking her off the edge of the world.

"It builds up in me," she said. The words dripped from her like a cold syrup. "It's like my chest is going to explode, like my skin is going to crack open. And either I go running into the street or... That's when I..."

Rita's eyes never left Daisy's. Her glasses caught the light as she nodded. "Try this," she said. "Take a deep breath. Now hold it. When you let it out, envision blowing a bubble in front of you. Make it any-thing—soap, crystal, bubble gum. Make the shape with your breath. Hold it in the air or in your hands."

Daisy slowly exhaled and envisioned her breath flowing down a long tube, like a glassblower's pipe. A glowing red sphere emerging from the end, cooling into pale, transparent blue.

"Do you have it?"

It shimmered through the air, floating iridescent in front of her. Her hands rolled up in her lap, cupped like a base for it. "I have it," she said.

"Put the words into it. Start with when your skin is going to crack open. When you want to run into the street."

"That's when I want to cut myself," Daisy said. The words floated into the sphere. Black obsidian letters, slimy with mold and moss. The bubble flared once, alarmed, then its blue intensified. The black letters burst into flame.

"Now pinch the bubble off, like you're tying a balloon. Do you have it?"

Daisy nodded. It didn't work with her visualization, but she got the idea.

"Now let it go."

In her mind, Daisy simply threw the ball against the wall and watched it shatter with a detached satisfaction. Her shoulders relaxed. The next breath into her chest was warm and soothing.

"That's a good trick," she said.

She listened to the silence, dissected all the layers of sound within it.

"Sometimes it's like my skin is begging me to cut it," she said.

"To release it."

Daisy nodded, her eyes dissolving. "I haven't cut in five weeks but I can't stop *wanting* to. I think about it all the time. The therapists at the hospital gave me all these tricks and I try them. I run a nail file on my fingertips. I use a stress ball. I cut paper. It does nothing. I draw on myself with magic markers but it doesn't come close. I need the *slice*. I need to hurt and I want to bleed and I want..."

Rita steepled her fingers beneath her chin. "You want," she said. "Yet you haven't cut yourself in five weeks. That's tremendous."

Daisy stared.

"I'm not being sarcastic," Rita said. "I hear *want* and I hear *need* but I don't hear *I did it.* If you were stripped and searched right this minute, would we find fresh cuts on your body?"

Daisy shook her head.

"Then that's fantastic."

"But I want to do it. Every day I wake up wanting it."

Rita spread her hands. "I want to eat a bag of potato chips for breakfast every day. I don't. You want to cut every day. You don't. Wanting and doing are two different things and in this scenario, your not doing kicks want's ass."

Daisy sat back, slightly stunned.

"How do you keep from doing it?" Rita said. "What stops you from caving into the want?"

"Well, I'm seeing someone," Daisy said. "He's the one who made me get help. So he knows. And if I cut, he'll see. He'll be the first to know again. And it stops me."

Rita nodded. "It's good you have him."

"No," Daisy said. "I'm a shitty girlfriend. I have no business dating anyone. I'm not over Erik. I still love him. I cheated on him and I may as well be cheating now. I hate what I've become. I want myself back. I want it back the way it was before. And I want Erik. I want him back so bad."

Shoulders heaving, she buried her face in her hands, rubbing against the hot saltiness puddled in the creases of her palms.

"He doesn't know where I am. He doesn't care where I am anymore. I ruined everything. I want to cut away the part of me that wrecked it. Cut that part of my life away, make it go away. Just make this all go away."

Soft footsteps on the rug and Rita set a box of tissues down on the seat of the couch. "What you do in here, Daisy," she said. "In this office, is a safe form of cutting. A productive form of cutting. You slice yourself open, not physically, but mentally. Because this isn't about who you are or what you do. This is about how you feel. Cutting into your physical entity isn't going to make how you feel go away. Cutting into how you feel, though..."

"What I feel has no name," Daisy said, crying hard.

Sobs like glass bubbles burst from her lungs and smashed in pieces on the floor until she was spent, a sodden lump on the couch. Her forehead felt swollen and heavy.

"I'd like to help you find names for what you feel," Rita said. "I'd like to help you find yourself."

Daisy nodded, perplexed that the woman seemed to be asking permission to work with her, instead of the other way around.

Rita took a casual glance at her wrist. "We're nearing the end. I don't want you to leave here this upset. Let's do some breathing, try to get you back to harbor."

"All right," Daisy whispered, taking another tissue.

"Do you feel like you could come back and see me?"

Daisy wiped her eyes. She looked over at the bookshelf and the *Betsy-Tacy* series. Sweet little girls in pen and ink, arm-in-arm. Braids and curls flying. Simple and carefree.

She looked at Rita. The crazy curls and funky glasses and chipped orange toenail polish.

"I want to," Daisy said.

HUMBLE INVISIBILITY

WILL AND DAISY stood at the bulletin board outside studio A. It was a week after auditions for the conservatory's fall dance concert and roles were posted that morning.

Will let out a slow, soft whistle. "Well, well, well. A little shakeup is good for everyone but this is a small earthquake."

Daisy stared at the cast list. Marie was choreographing a new ballet to works by Johann Sebastian Bach. Daisy found her name in the two ensemble pieces: the opening Bourée from the Suite in E Minor and the finale to the Brandenberg Concerto. Being a freshman, it was what she expected.

But in the middle of the cast list her name appeared again.

Prelude in F Minor: Kathy Curran, Christine Chung, Jessica Barnes, Meghan Lamb, Daisy Bianco.

"This doesn't happen," Will said. "No slur on your talent. But freshmen don't get solos. Brighton or no Brighton."

A little further down from the Prelude line, the surprises kept coming.

Siciliano from Sonata #2: Kathy Curran and Matt Lombardi. (Understudy/matinee Will Kaeger and Daisy Bianco)

"Do you think Marie made a mistake doing this?" Daisy asked quietly.

"Mistake? No. Rules, especially unwritten rules, are meant to be broken. Your technique runs circles around some of the upperclassmen and they know it. All the same, I don't exactly envy you. People are going to be pissed."

"What's the best way to handle this," Daisy said. She had an idea but wanted to hear if Will's matched.

"Head down, shut up. Stay in the back row and dance well. Be nice but don't try to be one of them. Don't show off and don't show them up if you can help it."

"Exactly what I thought."

"And listen." In what had become a familiar gesture, Will put his palm flat on the crown of Daisy's head. "Marie might be testing you. See what you're made of. Know what I mean?"

Daisy nodded.

"I won't shadow you like a bodyguard but I got your back. Don't let them see you cry. Come cry to me afterward."

Daisy took the pen attached to the bulletin board and initialed the four places where her name appeared. She hitched the strap of her dance bag further on her shoulder and prepared to embark on a campaign of humble invisibility.

"Let me go in first," she said. They exchanged three quick kisses: left cheek, right, left again.

"Fuck 'em," he said.

Walking into the studio, Daisy told herself she was only imagining the break in the buzzing conversation. The eyes turned in her direction were mere coincidence. *Head down, shut up,* she thought, her own eyes scanning the ranks for one familiar and friendly face.

From one of the back row barres, Taylor Revell, a fellow freshman, put down her knitting and raised her palm. Her foot nudged aside the dance bag she'd set on the floor, holding a place for Daisy. Suffused with relief, Daisy walked over, smiling and saying hello to anyone who looked at her.

Taylor had corn-colored hair with bangs, and a smattering of freckles across her long nose. Her teeth were long as well, making her slightly horse-faced. She was convinced her chin was too weak for ballet, an insecurity which gave her the mannerism of sticking her bottom jaw out. Marie lovingly called her Il Duce.

"You've got about five red laser dots on your back," Taylor said out the side of her mouth. "You're in the crosshairs."

A quick glance confirmed Jessica Barnes was staring and whispering behind a hand to Meghan Lamb.

"Where Barnes goes, little Lamb follows," Taylor said.

"You might not want to stand too close," Daisy said, pulling on her canvas slippers. "Dancers have notoriously bad aim."

SHIPWRECK

"I REMEMBER SAYING IT," Daisy said. "'Dancers have notoriously bad aim.' How's that for irony?" Her chuckle fell flat and Rita's mouth barely twitched in a smile.

"Anyway," Daisy said, tucking a foot under one knee. "It was tough adjusting that first month of school. I felt a little lonely."

"Did you have a roommate?"

"I did. Sarah. But she... Looking back now I wonder if she was depressed. She left school by the beginning of October and I barely got a chance to know her. I'm not the type to leap into friendships anyway. I remember seeing girls in my dorm who were pricking their fingers and exchanging blood two days after they'd met. A month later they were barely on speaking terms or rooming with someone else. I'm more cautious socially. Sometimes I wonder if it came across as cold."

She picked at a loose thread in the brown chenille pillow that was becoming her best friend during therapy.

"A lot of times high school felt like a shipwreck. A social shipwreck with everyone in desperate survival mode and only one lifeboat. Everyone fighting for a seat, clinging to the sides and beating each other with oars to keep their spot. I can't stand that kind of chaos, when people create drama for the sake of it. Dance was always my haven in that regard: a solid pontoon boat that never tipped over. Then I got to college and everything reversed—socially it was more chill, but dance became a complete shipwreck."

"Was it more competitive?"

"Competitive to the point of toxic," Daisy said. "And catty. These ridiculous, unwritten rules in class about who stands where at the barre. All this idiotic posturing within a dumb pecking order. The boys weren't so bad, but the junior and senior girls were a pack of bitches."

She was pulling the loose thread in the pillow too tight and making the stitches pucker. She smoothed it out, taking a deep breath. "The company I danced with in Gladwyne had a hierarchy but it served a purpose. You were mentored by older students. They'd help if you were struggling or applaud your accomplishments. At Lancaster your accomplishments got a shrug and an eye roll, like it was beneath upper-classmen to recognize talent. And if you were struggling, Jesus, they were almost gleeful about it. What's that word when you take delight in someone's misfortune? Schaden…"

"Schadenfreude," Rita said.

"They adored someone's bad day. I swear. I spent the first month of school thinking I'd made a mistake. I was really unhappy." She took a sip of her coffee. "It got worse after I was cast in *The Bach Variations*. I felt targeted, disliked and for no good reason."

"Did you talk to Marie about it?"

"No, that's not how it works in ballet."

Rita raised her eyebrows.

Daisy tried to explain. Dance trained her to be fearless of physical pain and struggle, and to recognize the gulf between difficult and impossible. Ballet favors not only the brave, but the smart.

"No stupid girls are in ballet." It was the motto of Daisy's Russian teachers at Gladwyne Ballet. Usually shouted as a hand slapped your butt after a careless mistake. Sometimes muttered under the breath as trembling limbs were shoved into alignment. Even spoken affectionately with a pinch on your inner thigh that pushed your extension into something you didn't even know possible.

Marie Del'Amici didn't subscribe to such corporal teaching methods, but she was no less demanding. And not averse to an occasional, shouted harangue when her students got lazy. Fortunately, her language restrictions took some of the sting out. She ignored the pecking order unless it became an unacceptable distraction. Her job was to teach and the students could sort themselves out.

"Will said Marie might have been testing me," Daisy said. "Another thing about ballet. If a teacher is hard on you, it means they care. Marie cast me in the Prelude for a reason. I didn't want to let her down so I dug in and went to work. Maybe that's why I said yes to David when he asked me out."

"This was before you met Erik?"

"A month, maybe six weeks before," Daisy said. "During the time I was so tired, lonely and distracted. Maybe I didn't handle David as well as I could."

"What do you mean?"

"Maybe I said yes because I didn't have the energy to tactfully say no. Or because I wanted some validating attention."

Rita's smile was soft as she shook her head. "Nothing wrong with that."

"Will suggested we double-date, go out as a foursome. But David objected for some reason."

STORIES IN MY HEAD

"I GOT NO OBJECTION to Will," David said. "Shit, the guy gets more pussy than the ASPCA. He probably goes with men just to get a break."

Daisy didn't quite know how to answer.

"You sleep with him yet?"

Silverware frozen in hand, she looked at him. "This is charm, right? Clarify for me because I think it's charm but your accent is hard to understand." Actually it wasn't. Will's Canadian accent and slang were sometimes sludgy in her ears, while David, who was born in Belgium, spoke perfectly decent continental French.

"It's curiosity," he said.

"But if you know I'm a virgin, and you do, then why ask if I've slept with Will? If you're curious, ask why I haven't slept with anyone. Or if you're ballsy, ask if I'll sleep with you."

"Will you sleep with me?"

"No."

His smile didn't waver yet his face changed. As if a mask dropped. Or a single-celled layer of skin melted away, revealing beneath it a gentler, more thoughtful David.

"Will said you didn't bullshit easily," he said.

She smiled and returned her attention to the plate, twirling a careful portion of linguini against her spoon. It was hard enough eating pasta neatly. Even harder with a boy staring at you like you were his dessert.

David was a brisk eater. He set his fork and knife neatly across the empty plate and pushed it away. "Anyway, I don't know many virgins."

"You make it sound like I'm an albino or some other genetic rarity."

"Well, you must have had boyfriends."

"Why?" she said behind her fork, chewing.

"Because you're fucking gorgeous."

"But I could be a total bitch."

"Doesn't matter."

"The pretty girls always have sex?"

"Speaking from my observational experience? Yes."

She finished chewing, looking across the table at him. Compared to sparring verbally with Will, which felt like a tango, this was fencing. Moving blindly backward as she kept up a parry to his thrusts.

She tried a soft riposte. "I've had boyfriends. And since you're curious, and buying me dinner, I'll tell you I'm not all that blank of a slate."

He smiled. "I'd love to fill it in."

His words filled her face with a swift heat. His manner was bold but she couldn't deny a small part of her was flattered by it. Attention was attention.

So she smiled back. "Listen, you want to take me out to get laid, then I'm not your girl."

"I never said that."

"But you're not saying much else."

"What do you want to talk about?"

"Anything but sex." She looked at her watch. "Three minutes about you. Go."

He rearranged the salt and pepper shakers, thinking. "I love music," he said, running his fingertips around the rim of his water glass. "Both my parents were classical musicians."

Daisy went still. She knew David was an orphan but not the circumstances of his parents' death. She looked up to meet his eyes but he was looking down now, playing with his spoon. Fiddling with the latch at the gate of his most private self.

"Music talks to me," he said. "It makes me tell stories in my head. It was how I dealt with a lot of things when I was young. Know what I mean?"

She nodded, wishing he would stop fidgeting. "Go on," she said quietly.

"The first time I saw you dance... I was watching a class and Marie was having you do something to the music from *Nutcracker*. The second act pas de deux."

He hummed the descending notes of the grand adagio, in a voice that was soft, but right on tune. "I love that theme. My mother told me a story about it. Someone bet Tchaikovsky he couldn't compose a piece using the notes of a scale in order. They assumed ascending order. But Tchaikovsky, being a genius, chose descending and the result was the *Nutcracker* adagio. The rest of the score gives me cavities but that piece always makes the hair stand up on the back of my neck."

"My ballet teachers told me a different story." Daisy said. "Tchaikovsky's sister died while he was writing the score. And the adagio's sadness is in tribute to her. The descending scale is her death haunting him."

David pointed the spoon at her, mouth slightly open. "I knew it," he said. "I *knew* you knew that story. The way you were dancing. Everyone else was bringing the sweetness but you tapped into the sadness. I knew you knew."

"It has a righteous anger to it, too. Toward the end, when he brings in all the brass and lets rip. He's pissed. Shaking his fist at the sky and cursing God."

"Yes." His eyes held hers, filled with a pleased wonder. The moment flickered warm between them. A small, complicit campfire. Then it was as if David became aware of the taste of vulnerability in his mouth and he gave the spoon in his hand a tiny toss. It plonked onto the table and bounced onto the rim of Daisy's plate. It was a defiant gesture, and his cocky expression was back as he glanced up at her.

"I have a bad habit of falling in love with dancers," he said, grinning.

"What do you like about us?"

"The flexibility."

She touched her tongue to the inside of her cheek and raised her eyebrows.

"What I don't like would be a shorter list," David said.

"Do you dance?"

He laughed. "No."

"What do you do?"

Over the rim of his water glass his eyebrows wrinkled. "Is this curiosity or your cocktail hour conversation?"

She put her chin on the heel of her hand. "What do you love?"

He tapped the base of the glass on the table, shaking the ice cubes. "I love the five-minute call," he said after a moment. "All the action before the show finally starts. I like the little pause when my hands are on the rope of the curtain and I hold the whole thing captive. It doesn't start until I pull. I love that last moment. I love being in line for something and it's not yet my turn, but I'm next."

"Why?"

"Because everyone wants to be me right then. Lucky bastard, he's next."

"What else?"

"I love the moment before you kiss someone new. The almost-kiss. You know it's going to happen but hanging tight with your faces together and not kissing? It's my definition of magic."

He likes to get there, Daisy realized. *Not be there.*

"Did I make it?" he asked, taking her wrist and looking at her watch.

"Close enough."

"Can I kiss you?"

She hated when boys asked beforehand and what exactly was he planning to do if she said yes? Plant his hands between the plates and lean over the table to her? She smiled into her pasta. "Maybe."

He took his time letting go of her arm and she noticed he wore rings on both his index fingers. One was dull silver and textured, the other plain gold. When she asked, he took the silver one off and handed it to her with a little shake which seemed to make it fall apart. She saw it was a puzzle: five separate bands that fit together in one. She attempted to put it back together as he lit a cigarette and watched her.

"It was my father's."

"Oh?"

"And this," he said, pointing to the gold ring, "was his wedding band."

"What happened?" she asked.

"Car accident. He and my mother together."

"I'm so sorry."

He shrugged.

"How old were you?"

"Eleven."

She couldn't solve the puzzle. He took it back. Elbows on the table, eyes squinted against the cigarette clamped in his mouth, he put the rings together in ten seconds. "Took me about a month to crack it," he said, shaking it apart again and putting it in her hand.

"When did you come to the States?"

"Right afterward."

"Was there no family in Belgium who could take care of you?"

"My mom was an orphan. She only had one sister, Helen, who lived in New York. My dad was the youngest of eight children. He was an afterthought. You know, seven kids, then ten years go by and oops."

"Surprise."

"So when he and my mom died, my father's parents were alive but they were old. And all his siblings were older, too. Older and scattered. Only one of his sisters was still in Belgium and she wasn't even in Brussels. I was going to be uprooted no matter what and my parents must have had the foresight to realize it. In their will they made Aunt Helen my legal guardian. It was never contested." A bitterness in David's tone made Daisy wonder if he resented nobody fighting to keep him in Europe.

With an exasperated sigh she gave the ring back. "I can't do it."

David's expression was thoughtful as he reassembled the ring and slid it onto his finger. He was cute. And when he calmed down, held still and showed himself, he was actually interesting.

"Want to go somewhere else?" he asked.

"No, thank you. I had a good time but I'm kind of tired. And I have class tomorrow."

Little was said on the drive back to campus. He held her hand as he drove and it felt phony. His attraction to her sat in her lap. So did the certainty he'd want to kiss her goodnight.

"So quiet," he said, squeezing her fingers. "What are you thinking about?"

"Nothing, really," she said, wondering if going with the slightly-stretched truth—*I don't kiss on the first date*—was the best tactic. She considered a fake coughing fit or cooking up a scratchy throat.

"The quiet ones are always wild in the dark."

"Is that also your observational experience?"

"Personal experience."

A cold sore would be ideal right now.

"Is your roommate around?" David asked as he walked her to her dorm.

"I don't have one," Daisy said absently.

"Oh?" David was a master at putting seven kinds of innuendo into one syllable. "How'd you pull that ideal situation off?"

Inwardly Daisy kicked herself for the slip. "I had one. But she left school."

"And now you have the swingle."

"Well, I'm not getting too used to it. I'm sure housing will transfer someone in. If I don't find a new roommate myself first."

"Well, don't hurry."

They walked the rest of the way in silence. It was a weird, humid night, with a drizzle that couldn't make up its mind whether it wanted to be rain or mist. With David's arm around her shoulders, Daisy was painfully aware of how the rules had been ratcheted up a notch. She was on her own. No curfew or school night excuse as a safety net. No "my father will kill me." And no roommate to blame. Not even a fake one, thanks to her idiocy.

"I had a good time," she said, glancing up at the skies as the rain starting coming down heavier. "I'll see you around Mallory tomorrow?"

He nodded. "Can I kiss you?"

"I don't know," she said. "Can you?"

A long staring moment and then his hands slid around her face and tilted it up to his. His eyebrows and eyelashes were wet. His face came closer and he rolled his lips in, then out. A hesitant, almost shy gesture and for an instant it made her toes curl in her shoes. She understood how he loved the almost-kiss. The moment before his lips touched hers was magic. Then his mouth opened and his tongue slid against hers and it was all wrong. He felt wrong. He tasted wrong. He kissed wrong.

"Goodnight," she said, half-backing and half-ducking away. Pretending she didn't see his disappointed expression. Feeling seventeen, foolish and virginal.

BLIND AND STUPID

THOUGH HER MAJOR was ballet, as a BFA candidate and a Brighton Scholar, Daisy had to study contemporary dance as well. In this arena the classroom atmosphere was warm and supportive. It was with her own body Daisy found herself fighting an entirely different battle.

All her experience with modern dance had been fleeting. A class here, a workshop there. She never pretended it was her forte and may have subconsciously thumbed her nose at it by maintaining a certain pretty lyricism in her movements. Always a bunhead first.

Now she was faced with modern technique five times a week. Naked feet to the floor and on the other side of her body's equator where everything was opposite to ballet. Legs and hips turned in instead of out. Arms thrown at angles instead of curves. Working on the plane of the floor as well as the air.

"Floor is ugly," said one of Daisy's teachers at Gladwyne Academy. "Ballerina only touch floor when necessary. Only lie on floor if sleeping princess or dead swan. Floor dirty. Not pretty."

Now, in Cornelis Justi's modern class, pretty had an entirely new definition. Plus Daisy's body was finding new ways to define pain. Muscles she didn't know she possessed bitched and moaned. Dancing barefoot was making the callused skin on her toes split into deep, horizontal cracks. Dirt got into the cracks and wouldn't let them heal. Clutching at the floor with these pained, uncertain feet gave her a nasty case of shin splints.

"Those will pass," Cornelis said. "A little more time and your feet will stop trying to do all the work."

Everyone at Lancaster Conservatory—male, female, straight, gay or in between—was in love with Cornelis. Everyone lived for the tiny rite of passage when they were invited to use his diminutive name.

"Call me Kees." It rhymed with lace. "Or Keesja. But only if we're dating."

He was the most gigantic person Daisy ever encountered. His tall frame and broad shoulders gobbled up the studio floors. He moved like a hurricane, even when demonstrating from a chair. He ate life and spit out the bones. Unlike the scatterbrained Marie, he knew every student by name and his greetings in basso profundo echoed throughout Mallory.

"William, my friend."

"Good morning, Christine."

"Look who's here. Daisy, our little flower."

Born and raised in Amsterdam, he could converse, joke and curse in several languages. Prior to Lancaster, he taught for a spell at Louisiana State University. A bit of an evangelic twang had accompanied him to Philadelphia.

"Will you look what the good Lord hath brought to me?" he cried when he saw you in the halls, scooping you up in a rib-crushing embrace as if only you existed for him at that moment. He was a happy creature. A shaken-and-stirred cocktail of black and gay, cultured and cosmopolitan, down-home and up in the stars. Poured out into as many shot glasses as he could afford and thrown back—L'chaim!—with an unapologetic belch before he sent his glass smashing into the fireplace.

Daisy adored his classes, though she often felt hopeless there. Hopeless and helpless. Her feet continued to clutch the floor while her limbs wrapped around the unfamiliar technique and failed. Kees chased her across the studio in combinations.

"Bigger," he said in his booming voice, breathing down her neck. "Bigger. More. Be sloppy. Fall down."

She sucked at sloppy. The older modern students patted her shoulder sympathetically. "Tutu lock," they called it. She laughed even as the frustration gummed up her throat and tears threatened the back of her eyes. This upset her more than the whispers and sneers from the ballet girls.

Kees was implacable. He kept her after class, patiently worked alone with her, trying to exorcise the ballerina's marrow-deep need for perfection.

"Quit wiping your hands off on your tights," he said. "It's dirt, but it's washable. Come on, try again. I don't care what it looks like, Dais. I care what it feels like. Give me a mess. Show me ugly and hungry then you can show me perfect."

One day, he blindfolded her before a combination. Only with a light piece of gauzy material but it was enough to her small comfort zone. She could just perceive light and dark, walls and floor. It wasn't enough. With no visual cues, no depth perceptions, she was terrified. Not only was she going to fail, but she was going to *fall down.* On the dirty floor. Her body stiffened in a primal attempt to survive.

"Follow my voice," Kees said in front of her and slightly to the side. "Don't be afraid. And if you start to fall, the floor will catch you. Make friends with the floor. Trust your body, Dais. It knows where it is."

She was alone with Kees in the studio. Even the classroom percussionists had left. She breathed in and dropped her shoulders. Like a horse switching at a fly she flicked off her fear. It was dancing. She had nothing to fear. Kees wanted a mess? He wanted her stupidity, her mistakes, her dirty hands and everything else the Russian Mafia swatted her ass for?

He could have them.

She lifted her arms and moved into the silent space. A blind idiot. She reached for the movement but at the last second decided to let the movement reach for her instead and not give a fuck what happened.

And something happened.

Her body seemed to peel open. The not-caring-anymore spilled from somewhere beneath her sternum and exploded out into the dark.

"That's it," Kees said. "Beautiful. More."

She understood. The dance wasn't a jacket to stuff her limbs into and make fit. It was a jacket that would self-tailor to whatever emotional color she wanted. But the emotion had to come first—good, bad and ugly. And even ugly could be beautiful.

She was dancing full out and fearless now, coming out of a turning leap and following the momentum downward. The floor put up its dirty hands and caught her, counterbalanced her rolling weight and pushed her back onto her bare feet. She did the step again. Did it bigger. Did it too big, pushing the limit and breaking the rules. Reckless and imperfect, borne on invisible hands of feeling, pushing from behind and pulling from ahead.

"Yes," Kees cried. "Will you look at this girl?"

One of his hands was gentle on the back of her neck. The other peeled away the blindfold and he brought her to a stop, picked her up and twirled her.

"Oh my dear, you are going to be something else," he said.

COURAGE TO BE A MESS

"I FIND THAT SO interesting," Rita said. "The courage it took for you to be a mess."

"It was one of the hardest things I've ever done in dance," Daisy said. "Learn to let go of pretty. But it changed everything. By the end of my freshman year, I was a completely different dancer."

Rita nodded slowly.

"You look on the verge of an epiphany," Daisy said.

"I keep coming back to the courage to be a mess," she said. "And I wonder if you allowed yourself to fall apart after the shooting."

"I did. I *was* a mess." Daisy looked around, confused. "That's why I'm here."

"What I mean is... I'm sorry. I'm trying to articulate something that's still forming in my mind and not doing a good job. Let me table it for a bit." She scribbled something in her notebook. "You go on."

Daisy sighed. "I forgot what I was saying."

Rita went on writing.

"I'm all over the place," Daisy said. "I'm talking about everything but Erik. But I didn't meet him until November. God, I haven't even told you about Lucky..."

Rita looked up. "You don't have to present me with a perfect story arc," she said. "You're not here to entertain me. You can give me the ugly mess."

Daisy laughed. "If I have the courage."

PRETTY PRINCESSES IN TUTUS

THE SHIN SPLINTS worsened and Daisy was sent to Mallory Hall's training room for treatment.

She reclined on one of the padded tables, heating pads on both legs. Next in line for ultrasound therapy, she was trying to get some reading done for American Literature but the words kept swimming in front of her eyes. Yawning, she rested the book open on her chest.

On the table next to her, Aisha Johnson had her nose in a magazine and an ice pack on her Achilles tendon. She was the other recipient of that year's Brighton Scholarship and a rising star in the contemporary division. Her six-foot sculpted body gave off an energy and presence that made Daisy back up a few steps in class. She watched Aisha with half awe and half despair, wanting to emulate something she could barely define.

They were friendly in class, but not friends. Aisha was fierce, proud and independent. Her circle was predominately black and her loyalty pledged to only a select few. She always held her face like an immutable facade yet often snuck wisecracks out a side door.

Daisy liked Aisha's dry humor, and had extended a few overtures, all politely received but not returned. Daisy retreated with no hard feelings and accepted the benign neglect.

"Everyone has a social bell curve," her father said once. "And sometimes you are nothing more to a person than scenery. Neither cherished nor detested. Don't take it personally."

One of the student trainers came to Daisy's side. "How we doing here?" she said. "The royal we. Already I'm talking like a nurse."

"We forgive you," Daisy said.

The trainer laughed. She was short with a Southern Belle's hoopskirt figure. Her blonde hair exploded from her scalp in crazy spiral curls, some of which were captured in a hair elastic at her nape while the rest bounced around her face. She took the heating pads off Daisy's shins and started pressing gentle but competent fingertips up the length of muscle lying against the bone.

Daisy pulled a quick, concentrated breath into her nose.

"Be brave," Aisha said.

"Jesus," Daisy said, wincing.

"I'm sorry," the trainer said. "This is the injury that makes the athletes cry. You dancers are so much tougher." One of her hands took Daisy's ankle while the other flexed and pointed the foot, letting the shin muscle stretch and contract. She put the heating pads back on and gave Daisy's legs a reassuring pat. "Ultrasound machine will be free in about five more minutes. Let's kept them warm."

"Yes, let's," Daisy said.

Smiling, the trainer reached toward the chair where Daisy had set her dance bag. She found one of Daisy's pointe shoes. Daisy nodded permission and the blonde girl drew it out.

"I love these," she said quietly, smoothing the satin with her fingertips. "What little girl doesn't dream of pretty princesses in tutus?"

Aisha turned a page of her magazine. "Ballet broke my heart."

"It breaks a lot of hearts," Daisy said.

"Being black was strike one," Aisha said. "Then I was six feet tall in eighth grade. And pointe class was my nemesis. I don't have the feet for ballet." She extended one muscular leg.

"What's wrong with your feet?" the trainer said, eyebrows wrinkled.

"They don't point," Aisha said. She was extending her toes as much as possible but her foot didn't curve. "Ugly enough bare. In pointe shoes, they're horrendous. Not like hers."

She flipped her thumb to Daisy's feet. Daisy pointed them: a ripple from ankle to taped toes, the backs of her legs not stirring from the table top. Her feet curved until her toes touched the vinyl upholstery, perfectly lined up with her heels. Twin arched tunnels you could roll a matchbox car through.

"I hate you," Aisha said. She put her magazine back up, excusing herself from the conversation.

The trainer was still looking at the pointe shoe with a reverent expression. "God, I wanted ballet lessons so bad when I was little."

"Did you get them?" Daisy asked.

"No, my mother said I was too fat and too much of a klutz." The girl's voice was conversational, stating a fact and not looking for pity. Daisy studied the face under swinging wheat-colored curls. Its wide cheekbones and pointed chin. The line of tiny studs up one earlobe and a single silver ring through the ear's cartilage. Her hands weren't klutzy. Nor was she fat.

Daisy smiled at her. "I'm Daisy," she said. "Flatfoot over here is Aisha."

"Up yours, bunhead," Aisha said from behind the pages, not unkindly.

"I'm lucky," the trainer said.

Daisy tilted her chin. "Why?"

A triangular grin unfolded, wrinkling the blonde girl's nose. "My name's Lucia," she said. "Lucia Dare. Lucky for short."

AN OPEN–ENDED PURSUIT

"LUCKY BECAME MY CLOSEST FRIEND," Daisy said. "My roommate for the rest of college and still my best friend today. Aisha was... She was never my friend but she was an ally. I knew she'd be there if I needed her. Taylor Revell and I began to get tight, both in class and outside the theater. It slowly started to turn around."

She stared down at her hands, remembering Taylor's grey eyes under her thick blonde bangs, taking in the world over her knitting. A high-strung girl, Taylor was never without a skein of yarn or her needles. Knitting kept her anxieties grounded, the repetition of needle through and yarn around soothing her whirling thoughts into peace.

"Knit one, purl two," Taylor would chant to the stitches. "Don't forget, I love you."

Aisha Johnson, tall and proud, the unruffled apex of the social bell curve. Neither friend nor foe. Neither cherished nor detested. Yet before every performance, she and Daisy put their palms and foreheads together and whispered, "Merde" for good luck.

"Besides Will," Daisy said, "I often danced with this other freshman boy, Manuel Sabena. We had choreography and composition classes together. He was little—five feet five, the same as me, which is short for a male dancer. He couldn't partner me the way Will did, couldn't lift me over his shoulders or do all the showy throwing and catching. But we'd hear music and have identical visions of how it would translate into movement. And we developed our own way of partnering that was based on mutual strength and a much more grounded style. Showy floorwork instead of airwork. The creative aspect of my art began to open up and develop. Plus all the ways Kees was teaching me to be more raw and unrefined and nakedly passionate with my dancing—those are the things I was able to work on when I danced with Manuel. Like we were lab partners, if that makes any sense. It's hard to explain."

"Well, what I'm hearing you say is you found your tribe," Rita said.

"I did." Daisy picked at the fringe on her favorite pillow. "I found them but then I lost them. Aisha, Taylor and Manuel were all killed in the theater."

"And Marie," Rita said. "Your teacher. I'm sure she was your good friend by that time as well."

"Yes."

"I'm so sorry, Daisy. It must have been devastating. I can't imagine..."

Daisy nodded, chewing her bottom lip. "I still have Lucky," she said. "She lives in Fort Lee and works in the Bronx. We see each other as much as we can. Will's in Europe now, dancing with the Frankfurt Ballet."

"What about David?"

"I don't know where he is."

"Was he in your tribe?"

"He was, but he fluctuated between the extreme ends of the bell curve. He was moody as hell and a terrible tease. Then he had moments when he was chill and approachable and let his guard down. We could speak French together. We had the theater in common. I didn't dislike him but I didn't want to date him. And...I don't know. I tried to be kind about it. Nothing you can say makes it easier when you're rejecting someone, but I couldn't keep going on dates and letting him think something was going to come of it."

"From the way you described David, maybe he would've enjoyed an open-ended pursuit," Rita said, smiling.

"You may be right," Daisy said. "He got off on the chase. He wanted things so badly and then he'd toss them aside. He liked getting there, not being there. Anyway, he took it hard when I said I wanted to be friends and that's when he started calling me Marge."

Rita raised her eyebrows. "Marge? Oh. From Marguerite?"

"Yeah. I let him. I didn't like it, but fine. Call me Marge, it'll be our little...thing. And I learned to ignore his moods. Ignore when he'd get a smarmy look on his face if he saw me talking to a guy. It was a lot of passive bullshit, nothing overtly mean. But one night I was out with my girlfriends and I met this guy. God, what was his name? Ryan? Rob? Rob, I think. It doesn't matter. It was a random meet. Our groups merged and it was on. Rob and I were talking and flirting and digging each other. And David happened by. He was drunk and belligerent and made a scene."

Daisy crossed her arms, hugging the pillow and remembering.

"It got ugly."

VESTED INTEREST

"IS HE YOUR BOYFRIEND?" Rob said.

"No," Daisy said. Her face burned with anger and embarrassment. "Look, maybe I can see you another time. Let me go handle this."

Rob looked over her shoulder with wrinkled eyebrows. "Are you sure? He looks pretty shitfaced."

"I'm sure. I'd actually appreciate it. My friends are with me. I'll be fine."

"All right. It was nice talking to you."

"Yeah. Sorry about this."

"Not at all."

Rob walked away. Looked back once and waved.

"Don't feel bad," David yelled after him. "I couldn't bust that cherry either."

"Jesus, Dave," Lucky said.

"Come on, let's go," Taylor said.

Daisy started to step off the curb but the light was red. She was trapped. She stepped back, staring through the passing traffic. As David approached, she closed her eyes, breathing slowly through her nose.

Don't engage.

She opened her eyes and the street scene was blurred and trembling.

And don't cry.

She felt all at once lonely and tired and depleted. Wanting her mother came like a punch to the gut. Which made her feel like a baby. She bit down on the inside of her lip and didn't move.

"Marge." David was beside her now, despite the efforts of Taylor and Lucky to thwart him. His hand pulled at her elbow. "Marge. Dais. I'm sorry."

She turned her head slightly from his fruity breath and cigarette scent. "Go away, David," she said.

He tried to take both her arms. She kept her hands in her pockets and stepped away. "David, please don't touch me."

He followed. In her face, babbling apologies in French and pulling at her.

"Dude, knock it off," Lucky said. "You've upset her enough."

"C'mon, honey, be nice," Taylor said, putting an arm around him, playing good cop.

He bucked backward, pushing Taylor away.

"*David,*" Lucky cried.

Daisy felt her eyes widen and her hands came out of her pockets. She planted them in David's chest and shoved him, hard. "What is *wrong* with you?" she said, her voice raised and echoing down the street.

He grabbed her wrists. She dug her heels and pulled out of his grasp. He released her and she skipped backward, fell flat on her ass.

I hate you, she thought, and the tears spilled down her face.

Strong hands scooped under her armpits then and she was being picked up and put on her feet as a voice spoke over her head. "Evening, ladies."

It was Will. Tall and fresh in jeans and a tight black shirt, his hair down and a crackling, sexy energy in his stance. He brushed off Daisy's back. "Your tailbone all right?" he said.

She nodded, smearing the heel of her hand across her eyes.

"Let me handle this." Will tucked her beneath his tattooed arm and sauntered with her over to Dave. "What's up, asshole?"

"What do you want, faggot?"

"Hey, hey," Will's voice was mild. "Don't get all pissy with me."

"Why don't you and your boyfriend get lost?"

Daisy looked back and saw Matt Lombardi, one of the senior dancers who was apparently out with Will tonight. He flicked his brows up and rolled his eyes.

"Why don't you explain why you're shoving girls around?" Will's hand rested strong on the back of Daisy's neck and her heart began to slow down.

"I wasn't shoving her."

"Looked like it to me. I don't like seeing that shit, Dave, least of all with my partner. I happen to have a vested interest in her ass."

"Yeah, I know where your interest in asses is vested, Kaeger."

Lucky came by Daisy's other side and threaded a possessive arm with hers. David had his back and the sole of one foot against a lamp post, lighting a cigarette.

Will's arm slid from Daisy's shoulder and he took a step toward David. But then stopped and looked back, not at Daisy but beside her.

"Hi, I'm Will," he said.

"I'm Lucky."

A breeze came down the street and blew Will's hair back from his face. His bottom lip retreated a fraction, then his smile unfolded.

"So am I," he said, painfully beautiful under the streetlights.

Lucky's expression was unreadable, but her fingers curled like talons into Daisy's forearm.

Will turned back to David. "C'mon, man. You should go home."

"Don't tell me what to do."

"I'm not. I'm just giving you some advice. Can I bum one of those?"

"Jesus," David muttered, but he reached back in his inside pocket.

"I brought my own," Matt said, sidling up and lighting up.

"Great," David said, exhaling smoke. "The hags and the fags. What a banner fucking night."

Will leaned back from the trio and looked at Daisy. "Go home," he mouthed. He pointed at Lucky with a you-go-with gesture.

The girls moved a few steps away.

"Dais, I'm sorry," David said.

Daisy looked back. He was between Matt and Will's shoulders, trying to follow her, but they were having none of it.

"Tell her tomorrow," Matt said.

"Yeah, apologies are better given sober, man."

"Come on, children," Taylor said. "Let's find a party."

But Daisy had lost interest in the evening. "I'm going home."

"Yeah, I'm done, too," Lucky said, patting back a fake yawn.

Taylor shrugged, kissed them, and set out alone. Her chin out, long stride and boots echoing clacketa-thump, clacketa-thump behind her.

"Oh my God," Lucky said, still squeezing Daisy's arm. "Oh my God, who is he?"

"He is Will."

"Did you feel it? Am I crazy? Did you feel that chemistry?"

"I felt it," Daisy said.

"Jesus," Lucky said, looking back over her shoulder once more. "The way he took control of the situation without throwing his dick around? It was hot. David was eating out of his hand."

"He's got a charm."

"You all right? How's your ass?"

"My ass is fine and I'm pissed off."

"Let's go get a Sara Lee cake. Take it back to your room and get fat."

Daisy shook her head. "I have a costume fitting tomorrow."

"Ugh, you dancers. Fine, I'll get one and you can watch me get fat."

As a consolation, Daisy got herself an ice cream sandwich. It soothed for about five minutes and then she was chilled off. Back in her room, she pulled on her warmest sweats and flopped face-down on her bed.

"I hate boys."

Lucky cut a generous slice of chocolate cake. "David is not all boys. Clearly he's nuts about you, but he can't hold his emotional liquor. Which is not sexy." She licked her fingers. "Will, on the other hand..."

Daisy rolled on her elbow. "You've got him in your crosshairs."

"God, he is sexy. But what was all David's gay blather? Is that an inside joke?"

"I hear it a lot," Daisy said. "That he bats for both sides."

"You've seen? Or only heard?"

"Only heard. The consensus is he's straight with a slight bend."

Lucky carefully ran the blunt side of the icing-encrusted knife along her tongue. "What's your thought?"

"He's comfortable in anyone's company. An equal opportunity flirt. Actually, no, I take that back. I wouldn't call him a flirt. He's not an attention-seeker and nothing he does is for shock value. He is who he is and honestly doesn't give a shit what other people think."

"Interesting," Lucky said, setting the lid on the tin and folding the foil edges down. "Straight with a slight bend and no fucks to give."

"Would it bother you if he were bisexual?"

"No." Sitting on the floor, ankles crossed, her arms stretched wide along the iron bed frame, Lucky looked both sated and hungry. "He could sleep with trees for all I care. I just want to taste his tattoos."

Daisy laughed, rolling onto her back.

"You don't mind me going after him, do you?"

"Mind? No. He's my partner. And not to dismiss your crush but, he's not really my type."

"What is your type?"

Daisy opened her mouth, stuck for an answer when a knock sounded at the door. "Come in."

It was Will. "Just checking that everyone's ass is accounted for," he said.

"Speaking of which, where's David?" Lucky asked.

"Passed out. No longer a threat to society."

"Is he always such a douche?" Lucky said, tossing her curls back.

"He's an orphan," Daisy said and Will glanced over at her, nodding, his expression thoughtful.

"That's how I look at it, too," he said. "He wants to be loved. He just has a terrible way of asking for it."

"Well, thanks for coming to the rescue," Daisy said. "Your timing was perfect. As usual."

Will's broad shoulders shrugged. "I could've kicked his ass but I wanted to spare him the humiliation. I'm kind of stupid that way. Hey, is that cake?"

"It is," Lucky said, getting up. "And I need to get it into my fridge."

She put the cake box into Will's hand and shrugged into her jacket. As if they'd been acquainted for years, Will reached to help with a sleeve. His eyes slid up and down her back. He looked hungry as well.

"Want me to walk you home?" he said.

Lucky winked at Daisy. Turning around, she drew her hair out from beneath her collar and took the box from Will. "Sure."

Oh boy, Daisy thought, but said nothing as she lifted her face, first for Lucky's kiss, then Will's.

"Bonne nuit," Will said.

"Doux rêves."

"C'est la vie?" Lucky said.

"It's a start," Will said. And the door closed.

FOOD AND FRIENDSHIP

THE NEXT MORNING, Mallory Hall's costume department was a zoo.

"Can you come back in an hour?" the frazzled wardrobe mistress asked Daisy. "Three of my slaves called in sick. It's not even Mardi Gras."

Dancers knew it wasn't wise to be disagreeable with the woman who handled your costume. Daisy assured her it was no trouble and headed over to the campus center to get some breakfast.

She saw David sitting in a booth. Plugged into his Walkman, he was hunched over a Styrofoam cup as though judging whether it could hold the weight of his head.

No other tables were free. Without thinking twice, she slid into the bench opposite David and gave him a small smile. He looked like hell, his wet hair combed straight back from his face, revealing bloodshot eyes. A tremor in his hands as they reached up and took off the earphones.

"Hi." His voice was sludgy and he cleared his throat.

She smiled again, blew on her hot tea and took a careful sip. "What are you listening to?"

"Beethoven. Helps with a hangover."

"Does it?"

"No."

She held out her hand and he gave her the earphones. He rewound the tape a little and hit the play button. Cellos and violas filled her ears. A somber two-note ostinato repeating, unfolding into a theme. Simple. Like the tune to a child's nursery rhyme. The theme was handed off to the violins and a second variation played under it. The phrases wound together like two dancers.

She took one earpiece away. "What is this?"

"Second movement of the Seventh Symphony."

"It's beautiful," she said. "When one theme plays on top of the other, it's so simple but it's..."

"A string of beauties hand-in-hand," David said.

Her eyes widened. "Yes."

"Someone famous said that, I don't remember who. Christ, my head." He lit a cigarette and slid the pack across to her. After a few more measures, she stopped the tape and put the earphones back on the table.

"My parents loved the Seventh," he said in French, running his fingers along the edge of the Walkman.

"You said they were musicians."

He nodded. "In the Orchestre National de Belgique. My father played cello, my mom the violin. They used to play the second movement all the time. Or sing it. Sing all the parts." He put the cigarette in his mouth and ran both hands through his thick hair. Exhaled a ribbon of smoke and flicked the ashes. "Yesterday was the anniversary of the car accident."

"I see," she said. "I'm sorry."

"I should know better than to go out in public. I usually hole up alone or something."

"You shouldn't be alone," she said.

He shrugged.

"I'm glad you told me."

He looked over her shoulder, smoking. "I'm sorry I was a dick," he said softly. "I hope I didn't ruin anything you had going on. It's just... You smell like sugar and you're the prettiest thing I've ever seen in my damn life and I don't know why it makes me act like such an asshole."

She smiled. "Could I see the ring again?"

He slid it off, shook apart the silver bands and handed it to her.

"Do you have any pictures of your parents?" she asked.

"Sure."

"Will you show me sometime?"

From under the visor of his hand he looked up at her. Slowly, he nodded.

A boy walked up to the booth, indignant and annoyed. "Dave, what the fuck, I'm looking everywhere for you."

"Shit, what time is it," Dave said, exploding into action, gathering Walkman and jacket.

"Half past your ass is late," the boy said, then looked at Daisy. "Hi, I'm Neil."

"Sorry, sorry," David said. "Neil Martinez, my roommate. This is Daisy. My...friend."

"Oh, you're Daisy," Neil said, his smile turning up. "I've heard—"

"Nothing," David said, smacking the back of his hand against Neil's chest. "You've heard nothing."

"What are you late for?" Daisy asked.

"String ensemble concert," Neil said. "We're running lights."

"And we're late," David said, nudging Neil along. "Say goodbye."

"Good meeting you," Neil called over his shoulder. "Finally."

Shaking her head, Daisy continued playing with the ring another minute before it dawned on her David left without it. And his smokes. And his coffee.

She drummed her fingers on the table, thinking, then gathered the smokes and ring into her pocket. She went to the deli and got an egg and cheese sandwich, topped up the coffee cup and walked out of the campus center into the cold morning sunshine, toward Mallory Hall.

The theater was filled with the echoing bangs and clangs of chairs being set up onstage. In the glassed-in booth at the back of the house, David and Neil were organizing papers and equipment. Daisy tapped her fingernails on the door.

"Room service," she said, putting down the sandwich and coffee.

David's head whipped around and he got to his feet, staring. She found herself smiling at his stance, knowing it was unconscious and ingrained: he was raised to stand when a lady came into the room.

"And lost and found," she said, adding the ring and pack of cigarettes. She glanced at Neil's interested expression and decided she didn't want to embarrass David any more than necessary.

"I bring food and friendship," she said in French. "It's yours if you want it."

He nodded with a closed-mouth smile. "I want it."

"Ça y est." With a wave she left the booth.

GENTLY BACK TO YOURSELF

"EVEN WHEN DAVID was being an asshole something always tapped the back of my mind and reminded me he was an orphan," Daisy said. "He lost his parents. He was taken away from the home he loved, away from music and art and this magical childhood. He did show me pictures of his years in Belgium and they broke my heart. I couldn't love him, but I wanted to be kind to him. Anyway, am I losing you?"

"No." Rita smiled. "And it's not about my entertainment."

"I know. Where was I?"

Rita didn't answer and by now, Daisy wasn't expecting her to. She sat and waited for her train of thought to circle back around. Or for a new thought.

"So I reached a truce of sorts with David. Food was a thing with us. I'd bring him a snack or lunch and we'd have a running gag about the tab and who owed who money. And his roommate Neil would call me Marge and Dave would get possessive. 'Hey, only I call her Marge.' So we had our bits and our jokes and it felt like we were friends. Or at least friendlier."

"Must have been a relief."

"Lucky moved in with me. And I loved having her for a roommate. We got along so well. Meanwhile she and Will were having the mother of all affairs but not in a way that was exclusionary. Sometimes I'd see these couples hook up and they'd get sucked into a black hole. Drop out of sight for three weeks and then emerge looking like they'd been on a bender in Vegas. Lucky spent a lot of nights at Will's suite—he had the single room so they could be alone at night, but he'd also come hang in our room and sleep over sometimes." Her eyes turned to the wall, looked through the sable grey to the past. "I liked when he did."

"How so?"

"It made me feel included. And it was a different side of Will. He projected such an aura of self-confidence. It was interesting to see him tender and sweet and a little vulnerable. I'd watch them sleep, fascinated by how they held each other and how their breathing matched. His hand in her hair and her face in his chest. I was trying to imagine what it would be like. A boy sleeping with me, sharing my covers and pillows. Breathing on me."

Rita laughed. "I'm sorry," she said, a hand to her mouth. "I'm only laughing because I had the same moment in college."

"I liked Will being in the room. I trusted him so much as a partner and it felt natural with him sleeping close by. Sometimes we'd all lie awake talking in the dark before we fell asleep. Goodnight, John Boy. Goodnight, Mary Ellen."

She ran her fingers through her hair, gazing back at the past again. "In high school you were never quite sure who was or wasn't doing it. In college, it was out in the open. People made and arranged and rearranged their sleeping conditions to suit them. Sex was everywhere. And I would watch Will and Lucky together and it made me want..."

Her thoughts trailed off and her eyes softened, remembering Will's tattooed arms crossed over Lucky's body. How small Lucky looked in his embrace. Lucky, whose mother told her she was fat.

"Will made her feel beautiful. Everything Lucky's mother found fault with, Will loved. Her body. Her hair and her curves. Her style and her manner, her thoughts and dreams. She said to me once, 'It's like he's given myself back to me.'"

She looked up at Rita. "I love that. Someone who gives yourself back to you."

Rita leaned in her chair and trailed a finger along one of the lower bookshelves. She pulled forth a hardcover book and turned the front to Daisy. *The Collected Works of Antoine de Saint-Exupéry.*

"Have you read any of his work?"

"Only *The Little Prince.*"

"He says essentially the same thing. 'Perhaps love is the process of my leading you gently back to yourself.'"

Daisy took the book and ran her thumb across the page edges. "Can I borrow this?"

"If you like."

Daisy tucked it beside her. "Do you believe in love at first sight?"

Rita smiled. "What do you believe?"

"With Erik, it wasn't love. More like a knowing. A feeling. It was the start of tech week, when we go into the theater and set the ballets on the stage and do the lighting design. Sunday to Wednesday is tech. Thursday is dress and Friday is opening night. I was bringing David a sandwich Sunday morning. I went into the lighting booth and there he was."

"Erik?"

Daisy nodded. "He spun around in his chair and looked at me. And I looked at him and it was immediate." She looked at Rita and smiled. "It's impossible to tell this story without sounding like a Hallmark movie. The truth is I never believed in love at first sight. Love is built over time, it doesn't magically appear ready-made. And even connection at first sight? *Recognition* at first sight? I don't think I believed in those, either. But I walked into the booth and..."

The memory was like a looped movie clip. Erik turned around in his chair. Turned again. And turned again.

"There he was. It was him."

HIS NAME THROUGH HER MIND

A NECKLACE OUT OF LOVE

A BOY WITH DARK BLOND HAIR, dressed in jeans and work boots. Sleeves of a dark blue T-shirt pushed up along his forearms. A pencil jiggling in the fingers of one hand.

"Yo baby, what's up?" David said.

She looked at him, forgetting why she was here. The heat of the paper bag in her hand reminded her.

"They didn't have the chicken parm. I got you the meatball sub." As she handed the bag to David, she was conscious of her voice. How did it sound in the blond boy's ears?

She glanced at him. His eyes got a little bigger, his eyebrows coming down a hair. He looked away.

"What are you doing walking around barefoot?" David said. "Marie will kill you."

The three of them looked down at her feet. Daisy hid one behind the other calf. David was right—she needed to get her shoes on. Too many sharp things littered the theater.

She wasn't leaving until she knew his name.

"Dais, this is Erik. He's running your follow spotlight so be nice to him."

Her mind folded like protective hands around the words.

Erik.

Be nice to him.

She took the bag of food away from David and handed it to Erik.

He smiled like the sunrise, mouth stretching to show his teeth, cheekbones lifting to narrow his brown eyes. Their color made her think of the honey her mother drizzled into a shot of cognac—the Bianco cure-all for head colds and heartache.

Her heart ached with revelation. Looking at him, she felt an assembly within her body. As if she had lived up until this minute in four or five distinct pieces, each complete and content. But disconnected from the others. Now the pieces joined with a satisfying shift and click. Here. Next to here. And this fit here. Yes.

She pulled herself together.

You, she thought.

Leaving the booth, she should have been stumbling. Because love, from what she heard, shoved you from behind, knocked you sideways. Rocked and rattled you. But as she moved down the carpeted aisle, her forbidden bare feet were solid underneath her. Her mind felt fresh, like the first wide-open window of spring letting in soft, damp air.

Erik.

The company gathered onstage. Down in the orchestra, David slipped into one of the rows and Erik followed. She couldn't take her eyes off him. Every time she looked to where he was sitting, he seemed to be staring back. Not coyly or flirtatiously. Not with David's direct hunger. He looked as thoughtful as she felt.

They started the Bourée. Her feet danced. Her eyes stole glances into the audience. She felt him watching.

Who are you?

During a break, she came down off the stage and slipped into the row behind him, just over his right shoulder. His head turned a little. Then a lot more. His eyes widened and his smile unfolded.

"Hey," he said.

"Hi." She crossed her forearms on the empty seat next to him.

Further down the row, David and Kees were bickering in Dutch and Erik stared curiously at them while drinking a soda. She wanted to touch him. She wanted to kiss him. She asked for a sip just so she could put her mouth where his had been. Their fingers touched when she passed the bottle back.

She watched his hands take notes and twirl a pencil. His fingers, with their short clipped nails and ragged cuticles, scratched the back of his neck. He had a cut healing on one wrist. When he was thinking, he ran his left thumb along his fingertips, the nail worrying at the edge of a callus. Daisy's head tilted and her eyes squinted. Callused fingertips on the left hand. This boy played guitar.

She stared. The lights picked up the fine golden hairs on his forearms. She looked frankly at his body, his legs in jeans, his feet in workboots. She studied the bit of gold chain peeking out of his T-shirt collar. She could pick up a scent from the back of his neck. Skin and soap. Citrusy with a mint overtone.

He passed her the soda again and smiled. Something flickered in his eyes. A courageous attempt to communicate the unknown. She could hear him think what she was wondering.

Are you feeling this? Am I crazy?

She must be crazy.

Yet she felt so calm. Filled with the strangest compulsion to lay her hand on the back of his head and stroke his hair. And the even stranger conviction that he would lean into her touch, not shy from it.

She watched him all day. Eyes and ears straining for anything he said or did.

Erik. She threaded his name through her mind.

"Fish." Leo Graham, the technical theater director, called from the wings. "Come over here, I need you." And Erik went.

"Fish, catch," David said later, and Erik caught the hank of cable tossed.

Fish, Daisy thought. She didn't know what it meant or why he was called that. Asking David was out of the question.

She sidled up by Allison Pierce, one of the female techs, an overweight girl with straw-colored hair in braids. "Why do they call Erik Fish?" she asked.

"I think his last name means fisher," Allison said. "In Norwegian or something. Not sure."

"'Scuse us, coming through, ladies. Step aside." David was carrying the top end of a boom stand through the wings. Neil held the middle and Erik brought up the rear, lugging the heavy base.

"How you doing, Marge," Neil said in passing, his grin flashing wide.

"Hey." David looked back. "You don't call her Marge. I call her Marge. Inside joke."

Now Erik looked back. "Marge?" he mouthed.

She rolled her eyes and shook her head.

He smiled as if the joke was theirs.

SHE LAY ON HER BED THAT NIGHT, hands behind her head, staring up at the ceiling. A vague confusion had closed a fist around the serenity of the day and squeezed everything into a tight lump. Within it, her thoughts smashed and stuck together. She didn't have a word for what she felt. She knew nothing but his name.

Erik, she thought. *Fish.*

Lucky breezed around collecting clothes and her wash kit. Will this and Will that and Will something else. Daisy stared at nothing and made engaged noises.

"Hey," Lucky said, coming to sit on the edge of the bed. "What's wrong?"

She was going to say, "Nothing" and let Lucky be on her way. But the word stumbled in her throat, leaving her staring open-mouthed at the ceiling.

"Dais, what happened?"

"I don't know," she whispered, managing a smile but tears flooded her eyes.

"Tell me," Lucky said, sliding to her knees on the floor and crossing her forearms on the mattress.

"I met someone."

"When? You were at rehearsal all day. I turn my back a minute and you take an arrow between the shoulder blades?"

"He's running lights. He's working with David."

"One of Leo's rats?"

Daisy smiled at Lucky's use of theater lingo.

"All right. So, you met. And...?"

"That's all," Daisy said. "God, I sound so stupid."

"Excuse me? You had to practically tie my shoes after I met Will."

Daisy looked over at her friend. Lucky was blurred by tears but smiling gently. Her fingers smoothed Daisy's hair. "Funny when it happens, isn't it?"

Daisy shook her head. "I don't know if I can talk about it."

It was too fragile. A wad of tissue-fine papers she had to pick apart without tearing.

Lucky caressed her cheek, then leaned up and over and kissed it. "It'll be all right. It's like a fever. Take a couple of Tylenol and get some sleep."

"Sure," Daisy said, snorting, curling on her side toward the wall. She felt like jogging. She doubted she'd ever sleep again.

"Take a shower, take a Sominex. That's what my mother always says."

"I'll try it."

"Hell, if nothing else works, try masturbating. My advice, not my mother's."

Daisy looked over her shoulder. "I would if you'd go away already."

Lucky laughed. "Night, honey. Love you."

"Love you," Daisy said, as the door softly shut.

I love you, she thought, sliding the words like beads onto a brightly colored string. Abruptly she rolled the other way, clicking her tongue. A dozen glances and six words exchanged and she was making a necklace out of love. Her hand flicked the air, as if to cut the string and send the beads rolling. She was being ridiculous.

His soft brown eyes. Legs in jeans and a gold chain peeking out of his collar. The touch of his fingertips when he passed her a soda. And she put her mouth where his had been.

As if we kissed.

His smile. His direct, expansive gaze on her.

Every cell in her body whispering, *You.*

She rolled over again. Picked three beads and strung them.

Who are you?

HE'S SO YOUR BITCH

"SIX DAYS," DAISY SAID. "We met on a Sunday morning. We were together by Friday night. It sounds so cornball when I say it out loud." She lifted her shoulders and let them fall. "But we were together three years. *Something* happened in those six days."

"And I'd like to hear more about it," Rita said. "Next time."

The session was wrapped up and put neatly away. Daisy pulled her hat over her ears as she stepped from under the awning of Rita's building. As she turned off 82nd Street, the wind came whipping down the canyon of Broadway, grabbed her breath like a purse-snatcher and ran. Eyes watering and teeth chattering, she pulled her collar up and sighed at the grey streetscape. Stripped of holiday decorations, New York in January was a weary debutante after the ball, tired and disappointed with nothing to look forward to.

Daisy frowned at her watch. This wasn't her usual appointment slot and it threw off her schedule. Not enough time to go home for a nap, and too early to be at the theater. She hated having time to kill. She'd get a cup of coffee somewhere, head over to the Met and if a couch was free in the ladies' lounge, she'd close her eyes a bit.

In a bakery, she ordered coffee and a chocolate croissant, sat down at a little table in the window. She had no book with her, but she had her music. She slipped her earphones on and people-watched, letting the brisk first movement of Mozart's clarinet concerto accompany the hustle outside.

With the slower second movement, her mind pulled inward and her eyes stopped seeing beyond the window. She advanced the CD to the next track. The Bach Prelude in C.

"C Major," Erik said. "The friendliest key."

She took a sip of coffee, swallowing as slowly as possible, letting the warmth soothe her throat.

Erik passing her his soda.

The callused tips of his fingers.

Her mouth where his had been.

As if we kissed.

Six days.

Six hexagon beads on a string.

All day Sunday in the theater. No meaningful conversation, just a lot of exchanged curious glances and shared sips. And a feeling something was going on. Something that was beyond everything.

Monday afternoon was the focus session, when lighting for the concert was designed and the instruments and lanterns set in place. The dancers mostly stood around—talking, reading, knitting, dozing— while the stagehands were run ragged.

Daisy pretended to read while her eyes followed Erik. He went from stage left to stage right and back again, climbed up to the catwalk or crawled beneath the stage. He disappeared on errands for a length of time, then reappeared up on a ladder. Hauling, carrying, lifting and heaving. Far too occupied to be looking at girls.

"Dais, don't move or turn your head," Taylor Revell murmured over her knitting. "But the gorgeous blond stagehand can't take his eyes off you."

"He's been staring at her for five minutes," Manuel Sabena said. "I'm timing."

"Matt Lombardi already sniffed him out," Will said. "Thinks he's the love child of Bryan Adams and Sting."

Heart pounding hard, Daisy made her mouth into a vague smile. She counted to ten then looked over at the wings. Erik quickly looked away.

"Five minutes, fourteen seconds," Manuel said, digging Daisy's side and showing her his watch. "He's so your bitch."

Daisy's eyes narrowed. Erik was holding the ladder, a foot on the bottom rung and his arms braced. He pointed up, said something to his comrade, then put his forehead against his elbow and his shoulders went up in down in a tired sigh. He turned his head and met Daisy's eyes. He smiled and the fingers of one hand rose up in a tiny wave.

"Un régal pour l'oeil, hé?" Will said under his breath.

Easy on the eyes.

Later, while rehearsing the Prelude, Daisy went into an arabesque, gazed over the fingers of her extended arm and saw Erik in the wings. His eyes were easy on her as she hit the sweet spot of the pose and held the balance, suspended perfectly above the music, as if his gaze was supporting her. Then the music called and she had to go, pulling back from his eyes and moving, reluctantly into the next phrase of the dance.

At the end of rehearsal, she was sitting on the floor, untying her shoe ribbons when Will came and crouched down by her.

"I had a nice chat with your little friend," he said, peeling the hair elastic out of his ponytail.

She looked up at him, irritated. "You know, Will, I—"

He reached a finger and set it on her lips. "He talked me up in the wings. I went for a smoke, he came with. Want to know what I think?"

"No," she said, untying the other shoe.

He held still, balanced on the balls on his feet. Elbows on knees, fingers laced between, composed and patient. She knew his leg strength. He could squat there indefinitely. She sighed.

"Yes," she said.

"I think he likes you." He put his hand on her head. "Furthermore, I think he watches and listens more than he talks. Which means he's just like you."

Tuesday, she and Erik spent an hour alone in the empty theater before rehearsal. She sewed her shoe ribbons and he surprised her by sitting down at the piano with some sheet music he found in the bench.

She started warming up, accompanied by his playing, and they talked. Or rather, she asked him a lot of questions he didn't seem to mind answering. She learned his younger brother was deaf and his mother was the musician—she taught piano for years before his father left them. Then she had to sell the piano and go to work.

Daisy had a leg up on the piano, stretching out over it. She frowned against her knee. "Your father left you?" she said.

"Went out one night and never came back."

She picked up her head. He looked at her over the music stand, the tiniest bit of confusion in his expression. As if he couldn't believe what he just told her.

She took her foot down. "How old were you?"

"Eight."

"You haven't seen your father since you were eight?" He shook his head and she probed a little. "No word, no contact? No nothing?"

"Nothing."

Taken aback, she picked up the unfamiliar garment of his experience and tried it on. Clothed as she was in the strong, unwavering love of her own father, it was a poor fit. She squirmed and itched in it, trying to be eight years old, when the world is easiest understood in black and white. Except when black and white becomes here and gone. Overnight. With no explanation.

"Is he alive?" she asked.

He didn't know.

Sitting straight and proud on the bench, he looked at her, letting her in through his eyes. She looked back, breathing him in. Her heart pulsed, dressed in his pain. They went on staring, caught up in the strange, delicate moment.

Look away, she thought. *You're freaking him out, stop staring.*

Neither moved.

"My real name's Byron," he said. He shook his head, smiling. "Since I seem to be telling you everything."

"Does anyone call you Byron?" she asked, putting it with Erik and Fish. A trinity of identities attached to this boy.

"Rarely," he said. "It's his name, too. My father's." Then he looked away.

She told him her real name. "It's French for daisy."

His chin went up and down in understanding. As his lips shaped Marguerite without a sound, she wanted to kiss him.

I want to taste my name in your mouth, she thought. A fiery blush raced up her neck and into her face. She bent over her outstretched leg, hiding. "Play the Prelude again," she said.

Wednesday night, after rehearsal, they went to the campus center for dinner: Daisy, Will, Lucky, David and Erik. The embryonic stage of the circle. By the end of the night, it was Daisy and Erik alone in the booth. She had chapters to read. He had his cue sheets to finish. The work went undone because they couldn't stop talking.

Couldn't stop staring.

His eyes were magnetic, attracting and trapping hers. They weren't aggressive like David's. Or lined with confident self-awareness, like Will's. They were gentle eyes. Vulnerable and curious. And when she looked into them, she was filled with an indefinable sensation. It was greater than joy. More precise than peace. Not quite love but close.

She felt understood.

He showed her his necklace—the gold chain she'd been admiring since Sunday. He unclasped it now and coiled it into her palm. It was warm from his skin. A handsome piece, square-linked and masculine, with three small charms. A saint's medal engraved with an ancestor's initials. ("She's Birgitta," he said, "the patron saint of Sweden.") A gold fish and a flat-bottomed boat with Fiskare engraved on its bottom.

"Fiskare means fisherman."

"I thought it meant scissors. The ones with the orange handles."

He laughed. "I get that all the time."

She asked if his father wore the necklace. Erik remembered playing with it when he was a little boy. He would sit on his father's lap and make up stories about Birgitta and her boat, catching the magic fish. He reached behind his neck to fasten the chain again, telling Daisy how his mother had met with his father one last time, to sign divorce papers. And the father had given the gold chain over.

Listening to him, Daisy put her hand out on the table. With no break in his words, Erik put his on it. Curled his fingers around hers and went on telling her things. He was only ten when the divorce was finalized. It was more than five years later when his mother gave the chain to him to keep.

"But I had to be sixteen about it," he said, now holding her hand in both of his. Under the table their calves and ankles were hugging. "Prove he was no big deal to me."

He was everything to you, she thought, her palm warm between his. He was running his callused fingertips along the edges of her nails. She looked at him, balancing on his gaze.

"I like you," he said.

As she did over the lid of the piano yesterday, she reached invisible hands to try him on. And found the warm jacket of his simplest self fit her perfectly. She pulled it close around her shoulders, drew her hair out from beneath its collar.

"I like you," she whispered, lost in his eyes.

You fit me, she thought.

Thursday was dress rehearsal. She was standing in the wings while the wardrobe tech sewed up the back seam of her dance dress when she saw Erik. She held her hands out to him and he came to her, took her hands in his. They stood still, the hustling current of production parting and passing around them as their eyes held in a silent, staring communion. He reached shy fingers to play with her earring, then trailed them down her jaw, touching her like a lover.

Her mind wrapped arms around the moment and slowly pulled it horizontal, drawing Erik's longing to lie down with hers. She felt it then—the ache of her negative space needing a positive to fill it. Craving for the first time a closeness that conjoined, male and female. Away floated the last bits of adolescent revulsion toward the notion of a man being inside her body. Her thoughts became fists. They dug their nails into Erik's presence and held on with a quiet, greedy revelation.

I want him.

Friday was opening night.

The night her life opened.

 I CAN'T BREATHE

THE DRESSING ROOMS LINED the space beneath the stage like cat-acombs. Beneath the low ceiling, the air was warm and dry. A little musty. Layered with the smell of hairspray, makeup, sweaty costumes and illicit cigarettes. (They weren't supposed to smoke down there but everyone gathered around the one transom window that opened and did anyway.)

Because it was opening night, the strong scent of roses and carnations wafted down the row of dressing tables as the girls exchanged flowers and notes. Personal possessions and good luck charms crowded the Formica. Pictures were tucked into the mirror frames and trinkets were arranged in mystical, superstitious order.

Wrapped in her mother's black shawl, Daisy sang softly to the music from someone's boom box while she made up her eyes. Among her cosmetics was a bud vase with two yellow roses—one from Will, one from Manuel. At her elbow was a tissue-wrapped package: Taylor knitted her a hat.

"Hey."

Lucky's reflection appeared in her mirror.

"A little Fish was swimming around your mailbox." Lucky reached over Daisy's shoulder to set something on the dressing table. "But so was a shark named David."

Daisy half-turned to look back at her, eyes wide.

"I don't trust him," Lucky said, smiling. "So I went with my gut and brought it down."

"Thank you," Daisy said. She turned back to the table, heart spinning in circles like an eel. Erik left a bag of Swedish Fish in her mailbox. Two daisies taped to its top and a folded piece of paper beneath. Lucky slipped away as Daisy unfolded it. The note was short, only ten words clustered in the center of the page.

The library had a Swedish-English dictionary.
Sax = scissors.
Merde.

Lucky came back and set a paper cup of water on the counter. With a careful fingernail, she picked the tape off the daisy stems and put them into the cup while Daisy read the note again.

Lucky pulled out the chair at the next table and sat. "You got a nail file?"

Daisy gave her one then tapped her eye pencil on the table, thinking. She waited until Lucky was engrossed in filing to speak.

"Can I ask you a personal question?"

"No. You can buy me tampons at the drug store and throw my dirty underwear in with your load of laundry, but no, you may not ask me any personal questions."

Daisy smiled, loving her. "When did you have sex for the first time?"

"Actual intercourse?"

Daisy nodded.

Lucky put her hands down, fidgeting with the emery board. "I was fifteen," she said. "And I didn't do it for love. I did it to piss my mother off."

"Do you regret it?"

Lucky rolled her lips in, nodding. "A little. I got nothing out of it."

"Who was he?"

"A boyfriend. Sort of. Don't get me wrong, he was a nice guy. But not the one who should have been my first. And I should've gotten pregnant but I didn't, thank God. And by the way, since we're having this conversation and you have a funny look in your eye, I keep the condoms in my top drawer. Help yourself."

"Thank you, I have my own."

When packing Daisy up for school, her mother had thrown a box of Trojans into the carton of drug store supplies. Right in with tampons and witch hazel. They went into Daisy's top drawer and hadn't seen the light of day since.

Lucky's nose wrinkled. "In case you haven't figured it out, I like to take care of the people I love."

"In case you haven't figured it out, I trust you."

Lucky smiled at her. "What's going on, Dais?"

"Everything." Daisy leaned toward her mirror, lining her eyes. Cloaked in a mild confusion. She wasn't sure if Lucky gave the wrong answer or if she asked the wrong question.

"You really like this guy."

"I can't stop thinking about him. And I'm thinking about him in ways that I... I've never felt like this about a boy."

"Like what?"

She looked at Lucky. Put one foot on the trust, then the other. "Everything I like about him," she said, "I want to feel inside me."

Lucky nodded. "You're smart."

"Am I?"

"I think too many girls jump into sex before they even know what they're feeling. Or feeling anything at all, for fuck's sake."

"I have no shortage of feeling right now," Daisy said to her reflection.

"My thought is you don't have to hoard your virginity until marriage but it's not a thing to get rid of either. It's a gift. Not only to him but to yourself."

Daisy turned, pointing the eye pencil at her friend. "You're gifting him your history."

"Exactly. No matter where you go or what you do, that guy is the first and there's no erasing it. And that's what I could kick myself for. What's done is done. I'm not going to die of regret. And I'm not trying to sound like I know everything about sex. But the way it is with Will? I'm telling you, Dais. Don't do it because you're in college and everyone else is doing it. Do it because it feels right. When it's the right person, Jesus, it's so fucking good."

Daisy nodded as she touched the two daisies on her table.

"You'll know when you don't have any inner monologue going on in your head," Lucky said.

The cloak of uncertainty fell from Daisy's shoulders. Nothing was wrong with waiting. And nothing was wrong with knowing it was time. Not wanting sex didn't require an apology. Neither did wanting it.

"Thanks, honey," she said.

Lucky hugged her. "Good luck. I mean, merde. Will taught me you say merde to a dancer."

"I'll teach you a few things to say to him."

"Which is why I love you."

AS DAISY WARMED up at the backstage barres, her thoughts kept returning to the night in the campus center. When Erik unclasped his history from his neck and set it into her palm. Let her hold it. Let her touch some of the keen sadness that came with it. As if he stripped off the armor of adulthood and let her see the little abandoned boy within.

Nothing could be done about it except to hold it in her hands and witness.

I don't know what else to do, she thought. *You let me touch some of the sadness you carry in your heart. Now your happiness is something I need.*

Slowly she took her foot off the barre. She was filled with words piling on top of words. She went back to the dressing room, sat down and turned Erik's note over to the blank side, reached for a pen. She'd never written a love note. It always seemed to her a foolish thing to empty yourself onto a piece of paper that could fall into the wrong hands.

I don't do this, she thought. *I don't bleed my feelings on paper to someone I barely know.*

She looked down at the white expanse behind Erik's words, hearing its plea to be filled with hers.

I don't know what to do, she wrote, vulnerable and trembling. But the paper was kind to her thoughts. She saw herself between the words and lines. She trusted the blank space. Trusted the little gift Erik had given her tonight. Trusted the moments they shared so far and what he let her hold in her hands. She wanted more of it. Wanted to hold all of it.

I'm looking for you all the time, she wrote.

She exhaled, breathing herself onto the paper. She dared to tell him he filled her head like a dream. Not just his body but his mind. His heart and his pain.

I want to talk to you about everything.

She ate the candy and wrote until the stage manager called fifteen minutes. She wrote a little more after the Bourée, arranging a circle of red gummy fish around the paper cup. She wrote after the Prelude and the Siciliano, the words rolling through her head to her hand.

I didn't know love would be like this.

She stopped, pen poised over *love.* Too soon? What else would you call it? Her fingers traced over the lines she penned. They were in ink. They couldn't be erased. Either she gave him all of herself or nothing.

No apologies, she thought.

After curtain call she was free to leave. She changed out of her costume, tidied the top of her dressing table. She would go back to her room. Tell him in the note where she was and ask him to find her. If he felt the same. She picked up the pen.

If you don't feel the same, please be kind. But if you are thinking "Me too" please come find me.

Excitement pressed her, front and back, squeezing her lungs between.

"God, I can't breathe," she whispered.

She hesitated before confiding this last secret. In a way, it was the most honest part of what she felt right now. And she told him.

God, I can't breathe.

She folded the paper, slid it and her heart back into the empty bag of Swedish Fish, which was now an envelope, and placed it in Erik's mailbox. Gave it one last caress.

Please be kind.

She went to her dorm, showered and put on sweats, called her mother. Acted as if it were a normal night. She turned out the overhead light, leaving her reading lamp and the Christmas lights around the window. Her body was tired. The adrenaline of performance seeped out of her muscles, leaving them limp.

She dozed until a knock at the door woke her.

Slowly she got up.

No apologies.

The cold came off his clothes. He was breathing hard and trying to quiet it. The color was high along his cheekbones. And she knew he ran the whole way. He came running to her.

"Me too," he whispered.

SOMETHING UNDER IT

THE SKIN OF HIS FACE was cool but his mouth was warm. He was shaking all over, as was she.

His kiss was perfect. She touched his mouth, felt his breath catch against her fingers. He tasted like everything she wanted. He was beautiful, golden and tousled and trembling. She stroked the back of his neck, ran her lips over his head where the cold still clung.

"I have so much to tell you," he said.

"Lie down with me," she said. "Tell me everything."

Under the covers of her bed, still dressed, still shaking, they kissed and talked, falling asleep mid-sentence. Woke again to pick up where they left off. Kissing and talking until the thin hours of dawn.

"I want to talk forever," she said.

He pushed up on his elbow and slid his hand into her hair, pulling her face to his. "You know what I want. I don't have to tell you. But I'll wait for it. I don't care how long. Whenever you're ready for me. I'll wait."

As the days gathered speed and collected into weeks, as they explored each other's hearts and bodies, he said it often.

"I'll wait, Dais. I'll wait for you." He sighed, the circle of his arms tightening around her naked body. All of his skin lay along all of hers and it wasn't close enough for her. Not anymore.

"It's the first time I understand how love can have a physical expression," she said. "Because everything I like about you I want to have inside me. I want to put it with mine and make it us."

"God," he said, running his hands down her bare back. "Exactly like that. I want to be inside you. I mean all of you. Inside, looking out..."

He rolled her down, her head tucked in the crook of his elbow and his other hand on her face as he kissed her. His kiss was soft and hard at the same time, deep in her mouth yet hovering. The smell of his skin and the taste of his tongue. His palm sliding to curve around her breast. Gliding down to draw her leg around his hip. She felt him hard against her stomach. Hard for her all the while his mouth and hands were so relaxed and meandering.

"You feel so good," he whispered. "You make me feel so good and I want inside it. All of it around me."

"I want it too but I—"

"No buts. Stop." His finger wormed between their mouths. "Stop kissing me. Listen, this is important."

Smiling so wide it hurt, she nestled her head into his chest, her hand running down the soft skin of his back.

"Everything we've been doing, Dais, it's not like it doesn't count. I don't think of it as a consolation prize or second-best or something to make do with until we start having sex. If we're making each other come, then it *is* sex. It's making love to me. All of it. Even when we're lying around just talking."

"Even all my questions?"

"Especially those," he said against her neck. "You reached the tipping point with me. I mean, nobody has ever known me the way you do. And maybe... Give me a second, I'm kind of figuring something out."

He rested back on the pillow and ran his hand through his hair, eyebrows furrowed. He was so beautiful then, so endearing and thoughtful she wanted to throw herself into his experience. Melt and meld into his body so she could work it out with him.

"I'm so happy right now," she said, caressing his face.

He bent his head, rubbing his brow against the heel of her hand. "I'm trying to pay attention to it all," he said. He put his mouth into her palm a moment. "I've never fallen in love before. I want to remember this." His eyes flicked up to hers. "You know?"

She ran her hand along his cheek. Her thumb glided across his lips, then along his cheekbone. "I know," she said. "I want to remember the falling."

"I've never been anyone's first. And from what I hear, the first time isn't always such a great thing physically for girls. That kind of bothers me. Or worries me. I just want it to be... Not perfect, but..." His hand cut a level line through the air over their heads. "I want something underneath it."

"Build the bed first, before we get into it."

"Yeah. I want you to trust me. Maybe that's why I like your questions so much. Answering them lets you know me. Lets you trust I'll always give you the truth about myself. It means more to me right now than sex. It's how I'm a virgin. And I'm as cautious about giving it up as you are giving me your physical experience."

His smile flashed around a nervous laugh, his eyes grew wide. "Jesus, sometimes I can't believe the shit that comes out of my mouth when I'm with you. Did any of that make sense?"

Her heart was caught up in her throat, her eyes caught in his. "I love you," she said.

The smile faded. His fingertips came up to trace her face. They stared, peeled wide open to vulnerable bones.

"I love you," he said. "And I'll wait for you."

"Then I'll wait for you, too," she said.

HUNGRY FOR EVOLUTION

FOR FOUR WEEKS THEY built the bed beneath them. Constructing a bower of intense exploration. Sometimes her questions made him blush or chuckle. Sometimes he hesitated before answering, self-conscious about the truth or struggling to find the right words. But he always answered, making her more and more hungry for the arc of his life.

Running her hands over his body in the dark she purred with curiosity. Feeling him get hard against her body or in her hands, she was hungry for evolution, wanting to know all of Erik's journey through sexuality. How his body had woken up, started to respond to girls. The ways they would look or things they said and how he would get hard for them. She wanted to know how it came to be—from his experience of thinking about sex in the aching, preteen dark of his room all the way down the road to arrive at this place of being her lover.

"When was your first wet dream?" she asked.

He gave a bark of laughter. "Oh, God. Thirteen? Thirteen or fourteen, sometime in there."

"Did you know what it was?"

"I knew what they were as a concept, sure, but it's different when it actually... For a minute you forget and it's *what the fuck just happened?*"

"But you were already jerking off by that point, I guess."

He laughed again. "Well that started in like seventh grade."

"Lightbulb moment."

"Huge moment. Kind of a sad moment because any semblance of intelligence you've put together by that point is shot to hell. You get really stupid. All you think about is sex."

"Really?"

"Pretty much, yeah," he said, laughing softly.

She loved his smile, loved the shape of it and the flash of his teeth within. Loved how he lolled like a cat under her touch. She pushed up on her elbow, running her hand over his bare chest, hooking a finger-tip under the gold chain at his neck. She picked up the tiny fish charm and set it in the hollow of his throat.

"Would you do it every night?" she asked.

"Well not every night but..." His head bobbled around. "For a while it becomes part of the shower routine."

She laughed. "Convenient."

"Easy cleanup."

"What would you think about?"

He shrugged. "Girls."

"Girls you knew?"

"Sometimes. Movie stars. If the swimsuit edition of *Sports Illustrated* was out then it was always a hot month."

"You don't mind me asking all these things?"

"As long as you don't mind dealing with the answers." He took her hand and slid it against his erection, making her forget what she was going to ask next.

Another night in the dark of her room. Erik going down on her, his tongue like velvet, making her turn inside-out. Her hand rested on the side of his face, feeling his mouth work with and against her, the roll and shift of his jaw. Feeling how he made her come. Her heart pounding blood like gold through her veins and the Christmas twinkles blurring into an underwater galaxy. She dropped her hand on his head, holding him still. Catching her breath.

"What do I taste like?"

His hands slid up her legs and curled around her hip bones, his cheek on her inner thigh. She could feel his eyelashes against her skin and the damp warmth of his breath.

"So sweet," he said.

"Really?"

"But not right away. It's tart in the beginning. The sweet comes after a few minutes."

"Which do you like better?"

"Both," he said. "I love when my tongue first touches you and you make this sound. And when it goes sweet... I love that, too. And it kind of changes just before you come."

"It does?"

"Yeah. Like I can taste when you're going to come. I think I can, anyway." The shape of his smile became mischievous. "You know, six seconds after meeting I wanted to go down on you."

"Shut up," she said, running fingers through his hair.

"I swear. First time you got close to me and I smelled your skin? I thought, *she's got to be so sweet.* It was crazy. I'd never met a girl and immediately thought of doing that."

She smiled. "I thought it was every guy's go-to."

"Not mine. But I saw you and it's what I wanted."

"Go to, then."

His low laughter soft and cool where she was warm and wet. His tongue slid against her. Curled and coaxed. Her hand in his hair tightened. The lights around the window blurred again. More nights blurred together. More whispered questions blooming in their depths.

"What's the best part about getting head?"

"Everything," he said.

She'd gone down on boys before, but never with this kind of greedy ardor. She went for Erik with her passion ablaze. Lay on her stomach between his legs, up close and personal as she undid his belt, worked the snap of his jeans through the buttonhole and slowly tugged his zipper down. She didn't want to miss a thing. Not the heat of his skin or the soapy musk smell of him under his clothes or the line of soft brown hair extending down from his belly button and under the waist of his dark blue boxer shorts. How he dug in his heels and lifted up his hips as she worked shorts and jeans down his legs. The sharp inward tug of his breath. The clink of the charms on his necklace as his head fell this way then that on the pillow.

"God," he said as she ran her tongue along him. His body stopped and started, air caught up tight in his chest and his shoulders twisting down into the mattress.

"Your mouth feels amazing," he whispered.

She pushed him along the boulevard of pleasure. He put his hands over his face then pulled them back through his hair. They tumbled onto the covers, open and helpless as she pulled him over and over into the warm wet behind her teeth.

"It'll make me come soon," he whispered, his warning fingertips touching her forehead.

"I know," she said, taking his hand and gently putting it down on the mattress.

His voice was a keen blade slicing her name from the air one last time. Then his head fell back, his throat bared, the charms of his necklace sliding. The fingers of one hand gripping the sheets, the other hand curled into the dark as he came and she caught him.

After a minute he reached down, took her under the arms and dragged her up to him. Folded her into his elbows, gasping and shaking. "I swear..."

She put her fingertips on his lips. She was his everything at that moment and she didn't want any more words. She wanted the tremble of his limbs and the choppy breaths that gradually grew smoother. The slight lifts of his head off her chest and the attempts to speak, only to put his head back down again. She held him. Her tongue tingling. The skin of his bare back warm and gorgeous under her hands. His tight, hard body growing soft and still.

THE NIGHT OF HER EIGHTEENTH birthday, Erik gave her a set of Russian nesting dolls, Matryoshka, which she lined up along the edge of her dresser. Fat round sentinels watching as she gifted Erik to herself, to her history, to her life.

"Are you nervous?" he asked.

"No," she said. "Are you?"

"I can barely breathe and I don't want it to hurt you. I'm not scared but I'm shaking pretty bad here."

It made no sense—she should've been the one trembling with nerves. Instead she was undressing with a calm, steady burn. A candle inside the bell jar of his love. "Even if it hurts, it's still ours," she whispered. "I want you nervous. It tells me you care."

Her hands moved over his skin. As they kissed and touched, she felt the tremors in his body subside. Anxious or not, he was hard for her, bucking and straining as she unzipped him and helped him out of his clothes. Only the littlest hitch within his breathing gave him away.

Then she was sitting on her bed and he was kneeling between her calves, tearing open the foil of a condom. She took it from him. "Show me how," she said. "I'll be doing this a lot."

Laughter in his breathing now. The smile she loved shining on her head as his hands guided hers. "Not much to it. Just leave a little bit at the top here. Then roll it..."

"Can you still feel after it's on?"

"Don't worry about me. The less I feel the better. I have no idea how long I'll be able to make this last."

"I have nothing to go by," she said, lying back. "Come inside me."

As he crawled along her body, hard and intent, a wave of adrenaline splashed her chest. All at once she wasn't quite so fearless. Not sure where to put her arms or legs. Green and trembling in the shadow of his experience and needing him to partner her through this unfamiliar ballet.

"Now I'm shaking," she said, searching for his eyes, which had never led her wrong.

His hand was so soft on her face. His gaze steady and strong, filled with tiny gold lights. "This is the best thing I've ever done," he said.

"Show me."

"Put your arms up around my neck. Hold onto me."

She wound her wrists behind his head. He dropped down on one elbow, kissing her, the other hand reaching confidently between them and finding the way. He started to push into her, his hand now sliding under the small of her back, tilting her up to him. "Hold tight. I'll go slow."

She let her breath out and opened to him, fully expecting pain. He moved further up in her and she felt it, thick and warm, filling her up. Her mouth fell apart at the sensation, stunned. She knew he fit her but she had no idea he would *fit* her. She didn't know her body would give way like this, make room and then cleave to him, letting him in deep. It was tight. It stretched her. But it didn't hurt. It was Erik inside her and she made a noise she'd never made before in her life.

"Oh my God," she whispered.

He drew back. "Is it hurting you?"

She pulled him down and in. "No," she said. "No, it's good."

"Is it?" he said, sliding his hands underneath her back.

"Oh my God." Her knees inched up his hips. "It feels so good."

It felt too good. As the blur of pleasure drew into solid, sharper focus for her, it began to crumble through Erik's hands. She arched up and he moaned. She moved along with him and he pressed her still, begging her not so fast, not so much, it was too much.

"I can't hold onto it," he said. "It's too close."

"Go," she finally said. "Just go. We have all night."

"No, not yet."

"Yes." Tasting this new power of hers, she ran her mouth up his neck toward his ear and pushed him over the edge. "Let me see you come. Come in me. Fill me up."

A stifled, strangled cry in his throat and he was gone. He clutched at her and came, a writhing, grinding dervish. Gripping her so hard the charms of his necklace dug into her skin. She clung to him, wrapping him in arms and legs, mouth open against his temple as he came down. His body shivered. He laughed a little. Then he lay still, shoulders rising and falling as his breathing smoothed out.

He picked up his head and looked at her. "Don't cry," he said.

She touched her face, surprised at the tears. "I'm just happy," she said.

When he rolled off her, the condom was stained with blood. They both stared at it, a little confused.

"You're not hurt?" he said.

"No," she said. "Not at all."

He went on staring curiously, then he dipped a finger inside her and wrote his name on her leg. In her blood.

And she was his.

The second time was longer, their bodies more relaxed, and afterward they fell asleep in a mess of limbs. The third time, in the wee hours before dawn, she rolled another condom on him and climbed on top.

"Is this all right," she said and he nodded, eyes wide, hands coming up to cup her breasts and slide up and over her shoulders, down her arms.

"You're so beautiful," he said, palms spreading wide across her leg muscles.

She slid her hand between their bodies and guided him inside, kept her hand there so she could feel him moving along her fingers.

"I like this," she said. "I like you under me."

"Christ, I could look up at you forever..."

He had a tight leash on his desire now. He sprawled on his back like a god, letting her have at him. Taking the weight she leaned on him, watching as she tilted her hips this way and that. Confident in her body and secure in his love, she experimented with how he felt and fit inside her, rising up or leaning back or curling down.

"It's so good," he said, his eyes full of the sunrise. "I knew it would be."

They made love for a long time, kissing, touching and whispering as the windows filled with morning. She felt herself dissolve and melt into his body, felt her awareness flow back and forth between his body and hers.

It really is one, she thought. *It's one. It's all one. We are one. We are meant. We were born. I am him and he is me and we are us.*

"I love you in me," she said. "Making us. I love us."

His hands reached up, plunged into her hair and brought her down to kiss him.

"I love us," he whispered against her lips. Over and over. He was beyond calculated, conscious thought. He was babbling, a sing-song of impassioned feeling filling her mouth and flooding her throat and chest.

"I love you, Dais. I love it I love us I love you..."

A HOUSE LIKE THIS

ERIK'S HOUSE WAS A SIMPLE Cape Cod in one of the suburbs of Rochester. Homey and cluttered with a netless basketball hoop over the garage door. The downstairs was wall-to-wall carpet—a luxury for Daisy, who grew up on wood floors. The kitchen was open and sunny, the heart of the house. A banquette table was built under the corner windows and Daisy sat here with Erik and his brother while his mother cooked dinner.

Christine Fiskare was honey blonde and olive-skinned, with Erik's brown eyes and a husky voice. She was tall and broad-shouldered—besides being an accomplished pianist, she was also a competitive swimmer in high school.

Peter was dark blond as well, with blue eyes. Daisy thought Erik was guarded, but next to Peter's closed fist of a face, Erik was an open palm. Peter observed the world from a private and fortified fortress and no amount of friendly overture could make him come down until he was good and ready. Daisy sat quietly and let him get used to her, all the while covertly watching him under her eyelashes.

Pete was completely deaf in his left ear and a hearing aid allowed a bit of sound into the right. He wore the device at school and soccer practice and chucked it off as soon as he came home, preferring to divine the world through his keen sight and the assistance of his guide dog, Drew.

"He can pick shit up through his body," Erik said. "Like a giant antenna. I'm not kidding—he can be in his room and still tell the difference between me walking down the hall and my mother walking down the hall. He says the house vibrates differently around us."

Christine made pulled pork for dinner, and her face was a mixture of pride and despair as she watched her boys eat sandwich after sandwich and bicker over the last handful of fries on the baking tray. She rarely called them by name: Erik was *this one* and Peter was *that one.* Collectively they were *these two.*

"These two," she said to Daisy. "Keeping them fed keeps me just above the poverty line. I grew up with four brothers, all football players, and I have no idea how my parents didn't go broke."

"Your parents were broke," Erik said, spooning more coleslaw on his thrice-emptied plate.

"This one," Christine said. "Grew four inches in eighth grade. If he wasn't eating or complaining about his sore knees, he was sleeping. Weekends at two in the afternoon, I'd find him still in bed." She took the empty bowl of slaw to the sink and ran water into it.

"Eighth grade," Erik said, tapping the tines of his fork on his teeth. "Yeah, I remember that year I really liked my sleep."

Christine continued talking over the running water. Without a break in eating, Pete nudged his brother's arm. Erik put down his fork to translate into sign language.

"You have three fears when you're a parent: something's hurting them, or they're destroying something or, the worst, you don't know where they are. Whenever I found Erik in bed sleeping at two in the afternoon, I'd think, well, he's not hurting anything. Nobody's hurting him. And I know exactly where he is. And I'd shut the door and be happy."

Daisy was only half-listening as she watched Erik's hands. She knew he was fluent in ASL. When asked he'd shown her signs or how to finger-spell a word—mostly assorted curses, which were fun to learn. But she'd never seen him actively converse. Now she stared with bald fascination as he spoke and signed simultaneously, his strong fingers molding and shaping the air. It was more than a language, it was a highly skilled art form, this ability to listen to words and transpose into gesture. To interpret.

He's dancing with his hands.

Christine finished talking but Erik continued to sign. Pete's mouth cracked in silent laughter as he picked up and pegged a sandwich roll at his brother. Daisy stared, taking in the composition of Peter sitting with his guide dog on one side and Erik on the other. One who alerted him to sound and another who translated it. Erik was fending off Pete's punches with one hand and rapidly spelling with the other, and their silent connection reflected the kitchen light like sun glinting off a sword. They were bonded by steel, these brothers, an affinity made all the more stronger by its lack of noise.

Pete looked over at Daisy with an eye roll and a palm-up sign with his thumb and index finger touching.

"Asshole," she said. "First sign Erik taught me."

A flash of wickedness lit up Pete's eyes. He signed something to Erik, finishing with what looked like the universal gesture for jerking off.

"Milkshake," Daisy said. "It was the second."

Christine clicked her tongue. "Have you taught her any useful signs, Byron Erik?"

"No, ma'am."

"Just all the curse words."

"They're useful," Daisy said. She looked at Pete, who seemed on the verge of saying something, but then his blue eyes ducked away shyly. He rarely spoke.

"Doesn't want to," Erik told her once. "He will if he has to. If he's upset or in danger. Or even if he's super excited about something. But after my father left, he pretty much went electively mute."

Later on, Daisy was watching close-captioned *Late Night* with the two brothers. Several times she put out a hand to pet Drew, Pete's beautiful Golden retriever. The dog ignored her. After Letterman's monologue, Pete got up, yawning, and left, smacking one hand against Erik's raised one in farewell.

Pete caught Daisy's eye and over his brother's head he made the sign for milkshake.

"Goodnight," Daisy said. And made the sign for asshole.

Pete's smile flashed in the dark.

"Nigh, Days," he said.

The voice was pitched high and scratchy from disuse, but the words were unmistakable. Erik turned his head in surprise as Pete headed up the stairs, the jingle of Drew's collar in his wake.

"Damn," Erik said. "That one never says goodnight to this one."

ERIK WENT HOME with Daisy over spring break.

The farm-to-market business was called Bianco's. The house itself was called La Tarasque, after a legendary dragon from the region of France where Joe Bianco was born. A stone replica of the creature squatted by the mailbox, where the private driveway branched off from the main road.

Erik's eyes widened as they took in the sweeping vista of orchards and vineyards, the rolling green hills of Lancaster County spreading beyond. His eyes nearly bulged when, after dinner, Francine showed him to one of the bedrooms in the renovated carriage house and Daisy tagged along with a pillow under her arm.

"Where are you sleeping?" he said to her.

"Here. With you."

"Goodnight, darlings," Francine said as she went down the stairs. "Sleep well."

"I think my head just exploded," Erik said.

He and Daisy walked the orchards, apple blossoms falling like confetti into their hair. Erik helped Joe clear fallen branches, prune and tie the grape vines. He held baby chicks and ducklings in his careful hands. Put his face to the tiny, fragrant pine trees dotting the acres which, in a decade, would allow Bianco's to be a Christmas tree farm.

And he ate a ton.

Francine adored a good appetite. She was amused one morning when Erik picked a gold grapefruit out of the fruit bowl instead of the ruby reds Daisy and her father preferred.

"I like things that are kind of bitter," he said, a little shyly.

"You do?" Daisy said.

"Yeah. It's why I let tea steep for such a long time. I like when all the tannins come out and give it that edge."

Francine embarked on a feeding campaign. Salads with radicchio or endive or chicory. He devoured them. Homemade pasta with broccoli rabe, which Daisy detested. He ate three helpings. Joe had him try a well-aged Cabernet Sauvignon, one of the highest tannin red wines.

"Wow," Erik said. His face was thoughtful as he took another sip. "It's slippery in your mouth but then bone dry after you swallow it."

"Exactement," Joe said.

Dark, unsweetened chocolate, however, was a bust. Erik screwed up his face and shook his head. "No, that's too much."

"So interesting," Francine said. "A sweet boy with a bitter palate."

"You don't like sweets, now that I think about it," Daisy said, back in the carriage house.

"Only yours," he said, sliding her out of her clothes, looking for his dessert.

Lucky drove down for the weekend. She'd had a horrible fight-laced week with her mother. Her eyes were circled. Her curls drooped.

Francine believed in the healing power of small, important tasks. Lucky was sent to gather eggs. She held the warm spheres to her a cheek a moment before putting them carefully into her basket, her face absorbed and purposeful. She cut flowers for the table, folded the napkins and sang to herself as she swept the back steps. After lunch, she and Francine made a cherry pie. As it baked the kitchen smelled brown with pastry and almond, sweet-sour with sugar and fruit.

"Check it out." Lucky's cheeks were pride pink as she set the bubbling, lattice-topped dessert on the windowsill.

"A pie on the *windowsill*," she said. "What is more all-American, I ask you?"

That night the three friends built a fire on the patio and sat around the flames, eating pie. Erik played guitar, sloppy in an old plaid shirt and a backwards ball cap. His face shadowed with three days of beard growth. Every now and then he stopped to take a sip from the glass of Cabernet at his elbow. He moved his closed mouth around in dry appreciation, smiled at Daisy and went back to playing.

The girls talked and sang. Wrapped in a quilt, her curls backlit by the flames, Lucky looked beautiful. At peace. Reborn with a new nickname. Joe called her Lulu.

"This place is magical," she said. "It's so full of love and kindness and support. Your parents, Dais. I mean they're... It can't have been perfect. Tell me they tortured kittens in your presence or something."

Daisy laughed. It was an observation she'd been experiencing since high school. Everyone wanted her parents to be theirs. She could either feel guilty about it or share them. She brought everyone home.

"Here?" Erik said. "No, your parents didn't move here until you graduated."

"Our old house in Gladwyne," Daisy said against her fingers. She'd found a pit in her cherry pie. She threw it into the fire. "And even before, in the house in Fairmount—it was a stream of people coming in and out. And food. My parents are rabidly social but they really don't *go* anywhere. They like people to come to them. Pop jokes that no dining room table is big enough for my mom. So I did as they did and brought my friends to me."

"You know what's funny?" Erik said, firelight in his eyes as he smiled at her. "You call your father 'Dad' when you're talking to him. But when you're talking about him to other people, you call him 'Pop.'"

"I know," Daisy said, laughing. "Like he has a personal name and an anecdotal name. I don't know why I do that."

"And you call your mother 'Mamou.'"

"It was my first word and it stuck."

"Just you, right?" Lucky said. "You're an only child."

"Their only child," Daisy said. "Pop has a son. In France."

"Really?" Erik said, his fingers stopping mid-strum. "Have you met him?"

"No. Pop got his girlfriend pregnant before he left France. I don't know all the details—whether he said he would marry her then or if she said she wanted to wait. He was planning to join the army because it was a fast track to citizenship and he could go to college on the GI Bill. Anyway, he went back to see her after he finished his tours and found she'd had the baby and married someone else. And I gather her attitude was 'move along, Joe. We'll pretend this never happened, goodbye and good luck.'"

"Nice," Lucky said.

"He's turned the earth over to make a relationship. And been thwarted at pretty much every turn. Passively by the mother and aggressively by the stepfather. So he did a little side-stepping and forged an alliance with the grandmother. She sneaks letters in. And sneaks pictures out. Pop has a couple in his study. I'll show you."

"And you grew up knowing this?" Lucky said. "It was out there in the open?"

Daisy nodded. "It was my job to dust pictures when I was little. 'Who's this?' I'd ask and Mamou would say, 'That's Dad's son. He lives in France.'"

"Jesus," Lucky said. "Something like that would be silenced in my house. Stuffed under the bed or buried in the basement."

"What's his name?" Erik asked.

"Michel."

He smiled. "Maybe he'll come here someday."

"He knows he can."

"I want a house like this," Lucky said, her shoulders rising and falling. "A house people feel safe coming to. Where they can be themselves."

NETSUKE

"I WOULDN'T SAY my childhood was magical," Daisy said. "Or perfect."

"Nobody gets out of childhood unscathed," Rita said.

"But I certainly wouldn't trade it for anyone else's. I knew I had it good. Better than a lot of my friends. My parents are special people. I was treated as an adult at an early age. I wasn't left out of decisions. I wasn't sheltered from problems. I knew when money was tight or when Pop was having one of his episodes."

Rita's eyebrows raised. "Episodes?"

"Something happened to him in Vietnam. It's one of the few things I was never privy to. Something he saw. Or did. Or had to do. And it involved children. He could not cope when a child was screaming. I don't mean crying. Crying babies don't bother him. It's the fine line between a cry and a...a shriek. A scream of genuine distress. My father goes pale. You can see the blood drain away from his face. And his eyes go to a place so far away. I don't know what happened there and I'm not sure I want to know."

"Soldiers are no stranger to PTSD," Rita said. "Unfortunately the more generations you go back, the less it's talked about."

"He's a lovely man," Daisy said. "I love him so much. But he needs to have things a certain way and as soon as I was old enough to understand, my mom made sure I knew it."

"What kind of things?"

"His personal things. My playroom could be a mess, the kitchen could be a mess—it didn't bother him. His office was sacrosanct space. Everything in his study at La Tarasque is alphabetized. Every knick-knack, every book, every object is placed in a deliberate spot and cannot be moved. The rugs are aligned with the cracks in the floor. The fringe on the rug is flawless—not one piece longer or shorter than the other. He maintains it himself. The cleaning lady wouldn't dare go in there. It's the holy of holies."

Rita nodded. "Traumatized soldiers are often painfully ritualistic. Or painfully reckless, in the other extreme."

"One time, I was about five. Maybe six. I went into his office. He had a set of netsuke—little Japanese sculptures. Tiny, exquisite things. Carved out of wood or ivory. Little people. Little animals. Little magic objects." Daisy's hands cupped, remembering their charm. "They begged me to take them down from his shelves and play with them. And I took them out in the living room and had a ball. And then my father found me."

"Oh dear," Rita said.

"I think it stands to this day as the angriest I have ever seen him. He hollered from his office, 'Marguerite Chantal, you come fix this *right now.*' You know when you hear your full name you're in deep shit. I almost peed my pants. He comes out with his hair on fire, standing over me and pointing at his office. 'You fix this. You fix this right now.' I'm grabbing netsuke with both hands, bawling my eyes out because I don't recognize this yelling man as my father. Hands full, I run out of the living room and crash into my mother. And now she's pissed because..."

A pause.

"Because?"

"We had certain rules in our house," Daisy said. "It was a relaxed atmosphere but good manners prevailed. Not just table manners or being polite to company. Certain little courtesies my parents insisted on. Like thanking my mother for whatever she cooked. I don't think I ever got up from the table once without saying thank you. And whenever I left the room where my parents were, either parent, I said 'excuse me.' I didn't have to wait for their permission. I just had to say the words."

"I see."

"So I crashed into my mother and she took me by the shoulders and kind of whirled me around to face my father again. She said, 'Say excuse me before you turn your back on your father.' And her voice was something I'd never heard before either. I said it. Or sobbed it. And Pop pointed at the office like 'Get out of my sight, stupid child. Go fix it.' And I turned around again and my mom caught my arm and smacked my butt. Wham. I don't need that kind of shit twice to learn a lesson."

Rita laced her fingers around her knee, looked about to say something but didn't.

"To this day," Daisy said, "my father's study is not a room I find welcoming. My mom has a nice comfy chair by the window where she reads the paper. But I go in there and automatically tiptoe."

Rita smiled.

"But look, it's one room in the house, not the entire house. It's knowing he's sensitive to certain things. Helicopter rotors make him tense up. Thunder makes him uneasy. If he goes to a crowded venue, he always searches for the exits. And screaming children stir some dark memory I'll never know." Daisy rolled her shoulders. "He never took his demons out on me. Ever. But I knew these things. They weren't hidden from me. And I grew up gravitating toward stillness rather than chaos. No big shock I turned out to be a homebody instead of a party girl. I wanted to help make Pop's life sweet and restful. I guess because I saw the kind of atmosphere my mother created so effortlessly, and I wanted to be part of it."

"You're quite fortunate. Your family and your home...whatever home it was, in Philadelphia or at the orchard today. You're bonded to it. You have a deep sense of belonging and, what did Lucky say? It's a place you can go to and be safe. And your friends felt that way too, apparently."

"I loved to bring them home," Daisy said, her voice a dreamy, silk ribbon of memory. "I loved when the porch light would go on and Mamou would appear at the door. Waving as we fell out of the car. 'Hello, darlings. Come in, come in.' Staggering into the hallway which smelled like lavender and lemon and whatever she was cooking. She'd kiss and hug and fuss over us, shoo us into the kitchen like we'd been pulled from a shipwreck. And within minutes everyone would be her kid. She'd have someone setting the table and someone else fetching a platter or the gravy boat. We'd sit at the big table and eat and laugh and talk. For hours. And I'd see my friends looking around the table, looking at each other like they'd never known anything like it. And I'd be so proud it was my house making them feel so good."

Daisy touched her eyes, filled with unexpected emotion. "Someday I want to be that woman. Waving from the screen door as my children and their friends come to our house because it's safe and lovely and fun there, with wonderful things to eat."

ACROSS THREE GENERATIONS

DAISY EMERGED FROM the library, taken aback as she heard the clock tower chime nine-thirty. She'd been holed up in a windowless study room, working on an art history project. Shut off from the outside light, the hours fell away.

An unexpected cold front had come through Philadelphia, along with a mean rain. Without an umbrella, gloves or a hat, the walk back to her dorm was brutal. The raw wind blew hard in her face and she tucked her mouth under the collar of her jacket. Trudging chin down through the damp chill, she reached her dorm and put her hand on the side door's handle just as it opened into her.

It was Erik.

He grabbed both her upper arms tight and turned in a quick half circle so her back was against the bricks. He stared down at her, his breath making clouds in the cold night. His face wasn't angry, but it was hard, as were the hands squeezing her upper arms.

"What's wrong?" she said, heart pounding against the wall of her chest.

"I didn't know where you were," he said.

Her mouth fell open, at a loss. "I'm right here," she said, stupidly.

"But I didn't know where you *were*," he said. His mouth was partly open too, working around words he couldn't find.

She looked in his eyes, stunned and confused. Jealousy wasn't like him. He blinked back at her, looking far younger than his nineteen years. Then she remembered what his mother had said: how a parent's greatest fear was not knowing where their child was.

Or not knowing where your father is.

Or not knowing where anyone you love is.

It hit her all at once. How for some people, the not knowing was a mere nuisance. For others, it was a dire strait.

Daisy closed her eyes as understanding flooded her. This wasn't resentment of how she spent her time or who she spent it with. It was her whereabouts. The fixed constant of her place in his universe. The knowing was dire for Erik, this boy who was abandoned overnight.

"I'm sorry," she said, opening her eyes. "I'm so sorry. It was thoughtless of me. I should have let you know."

His fingers let up and his shoulders dropped. He swallowed, looking away. "It's fine," he said. "It's fine, it's just that—"

"It's not fine." She put her hands on his face. "You need to know where I am. I didn't understand until now. I'm sorry."

Some deep, fear-based emotion had coiled around him like a snake. His eyes blinked rapidly in the cold. He wasn't crying but he was held up tight in a vise.

He was eight, Daisy thought, her cold hands running gentle along his shoulders and arms. *His father was there one night and gone the next morning.*

"I'm sorry," she said. "I won't disappear like that again."

He put his arms around her, pulled her tight to his body. "You're freezing," he said. "Come on, get inside."

HE LOVED HER HARD that night.

"Turn over," he said softly, digging a hand beneath her shoulder blade and rolling her on her stomach. He knelt across her legs and worked himself inside her, his palms warm on the small of her back. His hungry body a sweet, crushing weight pinning her to the mattress, fixing her in place.

"I want you all the time." His mouth whispered along the nape of her neck. His teeth touched her skin. "I want you right under me."

Finding the hook of an orgasm while Erik was inside and getting it to stay with her was more chance than skill. Often it slipped from her grasp, or danced just out of reach. Now something within her shifted and sank deeper. It put down roots in the cradle of her pelvic bones, and started squeezing. A hand into a soft fist. Beneath the pillow her fingers wove tight with Erik's.

"Don't stop," she said. "It's so close."

"I can feel you," he said. "Let it go."

It was on her, rising up as Erik pressed her down. He slid into her faster. Deeper. The Christmas lights swam in her eyes, a twinkling blur cascading through her chest and belly and head as he pushed her harder. Threaded her through the needle and pulled her out long on the other side.

"Come," he said, his voice collapsing. "Come to me."

Their fingers clenched. She reared back into him, kicked up her hips and came in pieces. Her teeth rattled together. All the air pulled back through her throat, leaving nothing but a thin cord of sound wrapped around the shape of his name.

"God," he said, gasping against her head. "It's so good..."

She lay trembling beneath him, closed up in his arms, his heart thumping on her back. Her own heart like tympani beneath her ribs. His mouth soft in the tangle of her hair. Little nonsense noises as their bodies and their breathing quieted down. Together they floated in the dozing zone of contentment where time had no place.

Her body shivered awake.

"Are you cold?" he whispered.

"A little."

He reached out of bed, got his flannel shirt and buttoned her into it. He loved when she wore his clothes.

"I want to show you something," he said.

He leaned down again, hooking the straps of his backpack and dragging it toward him. From inside he drew out a book, handing it back over his shoulder. Daisy clicked on the reading lamp and tried to read the title but it wasn't in English.

"They're folk tales," he said. "My grandparents gave it to me for Christmas one year. It's all in Swedish, I can't read it. I just like the pictures. But I really wanted to show you these..." From between the middle pages he drew out several photographs and passed them to her.

Daisy folded her pillow in half to make a wedge and leaned back, examining the pictures. The first was a man and a little boy at the edge of a dock, fishing. The boy wore a pair of plaid shorts and nothing else. The fishing pole was curved in an arc toward the water and the boy was pulling back on it. Eyes wide and mouth in a little O of surprise.

The man stood behind, bending forward a little, his hands on the boy's forearms, his face wide open with laughing excitement. His hair was blond and cut short. Lean arms and broad shoulders in a white t-shirt. Around his neck swung a gold chain.

"Is this your father?" Daisy asked.

"That's him. And that's me."

"I guessed," she said, smiling. "What did you catch?"

"Probably a bass. Or a pike."

She put the picture face-down on her chest. The next showed Byron Fiskare walking along a rocky beach. He held Peter in one arm. The other hand was palm-up, showing something within it to Erik. The wind blew pant legs and jackets into folds and ripples. The surface of the water behind them was full of white caps. A faint smile touched Byron's face as he looked down at Erik.

"Where was this taken?"

"Clayton. It's on the St. Lawrence River. The Thousand Islands."

"You lived there?"

"I was born there."

The next picture was in a kitchen. Erik, looking no more than five, sat on his father's lap, a big closed-eyed, closed-mouth smile mugging into the camera. A fork in one hand, a piece of cake on the plate in front of him. Byron had both arms curved around Erik's middle, his chin on his son's shoulder, looking hopeful for a bite of dessert.

Across the table, Peter sat in a high chair, his face smeared with chocolate frosting. His mouth open like a hungry baby bird, leaning toward the fork a woman was holding out to him.

Daisy peered. It wasn't Christine sitting next to Peter. This woman was older. Slim in a print dress. Grey hair pulled into a low bun. Horn-rimmed glasses. Not smiling, but not unfriendly.

"Who's she?" she asked.

"That's Farmor," he said. "My grandmother."

"Did you live with her?"

"Next door."

"And what did you call her?"

"Farmor," he said. "Swedes have different names for grandparents. Farmor is your father's mother."

He reached and turned the next and last picture up. Byron and an older man busy at a workbench and Erik sitting on its surface. He drove a Matchbox car up his father's arm and Byron's head was turned back, smiling at him.

"That's Farfar," Erik said, fingertip tapping the old man. "My father's father."

"Your dad looks like you here," Daisy said, her own fingertip circling Byron's face. "And even in your grandfather I can see the resemblance."

It was in the cheekbones and the shape of the mouth. And how all their hair was fair and cut short, showing a similar brow across three generations.

"Pete has more of my mom's side in him," Erik said. "Everyone said I was all Fiskare."

She hummed, rubbing her head against his. "But your grandfather's face, the way it's closed. He has a reserve. That's Pete's expression. Your dad's face is a little more open. Like yours."

Her fingers flipped through the pictures once more. In each one, Byron was wearing the necklace. In each one, he was looking at Erik.

She didn't know what to say. Every observation felt potentially hurtful.

He looks like a nice man.

Nice men didn't abandon their families.

He loved you. You can tell by his face when he looks at you.

Then why did he leave?

She tapped the edges of the photograph into line and gave the stack back to Erik. He put them and the book on her night table and clicked the lamp off, leaving them in the light of the Christmas garlands.

He rolled away from her. "Lie against my back?"

She moved up to him, curving herself around his body. She slid her hand up to rest flat on his bare chest, feeling his heart. He loved to be held this way when he was drifting off. And she loved the broad plane of his back against her stomach. Holding onto him like a raft through waves of sleep. It worked perfectly. They made so much sense together.

"When did you move away from Clayton?" she asked.

"About a year after he left. My mom wanted to be closer to her family in Rochester and have Pete go to school there. He'd stopped talking, I told you."

"Did you ever go back? To visit your grandparents?"

"Few times. But it got harder and harder. I remember those visits being sad and almost awkward. I moped through them. Everything I used to love about that place I hated. I didn't want to see my old house where we were a family. Didn't want to see my bedroom window where I watched his truck drive away for the last time. Didn't want the river where I fished with him or Farfar's boathouse where I'd play by the workbench. Just didn't want any of it anymore. It hurt too much. My mom would be so tense back in Clayton, and my grandparents were getting older and more reserved. It wasn't a loving place anymore. As Pete and I got older and more busy with sports and stuff, the visits dwindled away. When Farfar died my junior year, I hadn't seen him in... I can't remember how long. Long enough that when we got the letter from his lawyer saying he'd left me and Pete his money, I felt bad. Like I could've tried harder to make a relationship.

"A few months later, his brother Emil died. He was the last of that generation. It finally hit me with my father gone, I was the next link in the chain. And that's when I took the necklace out of my dresser and started wearing it."

He sighed. She rubbed her forehead between his shoulder blades, breathed in his scent.

"You know I never showed those pictures to anyone," he said.

"I loved seeing them," she said.

"I feel like I can tell you anything."

She rested her lips behind his ear. "Because you can."

"I'm so in love with you."

Her eyes grew warm and she felt her heart would burst. "I'm so happy," she said.

His fingers curled around hers.

Then he was still.

Emotion cradled her in soft arms as she lay awake, listening to him sleep, running a gentle fingertip along the gold chain at his neck.

After that night, she always let him know. Called or left a note, left word with someone else. And few were the moments when one of them didn't know where the other was.

HIBERNATION

THE ROOM WENT utterly quiet. The sound of no sound pressing against Daisy's eardrums. Her heart beat slow, as if she were in hibernation.

"When he'd tell me about his father," she said. "I'd feel so close to him. When someone shares the happy stories of their life, it's always beautiful. But when someone shares their pain with you, it's almost more profound. More valuable."

"I agree," Rita said.

"God, I loved him. It felt grown-up. But we were really just kids."

"Yet it sounds like you had quite a mature relationship," Rita said. "To hear you tell it, you and Erik were lovers and partners. You worked through problems together. You were attuned to each other's wants and needs. He trusted you implicitly and—"

"And I blew it," Daisy said.

Come back. Please come back.

Rita hummed, a soft note of attentive sympathy.

"I own what I did," Daisy said. "But at the same time, I wish to hell James had never come to Lancaster." She ran her hand along her damp eyes. "I get so tired and it's easier to blame him. If only he hadn't showed up, everything would be different."

Soundlessly, Rita turned a page in her notebook.

"When did James come?"

"Junior year."

"Can you tell me about him?"

A BROKEN
LITTLE BROTHER

BOTH ARMS

MARIE'S ADVANCED PARTNERING class was learning the balcony scene from Kenneth MacMillan's ballet *Romeo and Juliet.* The partnering was difficult, the lifts complex. Timing was critical and if Romeo wasn't where Juliet needed him to be, stars would not only cross but they would also end up on the floor.

"Sorry," James said, helping Daisy up. "That was my fault."

It was his fault. But one of the first things a girl learned going into supported adagio class was how to fall safely. The second was patience. Daisy fell plenty when learning to partner with Will. She had to keep it in mind as she was learning with James. She brushed off her hip and butt, pushing away her irritation.

"You all right?" James said, his apologetic grey eyes like storm-filled skies, threaded with lightning bolts of gold. He'd transferred to the conservatory from Juilliard and already made an impression as a brilliant but erratic dancer. His range was phenomenal—he could shift effortlessly from classical ballet to edgy modern to ballroom schmaltz and he was a credible tap dancer as well. Plus he had a kinesthetic memory: he merely had to watch movement to copy it. He recalled choreography and style after a single demonstration. What he couldn't seem to retain, however, was consistency.

They started learning this pas de deux two weeks ago. The lifts worked fine. Then for no reason, James blanked out on simple mechanics. In the next class, he had them down again. Today, it was a disaster. Tomorrow they might be perfect. Daisy had no way of knowing. His erratic nature made her nervous and cerebral and when she got too caught up in her head, her dancing went flat.

It drove Marie batshit.

"For the fortieth time, Jase." Marie hadn't gotten his name right yet. "You are trying to catch her with one arm." Marie's voice was quiet but it dripped intolerance. "You are going to either break your arm or break Daisy." Her tone left no question which she would prefer.

"Mark the lift, please. Walk through it, Daisy. Are you listening, Jase? Let her take your hand as she goes up. Let her let go of you during the throw. She will turn herself in the air and when the turn is complete, you catch. *Both* arms. Tight. You love her, for goodness sake."

James nodded, hands on hips, expression contrite. As she walked to her starting position, Daisy smiled at him and touched his damp shoulder. If Marie was intent on James partnering her, she had to find a way to connect with him, especially since Will was graduating this year.

If she were dancing with Will right now, her head would be filled with a Capulet-and-Montague narrative. She and Will would have read the balcony scene together. Acted it out and built a backstory. Murmured the dialogue as they practiced steps.

James barely looked at her. She may as well have been playing the nurse.

Marie cued them. "And…"

Daisy wiped the slate clean. Ran and took James's hand as he threw her. He was strong and the momentum let her turn over easily in the air. She should have been turning because she longed for his arms. Because it was too lonely in the air and down on the earth with Romeo was where she belonged.

But with the imagination-less James under her, her mind only knew one entreaty: *please, God, catch me…*

He did. With both arms.

"Bravo, Jase," Marie said. "Now do it that way every time, si?"

"Sí," he said, setting Daisy down. She turned to him but he wasn't looking at her. His hands were on his hips again and his gaze was intent. Within the goatee he sported, his mouth curved in a slightly predatory smile. He was looking across the studio to Will.

Who was looking back.

Class was dismissed. Daisy plopped down by her dance bag and untied her shoe ribbons, covertly watching James. He wore his dark brown hair cropped short. The goatee and the gold rings in both ears gave him a gypsy air. He stood by Will, arms crossed, with that intense gaze as Will dried himself off with a towel. Grinning, Will chucked the towel at James's face, who pulled it off with relish. Will dragged his wet T-shirt over his head and tossed it at James as well.

"Keep going," James said.

Will laughed, shaking out a clean, dry shirt and, Daisy noticed, taking his sweet time putting it on.

It wasn't a point for debate. At twenty-two, Will was a hunk. All boyish grin and chewy sex appeal. His skin flushed with sweat and exercise, the veins pushed up high in his muscles. His tattoos curled black, grey and green in the contours and cuts. Daisy knew them all: the Chinese characters, the compass rose, the yin-yang symbol and all the rest of them. Or at least the ones on his torso. The ones below the belt she'd only heard Lucky describe in dreamy tones.

"You know the iliac line really fit guys have? Will's got some Zen quotation running right along it. Fucking hot. It's my favorite."

Lucky wasn't at school this semester. She was up in Boston doing an emergency medicine course. Daisy didn't know if any kind of separation agreement was put in place while she was gone. But she knew Will and she'd been detecting a shift in his demeanor lately. A curious wind turning his interior vane in the opposite direction. Daisy watched him laugh as James peppered him with friendly punches and she grasped the situation unfolding in front of her.

James couldn't speak French, but he spoke dance and men—two of Will's languages. He was fit and built and definitely easy on the eyes. His tattoos had their own story. He liked Will.

And Will was digging the shit out of it.

AS SEPTEMBER SLIPPED by and James's presence became more frequent in Daisy's circle, she was positive Will was looking for some fun. A smug strut accompanied his presence, as if the confirmation he was attractive to both sexes had gone to his head. He was partying hard on the weekends, which was where Erik had to either disengage or throw everything off and dig in.

It wasn't his strong suit. James, Will and David had the heads and stomachs for boozing. Erik tried to keep up but usually ended up paying a hefty price—his hangovers were the stuff of embarrassing legend. And it wasn't only booze on the menu. David always had cocaine and James smoked more pot than Leo Graham.

Both Daisy and Erik declined the blow. They were curious about the high, but shared the same aversion to putting anything up their nose. They took the joints passed to them, but smoked in a methodical way, enough to get the edges of the world to giggle, but not enough to make their DNA disintegrate.

But it wasn't only substance intolerance bothering Erik. Other lines in Will's life, invisible up until now, were becoming obvious and testing Erik's social tolerance.

"It's not like there's never been speculation about Will batting both sides," Daisy said.

"Well it's one thing to speculate and another thing to see it in action," Erik said.

A perpetual wrinkle of worry seemed to be in between his eyebrows. He was morally and emotionally cornered in his masculinity. He respected Will's private business and had always chosen to deal with things he found personally objectionable by shutting the hell up. To butt in and say something was either to admit he had objections to Will's relationship with James or, more truthfully, that he was jealous.

"I'm jealous of James." He laughed as he said it but the admission was raw. "It's fucked up."

"Because he's getting all Will's attention," she said.

"What the fuck do I care who Will pays attention to?"

"He's your friend."

"David's my friend and I couldn't care less who he sleeps with."

"One, David is not Will. Two, I'm not a psychology major or anything, but I think you might have a *small* problem with people's attention being taken away from you suddenly and without explanation. Particularly people you care about. Possibly *male* people you care about but that might be too Freudian a stretch..."

Erik looked at her a long time, lips parted as if to deny. Then his eyes rolled to the ceiling and he ran a hand through his hair. "Stop knowing me," he said.

"I'll try," she said, putting arms around him.

"So what do I say to Will? 'Dude, I'm having serious daddy issues, could you maybe take me out to dinner or something?'"

"He'd love that," she said, laughing.

"Maybe I'll stand under his window and sing 'You Don't Bring Me Flowers.'"

"Come on, in all seriousness, all you really need to tell him is that you want to hang out more. Alone."

"Sounds so gay," he muttered, bristling like a cactus in her arms.

She let him go. "Tell him. Have a conversation. It's because you respect his private and personal life that Will will talk to you about damn near anything."

This she knew. She'd never directly asked Will about his sexual persuasions. As tantalizing and fascinating as she found the notion of him having male lovers, it was none of her business. But she'd had plenty of conversations about tolerance with her partner, and he'd made clear his philosophy about discourse.

"I'll talk about anything," he said. "Just don't be an asshole about it."

As a person who welcomed and honored love in all its forms, without regard for gender, Will could not be phased or shamed. He had nothing to hide. Which made him completely open to discussion and debate as long as it was done with a decent amount of civility.

"You want to sit and ask me stuff? Bring it. You want to ask if I've ever sucked a guy off or taken it up the ass, because you're genuinely curious? Go right ahead. We'll have a conversation. But don't try to corner me or confront me. Don't ask me shit with a sneer on your face, thinking you can shame me into some sordid confession just to make yourself feel better about your own doubts or insecurities. I don't have time."

Daisy was willing to bet the civilized questions turning over in Erik's mind contained the words "suck," "take" and "ass." But as for whether or not Erik would ever ask them, she'd keep her money in her pocket.

THE BUS

"HOW ARE YOU, darling girl?" Daisy said, switching the phone to her other ear. "I miss you."

"Do you?" Lucky said, laughing. "I thought Erik would be moved in by now."

Daisy and the boys had started renting off-campus that fall. They had the luck to find two apartments on adjacent streets, the backyards bumping together, and David shared an apartment with Neil Martinez around the corner.

"Oh, being the single occupant has its perks," Daisy said. "But I miss you. How's the course going?"

"Tougher than I thought." A sigh was in Lucky's voice. "I'll stick it out but I don't know if I have the stomach for this. The actual course-work is interesting, but going out in the bus is...pretty brutal."

"Bus?"

"The ambulance. We call it the bus."

"Ah."

"No lack of hot firefighters, however. As you said, it has its perks."

Daisy laughed and a slight pause flowed over the line.

"I, um," Lucky said slowly. "I had a date."

"Really? So you and Will made an agreement?"

"Yeah." The word was thrown out cavalierly but Daisy could sense a thin veil of uncertainty around it. "I mean, it seemed a natural and sort of sensible time to..."

"See what's out there?" Daisy said.

"Sort of. We agreed we weren't going to actively go out looking to get laid, but we didn't swear an oath of absolute social fidelity either."

"An experimental, emotional separation while you're physically apart. See what happens, see how you feel."

"Right."

"And?"

Lucky sighed. "I've been on a few dates actually. And every guy is... He's nice, he's funny, he's intelligent. We get along. He's good-looking. But at the end of the day, he's just not Will."

"Ah."

"I know he's having a good time."

Daisy spoke carefully, knowing Lucky was no fool. "I get the sense he's stretching his wings."

"He keeps talking about this James guy. What's he like?"

"He's a great dancer. But personally I find him unpredictable. He's an attention junkie. The kind with a deep streak of damage somewhere inside, like it's never enough. When he's in a good mood, he's king of the world. But when he's not, it's one passive-aggressive ploy after another to get someone to look at him."

"Sounds like he likes Will looking at him."

Daisy tapped her teeth together, thinking. "How do you feel about that?"

"It's not like I had no idea. Straight with a slight bend, right?"

"Do you know that for a fact? I'm not digging for dirt. Just curious."

"So is he. Curious, I mean. That's how he explains it to me. He loves women. His long-term emotional relationships have always been with women. But he has this physical curiosity toward men and he's never been afraid to pursue it. Nothing ever crossed the line and turned into love, though. He said he doesn't love men. Except Erik. The line gets a little blurry there."

Daisy laughed. "Really? Since when?"

"I don't know. Lately the line has a line. You know Will—nothing is off limits and he's incapable of being flustered. But sometimes if I tease or dig too hard about Erik, he'll actually blush. And clam right up."

"Stop."

"Hand to God. Super delicate subject so please, not a word about it to Fish."

Daisy drew two lines across her heart. "Entre nous."

"Good girl. All right, I have to hit the books. I'm lonely and I miss you like crazy. I miss all of you. Even David."

"We miss you too. Come home soon."

"Leave the light on."

TURNING ALL THE CHEEKS

"HOW DID YOU FEEL about Will's relationship with James?"

"Curious," Daisy said. "Kind of turned on if you want to be blunt about it. I kept hoping I'd see them... I don't know, at least kiss or something." She laughed as a bit of heated color swept across her face. "Come on, they were two hot, tattooed guys with amazing bodies. I'll just watch a little."

"What about Erik?"

"He had no interest in watching."

Rita smiled. "But he and Will lived together. How did he handle it?"

"Funny thing about Erik. When he wasn't entirely sure what the hell was going on, he was a moody, brooding bundle of angst. And then one night, we were at my place and we ran out of condoms so he got dressed and went back over to his place to get some. He walked in on Will and James. Not in flagrante on the living room floor, but he found a trail of clothes going up the stairs and when he opened his bedside table drawer, all his condoms were gone. Then Will came into the hallway wearing only a towel and it was out in the open. Erik went chill. He could finally organize everyone into their places in the universe and figure out how to make it work in his head. Will is Will. I am me. And live and let live. Lucky was away so Erik moved his stuff over to my place. He called it turning all the cheeks."

Rita turned a page in her notebook. "But in time the relationship between James and Will became tenuous."

Daisy nodded. "In the beginning, it was euphoric. That fall, Will was choreographing a ballet to Philip Glass's soundtrack to *Powaqqatsi*. James became Will's unofficial assistant and he was brilliant at it. So they were collaborative lovers and Will depended on him. At the same time, Will warned him things had an expiration date. When Lucky came back it was going to be over, no discussion. James supposedly said he was fine with it. But when Lucky came back second semester, James evidently was not fine with it."

"Did Lucky know?" Rita asked. "About the affair with James?"

"Will told her. I think he suspected James might be the type to use emotional blackmail. Also, both Will and Lucky hated secrets. They preferred the bald truth, even if it was brutal. So he told her. Lucky was upset, but she told me it was more for Will's choice of partner rather than the actual infidelity. James was clearly unstable."

She crossed her arms. "It's clear now. God, Rita, I can look back and see what a giant, emotional tinderbox it was. But, I mean, who the hell thinks it will drive a person to murder? Maybe on TV or in the movies, not in real life. Not in your school. Not in the middle of rehearsal."

"Was there even an inkling? Any violent altercation between Will and James?"

"Will realized he made a mistake keeping James as his assistant while he was expanding *Powaqqatsi* for the spring concert. James was being passive-aggressively impossible which drove Will crazy. Like I said, Will had no patience for those tactics. His philosophy was always 'If you have something to say, say it. Let's have a conversation.' And he finally had to ban James from his rehearsals. Then the tension started to spill over and ripple through the rest of us."

Daisy smiled, but it felt tight around her eyes. "It was a little house," she said, running her fingers along her jaw. "The walls were thin. And the four of us were comfortable with each other. We heard each other argue and we heard each other make love. We shared the bathroom and passed half-dressed in the hallway at night. So the situation was in a fishbowl. It was *our* problem, not just Will's."

"How did it become your problem?"

"Because I still had to dance with James. He was upset and erratic, which made me crazy when we partnered. So Erik was on edge because I'd come home from rehearsal stressed out and distracted." She unscrewed the cap from her water and took a long sip. "I was actually looking forward to the concert being over. Which sucked because it was Will's last one and I should've been savoring it. Enjoying it. I was dancing in such a great ballet too—Marie got the rights to stage George Balanchine's *Who Cares?* It's set to music by George Gershwin. Jazzy and stylistic and romantic. And tough. Balanchine's choreography is really hard."

"And you were dancing with James?"

"We had a pas de deux set to 'The Man I Love.' But it wasn't going well. I had no connection with the guy at all and after Will banned him from coming to *Powaqqatsi* rehearsals, I felt like I had to do something. To make him feel someone was on his side."

WATER IN THE DESERT

"HERE," DAISY SAID, setting a cup of coffee in front of James.

His hands curled around it. "Thanks." He took a sip, then shook out a cigarette each and lit them.

Daisy was quiet for a few moments, letting James get used to her companionship and her compassion. Their relationship so far had been confined to the studio and incidental occasions at her apartment. She couldn't launch into an intense share-and-trust exercise. It had no context.

"I don't know what to do," James finally said.

"I'm sorry," she said. "I wish I could help."

"You don't think you could talk to him..." His voice trailed off along with the impossible request.

Daisy made the shake of her head slow and gentle. "Best thing to do is back off. We have a concert in six weeks and frankly, you're making me nervous." She touched his wrist and met his eyes, giving him a taste of her concern.

"I know," he said, running a hand back over his head. "I'm sorry. I'll get it together. I just... I just hurt so damn much."

Tears filled his eyes and the wrist under Daisy's fingertips rolled. The pink of his palm up on the table, vulnerable and empty. Daisy put hers on top of it. It would do no good to tell him what he already knew and beat him over the head with platitudes or told-you-so.

"I feel like an idiot because he told me," James said. "He told me and I didn't... I went and fell in love anyway. It wasn't just the sex, Dais. It was the collaborating. That creative bond. Jesus, it was amazing. And it made me feel like... I really thought we had something. I thought something more was there. Something that would make him think twice or make it not so easy when she came back. But it's like he flipped a switch. Like none of it happened. I feel so fucking stupid. I feel used and thrown away, which is the story of my goddamn life."

His face dissolved. "I love him, Dais." He brought his hand up to hide it, keeping the other around Daisy's. She stroked his fingers and let him be. The campus center was largely deserted. They were tucked into one of the rear booths, with no one around to disturb or pry.

"What's it feel like?" he asked.

"What?" She let go his hand to rummage in her dance bag for some tissues.

"To always be happy. Thanks." He blew his nose.

"I'm not always happy."

"You're such a positive person. Nothing bothers you. Nothing upsets you. Everything comes so easily and you and Fish are in love like nothing I've ever seen. You've got like this charmed life. Do you even know it?"

Her life, charmed or not, wasn't the issue. Daisy decided it was time for some firmness. "I'll tell you what I do know," she said. "I know you love him and I know you're hurting. But sulking around when your work needs to be done isn't attractive. Being confrontational, dramatic and needy isn't attractive. Lucky's my roommate. Will's one of my best friends. I'm not going to insult your intelligence by acting like you don't know where my allegiance lies. That said, I'll tell you one thing you have that Will doesn't."

"What?"

She sat back and crossed her arms. "Me."

James's eyebrows drew down in confusion. He looked at her. She looked back, letting him think it over. And slowly his forehead smoothed out and she saw it sink in.

"I don't have the man I love," he said. "But I have 'The Man I Love.'"

She nodded. "And I won't further insult your intelligence by acting like I don't miss him. That not being partnered with him for *Who Cares?* isn't disappointing."

A little life was coming into James's eyes.

"You know the expression 'looking good is the best revenge'?" she said.

A smile began to stretch out the corners of his mouth.

"He'll have more respect for you if you get your dancing into shape. You have more chance for some kind of relationship with him if you get your shit together. You're perfectly capable of dancing 'The Man I Love' well. As good as if not better than him. And I'll help you. Because if it looks like I get everything I want, it's because I work my ass off for it. Now what are you going to do? Die? Or dance?"

He inhaled, exhaled. Tilted his head and looked at her as if truly seeing her for the first time.

"Your eyes are so pretty," he said.

She smiled at the irrelevance but said nothing. Only held his gaze, holding the flame she'd coaxed alight.

"Marguerite," he said. "That's your real name, right?"

"Yes."

"Funny. My sister's name was Margaret. I suppose Fish told you about her."

Daisy nodded. She knew Margaret was the buffer between James and the homophobic, verbal abuse of his father and brothers. The comfort for the alcoholic neglect of his mother. She was his champion. She was also a soldier. She was deployed to Saudi Arabia and died in a scud missile attack on the army barracks.

Daisy took her own deep breath and took a small risk. "What touched me most about her," she said. "It's just a little thing that stuck in my head. How she was in a water purification unit."

"What of it?"

"She died bringing people water in the desert. I don't know what I'm exactly saying, but it stayed with me. Like the opening line to a story. *She died bringing water to the desert.*"

"I'm a desert," James said. "Something in me dried up when she got killed. She was blown to pieces. Only things the army could send home were her guns and her dog tags."

"I'm so sorry."

He crushed the paper cup in his hand and attempted a weak smile. "You got brothers? Sisters?"

"I have a half-brother," Daisy said. "My father's son from a previous relationship. But I've never met him. Maybe someday he'll come..."

She stared over James's shoulder, an idea taking shape in her mind. *Someday he'll come along.*

The music for "The Man I Love" swelled in her head. Her feet shuffled on the ground, marking choreography.

"Let's go find a studio," she said.

"Why?"

"I have an idea. Come on."

"I don't have my bag."

"Doesn't matter." She stood up. "Come on, James. Trust me. For an hour."

They found some empty space. In their street clothes and socks, with their rehearsal tape on a boom box.

"Let's not dance this romantically," Daisy said. "Let's do it as siblings."

James's expression became interested. "Lost siblings," he said, nodding. "Like separated twins."

"You be the desert. I'll be water."

It took time, but as they marked through the steps, a current began to crackle. James started to look her in the eye. Instead of gazing back with longing, she made a face at him. Trying to get him in trouble at the dinner table. He laughed and gave her a shove.

Sometimes his eyes went distant.

"What are you thinking?" Daisy asked.

His mouth opened and closed around a wistful smile and a little chuckle in his chest. "I dared her to eat a stick of butter once."

"Did she?"

"Yeah. And spent about eight hours trying not to puke. I told her to get it over with. She'd feel better if she threw up. But she wouldn't. She was tough."

"So are you," Daisy said.

He looked down at her. "Kees Justi said something when he found out you and I were partnered for the concert. He said, 'You'll like dancing with Daisy. She's generous.' I really had no idea what he meant. I do now."

"Now I'm about to puke," she said. "Shut up and dance."

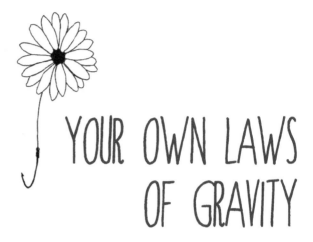

YOUR OWN LAWS
OF GRAVITY

They worked hard. Long hours of sweat and practice, finding a common thread to sew together the choreography of "The Man I Love" and make it their own. Daisy pushed James to imagine, to narrate his memories of Margaret out loud as they danced. In return, she listened to his advice and deferred to him on certain partnering decisions.

"What do you think?" she asked. Or, "What am I doing wrong here?"

His talent was immense. She got him to trust it again.

She started to trust him.

In the middle of the piece, she did a whirling chain of turns upstage to where James was waiting, the last one tilting off-balance to fall back into his arms. James waited for her to reach him with his hands behind his back. It was a schoolboy stance, but a teasing grin lifted a corner of his mouth. A hint of a dare in his eye. They weren't dancing: they were playing chicken.

Daisy spotted his face to keep her trajectory straight, whipping her head around with each revolution to focus back on him. As she turned faster, she pulled his expression into her, letting fear spiral off her like the contents of a centrifuge. She let her vision blur as she fell back, laughing out loud when James's arms seized her at the last second.

"Gave me a heart attack that time," she said, upside-down.

"Wimp." James brought her up into an arabesque, turning her in a tight circle, round and round. If it were Will, she would wind her arms about his shoulders and lay her head down in romantic surrender. With James she kept her chin up and her eyes locked on his, and gave him a playful swat on the jaw before she moved into the next phrase.

"This feels good," James said when they took a break. "I never dug into the story behind a pas de deux this way. Even if no one else gets it, it's cool."

"I think they will."

He paused. "My sister would have liked this."

"Did she come see you dance?"

"You kidding? She was the only one who came."

As they headed into the first studio run-through of *Who Cares?* Daisy prayed the connection would hold. She was eager for their work to be seen.

Up until now, everyone had been learning and rehearsing their solos and duets in private. Now the company gathered and opened the folding partition between studios A and B, making a double-wide performance space the size of the theater. Anticipation and excitement hung in the air. A keen interest to see the ballet as a whole.

Daisy sat under the barres, James on one side and a sophomore boy named John Quillis on the other.

"You feel good?" she asked James.

He nodded without looking at her or smiling. His gaze was across the floor to Will, who was sitting under the opposite barres with Taylor Revell. A faint sense of unease coiled in Daisy's stomach. She pushed it away and rubbed a few circles between James's shoulder blades. A suspicious herbal fragrance lurked in his T-shirt. She pushed that away as well.

In the center of the studio floor, Manuel Sabena was deep in his solo to "Bidin' My Time." A gymnast before he embraced ballet, he had a jump which defied physics. He hung in the air, gobbling up the space in turning leaps, bringing whoops and catcalls from the observers.

"Must be nice to write your own laws of gravity," John said.

John looked exactly like a young Ron Howard and the conservatory had baptized him Opie.

"Don't fucking call me Opie" was his perpetual, mumbled lament. Which only seared the nickname's brand deeper.

Daisy liked him. To safeguard against James's unpredictability, she'd discreetly taught James's roles to John all this year. Just to have backup.

"I'm impressed with Opie," Will said once. "He's like a vein of raw talent nobody's mined yet. He'll make a nice prince someday so handle him carefully. Make him feel like more than a convenient understudy, but don't kiss his ass. He's shy and he's crushy on you, but he's not stupid."

The endorsement did a lot for John. He was in the thick of his sophomore transition year and hungry for opportunity. He was also one of a handful of straight boys in the conservatory, trying to juggle the passion for his art against his still-developing male ego. As such, he shadowed Will—not only in class, but to the gym, building up both his confidence and his muscles.

With a bit of startle, Daisy noticed a subtle change in John's appearance. He'd been growing his copper hair out and experimenting with a more messy, tousled look. A couple days of beard growth gave him an adult air. Even at rest, she could see new mass and definition in his arms and chest, products of working out with Will. As he talked to her, he didn't blush as much.

Together they watched Will and Taylor's duet to "Embraceable You." It was sweet. Not much else. Taylor's technique was impeccable, but strangely soulless. Will's personality seemed too much for her—she kept pushing her chin out against it. If he tried too hard, he'd come across as lecherous, so he simply smiled and partnered her. Applause was polite at the end of the piece. Will sat back down under the barres, his face unreadable.

"All right," Marie called. "Where is the man I love?"

Daisy got up and reached a hand to James. His palm was sweaty in hers. As his head reached her level, she saw his eyes were bloodshot.

Jesus, is he stoned?

The idea reviled her. It was akin to spitting on the altar in a church, or some other desecration of religious property. The studio was sacred space and rehearsal was Mass. James wouldn't dare.

He simply wouldn't dare.

Within thirty seconds of music, she knew she didn't have his attention. The connection was dead and the pas de deux had gone flat. Flatter than Taylor and Will's. All the sibling playfulness, the backstory, everything she was so excited to reveal today—gone. It took every bit of professionalism she owned to tamp down her anger, make it sit on a chair in the corner and shut the hell up until she finished.

They reached the section she dreaded most: a run to James and a turning leap backward into his arms. She had to jump and rotate blind. And trust he'd be there.

Mid-run she had a premonition it wasn't going to work. Too late, she realized James wasn't even looking at her, much less prepared to catch her. But then she was in the air and turning.

He's not here.

"Jesus, James," John yelled.

"Dude," Will cried.

She shot right past him. Her hands instinctively went for the floor. Always help take the fall with your palms and then roll and aim for something cushy. Preferably your ass. You couldn't break your ass.

But momentum was carrying her backward and she couldn't get her hands down in time. All her weight collapsed on her left ankle, which rolled under with a sickening wrench. Crying out, she toppled full onto her left hand and felt a snap in her pinky.

Then she was down.

Everyone else was up.

"The hell is wrong with you?" Will yelled, taking James by the back of the shirt and flinging him into the barres which rattled in their brackets. "Are you out of your *fucking* mind?"

"Wheel, no," Marie said. "Stop it. Jase, you get out of my sight. Get out of this studio. Wheel, *stop*, that's enough. Basta."

That's it, Daisy thought as tears flooded her eyes. Not from pain. She was numb to the throb in her foot and hand. The agony came from the concert flashing before her, the curtain coming down on a stage she wasn't on. She fell. She was out. She was done.

"Margarita." Marie sank to her knees, pressing cold hands to Daisy's shoulders. "Where are you hurt, did you hit your head?"

"No. I'm all right," Daisy said, gasping and trying to sit up. Marie wouldn't let her until she turned her head, moved arms and legs and wiggled the uninjured fingers and toes. Will helped her up, his hands shaking.

"Give her some room, darlings," Marie said. "Let her breathe."

"It's my foot," Daisy said, wiping her face on Will's sleeve.

"Ankle's swelling already," John said, crouched by her feet, a soothing palm on her shin.

"Non te la prendere, cara." Marie's hand was firm around Daisy's. "Let's get her to the training room."

"C'mere, honey," Will said, scooping careful arms under her back and knees. He stood up, Daisy crushed to his chest. "I got you."

"I think my finger's broken," Daisy said, feeling a little sick as her brain decided to let the idea of pain down to her left hand. The heel of it was howling and her pinky felt on fire.

John gently touched her wrist and sucked the air back through his teeth, his eyes wincing. "You tore a nail off. Right down in the quick."

"Son of a bitch," Will muttered.

"Wheel, listen to me," Marie said. She put a hand on Will's shoulder and held up her other finger by his face. "Do not get into trouble. Capisce? I cannot replace you."

Will nodded without making eye contact. Marie twisted her mouth and looked over at John.

"Gianni, you go with," she said.

Once out in the hall, Will had other ideas. "Ope, go down to the shops," he said. "Tell Fish to come up to the training room."

"It's all right," Daisy said. "He's busy. I don't need him to come up."

"I do," Will said.

John crossed his arms. "Are you s—"

"Oh, knock it off, I don't need a shadow. Go get Fish. Jesus Christ, he'll fucking kill me."

Will strode down the hall with Daisy in his arms. His jaw clenched tight. His face filled with rage and something else Daisy barely recognized as shame.

"It's not your fault," she said.

"It isn't?" he said. "He was looking at me. You ran and jumped and he dropped his arms and kept looking straight at me the whole time. Motherfucker knew exactly what he was doing."

Her throat seized up in horror. "Will, this has to stop," she said.

His arms tightened around her. "I know. I'll handle it, Dais. I promise."

PARTING SHOT

WHEN ERIK APPEARED in the training room, he was out of breath and still wearing his safety goggles and gloves. But he knew what Daisy needed best in a crisis and his expression was mild as he sat next to her. He didn't fuss or pat her, which she couldn't stand. She needed to think. She could only think when everyone held still. She slid her head against Erik's kiss and returned focus to her foot in its ice bath and the whiteboard of contingency plans piling up in her head.

Lucky was brisk and neutral, speaking in the royal we. She wrapped a bit of gauze around Daisy's bleeding pinky nail, then bundled it up in ice. She draped a blanket around Daisy's shoulders, concerned about the chilled damp of sweaty practice clothes. Combined with the frigid waters around her foot, Daisy was starting to shiver.

"I want her in the ice another ten minutes," Max Tremaine, the head trainer, said. "Then we can take her over to the health center to get it x-rayed. I don't think it's broken."

Broken, Daisy thought. *Worst case is broken. Broken means I'm out. Sprained is at least two weeks. I have four. But it's my left foot. I can dance with a weak left foot. I only need my right for the hard stuff. I can do this. I can do sprained.*

"I'll get the car," Erik said, brushing his lips over Daisy's hair. "Be right back."

As he went out, he passed Will and his head gave a jerk toward the door. The message was unmistakable. *You. Outside.*

John, who'd been lingering in the doorway, moved out of their way and came to sit next to Daisy. They sat in silence, both their heads slightly tilted, listening. Every other sentence in the hall reached Daisy's ears, but she got the gist of it. The tone of Erik's voice, tight and hard, pushed through the wall of his teeth.

He was furious.

"Fish," Will said.

"Don't 'Fish' me."

Daisy's teeth chattered. John reached and tugged the blanket higher up around her neck.

"...Messed up over you to the point of coming to rehearsal high and injuring my girlfriend, it starts to be my business."

John rested his forearms on his knees, fingers interlaced, thumbs tapping together.

"I don't want him anywhere near her," Erik said in the hall.

Will's calm but hollow voice answered. "I don't either."

"You think he was stoned?" Daisy whispered.

John glanced at her. "Yeah, I do."

"Then he's out."

"He better be out. I can't imagine Marie keeping him in. Stoned or not, what he did was blatantly stupid."

She drew the air into her nose and released it, recalculating her plans. "If I can do it, will you dance with me?"

"Absolutely."

"It's a tough piece. The partnering is a bitch."

"So am I."

A smile cracked through. Then a small laugh.

"There you go," John said, pleased.

"Thanks, Opie," she said.

"Don't call me Op—" He faded out as he looked over at her and a flush crept over his cheekbones, blotting out his freckles. "All right, fine, you can call me Opie."

He looked away, rubbing the back of his neck, muttering under his breath. "Jesus, those eyes. How does Fish get anything done?"

"A BAD WRENCH, but nothing ice and a week's rest won't cure," the doctor said. Unfortunately, nothing could be done for her fractured pinky except tape it tight to her ring finger and let it heal. The nail bed throbbed for three days. So did the vein in Erik's temple whenever he looked at it.

James had been dismissed from the concert. John would take his place in *Who Cares?* and partner Daisy in "The Man I Love" when she was ready to return.

Lucky, now in her third year of sports medicine training, was stern. "A week means a week. And off your ankle means *off*. No sneaking into class and doing a right-foot barre."

The mini-vacation turned out to be the perfect remedy for Daisy's rattled spirit. With time to kill, she caught up on sleep for a couple of indolent days. When restlessness set in, she wandered into the catacombs of Mallory. Down into the warm shops with their engine-like thrum of buzzing activity. It smelled different down there, like furnaces and oil and sawdust. Paint fumes and metal. Constant hammering, banging and clanking. Voices over the din. And music.

This was Erik's world.

Leo Graham didn't take kindly to strangers intruding on his turf, distracting his minions and disrupting the rhythm of production. But he liked Daisy—she brought him coffee and discovered his fatal weakness for a York Peppermint Patty. She sat quietly and watched. Didn't intrude, distract or disrupt as the sets for *Who Cares?* were constructed. After a day or two, she became invisible.

The design for the ballet was David's senior project. According to his plans the crew was building a Manhattan skyline to stretch clear across the back of the stage. And no artist's interpretation of the Big

Apple either. David spent a whole weekend in New York, photographing the city from a dozen angles and at different times of day. The skyline was as true to life as he could make it, and the lighting design would take it from dawn to dusk.

Every building was meticulously outlined in tiny bulbs. Daisy looked up from her book and watched Erik, David and Neil slog at the thankless task. They stooped over the sets, laid out on sawhorses, drilling holes and placing the bulbs, wiring and taping and testing. They were punchy from the tedium, barbs and cracks flying. Then they fell into focused concentration, singing as they worked. After a period of calm, the horseplay started again.

Daisy was crutching downstairs for one of her visits when she finally saw James again. His appearance made her rear back in shock and distaste. Trudging up the open stairwell, he was strung-out, unshaven and gaunt. Red-eyed and jittery.

This is bad, she thought. *This is unstable.*

"Hi," he said.

More than a little disturbed, she tried to squeeze by with a cool, echoed "Hey." But her crutches made evasive moves impossible and his hand closed on her upper arm.

"Dais."

"I don't want to talk to you."

"Dais, I'm sorry."

"You're not," she said, louder. "You're not sorry."

"I didn't mean—"

Anger bubbled up like foam in her throat. "You did mean. You made a choice when I was in the air. You looked Will in the eye and dropped your arms, so don't you *fucking* tell me you're sorry. I swear I'll—"

"Hey."

Both Daisy and James's head flicked up to the top landing. John Quillis had one foot and both forearms on the railing, looking down on them.

"Leave her alone," he said.

James's lip curled. "Fuck off, Opie."

Unphased, John started down the stairs. "Let her by."

"I'm just talking to her."

"No, you're not. Move along." He'd almost reached them.

"Fuck you, I'll move along, punk."

It was hard to say who was more surprised at what happened next, Daisy or James. Quicker than either could register, John had James pinned against the concrete wall, one arm twisted behind. John's face was composed but a vein in his neck flickered. His eyes were hard. Something in his stance was both effortless and expert. Daisy's own eyes bulged, wondering if Will had been schooling John in more than workout routines.

"Leave her be," John said. "You're lucky it was me who came along and not Fish. Go on, Dais."

She crutched by, letting her knuckles brush John's back in thanks. She expected a parting shot from James to float down after her. Instead, when she glanced up, she saw only a broken little brother.

And in spite of her anger, it cracked her heart.

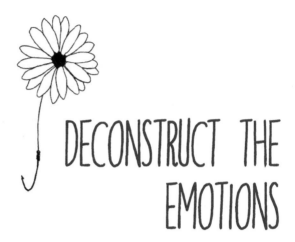

DECONSTRUCT THE EMOTIONS

"JOHN AND I STARTED REHEARSING 'The Man I Love,' but it didn't go well. I guess I was more shaken up than I thought. I'd never had any kind of serious injury before and it spooked me. When you're a dancer, your body is all you have. It's everything. You're *it*. You're the means. And one fall or break or bash and..."

"It could be over," Rita said. "Or at least put you out of commission for a long time."

"Yes. It threw me. But more than that, I was so damn discouraged. I'd worked hard to build a relationship with James. I gave him my time, my attention and my trust. I gave everything to give him a chance and at the last minute he..."

Tears stung her eyes. The demoralized disappointment was a rusty nail piercing her heart, as fresh as the day. Fresher. As if it had never been felt at all.

"I feel more upset now than I think I did then," she said.

Rita nodded.

"He took all that time and trust and work and shit on it. Made me a pawn in his little game to get back at Will. And then told me he didn't *mean* it."

"You must have felt used."

"I did. Now I had to start all over again with John and I had next to no motivation. I couldn't find it in me. It felt like I didn't have enough time to deconstruct the emotions of the dance. The steps were hard enough. We slogged away but it wouldn't mesh. After a week John went to Marie and asked if she would switch him and Will. Let Will dance with me."

She laughed, shaking her head at the memory of his nerve. "I don't know how he pulled it off. One thing Marie did not like was people complaining about casting or asking her to make changes. You take your role. You learn it and you dance it. You dance and you deal. Those were her rules. But somehow John convinced her. Or charmed her. So Will and I ended up dancing together after all."

"Which must have been a relief."

"I can't tell you." Daisy closed her eyes. "As soon as we got into the studio and touched hands... I was calmed, I was confident, I was back where I belonged. We didn't have to dissect a single feeling—we were dancing together again. The relief became the backstory."

Daisy had been seeing Rita for six weeks, telling her story. Now April of 1992 was on the stage in front of her. The sets were in place, the lights focused. Like David, she had her hands on the curtain rope, ready to pull and put the whole thing into motion. Nothing moved until she pulled. She held it all in her hands.

"We're getting near to when it happened," Rita said, echoing her thoughts.

"Yes," Daisy said. "About two weeks before, James showed up at our apartment. In the middle of the night. Lucky saw him out in the back-yard, staring up at the bedroom windows."

"What did he want?"

"He wanted Will." Daisy spread her hands. "You know I... I keep for-getting he was as young as us. I don't know why my memory sometimes makes him much older than he was. He was twenty-one. He was Erik's age. Just a kid who was in love."

"Did Will go down and talk to him?"

"No. Erik did."

"He wasn't afraid?"

"Afraid? No..." Her voice trembled. Cold swept her limbs. "Nobody thought James was dangerous. Damaged, yes. Needy. An attention addict. But not a vengeful murderer. And not suicidal. Erik came back upstairs after a while and didn't seem concerned for James's safety. I asked what they'd talked about and he said he'd mostly listened. Tried to validate James's feelings and get him back to a safe place for the night. He said, 'Everything's all right, Dais. Go back to sleep.'

"I remember curling up against his back and drifting off. Feeling so safe with him. Thinking about how he made everyone feel safe. And feeling a pride in him I'd never felt before. Proud of who he was and proud to be his. He was so good. He saw the best in people. He was pissed at James but something in his heart made him go down and talk to him anyway. What does that say?"

"That he had a big heart," Rita said. "Where I come from, we'd call him a mensch."

"But the next morning, they found James in the bathroom of his dorm. He'd overdosed on some pills his roommate had. They rushed him to the hospital. He survived. His parents came and got him, took him home to Pittsburgh. And it was the last we saw of him. Until April nineteenth."

"Are you ready to tell me?" Rita said. "What happened that day?"

Daisy took a deep breath. "It started the night before..."

SUGAR UNDER FIRE

ERIK CAME HOME LATE from the shop. Finally the damn sets for *Who Cares?* were done and he was tired, stressed and so horny he couldn't see straight.

"Say goodnight," he said, as he pulled Daisy off the couch and slung her over his shoulder like a caveman.

"Goodnight," she called to Will and Lucky. "Pray for me."

"We got rehearsal tomorrow, Fish," Will said. "Bring her back in one piece."

"And if you can't," Lucky said, "bring back *all* the pieces."

"You may want to leave," Erik said from the stairs. "This could get loud."

He kicked the bedroom door shut and pushed Daisy up against, it, kissing her with blunt, unapologetic greed.

She never loved him more than when he was like this. Always when he was in one of his moods, the air around him seemed to shimmer and press. If he wanted to make love, he put out a shining, warm aura, like twinkling starlight. But on a night like tonight, after long hours of working and keeping David focused and sweating a deadline, he was an impatient porcupine of need. His bristling, edgy mood piercing through his skin.

"Want you so bad," he whispered with a shaking mouth, his voice caught tight in his throat. She pulled his shirt off, threw it aside. He was working out all the time that semester and his body was spectacular. Ripped and lean and sexy. His hands unbuckled and unzipped and he burst out of his pants, rock hard, worked up and dying for her.

"Jesus," she said, closing him up in her fist.

"Tell me about it," he said against her neck. "All goddamn day I've been hard for you."

Her life was defined by the total and complete control she had over her body but that night she gave it over to him. Gave up as he turned her away from him, took her hands and put them flat on the bed. From behind he yanked her jeans open and pulled them down, like she was a bad girl who needed to bend over and be spanked. At the corner of the mattress, her jeans around her knees, he held her by the hips and groaned hard as he buried himself in her.

The noise she made that night. She who was usually rendered mute at the pinnacle of pleasure. Tonight she reversed her own polarity, opened her throat and let her voice turn itself inside-out. She spread her legs against the bind of her jeans, arched her back into his thrusts. Matched him moan for moan, sigh for sigh until she burrowed her face deep in the pillows and yelled her head off, not caring if Will and Lucky heard, not caring if the neighborhood heard.

"You feel so good," he said into her hair. He curled over her and got his hand around her hip, down between her legs and started rubbing her. Rubbing it out of her.

"So tight and hot on my cock," he said. "You have no idea..."

Her chest twisted around his words as his fingers locked in. She threw her head back and came, hard enough to make her vision double. And then came again. One orgasm linking to another. A chain of them. She couldn't breathe. Her being teetered on the edge of un-being. Her sanity dripped through her fingers like sand. She almost made him stop, almost reached out to take back the precious control of herself. But instead she put her trust into his hands, put her own hands behind her and let go.

Erik clasped her wrists, crossed them in the small of her back, pulled them up tight—not enough to hurt, but enough to hold her down. Enough torque on her shoulders to hold her still, hold her where he wanted her. He moved slowly, letting her feel every inch of him.

"Give it to me," she said, breath hitching in her chest.

"You like that?" His voice curled around the dark and squeezed hard.

"I want it," she said, somewhere beyond herself. "All night long. The rest of my life just keep... God, you fuck me so good."

Fuck was a piece of candy in her mouth. A hot cinnamon fireball on her tongue, almost too intense to bear. She had to pull in air to cool it.

"You fuck me so good," she said again, sucking on the night, feeling layers dissolve away, sugar under fire.

Over and over he slid into her, his strong quads battering her hamstrings. She writhed and came. Her body strained with wanting even as her hands stayed relaxed and open through the grip on her wrists. Both bound and free within his embrace.

"You're beautiful," he said.

"I'm so in love with you," she said, lips moving weakly in the damp sheets by her mouth. "I'm so in love..."

He stopped. His fingers melted from her wrists and slid up her arms as he gently pulled out of her.

"Erik."

"Shh..." He gathered her up against his body, letting her catch her breath. His chest hair soft on her back, his mouth running a tender line from her jaw to her shoulder.

"This," he whispered. "All I want. The rest of my life, I just want to make you come like this..."

She turned to liquid in his arms as he smoothed her hair, tilted her chin and kissed her. She could taste cinnamon and knew he was being pulled by a different gravity too. Orbiting a different dimension of his sexuality.

He helped her out of her shirt and bra, steadied her as she kicked her trembling legs free of her jeans. Her fingers pulled at her earrings and bracelets and rings. She wanted nothing between her body and his. She could feel his heart thudding against her back.

Me, it seemed to say. *Only me. Only I see you this way. Hear and touch you this way. Fuck you this way.*

"Erik." She closed her mouth around his name, pressed it tight to the roof of her mouth.

"All right?" he said, his hands gliding over her naked skin.

She nodded, her mouth against his, her thoughts rolling and folding like a lazy syrup. *I love you and only you and you have everything and nobody but you for me and you and I...*

"More?"

"Please." And she bent over for him again, put her hands behind her back and begged. More. More. An itch no amount of scratching could relieve. It was the scratching itself she craved.

An hour later, when they were sprawled in the sheets, slick with sweat and teetering on the edge of consciousness, Erik put her hand against his face, his swollen candy mouth breathing into her palm.

"I love nobody and nothing," he said, "the way I love you."

MORE THAN I WANTED TO DANCE

"WHY DO YOU SAY it started then?" Rita asked

"Because the next day at rehearsal," Daisy said. "I was..." Her face seized up, twisting with some unnamable emotion, wringing tears from her eyes and nose. "I was..."

"Stay with me, Daisy," Rita said. "You're safe here."

"I was sitting on Erik's lap in the lighting booth. We were talking about the night before. Laughing at ourselves. At how incredible it had been to fuck like that. Complete openness, complete trust to do anything and say anything. To show the sides of ourselves that were raw and..."

She stared, mouth parted in memory. Warm wet on her face and she touched it with her tongue, looking for cinnamon but finding only salt.

"To love like that," she said. "Maybe you're thinking, *So what, you got spectacularly laid one night, big deal.* But it was more. He and I were so attuned. It wasn't two halves becoming a whole. It was two wholes becoming a greater thing. Erik called it a cathedral. It was like a giant structure we were continually building together."

"You were in love," Rita said. "And a love affair is never a finished thing."

"No, it's not. I think that night I finally understood what it meant. And the next day, in the lighting booth..."

"Tell me."

"I wasn't finished. I was joking with him about ditching rehearsal and going back to bed. Joking but not joking... I wanted him."

"And then?"

A stab of anxiety pierced her chest. A wave of heat slid up her neck and reached sinister hands around her cheeks. Clapped invisible fingers over her mouth even as the bile rose up in the back of her throat.

"Oh, God," she said, her voice nothing but an airless hiss.

Rita leaned forward a little. "Tell me what's happening."

"I don't know..." She sucked air through her nose, fought the urge to flee the office and go running into the street. Her fingers clenched, desperate for a sharp edge to cut it out of her.

"What happened in the booth?" Rita aid.

"I can't do this," Daisy said, half-rising off the couch.

"Listen to my voice." Rita leaned further into the space between their chairs, elbows on knees, hands clasped. "Stay with me, Daisy. You're here with me and you are safe."

Daisy sat back as the panic intensified. She'd never known such terror. Her heart strained and squealed, hammering fists against the wall of her chest. She had to get out or she was going to die here. Her feet beat against the floor, like a child having a tantrum. "I hate this," she said through her teeth. "I hate it, I want to run, I want to cut it *out* of me."

"I know. You are pure fight or flight right now. But listen to me, because you have a third option. You can stay still. Not flee. Not fight. Just stay here and let it come to you."

"I can't."

"You can. You can let it come to you and go through you. Relax your jaw. Let go your hands. I'm right here with you, Daisy. Tell me as it happens."

"I feel like I'm dying."

"You are living right now. Don't pull back away from it. Just hold still and live."

Hold still, Daisy thought. *I can do that. I'm good at that.*

"That's it," Rita said. "Let it sit right in your lap. Bring it on. Deep breath. Let it come. Breathe and come out the other side."

Daisy breathed, counting inhales and exhales. Calmness put a hand on her shoulder. Then yanked it away and the bottom of her stomach dropped out.

"Fuck, I hate this," she said, torquing and twisting again. "I hate feeling like this."

"I know but trust me, if you don't fight it, if you let it come to you, it will leave faster. Deep breath now. Let it out."

Daisy was starting to shiver. "My skin hurts." Her teeth chattered so hard she could barely get the words through them. "It's like nauseous in my *head.*"

"That's it," Rita said. "Tell me as it happens. Narrate it. You're doing great."

In spite of the violent trembling, a single wretched chuckle escaped. "You're always praising my worst moments."

"Who's to say they're not your finest moments?"

"I feel so stupid."

"Then feel stupid. Feel afraid. Feel whatever you w—"

"I feel like such shit. I want this to stop."

"And it is. It's stopping. Every second you get through is a second closer to stopping. You're going through it and you will come out the other side."

"Promise?" Daisy said, the P catching between her shaking lips.

"I promise," Rita said, and in two words she blew a bubble, a protective force field around the small office, enclosing Daisy in trust.

"I'm so scared," Daisy said, putting the words inside the sphere.

"Then be scared and keep telling me about the day."

"I can't."

"You're going to feel like shit whether you tell me or not, Daisy. You may as well let it out, throw it on the pile."

Her head teetered back and forth on her neck. "I can't remember."

"Try."

Half a laugh mixed with half a sob. "You're so mean to me."

"I know, and you pay me to be. Drink some water."

Teeth still clattering in her jaw, Daisy took a sloppy sip from her bottle. Her stomach agreed to keep it and even allowed another.

"You were in the booth with Erik," Rita said. "Is it truly the last thing you remember?"

Daisy exhaled roughly and closed her eyes. "Marie called me to run 'The Man I Love' with Will," she said, following the last thread of memory, a ball of yarn down to a few final loops.

"I left the booth. I walked down the aisle. And I turned back to wave at Erik. I remember looking back and wanting him more than I wanted to dance. God, I wanted him so bad."

Despite anxiety's relentless chokehold, she was deep in another moment now. A ribbon of remembered pleasure weaving through the angst. Her heart blazing with joy. Her belly filled with heat. Secure in her love and her talent and her passion. Her life bursting with accomplishment and contentment. Erik slowly shaking his head and smiling on the other side of the window.

"He was so beautiful right then," she said. "And he was mine."

Gorgeous, sexy and hers. *Hers.* His smile and his body and his love—ardent, raw, passionate or savage, all of it was hers. Through the glass she saw him coiled up with hot longing and not even trying to hide it. Chin on the heel of his hand, a thousand promises in his expression: *Tonight, when I get you alone, I'm going to make you forget your name.*

"And then?" Rita said.

Daisy tried to rise above her stomach and follow the trail. Eyes still closed, she gently scratched her nails along the bottom of her memory's barrel, making sure no scrap had gone undetected.

"I think I remember grabbing my dance skirt from my bag," she said. "Tying it as I walked down the aisle. It seems like a real memory because I can feel it on my waist. But then... I don't know, I have some little glimmers but I'm not sure if they happened or if I'm adopting other people's experience and making it mine. Like I know where my friends were standing because I was told later."

David with Neil behind the Manhattan skyline set, fiddling with cables and wires. Lucky in the stage right wing, rolling an ace bandage as she talked and laughed with John. Taylor in the opposite wings, her chin pushed out in concentration over her knitting. Near to her, the six-foot Aisha stretching with a hand on the diminutive Manuel's shoulder.

And James, her broken little brother, who must have been a hundred yards from Mallory by then.

Daisy's hands slowly pulled the curtain rope. But instead of lights coming up, they began to tunnel out.

"It becomes like a dream," she said, letting her mind ramble. "I can see the tall black shapes of the curtains and I can sense the stage lights and feel their heat. The lights are Erik. His hands make them go on and off and fade and brighten and turn different colors. I dance in the light he makes and the warm heat on my skin—that's him. The lights are his love.

"Then noise. Noise and commotion and I'm lying on my back and... I don't remember pain. Just confusion because Will was lying next to me and I could see all the blood but it wasn't registering. I didn't know what was going on. I pushed up on my elbow and tried to look around. And I saw a man in the aisle. He raised his arm and the windows of the booth started exploding and Erik was in there but I couldn't see him anymore. He was gone."

A long breath-held moment, so utterly still she could hear Rita's wristwatch ticking. Before her remembering eyes the spotlight faded to a diamond star and winked into black.

"Then nothing," Daisy said. "It all went dark. I woke up and I forgot what I saw. For a little while... I even forgot my name."

LIME AND MINT

SHE DREAMED BUT didn't know she was dreaming.

She half awoke and knew she'd been moved from one place to another place but the dreams that weren't dreams came again and she was no place.

Her eyes were closed and she didn't know she had eyes to open.

Sounds found her ears and waited to be recognized, and then fell out upon her shoulders and she slept again.

Smell sliced through the non-dreams like an organ pipe piercing the quiet of a church. Scent reached hands through the muck and mire of her tired brain. It wafted warm and cool at the same time, passing behind her fastened eyelids and loosening her tongue. The smell curled fingers around her jaw and drew her head over to the side, where it became stronger.

Her tongue fell free into her mouth. She became aware of breath in her nose and lungs. A high-pitched thrum in the center of her chest when she released air, an involuntary sound of recognition. She knew this warm-cool scent.

Awareness prickled from the center out. Nerves frantically stretched feelers across her brain, reaching for a matching set to make a handoff, hopefully a connection. Arm. Hand. Fingers. A quantum leap and she realized her hand was not alone. Another hand. Attached to the scent.

Her fingers squeezed. She made the noise in her chest again. Turned her head further and met with a solid warmth.

"I'm here," someone whispered.

She didn't know here and couldn't put a name with I.

"I'm here, Dais. I love you."

Dais dropped into the center of her head like a burning star and her thoughts began to swirl around it like a galaxy. *Dais* was the you.

She knew herself now.

And her self was tired.

She held the hand, settled into the tight strength at her side. She breathed in its scent.

And slept.

SHE WOKE TO HER mother's hands on her face.

"Hello, darling." The voice like wind chimes. "It's all right. Mamou's here."

Her lips pressed into Daisy's forehead, a waft of face powder and a little perfume. As Francine leaned over her, Daisy realized she was in bed. Not her bed. But Mamou was here. That was good.

"Hi," Daisy whispered. The exhaled syllable took no effort. She pressed her lips together, trying to push the M. She couldn't. Her mouth was dry.

A man's hand now on her face. A bass note of aftershave. Spearmint chewing gum and a little cigarette smoke in his cuff.

"Dézi."

"Da," Daisy said. It fell out as she separated her tongue from the roof of her mouth.

"Sweetheart," he said.

Her head turned right and left and she summoned the will to make her mouth say what she needed. "Thirsty."

A bustle of purposeful activity and a woman appeared by her father. She was dressed in pink. Daisy stared. Her brain turned over like a rolodex. Finally it plucked a single card with a single word and turned it up: *nurse.*

She was in a hospital.

Open-mouthed and parched, Daisy stared as the pink woman gave over a paper cup with a spoon sticking out the top. Her father took the spoon and offered it.

"Here, sweetheart."

A single ice-cold jewel in her mouth. A wet diamond melting. Her eyes closed in relief. Her tongue danced through the silver cold. Too soon it disappeared. The dry heat took over again. She opened her mouth. Joe gave her another jewel. Cobalt blue cold.

"Nice and easy," Francine said. "Don't rush."

She didn't rush but her mouth devoured the ice. Seduced and ravished it, leaving only the barest trickle to find its way down her swollen throat.

A third cold spoonful. Two pieces this time. She kept one on her tongue and sent the other immediately back and down. The relief. She could swallow now. She could breathe.

She could think.

"What happened," she said.

Over her head, her parents exchanged glances.

"Mamou." She tugged Francine's sleeve. "What's happened?"

Joe's hand on her cheek. "Do you remember anything, Dézi?"

Her brain turned again in a waterfall of cards but none were revealed. She opened her lips for another piece of ice which she held in her mouth, wrapping herself around its cold clarity. Remember. To remember meant to know what came before now.

What was before now?

"What day is it?" she asked.

"Monday," Francine said.

Monday. Now the rolodex got excited and dealt a bunch of cards. Monday was intro to music theory at eight and early French literature at nine. Then she had advanced ballet technique class followed by partnering. Then lunch and a little bit of down time before she was due back in the studio for folk and character dance. Then it was over to the theater because this week was tech week for the dance concert and−

A flurry of faces, feet, bodies and music.

"Rehearsal," she said. "I have rehearsal tonight."

"It's all right, Dézi."

She tried to sit up, only now aware of the rest of her body. As if with the hydrating of her mouth and throat, the rest of her life came back to her. And her life was bound up in her body. She had rehearsal but instead of being in the theater, she was in this bed. Her parents were here for some reason and a pink nurse was handing out ice chips. Where were her legs?

"What's happened?" She clutched her mother's cardigan in both hands. "Mamou, did I fall down?" It was the only reason she could think of for being here. But if she fell, she would remember, wouldn't she?

And why were her parents here?

How bad did she fall?

Everything was in context except herself.

What came before now?

"Darling, something happened in the theater yesterday."

Yesterday. Sunday. She would have had rehearsal. She couldn't remember dancing yesterday. She squeezed her eyes shut, reaching into the black behind her lids and trying to pull it back. Faces to the bodies. Names to the faces. Her friends. Sitting in the rows of seats in the theater. The curved rows like a comb, embracing the apron of the stage. Sloped slightly downward from the rear of the theater. The lobby doors propped open and the tall glass windows of the lighting booth where−

I just want to ditch this rehearsal and go back to bed with you.

Her eyes flew open. "Erik?"

"He's fine, darling," Francine said, her hand gentling along Daisy's forehead. "Erik's fine, he's safe."

"But what's *happened?*" Daisy cried, again trying to sit up.

"Dézi, listen to me." With a clang Joe put down the bar on his side of the bed and sat on the mattress next to her right hip. "Yesterday, someone came into the theater with a gun."

She stared at him.

"Someone had a gun and they opened fire on the rehearsal."

He took her hand in his, and Daisy noticed then the IV line snaking from the top of her hand to the drip bag hanging overhead. The rough cotton gown she was dressed in. Her leg, the one by her father, looked small and slim beneath the thin covers but her left leg was...

She looked back at Joe.

"You were shot yesterday, Dézi."

"You and Will," Francine said, her hand spread wide like a starfish on the crown of Daisy's head. "He's fine, though. You're going to be fine, Daisy. I promise." Her voice betrayed her on the last word, fraying like a bent stick of green wood. Daisy's eyes flicked to her mother's face. Then down to her own legs. The covers over her left leg looked domed. Some structure underneath held them aloft over her leg.

She pushed up on one elbow and reached.

"Dézi, no." Her father's hand stayed her. "You're not strong enough yet. Not yet. It's going to be all right. We'll fix everything, I swear to you, sweetheart."

She looked at him. Closed her fingers around the sheet.

And pulled.

"Dézi..."

Above her knee, her thigh was swathed in gauze. Out of the gauze fed another tube, filled with an evil yellow fluid.

She kept pulling.

A wire cage, like a wigwam's frame, arched over her calf.

Her teeth pressed together. Her fingers clenched hard.

Her calf was flayed.

"It looks worse than it is, darling," Francine said, sliding arms around her. "Look at me. It's not forever. It will heal, I promise."

Daisy looked only at her leg. From knee to ankle on both sides, they had sliced her calf open. Diamonds of angry flesh and muscle. Red meat bulging from the edges of her skin which were hard and yellow in some places, black and blood-crusted in others. Her flesh was falling out of her leg. They ruined her.

She pushed her teeth together hard, feeling her eyes grow bigger.

Her parents were talking. They explained she was shot in the thigh. The bullet severed her femoral artery. The initial surgery seemed to have been a success but complications set in. Pressure began to build up in her leg. They had to cut her.

They took turns, finishing each other's sentences, slapping words like inadequate band-aids on the bleeding mess that was Daisy's life.

"To save your leg, Dézi," Joe said, taking her face in his strong hands. "Look at me, sweetheart." His voice was quiet and commanding. A soldier. He wasn't afraid of anything.

Almost anything.

He heard too much in the jungle nights. Saw too much. He still hadn't turned around and looked at his daughter's leg.

Daisy turned her head out of Joe's grasp and put her free hand over her mouth. She stared down at those red diamonds on her leg and wanted to scream. It was either scream or die.

"Where's Erik?" she said through her fingers.

She felt her parents exchange looks once more.

"I'll get him." The bed rocked gently as Joe got up and left.

Francine gathered Daisy's head close. Her clothes smelled of lavender. "I promise," she said. "You'll dance again. I promise, darling."

The door to her room whispered open, followed by the squeak of sneakers on linoleum. She smelled him first. Skin that wafted a little warm like lime, and a little cool like mint. He sat where her father had been. Said nothing as he put his hand on her hip and followed her eyes to her flayed calf. She heard him pull his breath in but not let it out.

Mouth still squeezed up tight in her fingers, Daisy looked at her mother. Always they had understood each other. Worked in tandem to keep Joe's demons at bay. Now Daisy bored her eyes up into her mother's pale face and thought, *take him out of here.*

Francine's head tilted. Her eyes closed a moment. She hugged Daisy's shoulders hard, reached to cup Erik's chin. She left the bedside, putting her arm through Joe's and coaxing him out into the hallway.

Daisy was crying before the door closed.

She fell back, hands to her face. Her throat was caving in. Her eyes were melting. Thick, molten despair and rage boiled up in her stomach and flooded her chest in a lament that couldn't escape. She wept but it wasn't enough. It barely penetrated. They cut her leg to release the pressure. Nothing could release her grief now. Her fingers dug into her face. Her nails found her skin and pressed. Ten hard crescents. Looking to punch a hole in the shock, puncture the fat balloon of loss swelling in her chest and head. Her eyeballs and eardrums bulged. Her teeth threatened to fly out of her gums. Her ribs strained against it. Something had to give.

Erik took hold of her. Finger by finger he peeled her hands away from her head, then took her wrists and put them up around his neck. He leaned down, making a wigwam frame over her body. His clean-clothes smell over citrusy skin. His arms and chest wide and strong. She buried her face in his sternum and screamed.

He didn't flinch. Didn't move. His arms were tight. She screamed again, down in the dark warm cave of his chest and arms. He didn't shush her. Didn't soothe her with words. Didn't make promises or swear. He held the frame. Stayed still and domed over her body as she drew in another ragged, terrible breath. Loading the catapult and setting it alight.

She exhaled, sliced the rope and yelled her bones apart.

The ramparts crumbled, the turrets fell and the moat flooded everything. It all came up from the depths of her and then she was choking on it. The pink nurse made it just in time, seizing a basin and sliding a strong, competent arm under Daisy's shoulder blades. They got her to sit up as the heaving waves exploded. Hot acid scorching her throat and nose. She was on fire now, her blood roiling and burning like lava along her limbs. She couldn't get a breath. Couldn't stop it. They cut her leg. She would never dance again. It was over.

The carefully-laid connections and context started to unravel. Without Erik over her to fix her place in the universe, Daisy was cut loose and drifting. She was falling down. Erik ran a cold cloth over her face and she clung to the sensation. He spooned her some ice chips. More cold jewels but it didn't help. She was falling. She was dying.

Erik set his hands on her shoulders and pressed her back.

"Look at me," he said.

She fought to focus. On the other side of the bed, the pink nurse fiddled with the IV line and a syringe.

Erik turned her face toward him. "No, look at me. Look only at me."

Blinking rapidly she put her eyes on his. He stared back. His pupils widened, eclipsing the honey brown. They shrank. Then widened again. She saw her face reflected in the black. There she was.

"There we are," the nurse said.

"Look at me," Erik said.

Daisy felt her chest start to smooth out. The distant edges of her mind grew blurry as she looked at her reflection in Erik's eyes.

"I see me," she whispered.

"Look only at me."

"Only at you," Daisy said. The edges were crumbling and drifting away like stardust.

His hand slid against her face, his thumb gliding beneath one eye. Warm like lime. Cool like mint. She barely blinked now. Her chest rose and fell easily. The last layers of her mind peeled away.

"Only me," he said.

Only you.

"This."

This...

She slept.

IN HIS SKIN

A DETECTIVE CAME into her room and asked her questions about what happened in the theater. She couldn't help him. She didn't remember. The brick wall across her memory frightened her. She tried to scale it, digging for toe holds and crevices to jam her fingers in.

"Who was it?" she asked.

James, he told her.

James shot her. James tried to kill her.

"Do you know why he would target you?" the detective asked.

"No," she said. "I was water in the desert..."

She grew frantic and hysterical under the questions. She wanted Erik. He wasn't there. She needed to know where he was. It was dire. A tickle at the edge of her memory which became a scrape. Then a slice. She couldn't remember. She began to call for him. Then scream for him. The detective rang the bell and the pink nurse came to inject something in the IV line.

Daisy didn't fall gently into sleep. She was sucked down into a black void, clawing and fighting. It was so dark behind her eyelids. So big, with no frame to support it. It would implode, collapse, crush her in an airless vacuum.

Where are you? The words coiled into a whirlpool. The gelatinous black curved around her with sharp edges to peel the rest of her skin off.

Where are you...?

HER MIND AWOKE and her awareness unfolded. The silence leaned against her ears and she smelled Erik. Her eyes slowly opened.

"Hey," he said. He leaned one forearm on the mattress by her shoulder, rested the other palm on her cheek. She closed her eyes. Opened them again. She could see herself in his pupils.

"Feel better?"

She nodded, looking at herself in him. Her chest was serene. She felt no pain. She even managed to lift the corners of her mouth in a weak smile before thinking *What am I going to do?* The smile faded. Erik's hand continued its gentle path over her face and hair. She shut her eyes, moved her forehead into the cup of his palm. He held her still.

She breathed him in, listened to the sound of nothing.

What will I do?

Her eyes opened. Breathing deep, she stared down cross-eyed at his arm, not seeing.

And then seeing. Beneath the heel of his hand a blob of color swam into focus.

Her hand took his wrist, slowly drew it away from her head. She stared at the tattoo. While she was sleeping he had a daisy inked under the heel of his hand.

Her fingertips came up to touch it. Touch where the skin was still pink and puffed around the black outlines and the yellow eye. A hint of white in each of the petals. One of them was slightly tattered.

"Erik..."

He said nothing. His fingers folded loosely onto his palm and then opened again. Like petals.

"Does it hurt?" Her voice broke apart. Her heart swelled in her chest, squeezed the tears out her eyes.

"Yes," he said.

She pulled his wrist against her neck as he leaned over her again. She nestled the daisy tattoo against her as she pressed her wet face into the safe warmth of his chest. His love was a frame around her. A dome over her. It was warm and cool and it held still.

I am here. In him. I will forever be in him now. In his eyes and in his skin.

"Nobody loves me like you," she said.

Under his tattooed hand she fell into beautiful, soft sleep.

THEY MOVED HER OUT of the ICU onto the main ward. Visitors were allowed and with the visitors came more pieces of the story.

Lucky came to her. She scooched onto the narrow border of mattress snug to Daisy's side, held her tight and told her Aisha Johnson, Taylor Revell and Manuel Sabena were dead.

Daisy cried hard, her face pressed into Lucky's spiral curls, in equal parts grief and confusion. She still didn't understand what happened, still couldn't came to grips with the gaping chunk of time ripped out of her memory where such violent and irrevocable things took place. Her friends were dead, her leg was sliced, Will was shot, Marie was in a coma.

But Lucky was here.

"You saved my life," Daisy said. Everyone said so: Lucky's EMT training and quick, level-headed thinking helped save both lives and limbs in the theater.

Lucky's hands were ice-cold. She trembled next to Daisy. "I was so fucking scared," she said.

"Where were you?"

"In the wings with Opie. He pushed me down and threw himself on top of me. But there's no exit on that side of the stage. We were penned in."

Daisy held her tight. "Opie would have done something."

"Jesus, is he a fucking prince or what?"

He was. John thoughtfully brought Daisy a book—Stephen King's *The Eyes of the Dragon*—and a big bag of Swedish Fish. One of his cheekbones was badly bruised. When he threw himself down to shield Lucky he hit his face against one of the boom stand bases. Daisy touched the greenish swelling and he gave a wincing smile but his eyes wouldn't meet hers. He seemed upset and fretful but unable to articulate if it was any one thing or simply everything. After a few sweet but awkward minutes, he slipped away.

Kees came. He was shot in the shoulder and his arm was in a sling. He took her hand and gently told her Marie Del'Amici had died. He held Daisy's head against his chest as she cried, then tenderly set it back on the pillow as she dipped and drooped back into exhausted sleep.

Pain in her leg woke her up. She opened her eyes to find David in the chair next to her bed, an ankle perched on one knee, engrossed in *The Eyes of the Dragon*. He closed the book around a finger and hitched forward, his eyes wide and happy. He touched the tip of her nose and his smile was beautiful.

"Look at you," he said. "Still the prettiest thing I've ever seen."

"I'm so glad to see you," she said. And meant it. "Tell me what happened. Tell me everything."

The smile faded as he took her hand. He told her how he and Neil hit the deck behind the Manhattan skyline set when James started shooting. Between a crack in the buildings they watched James jump off the stage and open fire, witnessing the ensuing stampede as people made it out the lobby doors.

Or didn't.

Silence descended on the theater, leaving only James standing alone in the aisle, gun in hand.

"We were about to make a dash for the wings," David said. "Then I saw Fish come out."

Thoughts of escape were abandoned as Erik came out of the lighting booth into the aisle, crawled a careful distance and then sat on the carpet, up against the seats.

"I couldn't hear anything," David said, his eyes brimming. "But I knew Fish was talking to him. Trying to talk him down. He was holding up his hand. Like he was showing James something. Even with a gun in his face Fish was in control of the situation. Fucking human valium, that guy."

David watched as Erik tried to talk to James. Talk him down, get him to stop. And James stopped by putting the gun under his chin and blowing the back of his head across three rows of seats.

Daisy swallowed hard. She had never known such weary sadness. A despair that was hollow and decayed like a rotting tree.

"Why?" she whispered. "David, I don't understand. What did we ever do to... Why did he do it?"

David's gentle fingertips touched the tear tracks on her cheeks.

"Because we were happy," he said. "That's all."

She squeezed her face hard, nodding against the crying. Her leg howled. Her heart wailed.

"It's all right, Marge," David said. "Don't cry, honey, it's over now."

The pain intensified and she broke down. The nurse administered another dose of morphine. David hitched his chair closer, opened *The Eyes of the Dragon* and read aloud until the drug took hold and she was asleep again.

AN ORDERLY BROUGHT WILL to Daisy's room in a wheelchair, parked him close to the bed and left them alone.

They were desperate to embrace but they could only awkwardly reach around their injuries and rest their heads together, weeping.

"I'm sorry." Will's voice was a tatter of sobs. "I'm sorry, Dais, I'm so sorry."

"It wasn't your fault," she said.

"It was."

"No, don't say that."

"He was coming for me. Coming for everything I loved."

"I know. It's all right."

"Everyone's wondering why he didn't go straight for Lucky," he said. "Don't they get it, Dais? Don't they see? He knew what he was doing. He knew what would kill me and he went after it. He fucking went after *Fish*."

"It's all right," she said, stroking his head.

"I don't know what I would've done if he... Jesus Christ, I watched him do it. Watched him put the gun right in Fish's face and I swear to God, Dais, I—"

"Will, please," she said. "Don't talk about it anymore."

"I'm sorry." Will sat up, sniffing hard and shaking back his hair. When his good hand took Daisy's, it was with the grip of a partner.

"You're going to get through this," he said. "You're strong and you'll get through this and you'll dance again. I know you will. And I'll be there with you. All right? We're going to make this work. We can do anything. Don't cry, Dais..."

ERIK CAME EVERY DAY and every day he seemed thinner and paler. His eyes were circled and his hands shook. He squeezed beside Daisy's good leg, his head on her shoulder and she picked up the cigarette smoke in his hair and clothes. She only knew him to be an occasional social smoker but what she smelled now was pure, habitual need.

She couldn't hold him in her arms, only lace one hand with his and run the other over his head. His jaw snugged in her palm and his tears wet on her fingertips.

"Everyone's saying I was brave for leaving the booth," he said, sounding choked and hoarse. "And it's bullshit. I left the booth because I thought you were dead. I left the booth because I'm a fucking coward, because I'm afraid to live without you. I went out of there to die. Not to stop James, not to save anyone. I went out of the booth because I can't breathe without you. That's the truth."

"Shh," she whispered. "It's all right."

"I can't breathe without you," he said, his voice dissolving now.

"I can't either. Hold onto me, honey. It's all right."

He dug the heel of his hand into his streaming eyes. "I'm sorry. I shouldn't be doing this, it's not fair to you."

"Listen to me," she said against his hair. "I don't remember anything. People are telling me what happened and it's like they're talking about a movie. I don't remember any of it. I woke up and nothing was fair, nothing made sense until you walked in the room. Don't ever be sorry for needing me. If I'm your air then you're my..."

The sentence trailed away. She was weary and grieving and her leg hurt. She picked up his hand and ran fingertips over the tattooed daisy.

"This," she said. "I'm in your skin now. You keep me alive."

A shiver swept over him. "I thought you were dead," he said.

"Shh, honey. You're so tired. Close your eyes."

"I love you."

"I'm right here," she said. "I'm in your skin and I won't disappear, I promise. Close your eyes now."

He nestled into her shoulder. His hand in hers twitched a few times, then he was still, breathing soft and slow.

Her eyes were dry and alert as he slept. They looked daggers at her flayed leg, staring down the ugly red flesh and the blood-caked edges.

If I can't dance then all I have left is him.

She inhaled hard at the smoke smell in his clothes, desperate for a cigarette. Her nail worried at the calluses on the pads of his fingers. A nervous twist in her stomach. A feeling this was the price she paid for something.

But she couldn't remember what.

# AS A MOTHER

"IT WAS ALL PEOPLE talked about," Daisy said. "How Erik went out of the booth. Crawled through broken glass and went out into the aisle where James was with a gun."

"It was an incredibly brave thing to do," Rita said.

"They said he was a hero," Daisy said. "But he never believed it himself. Not even when my father gave him a medal. He gave Erik the purple heart he earned in Vietnam."

"What a beautiful gesture."

"Erik tried to talk to James. James trusted him once. But he was too far gone, I guess. And he shot himself."

She looked up at Rita. "I don't think Erik ever got over it."

"Nobody would."

"It changed everything. And everybody."

"Of course it did. It's a life-altering experience. And from what you tell me, neither you nor Erik, nor many of your friends, sought out counseling afterward."

"No. We didn't."

"Why do you think that is?"

Her shoulders circled vaguely and settled again. "We wanted to forget. Put it behind us. The worst was over. Right?"

Rita said nothing.

"Erik said the day of the shooting was nothing compared to the week after. When he and David went to all the funerals, four funerals in three days. It's what finally broke him down. The last service was Taylor's and then he cracked. His mother came to see me in the hospital. She sat on the bed and took my hands and said she needed to talk to me as a mother. I think she meant woman-to-woman. And I felt like an equal in the conversation, like we were conferring as the two women who loved him most. Erik was sick. He wasn't sleeping. He was losing weight and Christine was worried about what to do. And I said, 'Take him home. He needs to go home and collapse.' I knew him so well. I knew he'd go if she asked. Or rather if she told. He needed directions. He was waiting for someone to tell him what to do. And I was right: he cried when we said goodbye but he wasn't fighting either of us. He was so tired."

"And you?"

Daisy leaned to scratch her ankle. "What about me?"

"How long were you in the hospital?"

"Three weeks."

"In bed the whole time?"

"For the first week. Ten days, maybe. Then I started in-house physical therapy. Nothing for my left leg, I couldn't put weight on it yet. But stretching everything else, getting some movement and range of motion going. Little things."

Rita shifted in her chair. "What was that like?"

For a minute Daisy barely understood what she meant. The question knocked on a door long closed, the hinges and latch cobwebbed and rusty. The nameplate missing from the mailbox. "It was fine" formed on her tongue and she nearly said it. But the door cracked. She looked within and it wasn't fine.

"Awful," she said. "Scary. Frustrating. Painful." The words felt inept. Labels with the wrong name on mailboxes. Unopened deliveries.

A fragile silence. More fragile than the edges of skin around the perimeter of her fasciotomies. One hand stroked the line of scar tissue through her jeans.

"They never give you a straight answer," she said. "It's all might and maybe and possibly. Probably not. But a chance. We're cautiously optimistic. After a while I stopped asking if I would dance again. And I stopped listening to all the hypothetical, cover-our-ass bullshit. I thought who's going to win? Me, or James? *You dance or else he's got the last word.* Fuck that. Fuck him. It'll be hard? Fine. It'll be painful? Bring it. It'll break my heart? I'll break it my way. I hardened down. Erik would say I went into my war room. I could almost feel it...like a coat of shellac over my heart. No more crying, it's time for work."

She put her hand into the bowl of dried lavender and lemon verbena and let the soft, dusty leaves and tiny buds sift through her fingers. Then she held them to her nose, inhaling. Smelling her mother.

"I went home after three weeks. Finally home in my own bed. Mamou filled a big vase with lavender and put it on my night table. I remember sitting on the front porch, breathing in the sun and the flowers."

"And Erik was home then?"

"Yes, in Rochester. He was going to start an internship at Lancaster in June. Rebuilding the theater. So we had all of May to get through before we'd see each other. It was hard. We talked on the phone every night but... It was the longest we'd been apart."

She could remember the spring nights curled up to the telephone. Remember Erik's voice and the keen, frustrated longing that laced their conversations. But none of the words.

"I started physical therapy. Cardio training at first: wheelchair workouts, building my endurance back up. Three of us were under the same trainer: one guy who was a double amputee and another who was paralyzed from the waist down. And me. All working with Stef."

"Stef?"

Daisy nodded. "A former drill sergeant roughly the size of a redwood. Funny as hell. Pure take-no-prisoners motivation. The only one who said to me 'Yes' when I asked if I'd dance again. Actually the answer was '*Fuck* yeah.' But oh my God, he was tough. Brutal. I thought I'd survived being shot only to die at the hands of a sadist. I got so mad at him once, I said 'First thing I'm going to do when I get strength back in this leg is kick you in the nuts.' And he gave me a shit-eating grin and said, 'I look forward to it. I'll even hold still.'"

"Did you?" Rita said, smiling.

"No. By the end of the summer, I loved him too much."

Looking back was like flipping through a scrapbook underwater, a blurred collection of mementos stretching from May to August. Washed-out sepia tones. Pages stuck together, melding days into weeks. Weeks into months. She worked and trained and recovered. Fell down and dragged herself up again. Took faltering steps to the shouted approval of her war mates, neither of whom would ever walk again. She cried to the impervious ears of Stef, who waited with beefy arms crossed until the crying was over. Then threw her back into the battle.

The pool. The exercises. The weights. The steps. Ice therapy. Ultra-sound therapy. Heat therapy. Massage therapy. Life revolved around her body. Her body's feats measured in millimeters. Then inches. Then steps. Ounces turned to pounds. She could put weight on her left leg for seconds which gradually became minutes. Her gait smoothed out. The limp began to fade. One joyful morning in August she put her feet into first position and did a plié and a rise onto the balls of her feet, both knees straight and true. Stef had wagered she wouldn't reach this important goal until September. Both a good sport and a man of his word, he wore a tutu and tiara to work the next day.

"At the time I thought it was the hardest thing I'd ever done in my life," Daisy said. She turned ironic eyes around Rita's office, shaking her head the tiniest bit. "Little did I know..."

"Don't dismiss it," Rita said quietly. "It was an amazing and heroic accomplishment. None of what's happening here invalidates how hard you worked. This is simply different work."

Daisy smiled, tasting it. "It was a long summer."

"It must have been."

"I went back to Philly one weekend. And David met up with me."

"What for?" Rita asked.

"I needed him."

BLACK CAKE

SHE'D NEVER ASKED David for a favor before. But she called him now. "Will you do something for me?"

"Anything," he said. "It's done."

He drove her downtown to the tattoo parlor Will frequented and where Erik got his daisy. The shop was next door to a West Indian grocery. They appeared to be co-owned, or at least on friendly business terms. The adjoining wall within had been opened up and the smell of spice drifted around the artists' stations along with the hypnotic offbeat of Reggae.

A gorgeous black couple lounged by the front desk, the woman sitting on the man's lap. His hair was in dreadlocks. Hers was barely fuzz along her perfectly-shaped skull. She wore not a shred of makeup or jewelry, except for a single, delicate silver ring in her nose. As the bell rang on the door jamb, she looked first at David then at Daisy, who was on her crutches today, letting her leg rest.

The black woman smiled. "Hello, sister."

With her eyes Daisy asked David to hang back and he did, taking a seat on one of the chairs by the front window. Daisy crutched smoothly to the desk and asked if she could see Omar.

"I am Omar," the man said, reaching past his lapmate's body to offer a large hand.

"My name's Daisy," she said, shaking it. "You know my friend Will—"

Omar put up his palm, silencing her. The woman slid from his lap and he came around the desk and set both his hands on Daisy's shoulders. His eyes swept from the crown of her head down to her feet.

"I know who you are," he said. "I inked your boy. William sent him to me after the shooting."

"Yes."

"He described your eyes." His hands still on Daisy's shoulders, Omar turned to his friend. "She was at Lancaster. She and her boy and William. Do you remember the daisy? This is she." His voice broke and he cleared his throat.

"I remember," the woman said. "How are you, sister?"

"Let's sit down," Omar said. "Tell me what I can do."

"Do you want me to come back later, Dais?" David called from his chair.

Daisy reached her hand to him, beckoning. "No, stay with me," she said. "This is David. Erik's friend." She squeezed the fingers that had crept into hers. "And mine."

The woman, introduced as Camille, brought David a cup of strong coffee and Daisy a cup of chai tea, an anise star floating on its creamy top. From her bag, Daisy drew out the sheet of paper she'd been doodling on for the better part of a week. "Don't laugh," she said to Omar.

"I never laugh at someone's vision," he said. "Bad for business."

She smoothed it out on his desk. "Erik's last name means fisherman in Swedish. Everyone calls him Fish. So..." She had attempted to make a fish shape from the letters spelling *Svensk Fisk.* Omar and Camille bent their heads over it, exchanging glances and nods.

"Oh yes, I see," Omar said. "I see it." He took a fresh sheet of paper from his desk drawer and clicked the end of a mechanical pencil. "Camille, love, get me that book. The one with the Norse runes."

Camille made a face but went over to the bookshelf. "I don't know, I think runes will be too angular and harsh. The fish won't ripple."

"It will," Omar said, drawing. "Think I'm going to ink something on a dancer that doesn't move?"

Camille's upper lip curled as she mocked him. Setting the book down on the desk, she inhaled by Daisy's head. "Goodness, you smell like black cake."

"Like what?"

"Jamaican rum cake. It's made with burnt sugar essence."

"Everyone thinks she smells like sugar," David said. He was walking up and down the panels of designs, arms crossed tight, looking both curious and fearful.

"Are you getting anything today, my friend?" Omar said, looking up from his sketching.

"Me?" David's head turned back. "No. No. She's the brave one. I'm just the chauffeur."

Camille, having slipped away, came back from the grocery side of the building with a small brown bottle with a yellow label. She unscrewed the cap and waved it first under Daisy's nose, then David's. A thick, singed smell wafted.

"Oh yeah," David said, closing his eyes as he inhaled. "You make cake with that and rum?"

"Black cake," Camille said. "You soak dried fruit in rum for three months beforehand. Then the essence is mixed in with the batter. It's religious."

"How much essence," Daisy asked, already composing a recipe for Francine. "Few tablespoons?"

Camille smiled. "The whole bottle, sister. And a dozen eggs."

"Jesus," David said.

"My aunt is a perfumer," Daisy said. "She made my scent for me when I was sixteen but I don't know what's in it."

"Well if the formula's ever lost you can dab a little of that shit behind your ears," David said.

"I have many friends who do," Camille said.

"What do you think?" Omar said, turning the paper around to face Daisy.

Daisy put her hand over her mouth. A little burnt sugar essence had spilled on her fingers and the smell filled her head as she took in Omar's design. The letters of *Svensk Fisk* cunningly drawn to evoke the shape of a fish. The first K making the dorsal fins, the last K made the tail. The letters hinted at runes yet they had movement. The little fish swam before her eyes. "It's perfect," she said.

David nodded, a smile playing around his mouth. "Will you color them in?"

"Red," Omar and Daisy said at the same time.

It took a half-hour for Omar to ink the fish into the hollow of Daisy's right hip bone.

"He usually works much faster than this," Camille said, a loving hand on the artist's head. "But he's crying too much."

"Two things make me cry," Omar said, turning his head to press his shoulder to his damp eyes. "Love and bravery."

Daisy's eyes were streaming as well, more from emotion than pain. She'd endured worse. She didn't need the hand David offered but she held it anyway because she knew he wanted to feel useful. His eyes were dry, but he looked a shade green. Every now and then, he unscrewed the cap from the bottle of burnt sugar essence and waved it under his nose like smelling salts before passing it to Daisy. Like the hand-holding, Daisy let him think it helped, touched by how he was caring for her today.

When all was done, Omar folded Daisy into his arms and held her a long moment. He smelled like sandalwood and strength.

"Take care of your boy," he said. "And come see me again soon."

"Come around Christmastime," Camille said as she hugged David and gave him the bottle of sweet extract to keep. "And have black cake with us."

"OH, DAIS," Erik said.

They were in her bedroom at La Tarasque, Erik kneeling at her feet. First his fingers traced the tattoo, then his mouth. Her pores were wide open and aching for his touch.

"Do you like it?" she said.

"I love it."

Her hand caressed his hair. "I thought a long time about where to put it. Somewhere only you could see."

"Only me." His forehead against her belly, arms around her legs. He exhaled. Now his cheek was wet against her skin.

"Nobody loves me like you," he said.

IN THE
DARK

HOLDING YOUR THING

WILL CAME BACK TO school shorn, his magnificent tresses cropped down to the scalp. His strong cheekbones leaped from his face like knives. With nowhere to hide, his beautiful eyes took center stage, liquid brown and haunted under thick lashes and brows.

He never spoke of James. Nobody did. Will never apologized for the affair or for his attraction to men, and nobody expected it of him.

But his eyes told a different story.

"I told him I trusted his hands," Erik said to Daisy. "I told him sometimes his hands were the only thing between you and a ten-foot fall to the stage and I trusted them. I trusted him with you. He could barely look at me in the hospital. He kept crying and saying 'I dropped her, I dropped her...'"

"He was shot through the back and nearly had his hand blown off," Daisy said. "It would've been a miracle if he hadn't dropped me. I don't blame him for this, I know you don't. Nobody does."

"It was nobody's fault," everyone said. "It was only James's fault."

Will wouldn't talk about it. His inner experience spoke through his sacrificed hair, his troubled eyes, and a fierce obsession with Daisy's recovery. His dire need to know the whereabouts of his loved ones surpassed even Erik's. Will wanted Lucky, Daisy and, especially, Erik, where he could see and touch them. He wanted the four of them together, all the time.

The circle pulled tight: the boys at Colby Street, the girls at Jay Street. David around the corner with Neil Martinez. And John dropping by with carte blanche.

They rarely went out. Crowded, noisy places made them uneasy. The world was unpredictable and strangers untrustworthy. Instead they gathered close at the girls' apartment and kept company, eating, studying or watching TV. They stayed up too late, delaying bedtime. All their sleep was sketchy and unpredictable, laced with nightmares they compared with a macabre one-upmanship.

John, who had knelt on the stage floor inches from Will's severed fingers, dreamed of dismembered hands in grotesque piles.

Neil dreamed of being lost in the caverns of Manhattan. Skyscrapers like teeth and the streets below full of blood.

Lucky, so heroic and competent in the theater, now dreamed of walking wounded, of having to make life or death decisions which were never right.

Will ran in his dreams. Ran and ran from an invisible looming danger behind him. He could feel its breath on his cropped head. Hear its accusatory laughter inches away. Sometimes he turned to fight, only to find the terror was still behind him.

Erik took a shot point-blank in the chest in his nightmares. He sat dying in the aisle as James went back to the stage to finish what he started.

David wouldn't tell anyone his dreams.

Daisy had two. One she told, the other she kept.

The shared dream was of blank space: a cavern of dark, yawning nothingness before her eyes. She could sense its dimensions but not its boundaries. It was endless and predatory. A gigantic oubliette determined to feed on her sanity.

The untold dream repulsed her: a bizarre sexual encounter with Erik where she devoured him. Her vulva unfolding like a Venus flytrap, sucking him inside. He went willingly to his death. His expression was one of happy relief while Daisy screamed in a helpless rage because assuming him into her body wasn't enough to save him.

It was never enough.

Her libido had been low during the summer but now it came back to her with a strange desperation, an almost frenetic direness to it. But she couldn't come. It was as if she wasn't allowed. Sex wasn't about frivolous pleasure, it was about protection. She had a job here: to save her man. And after making love, she felt sick to her stomach with a pervasive sense of failure.

Sex was playing strange tricks on Erik, too. He wanted it all the time, hungrily grabbing Daisy at every opportunity. He was edgy and passionate before, tender and loving during, but as soon as sex was over, anxiety came for him. Galloping over the hill of his mind like a pack of beasts on the hunt. And he fell apart in her arms, unmanned and shaking to his bones.

"Four A.M. when the wolves come," Daisy said.

She lay tight against his back, pressing his pounding chest with the palm of her hand and feeling responsible for his panic-laced body. Feeling helpless to stop it, feeling she missed the one chance to stop it.

Now, do it right this time, her body chided the next time they had sex.

It was always the same.

She didn't know what she was doing wrong.

The two couples slept at Jay Street every night and the house was rarely quiet in the darkest hours. Erik woke up shouting. Daisy woke up screaming. Down the hall Will bolted upright with a cry. Lucky thrashed in dreams and fell out of bed.

"I broke the lamp," she said one morning. "And for no fun reason."

They were brave in the light of day. They tried to laugh off the bad dreams, find the funny in the anxious vulnerability.

They were all sitting around late one night, watching a movie. Lucky went upstairs to get a sweater and came back down a minute later.

"Look at you," she said from the foot of the stairs. "One, two...three... *five* guys, and every single one of you has a hand down their pants."

As one the boys looked up and mumbled, "What?"

Daisy burst out laughing.

The boys exchanged mild glances, but not one hand moved from its place.

Lucky swung around the newel post, her curls bouncing. "All of you holding your thing like it's going somewhere."

"Hey, you never know," John said.

"These are tenuous times, Lulu," David said. "You keep your friends close and the junk even closer."

"I was being polite because ladies were present," Neil said. "But hell, now that you outed everyone..." He slid his other hand down his jeans.

"Both hands," David said, nodding approval.

"Get over here, Luck," Will said. "Get your hand down here too. For Christ's sake."

Erik said nothing. He'd toppled over with his head in Daisy's lap, laughing and laughing. One hand over his face, the other still down his pants. Peal after peal of laughter, and soon the knee of Daisy's jeans was damp with his tears.

"It's not *that* funny, Fish," David said.

"Yes it is," he said, his voice squeaking.

Daisy looked around, suffused with a hysterical happiness. The little living room was full of laughter as invisible golden threads knitted the circle together.

Knit one, purl two. Don't forget I love you.

We have to stay together, Daisy thought, stroking Erik's head, her lap full of his chuckling. *Hold onto these moments, make it last. If we stay together and find what's funny, we'll be all right.*

MARRYING ME

"WERE YOU dancing yet?"

"No," Daisy said. "Not in the fall. Still on disability, so to speak. Impatient as hell but I knew one reckless risk could blow everything. I started to teach, which was eye-opening."

"Teach what?"

"Mostly the beginner and intro ballet classes but whatever Kees needed me to do. We didn't have a replacement for Marie so he was running both divisions."

Another closed door materialized in her mind. Painted fresh and white but spots of rust seeping through. A pretty grille overlay, choked with dry, crumbling leaves. A pot by the jamb filled with dead flowers.

Ciao, fiorella.

Good morning, little flower.

Rita's head tilted, the light catching the lenses of her glasses. "Where are you right now?"

Daisy closed her eyes. "Marie used to say... If I was tired or slow in class she'd tease me. 'Margarita, darling, why so lazy today? You sleep with the fishes?'"

Rita's smile was sad.

"When you think about it, I never got any closure. I didn't go to the funerals. Marie didn't even have one to go to. Her husband had her cremated and took her ashes back to Italy. I never saw her in the hospital. Never got to go to her bedside and hold her hand or anything. I never saw her again. She disappeared. It didn't really hit me until I got back to school. It was like I almost forgot..."

She breathed in. Let it out, creating a bubble. "I kept looking for her. Looking for Taylor and Aisha and Manuel. It would hit me at odd moments. Come out of the dark to slap my face. They were gone. My tribe."

Rita nodded.

She touched her fingertips under her eyes. "Over the summer, David found one of Taylor's knitting needles backstage. I wrote to her mother and asked if I could keep it and she said yes. I have it on my dressing table. And I have the hat she made me freshman year, I keep that on my table, too. I like having her near me while I'm getting ready."

"She must like that, too," Rita said softly.

"Do you believe in spirits?" Daisy asked, not expecting a personal answer.

But, "I do," Rita said. "I believe they manifest as an energy around us. And I believe they are drawn to the little shrines we make for them."

"Will got a new tattoo for Marie. A wheel. That's how his name sounded when she said it. 'Wheel, darling...' What could I get for her? A margarita glass..."

She pulled at the fringe on a throw pillow. "I missed her so much. We, all of us in the ballet division, it was like we were mourning our mother. And when Kees asked me to teach some of her classes, I was terrified. Not so much of not being able to do it but of... I don't know, somehow intruding on her memory. It felt disrespectful. I balked and Kees said, sort of joking but not, 'teach the class or I'll flunk you.' And I saw how stressed and hurt and bleeding he was, and I realized he needed me. So I went in and I taught."

"And?"

She smiled. "I loved it. In a way it was the final touch on all my rehab. We have a saying in dance: to teach is to learn twice. When you're breaking down a movement or a step and explaining it to someone else, you're learning it fresh. Learning it better. And in November, when I finally got the green light to go back to class myself, I was ready and man..."

Her chest went warm with memory. "I walked into the studio that day and everyone gathered around me. Like I was the sun. Hugging me and kissing me and high-fiving. It was like coming home. It was the beginning of this little interlude, about two months, November into the first weeks of January, when it felt like things were turning around."

"In what way?"

"For starters, all the catty, cliquish bullshit in the studio was over. I walked back in and the place was completely shuffled. No more freshmen barres or unspoken rules. Seniors were next to sophomores, mentoring the new kids. It was a family. And I felt at the hub of it, the center of this galaxy of loving, creative energy. It spilled over onto everything else. Will and I were back in partnering class, figuring out how to work with his maimed hand. It was frustrating, but by that time we ate frustration for breakfast. Yeah, whatever, it's a problem. We'll find the solution."

Rita smiled. "I like that."

"Then we all went to La Tarasque for Thanksgiving. Erik, Will, Lucky. And David. Mamou made a beautiful dinner and the next day, everyone went with Pop to cut down the Christmas tree. Except Erik and I—we stayed behind and ended up having amazing sex."

Rita's chin lifted but she said nothing.

"Out of nowhere," Daisy said, a little sweetness creeping into her mouth. "It came back. The way it used to be before the shooting. We fell asleep afterward, completely peaceful and relaxed. Got up for dinner and then we all decorated the tree. Pop put Christmas music on and Mamou was baking—she found a recipe for these cookies Erik's grandmother used to make when he was little. David was singing funny words to the carols. It was the most perfect night ever. Erik and I made love again and didn't stop. We were stuffing our faces with it and crying in between, we were so happy."

Rita steepled her fingers beneath her nose. "Why do you think it was that way? At that time?"

"I don't know. Lucky always said La Tarasque had some kind of magic in it."

"A place where you could go and be safe, yes."

"Maybe that was it. We were away from Lancaster and in the safest, most loving place imaginable. No bad memories associated."

Beautiful, tactile images beaded the windows of Daisy's memory. Erik pressing her up against the shower wall in the carriage house's little bathroom. The tiles cool against her back. Thick steam in her lungs. Wet, soapy skin. The hot, hard slide of his cock, filling her up to her eyes. A Roman candle orgasm rippling through her belly, squeezing and pulsing. Then the softness of sleep afterward, snow beginning to fall outside the window. The butter-yellow walls of Francine's kitchen. Red wine and candles on the table, pine boughs and sparkling ornaments. Laughter up and down the table. Nat King Cole being drowned out by David's dirty lyrics to "The Christmas Song,"

Roast nuts chesting on an open fire. Nipfrost jacking off your nose...

Spicy orange cookies from Erik's childhood prying a name from his memory.

"Pepparkakor," he said, slapping a hand on the table. "I can't believe I remember."

Not only delicious but laden with magic. You put one in your palm, made a wish and pressed on the center. If it broke into three pieces, you were granted. If not, you still had a cookie.

"When we were in bed that night," Daisy said. "Erik asked if I ever thought of marrying him."

Rita nodded.

"We'd never talked about marriage. Not even hypothetically or jokingly. But he asked."

Do you ever think of marrying me?

"I said, 'If I marry anyone, it'll be you.'" She stared down at her lap. "Which still feels like the truth to me," she said. "I don't know who else I can love. You know, when I was in rehab, the fear of not dancing again motivated me. Because the alternative was unthinkable. I didn't know who else I was or what else I could do. I had one thing and it had been the only thing since I was five. I had no backup, no other hobbies or interests. No plan B. Nothing. Looking at my life without dance was utterly terrifying, and sometimes it feels like losing Erik is no different. Facing that fear in this rehab feels the same way, except now the alternative is all I have. I fought like hell to dance again and I won. And I fought like hell to get Erik back and I lost. I'm lost. He left and I don't know who I am. I don't know who else I can love. Jesus Christ, I don't know what the fuck I'm *doing*."

"You're finding out."

"I'm so afraid," she said, crying. Was this what her life was going to be—pining and longing and mourning and crying?

"You've been afraid before. It's a problem. And we'll find the solution, Daisy."

Daisy sniffed, wiping her eyes. "Stop quoting me."

"You have good lines."

"Lines," she said. "I haven't talked about that yet, have I?"

Eyebrows wrinkled, Rita shook her head.

Daisy chewed on her bottom lip. "Over Thanksgiving, Lucky got pregnant. Of course we didn't know until weeks later. Meanwhile December continued on this easy, pleasant trajectory. Life stayed sweet, nobody was having nightmares. Everyone was having sex."

She blew her breath out. "But it was short-lived. We came back to school in January and everything fell apart. Lucky had a miscarriage. She bled out all over our bathroom floor and Erik went in to help her. The sight of the blood... It unlocked something in him and he unraveled. We all were shaken up by it and then started the drugs."

"Ah." Rita turned a page. "What were you doing?"

"In the beginning, mostly cocaine."

"Where were you getting it?"

"From David. He was always into some kind of shit and we got into it too. Coke during the week. Weekends we did a lot of ecstasy. And then David introduced us to the high roll."

WHERE DID YOU GO?

"DAIS."

A finger snapped in front of her staring eyes.

Daisy shook her head and looked at the boy next to her. A tilted chin and sunny smile. Brows furrowed above questioning eyes.

"Where did you go?" he asked softly.

Open-mouthed, she shook her head and gazed in slow-motion. Her brain took an eternity to identify this as the living room.

I live here.

I am.

I exist.

She stared at the beautiful boy next to her. Another oozing interval of time before she remembered he belonged to her. Her atoms stirred in interest and her mouth grew wet.

"Erik," she said. As if she hadn't seen him in years.

"Come back," he said. "Don't leave me." He fell face-first into her neck, giggling. "Oh my God. I'm so fucking high."

"Me too," she said, pushing the words through a mouth that seemed full of buttercream frosting, so rich it made a nauseous thrum in the back of her throat. Her hand went to Erik's head. She felt all his hairs on her palm. She could count them. In fact, she could gladly sit here the rest of her life and count every single one. Differentiate the blond, the ash, the brown and the gold. She ran her hand along the velvet nap at his nape—she giggled at *nap* and *nape*—mesmerized by push and pull of tiny hairs.

Nap. Nape.

Push. Pull.

Pill.

David gave them a magic pill.

He called it a high roll—smoking a joint and then doing a hit of ecstasy. Now Daisy's mouth was a cake and Erik's hair was a waterfall. A field of wheat. An army of fine lines. Legions purring under her palm.

"Touch me forever," he said, his smile a delicious thing.

She wanted to eat him. She was beyond high. No greater vertical existed. She was at the apex of consciousness where the air thinned into cosmic dust. She was a star. She burned. No need for molecules of oxygen. She was breathing the universe. It was so beautiful.

David was gone. Like Santa Claus he bestowed his gifts upon them and then disappeared up the chimney. Will and Lucky were making out on the floor. Writhing and heavy and oblivious. Daisy stared, full of love and fascination. Shirtless and tattooed like a serpent, Will slid beautiful hands up into Lucky's sweater and drew it over her head. And Lucky, who had barely cracked a smile in weeks, was laughing around his kiss. Even her curls were laughing snakes...

Erik was kissing Daisy's neck. Moving her hair and sliding hot, shaking lips along her skin. She turned her head, caught his mouth. The kiss swirled and meshed like a kaleidoscope. Kissing was magic. Had she ever truly appreciated it before tonight? A sigh echoed within her head as she pulled his tongue against hers. She could do this forever. Thank God for kissing. If only everyone on earth would kiss like this, it could be the end of war and...

She opened her eyes. Her sighing head melted into laughter as she realized it was her own tongue she was orchestrating world peace with.

"I'm kissing myself," she said, fingertips against her mouth. She had a mouth. She was a mouthed human being inhabiting earth. A planet hurtling through space and time and how did it all begin?

"Kiss me," Erik said, pulling her into him. His mouth grabbed hers, catching her lip with the edge of a tooth. The bite of pain was a sword thrusting blue through the gooey coral and gold in her head. His hands curved around her breasts, thumbs moving in small tight circles. A prickling excitement radiated out from between her legs as she kissed him harder, chafing the little scrape on the inside of her lip. Pain and pleasure swirled together in a double helix and she came. Just a little one. But deep. A single, quick squeeze at the crux of herself.

"Do that again," she whispered.

Erik took her soft, electric hands and pulled her off the couch, stumbling backwards. His face was wide-eyed, laughing wonder. "It's all caramel in my head," he said.

He pushed her up ahead of him on the stairs. Every other step she turned to kiss him, wanting the edge of his teeth again and the blue squeeze down in her belly. Her mouth had never known such hunger. She was so high. So skinless and wide open and floating in a dimension of desire utterly foreign to her.

Do it again. Make it hurt.

Part of her had sliced itself off and now circled her ankles with the frenetic figure eights of a cat in heat. Trying to formulate a request she barely understood.

Do it.

Closed up in her room, they kissed in the Christmas lights. Erik reached behind, took hold of the back of his shirt and drew it forward, over his head. Her chin tilted in wonder. She had never noticed before how a boy took his shirt off from back to front. He slid one beautiful arm then the other out of the sleeves and it was a revelation. Her own arms crossed, took hold of her shirt at opposite sides and took it off the way a girl did: from the hem up.

He was a boy. She was a girl. They touched. His skin was bronze and copper and gold. Her hand made ripples over his chest and shoulders and melted into him. She could reach within and put her fingers gently around his heart like it was the fragile, unfused skull of a newborn baby.

She watched him take the rest of his clothes off. Belt and snap and zipper. A snake shedding its skin. Naked like that newborn, but strong and male and forged from metal. She ran her finger along the chain around his neck. St. Birgitta smiled at her. The fish winked its single golden eye. The beauty of the links and a legacy passed from man to man.

Father to son.

"I'm having your baby someday," she said. "You know that, don't you?"

"Only one?" His hands slid down the back of her opened jeans, pushing them down and pulling her belly against his. His mouth running up her neck, over her chin. He kissed her top lip. Then her bottom. And whispered into her mouth. "Have two."

She kicked her legs free of her pants. Pushed Erik down on the bed and knelt across one of his legs. Drew his shaking lips up into hers as she ground her hips down on his thigh. Sliding and rubbing. Catching the sweet spot. It wasn't working. Something was missing.

"Come, honey," he whispered.

I can't, she thought, writhing in frustration.

His hands slid along her head. Ten fingers wove into her tresses. Folded into fists. A crackle of blue light as he pulled her hair.

"Yes." Her eyes closed as the S stretched out long, the hiss of a tattooed serpent.

"Come for me," he said. He released his grip and the bite of pain at her scalp dissolved.

"Do that again," she said.

"What."

"Pull my hair."

He did.

"Harder," she said, making her voice swirl a finger in the caramel inside his head.

She felt his hesitation. Then he pulled.

"Feels good," she said into his mouth, kissing him with open eyes. Feeding him her burnt sugar fingers to suck. "You're so good."

He tugged, slow and hard. Her follicles howled and a sharp noise slipped out of her chest.

"Too much?"

"More. I love it." She pressed her teeth into his bottom lip and an involuntary groan, much like her own, tumbled out of him.

She held his face in her hands. "Make it hurt," she said, pushing him along, coaxing a child toward the classroom door. "It's making me crazy. Feel how wet I am..."

He dragged her head onto his shoulder. She slid along his leg, slippery and swollen. Letting it build.

"You're such a good lover," she said. Her tongue traced the seashell whorls of his ear. "Nothing makes me come like you."

Another groan in his chest and his mouth grabbed hers, hard and smug. She had him by the ego. He loved to be called good. His hands pulled. His teeth stabbed. He was shedding his skin. Turning inside-out and transforming under her. Rebirthing. A hero. A god.

"Come," he said, his breath like cinnamon now. "Make that sweet little pussy come for me."

"You're so good. Pull hard. Don't stop. Erik..."

The K splintered on her tongue and the world exploded under her eyes. Her hands hooked into claws, her nails pressing down into his skin. Deeper.

Erik's laughing delight filled her bones. He crooned her name over and under his breath, sing-speaking praises. "I love watching that. *God*, you're beautiful."

He released her hair and wrapped his arms around her twitching, convulsing body. Her scalp throbbed with pain as the last bits of pleasure rippled out of her and onto his leg. She ran her mouth along his neck. Salt and sweet. The springs groaned as she toppled off him and fell down in the sheets.

"I love when you come like that," he said. "And tell me things like that."

She put her forearm over her eyes, pressed down until the back of her eyelids turned to swirling patterns of gold. "I'm so high," she said.

His hand ran over her head. "Did I pull too hard?"

"Not hard enough." She felt his thumb glide on her mouth and she touched her tongue to it, expecting to taste blood. Only skin and a hint of herself.

I'm kissing myself.

"Look at me," he said.

She took her arm away. Waited until a blob of black bloomed like a flower in her gold vision. Opening its petals to gradually reveal his face.

"What just happened?" he said. "Why was that so good?"

"I don't know," she said.

His smile flickered, indulgent and knowing. *Nice try,* his eyes seemed to say.

"Tell me," he whispered.

Her own eyes welled up. The space between their bodies shivered. Warped and rippled in tiny pinpricks of light. She was seeing their bond. It was real. A physical thing that existed between them. *I was born for you,* she thought. *My voice was born to reach your ears. You were born to hear everything I have to say.*

"It was the hurting," she said. "It's all I can feel."

He nodded, his profile leaving trails in the sparkling air. "Me too."

His hand ran along her stomach, touched the fish tattoo. "I felt so alive just then," he said. "Making you come. I felt like who I used to be."

"I can see us," she said, moving her hand through the glittery air. He caught it in his and held it to his face.

"Lately I feel like I'm either numb or dying. Nothing in the middle. Numb scares me. I'd almost rather die. At least it's something."

"This is when you usually get anxious," she said. "Are you? Right now? Are the wolves here?"

"No," he said. He slid against her body. "Feel how hard I am."

"You are." She stroked his head.

"I don't want to stop feeling like this. I don't care what it takes."

"Come here," she said, pulling at him.

"What is happening?" he said, pushing into her.

"I'm not afraid. I want it." She rested her hand on the small of his back. Felt skin ripple over muscles. Felt muscles move like continents, obeying the commands his brain sent along nerves, tendons and bones. Making his body move in her. He knew what to do.

He was born for me.

"I'm scared it will go too far, Dais."

"It's just a different room in the cathedral," she said. "It's still ours. We built it. It's all making love, remember? Nothing we make scares me."

He looked at her a long time. Then he began to nod. She had him. She held his face, kissed him deep, then let her arms drop over her head, finding the headboard. "Tie my hands," she said.

He got one of her scarves and bound her wrists tight. Knots were his friend. He knew how to tie off cables above the stage and secure the fly ropes in the wings. He wasn't fooling around. He set his palms on her bowed elbows and leaned his weight down on her, his face hovering above hers. Something new and dangerous and beautiful in his eyes.

She brushed her mouth against his. "I love you. Show me every-thing. Let me taste it. I want to feel you dying."

He stared at her. Swirling pinpricks in his eyes.

"Do you trust me?" she said, as if he was the one tied up.

He nodded, the tip of his nose brushing hers. "I only trust you. If I step too far off the edge of myself, you're the only one who can pull me back."

"Unplug the lights," she said. "Come into the dark with me."

Like a snake his arm slithered between the bed and the wall and the Christmas twinkles died. He leaned and yanked the drapes across the window, cutting most of the light from the street. He crawled up and over her again. His hands circled her tied wrists. She couldn't see his face but somehow she knew it looked older. She felt it. The months since the shooting etched hard under his eyes.

"Promise you'll tell me when it's enough." A little bit of light flashed off his teeth.

She licked his mouth. "I'll tell."

It wasn't enough. He came at her like a night terror. Backhanded her with his raw, brute need. His unchecked strength astonished her, then filled her veins like another drug. She pulled against her bonds and begged for more. By morning her wrists were ringed red and her upper arms wore his fingerprint bruises like a new tattoo. He fucked a hundred words out of her throat and not one was "stop." They limped from bed, scratched and scraped, bone dry, hung over and wrung out black and exhausted.

They didn't know what it was.

They knew it wasn't enough.

NOBODY SCARS YOU BUT ME

"HE SURPRISED ME," Daisy said.

"How?" Rita said.

"Erik never had much artifice. He was drawn to the theater world but he wasn't a theatrical person. Not a daydreamer or a pretender. But when he was high, he would shrug himself off and do anything. He liked cocaine more than I did. He really liked the confidence of that particular high. Coke made him a nut, a hyper goofball. He'd *dance* when he was coked up. But he dug the ecstasy too and on a high roll, he was sexually fearless. He'd play games, play any part. Be someone else. Tie me up. Even pretend he was raping me." She drew her breath past her pounding heart. "I've never told anyone about this."

"Can you tell me?"

She looked down at the ball of her clenched fingers. "It was... Something about the hurting. Something about when sex was rough or violent or even painful. I began to want it. Like another drug. I wanted him to hit me. To hurt me. Not in anger, though. It's like..."

She pulled one hand free and dug the heel of it against her eye, trying to press the idea into place. "It's so hard to explain. So confusing and twisted because it was like him hurting me helped me feel safe. Does that even make sense?"

"Don't worry about sense," Rita said. "You spill. I sort."

"If he hurt me, then nobody and nothing else could. Like violent sex was a vaccine against the world. One time, we..." Daisy stopped as a cold, nauseous wind blew through her chest. "Fuck," she said, beginning to shake.

"It's all right," Rita said. "Let it come to you. You've been here before and you always come out the other side."

Daisy pulled the chocolate brown pillow into her lap, holding on. Her arms were struck with the sudden need for a live being to clutch. A wise, sober dog. She needed to feel a heartbeat.

"One time he was kissing me...and I bit him. Bit his lip. The blood was in our mouths. Not a lot but enough to taste."

"Were you high?"

"He rolled, I didn't. We'd smoked a joint but only had one ecstasy pill so he took it."

"I see."

"And when I made him bleed, he went off. Threw me face-first down on the floor, held my hands behind my back and gave it to me. And for the first time, I felt an edge of fear. Like I understood what he meant about going too far. I could *see* too far. See the line, the boundary. When you're high like that, you get really visual and sensory. Existentially descriptive, you're in the moment and narrating your life. I could feel my mind split down the center and one half was in pain. He was coming into me so hard, my eyeballs rattled. He was holding my hands behind my back and putting all his weight on me. I'd lost weight and I'm not built with a lot of cushion to begin with, so my hip bones were grinding into the floor, my shoulders were screaming. My face was against the throw rug so one cheekbone was taking the brunt of it all..."

"And the other half?"

"The other half was like the referee. Whistle in the mouth, eagle eye on the line. With this calm dry voice reminding me I was the only one who could pull him back. All I had to do was say *stop* or *too much* and he would back down."

"And was it getting to that point."

"Yes. But flirting with the boundary, seeing how close I could get to it." She shook her head and spread her hands, holding the enormous bubble full of her confused, shameful secrets. "I don't know how else to say it. Those nights up in my room, walking the line... I had the greatest orgasms of my life. I haven't come that way since and I'm terrified I never will again. Under any circumstances. Whether it's straight or sober, fucking or loving... I don't know if I ever will feel the way I felt with him."

"Hold that thought a moment," Rita said. "Don't close the bubble yet. I want you to finish the night. You were flirting with the line. Did it get crossed? Did he stop when you told him, or did you even tell him?"

Daisy closed her eyes. "I remember... My mind kind of took inventory. Triage. What was hurting me the most? What simply had to stop? And it was my shoulders. I think it must've been my ballet brain making the call. If he kept pulling on my shoulders like that, I wouldn't be able to get them into fifth position the next day."

She raised her arms to illustrate, shaping a curved wreath around her head. "I said something. 'Stop' or whatever but he kept going. I remember turning my head as much as I could and my cheekbone was raw against the rug. I spoke the way you do in a loud nightclub—shouting is useless, you have to throw your voice down into the middle of your chest. I didn't yell, but he had a hurricane in his head and I had to slice my voice through it and say, 'Honey, let go my hands, please.' I knew the *honey* and the *please* would get him. Send a signal. He let go. Being able to get my arms under me and the grinding pressure off my shoulders and cheek let me finish. Or let me let *him* finish. I was done at that point. I had come to pieces. I had just enough strength to ride it out."

"How was he afterward? Did you share with him what it was like?"

Her mouth opened and closed as a stream of flickering particles passed by her eyes. "I didn't have to," she said. "I don't know if you believe me, I want you to believe me when I say I didn't have to actively tell him. He rolled off my back and lay on the floor a few minutes, catching his breath. It was dark, so I couldn't see him. He was a black-on-black silhouette. And he said, 'Turn on the lights, I need to see you.'

"I crawled over to plug in the lights—my arms could hardly hold me up. We dragged ourselves on top of the bed, gulping water and gulping air. Then we stared at each other forever. Everything was gold and bright and beautiful and peaceful. I fell into his eyes and never wanted to come out. His fingers came up and touched my cheekbone, which was sore and stinging but I thought, *It's all right when you do it.* And a second later he whispered, 'Nobody scars you but me.'"

Rita's head rose and fell as she repeated it. "Nobody scars you but me."

"I loved it," she said. "It literally made me feel safe and protected..." She snatched a handful of tissues and pressed them to her face.

"Are you all right, do you need to stop?"

"No," Daisy said, muffled. "I'm blowing a bubble and I'm finishing this."

"You're doing great. Whenever you're ready."

Another breath. The slow release of her lungs and a shimmering sphere came into view. Soapy and iridescent. But strong. Her hands opened like a cradle for it.

"Do you have it?"

"We pushed it too far one night," she said, feeding the words inside. "We went over the line and... He blew the whistle. Stopped the game entirely. He couldn't do it anymore."

"What happened?"

The bubble shook in her hands, threatening to pop. "This is hard," she said.

"One word at a time," Rita said. "Any words you want. I do not judge, blush or scare."

Daisy licked her dry lips. She was pure blushing judgement and scared flat. Trapped between clinical terms and juvenile peek-a-boo euphemisms. Unable to just spit it out.

"One night he..." She swallowed, hating herself for being such a stupid prude. "He wanted to...fuck me in the ass and I..." Her chest seemed to collapse, a fine sweat dripped down her back.

"Take a deep breath," Rita said, getting up and taking a bottle of water from the mini-fridge under her desk. Daisy drank a few sips.

"I don't know why it was so hard to say," she said. "I'm a grown woman."

"You are now. You weren't then. And parts of you are stuck back then, frozen at twenty years old. Let those parts thaw out now. You're doing fine."

Daisy sniffed hard, her face twisting. "That night..."

"Had you ever had anal sex before?"

Daisy shook her head and took another sip. The water bottle became her bubble, a tangible vessel she could fill. She aimed her words toward it.

"No, neither of us had. We were rolling across the ceiling and we didn't know what the fuck we were doing. No buildup, no foreplay. We didn't even use lube or anything. Just right to it..."

Rita said nothing but behind her glasses her eyes squeezed shut, then opened again.

"It hurt me awful. And I came so hard..." Her face burned as she remembered. Pain like a dirty spike into her belly, a caduceus of twin snakes spiraling up her spine.

Let me in.

Let me hurt you.

She was tearing and breaking. She cried down into the pillows, clenching his fingers. She felt bright, alive and beautiful. Wild and terrible. Dirt and gold in her veins, crackling blue behind her eyes. She left herself behind, left Erik behind. Nothing but the dark existed. It was the wolf. It had tracked her down and trapped her. At last. It curved around her waist, slid between her belly and the mattress and found where she was wet, wide and aching. She came, bucking up into the clawed fur on her shoulders. Its teeth closed on the back of her neck and pinned her. A feral animal, growling and groaning around the death grip on her nape as it came into her and killed her.

"I bled for a day and a half afterward," she said. "And then Erik was out. Done. I remember he yanked my bedroom curtains open and plugged in my Christmas lights and he was shaking. Not angry, but adamant he wasn't going to hurt me in bed anymore. That's when I looked down at myself and saw what I'd become. How he'd pulled on my hair so much, it was falling out. My cheekbone still bruised. I was bleeding, with scratches all up and down my back and my arms bruised with fingerprints. And my next thought should have been how terrible I looked. That it was horrifying. But no, I thought it made me look...complete. Balanced. I don't know what I mean."

"Like your outsides finally matched your insides?"

Daisy closed her mouth up in a hand and nodded through tears.

GET UP, DAIS

THE SLAM OF HER BEDROOM door. A chill on her bruised skin as blankets were yanked away. She guessed it was Erik, back again to try to get her out of bed.

"Get up."

Daisy opened her eyes. It was Lucky, hands on hips.

"Get up, Dais. Come on."

"Go away." Her head was pounding. Her tongue was an emery board. Everything hurt.

"Up." Lucky's hands seized her, pulled her to sit. Her palms were cool on Daisy's cheeks. Her bustling and brisk authority filled the room.

"What time is it?" Daisy asked.

"Three in the afternoon. You have to get up."

"Why?"

"Because Erik is downstairs freaking out that you won't get out of bed. Now come on. Stand up. Let's get you in the shower."

The royal we. Daisy stood on shaky legs. Her ass howled. Bunched between her legs, her underwear felt damp and sinister.

"I think I hurt myself," she whispered, staring at the floor.

"What did you do?"

Daisy told her.

"Jesus God," Lucky said, brushing Daisy's hair back. "You stupid girl. Never, *never* do that without lube. Never again."

Stupid was a slap in the face and tears sprang to Daisy's eyes.

"Don't worry," Lucky said. "The bleeding will stop. Come on, I'll help you."

Pee. Brush teeth. Get into the shower. Lucky breezed in and out, supervising like a nanny. A new razor to shave, a fresh cake of Ivory soap. "Nice and easy when you're washing," she said. "Don't go poking your bits any more than necessary."

Her bits begged for forgiveness. Her shoulders barely allowed her arms to raise and wash her hair. Thick strands collected in the drain. Scratches stung and bruises winced.

Lucky brought towels, antibiotic cream, some kind of topical analgesic.

"Keep it next to the john and put a little on your butt every time."

Two Tylenol. A cold soda.

"It'll settle your stomach."

She brushed Daisy's hair.

"You need a trim. Remind me later."

Picked clothes.

"You got this," she said. "Everything's all right. I told him everything would be fine."

He needs you.

He needs to know where you are.

You cannot disappear.

When the soda was gone, Lucky brought a glass of water. "Pound the water today," she said. "The damn ecstasy sucks you dry."

Water in the desert...

Daisy drank it then pulled on jeans and a shirt. She changed it for a different shirt—the one Erik loved because it made her eyes pop. The thought of her clothes being a costume gave her context. This was a show. She put a bit of makeup on, getting ready for performance.

You have to be all right. Don't scream. The men you love cannot bear it. If you can't be it, act it.

Scream inside. Smile outside.

"Good girl," Lucky said.

At the top of the stairs, Daisy pulled up tall, a ballerina in the wings. On the bottom step, Will and Erik sat side by side, Will's arm around Erik's bowed shoulders, his jaw on Erik's crown.

I hold it together. I have my hands on the curtain rope.

"I'm up," she said, and pulled.

The boys turned around. She smiled. Her feet were light as she went down. Her hand caressed the banister. She kissed Will on the cheek, Erik on the mouth. Strode with blithe, happy purpose into the living room, ignoring the pain like knives up and down her hamstrings. She pushed up windows, letting cool fresh air in.

"Look how nice it is," she said. "Let's go for a walk."

Erik's face exploded with a grin.

"It's all right," she said, as his arms came around her and his relief exhaled onto her shoulders.

She put his jacket on—he loved when she wore his clothes—and they walked out into the sunshine.

"Are you all right," he said after a few blocks. "Is it still bleed—"

"All better," she said. "Don't worry."

"Not one of my greatest ideas." His teeth worried at his bottom lip.

"Our idea. And we were tripping." She gave him a playful, forgiving nudge in the side. "Jumping off the roof would've been a worse idea."

He laughed a little.

They walked and talked about other small, meaningless things. She smiled and swung their joined hands between them. Acted like herself, or the self she used to be. She kept her other hand in her pocket, nails dug hard into her palm, pinning herself in place.

Hold still.

Don't disappear.

Hours into days. A week passed. She forced food down, forced pleasant words out. She wore Erik's sweaters. Her mouth gave and received kisses. She went where she was supposed to. At dance class, she danced. In academic courses, she listened and completed her work. In bed at night, she looked into Erik's eyes and held him, her hand running through his hair, his shirt on her back.

"I love you so much," he said.

"I love you," she said, holding on with everything she had. All the while, a wolf had its jaws locked on her ankle, dragging her away.

Don't disappear.

Don't scream.

The eighth day dawned bored and looking for trouble. And she woke up needing to get high.

NO PLAN

"I DIDN'T GO TO DAVID'S apartment to get laid," Daisy said. "Sex was nowhere near my mind. I went over there to get high. I can't say it just happened. Nothing just happens. I could have walked out. I had legs. And I had brains enough to hesitate. I knew it was wrong but I did it anyway. I fucked him. Maybe I was fucking everything for the first time in my life."

"Expressing a darker side of yourself. A less attractive side of yourself."

"To David, of all people. Someone I didn't even like that much... God, I suck at fucking up."

Rita raised her eyebrows. "That's quite a statement."

"Well, I do. I'm not allowed to make a little error of judgment and hide it away. No, the universe has to send my boyfriend to walk in on it. First time I ever played with fire, I go to strike one match and burn the house down."

"That's not exactly your inability to fuck up properly," Rita said. "If there is such a thing. I'd say it was fate dealing you a shitty hand."

"It was me fucking up," Daisy said. "Let's call it what it was."

Rita shifted in her chair. "Or we could look at it another way. Often people who are unaccustomed to showing weakness or asking for help, have to go about it in grandiose ways. Dramatic acts of...well, sabotage, you might say."

But Daisy was done looking at it. "I hated myself," she said.

Rita was quiet.

"I still hate myself."

Depleted, Daisy sat and stared at the past for a long time.

"You said 'hide it away,'" Rita said. "What if Erik hadn't walked in? Do you think you would have eventually told him?"

"I had no plan of any kind. Not before. Not after."

THE LAST GOOD THING

FIRST SHE threw up.

Then she pulled her clothes on and threw up again.

She wouldn't let David help her. "Don't touch me," she said, hissing it as he knelt down next to her on the bathroom floor. "Don't fucking touch me, don't ever touch me again."

She knew it wasn't his fault but she was raw and terrified and had to throw it somewhere. She heaved as much as possible into the toilet and threw the rest at David. He could hold it a while. He had nowhere to go.

She ran back to Jay Street, only vaguely aware David was following her. What would she do?

Fix this.

Running down the sidewalk, her father's voice rang in the vault of her memory.

"Fix this. Fix this right now, Marguerite."

She had taken the netsuke, the cunning little Japanese carvings. Before she learned her father needed to have those baubles in his study never touched. Ever. They were set in a sacred, particular order that kept the universe in place. And she had not only touched them but *taken* them. Out of the study and into the living room to play.

The sun beat down on her head. Her father's shaken anger loomed over her, tall and terrible.

"Fix this, Marguerite. You fix this right now."

The soles of her feet slapping the sidewalk. Scurrying to obey and bumping into her mother. Firm hands on her shoulders, turning her around. "Say excuse me before you turn your back on your father."

Excuse me, Dad.

A finger pointed to the study. Three smart slaps on her five-year-old fanny as she ran to put the universe back in order.

You stupid child.

No stupid girls are in ballet.

Now she had rearranged Erik's galaxy. Disrupted and disturbed it. She had to fix this.

She couldn't let Erik turn his back on her.

Breathing hard, she stopped by the hedge between yards. Go to Erik? Right now? No. She needed a minute. To shower, to be sick again. To get rid of the rest of the high and gather her thoughts.

I fucked up I fucked up I fucked this up so bad.

Just fix it.

She turned to head inside and smacked into David.

Get the fuck away from me, she thought.

"Excuse me," she said and brushed past him to go upstairs. She was going to throw up again.

You stupid girl.

"Stupid, stupid, stupid," she said between heaves. Smashed the side of her fist against the vanity as another wave of it wrenched her apart. She flushed, wiped her mouth on the back of her hand and reached to turn on the taps of the bathtub. Then a noise like a metal avalanche ripped through the house. Breaking, dropping, shattering. Wood against plaster, steel against wood. Down in the kitchen things were being thrown together and torn apart.

She crept downstairs, a child tiptoeing on Christmas morning, not sure of what she'd find.

Go fix this.

Fix this right now, Marguerite.

A voice layered on top of the breakage now.

"You like fucking her? Did it feel good? I bet it did, you son of a bitch."

Her kitchen was in ruins. Everything that could be on the floor was. A sea of broken dishes and glasses, silverware, pots and pans. A chair upended by the stove, the other by the fridge.

And blood.

Erik had David cornered between the sink and the door to the basement. Had him in a headlock and was punching him, over and over. Blood had spattered onto the wall, a chunk of plaster broken out of it, a jagged grey hole with a bit of the stud showing.

"Hope it felt good because it's the last good thing you're gonna feel in your life, Alto…"

"Stop," Daisy cried. Shards of porcelain and glass under her shoes as she darted into the fray. "Erik, stop." She got her hands on his shoulders, felt the muscles shifting like continents. All his power and rage going in the wrong direction.

"Let go of him," she screamed. "Hit *me.*"

He didn't turn his head, but his entire back seized up. He bucked and reared, just like Will did when he was shot. And just like Will he threw her off. She went down flat on her back in the wreckage, the back of her head banging hard against the floor. A spasm of pain between her shoulder blades.

Fix it, you stupid bitch. Fix it right now.

She got up, knees and hands pressing into sharp edges. The screen door exploded open and a new energy filled the kitchen.

"Get back." With the confidant hands that had partnered her for years, Will put Daisy aside. He strode toward the corner and got his arms around Erik.

"Let go, Fish."

Erik didn't let go. "I'll kill you," he cried. "I'll fucking *kill* you."

The veins on Will's arms popped as he heaved Erik back against him. "Enough," he said. Then he did something and Erik howled. A cry of frustration and agony that made Daisy sink to her knees. He threw his head back across Will's shoulder, his throat open and bared to the ceiling. His grip on David broke and David melted to the kitchen floor, blood streaming from his mouth and nose.

"Come on, Fish, let's get you out of here."

Erik kicked and writhed in Will's grasp, sucking heaving breaths between his clenched teeth, fingers opening and closing into fists as he was dragged out.

Daisy's fingers dug into her hair as she stared after them. She pulled hard. Harder. Out on the porch, Erik looked back at her. From the clasp of Will's arms, his eyes reached hers, stunned and enraged and disbelieving.

This, Daisy realized, *is the last good thing you're going to feel in your life.*

You can't fix this.

No love was in his eyes.

You are not excused.

Her mouth moved around his name but no sound came out.

Look hard.

You're never going to see him again.

"Erik," she whispered. Her mouth was dry now. A desert that would never see water again.

Oh God. I'm so sorry.

The screen door slammed shut. Through the mesh, she saw Erik throw off Will's arms.

He turned his back.

And left.

SLEEP ON IT

"WE'RE TAKING DAVID to the health center," Will said. "He needs stitches."

Daisy nodded, staring across the yard and through the hedge to the boys' apartment.

"Don't go over there, Dais. Give him some space."

She did as she was told.

She didn't shower, eat or sleep. Only smoked cigarette after cigarette, sitting out on the back steps of the porch, looking up to the windows of Colby Street. The minutes passed, measured in cigarettes. A constellation of ground-out butts collecting on the cement at the foot of the stairs. The buzz of insects gave way to the first song of peepers. The white skies darkened to grey and the streetlights came on, orange and sick.

She smoked her last cigarette.

Then she just sat.

She fell asleep with her head against the railing. Woke with a jolt when Will crouched down, his three-fingered hand on her shoulder.

"Come inside."

She obeyed, got up and went in. Like a little lamb, she followed Will through the living room and up the stairs, along the hall to the bathroom where Lucky was waiting for her.

"Get in the shower," Lucky said.

Daisy stared at her friend, trying to dissect her voice. Was it cold? Angry? She couldn't decide.

"Just get in," Lucky said. "You'll feel better."

"You don't have to be nice to me."

Lucky's hand was soft on her cheek. "Yes, I do."

She waited for Daisy, sitting on the closed lid and holding a big towel at the ready.

"Brush your teeth now."

Daisy did, wishing Lucky would make all her decisions for the rest of her life.

Clean underwear and a T-shirt were laid out for her. The covers were turned back. Daisy lay down. Lucky had a quiet conversation with Will at the door before it clicked shut. Like a sister, Lucky slid under the blankets, her compact curves snug up against Daisy's back. Her hand found Daisy's and held it tight.

"We all do stupid things," she said.

Daisy cried hard. Lucky held her.

"I love you," she said. "I still love you. He does too. It's going to be hard for a long time. But you guys are strong, you'll get through it."

"I'm sorry," Daisy said between sobs, over and over.

"I know. It was a shitty thing to do but I know who you really are. It wasn't you. You're not yourself. None of us are. Shh...I love you. You're my best friend. I'll stand by you forever."

"I need to go see him."

"Not tonight. Everyone needs to sleep. You hang onto me. You get through tonight and if the sun comes up tomorrow, you go see him."

"I need him."

"And he needs you. But you got to let him be tonight."

"I can't."

"You can. Hold onto me. Go to sleep."

"I need something."

"No. No more of that, either. You're tired, go to sleep. In the morning, we'll figure this shit out."

"I can't."

"You can." Lucky pressed a soft kiss on Daisy's temple. "You have to."

DANCE WITH ME

THE SUN CAME UP the next morning.

Her bedroom window faced east, partially blocked by an oak tree. In winter, the sun woke her at dawn if the drapes were open. In spring, the sun had to worm its way through leafy branches to get a ray in edgewise. First it tickled her closed lids with a creamsicle blush of orange. Forgetting all that transpired, she opened her eyes. The sun wore a wicked grin then, parted the leaves and glared hard and mean, rubbing its hands together in relish of what was in store.

It was already hot when she went through the hedge. Steam was rising from the pavement. It must have rained in the night. The bugs were out, meaner than the sun. She went up the back steps of Colby Street. The door was unlocked and open. Through the screen she saw Will sitting at the kitchen table.

He looked up, his expression blank. Daisy pulled her breath in through her nose. Pulled her shoulders back and down, pulled her stomach in, stood up straight with every bit of her dancer's training, locking her spine and core into place. If Will wanted to take the first shot, so much the better. It would be rehearsal.

Will didn't say anything, but his foot nudged the other chair out from under the table. Daisy sat as Will got up and poured from the steaming kettle on a back burner. He came back to the table with the remaining three fingers of his left hand wrapped around a mug of tea. He set it carefully in front of her, gave her a cigarette, took one for himself, lit both.

"He's gone, honey," he said.

Tight steel bands clamped around Daisy's eyes and throat. She nodded, inhaling hard. She pressed her lips together tight, looked out the window and let the smoke slowly seep out her nose.

Will put his maimed hand out on the table. Her eyes flicked to it. They took in the shiny and seared flesh where his ring and pinky fingers once were, the ropes and ridges of scar tissue along the side of his palm, extending down into the heel of his hand. It was a brave hand. Heroic and kind. She recoiled from the kindness. It wasn't for her. She didn't deserve it. Shaking her head slightly, she took another drag and looked away.

He moved his hand further toward her. Giving hand was one of the most elementary gestures of the danseur noble. Extending his hand to the ballerina, ready to provide her with support and balance.

Dance with me.

Let my strength be your strength.

All she had to do in class was take Will's hand and they were imme-diately connected. One touch of her palm to his and she knew if he was feeling well or not, if he was happy or distracted. Or angry.

Now she was afraid of his hand on the table, afraid to touch him and feel what he was feeling.

"Dais," Will said. His voice was low in his chest and firm.

Come to me, his hand said.

Let's have a conversation.

She put her palm on his. His three fingers wrapped around her five.

"It was a stupid and shitty thing to do," Will said.

She nodded, feeling his acidic disappointment splash her bones.

"Were you high?"

She nodded again, her shoulders curving over toward her ribs, hair falling forward to hide her face.

"High or not, it doesn't matter. You'll be eating this for a long time, Dais."

"I know."

"But you can work it out. I know you can. You just have to give him some space first."

"I don't think so..."

His fingers squeezed tighter. "You guys got through worse. This was just stupid and thoughtless. You're weak, everyone's weak right now. Weak and brittle. Combine all our good judgment together and you wouldn't came up with enough to fill a spoon. You're a strung-out wreck and David preyed on it."

"Don't blame him," Daisy said. "This is my fault, I own this. Don't excuse me."

"I'm not excusing you. Erik's my best friend and part of me wants to kill you. But you're also my best friend and part of me wants to kill David. Christ, what a fucking mess. Jesus, Dais, what were you thinking?"

She slid her fingers out of his grasp and stood up, tea sloshing out of her mug. She crushed out her cigarette.

"I'm sorry," Will said, reaching for her but she evaded him.

"Don't be sorry," she said, walking into the living room.

"Don't go up there, honey."

She had to.

She lay on Erik's bed in the hollow, empty room. Drawers tumbled from their runners, wire hangers askew on the rod in the closet. Corners of posters still scotched-taped to the walls. Her picture was left on his bedside table, the glass inside the frame cracked. His calling card. His last words.

Will came up and sat on the edge of the bed, elbows on knees, fitting his three fingers between the other five. Daisy pressed her face into the sheets, looking for Erik's scent. A hair, a fleck of skin, a fingernail. Anything.

"Go home, Dais," Will said.

"In a little while."

He left her. She lay there as the sun crept around the edge of the window frame and inched across the bed. She cried a little then slept a lot. When she awoke, the sun was gone. The sheet had been pulled up to her waist and a glass of water put on the bedside table. She drank it down then went back to sleep.

She woke again, soaked with sweat, her mouth dry and bitter with cigarette smoke. She sat up, brain clanging like a bell between her temples. The empty room glared at her. She looked away from the accusing walls and her eyes lit on the wastebasket next to the bed.

It was filled with her.

She reached and picked through the pile. Notes and cards and letters. More pictures. Bits and pieces left in his room: hair elastics, earrings, hand cream and lip balm, a pair of her underwear. At the bottom of it all, a plain white envelope. It held their three most treasured artifacts, their three most important firsts: the wrapper from the Swedish Fish he left in her mailbox. The love note she wrote in return—the first love note she'd ever penned in her life. And the condom wrapper from the first time they made love.

Daisy reached with both hands and pulled it all out of the garbage. Sat up and collected every piece of herself, making a neat, squared-off pile in her lap.

You fix this.

TREMBLING WITH ANXIETY, she called his house that night.

"He's asleep," Christine said. "He came home early this morning and went straight to bed, said he didn't want to talk. What happened?"

Daisy's face burned hot, her mouth metallic. "We...had a fight."

Christine laughed. "You two, a fight? Let me step outside and see if the world is ending."

Daisy dug her nails into her leg and managed a brittle laugh.

"What's the trouble in paradise?"

"I won't put you in the middle," Daisy said, her heart pounding. "I'm sorry. I'll...call a little later."

"All right, honey. Don't worry. It's never as bad as you think."

Daisy went to see Kees the next morning. "Do I have enough credits to graduate? Am I certified?"

"You had enough last semester. I already told you that," Kees said. "You've technically matriculated. Why?"

"I have to go home. I'm not staying for graduation. I have to go home now."

"Whoa, whoa, slow down, Dais. What's the matter?"

"I have to go." Her feet made miniscule movements backward, retreating, poised to flee.

Kees stood up. He looked older, drawn and haggard, but his eyes were kind. "Marguerite," he said. "Qu'est-ce qui se passe?"

He was kind. He loved her. And before she realized it, the story was spilling out of her mouth. She told him everything. A spasm of pain flickered through Kees's face and she immediately regretted it.

"I'm sorry," she whispered.

"Daisy," Kees said, his composure returned. "Come sit down, honey. Let's talk about it."

She couldn't. She didn't deserve his support or sympathy. She bit the inside of her lip hard, stepped forward to hug him and then ran away.

Get out of here.

Get out of this place.

Go home, Dais.

Like Erik, she packed swiftly throughout the night. Unlike him, she said goodbye.

She forced herself to go see David. He lay on his couch watching TV, his face still swollen and bruised, the bristling black sutures like spider legs along one cheekbone. He winced as he sat up, the broken ribs howling.

"Don't get up," Daisy said. "I'm just leaving."

He nodded, tapping a cigarette out of the pack on the coffee table. "Drive safe," he said.

She lit it for him, then set the Zippo down carefully. She opened her mouth to say something but no words came.

"Dais," David said, staring at the ribbons of smoke rising from his trembling fingers. "Dais, I want you to be all right."

"I will."

"I'm sorry."

"It wasn't your fault, it was mine," she said and turned to go.

"Wait." He stood up slowly. "Dais, if it's any consolation..."

"Don't," she whispered.

"I love you."

"Please..."

"I love you." He was standing in front of her then. One of his hands closed on her upper arm. The other ran over her face.

"David, don't," she said. His tenderness was more than she could stand.

"I know what everyone says, that I only want what I can't have. But I swear to God, Dais. If you stay with me I'll... I can... I mean I can't..." His fingers dug in her skin. His face twisted and he kicked at an empty soda can which skittered across the floor. "Goddammit," he said through his teeth. "Why'd you have to *come* here?"

She scooped up the blame and clutched it to her chest as she backed away. "I'm sorry, I'm going," she said. "I need to go home."

Take all this. Take it home and fix it.

He took a step as if to follow but then only raised his hand and slowly let the fingers fall down on his palm. "Call me," he said.

WITHDRAWAL

PSYCHOMOTOR RETARDATION

"I WENT HOME," Daisy said. "It was the safest place I knew."

"What was it like?"

Exhausted from her retelling, Daisy shook her head. The silence swelled and shrank. A quiet friend and even quieter enemy. She was grateful for a moment and hated the expectation within it.

"It sounds convenient when I say I don't remember much," she said, her tongue thick and tired. "It's actually a little amazing to look back. I don't know how I got through it. I don't know what happened to the days. They turned into weeks, months and it's going on years. I look back and huge chunks of time are missing."

"It's your mind's way to survive," Rita said. "If we remembered every detail from our darkest times, we'd quickly break down. What you remember is usually what's important."

"I remember things but I'm not sure what order they happened in. I know I don't have to tell you a neat story, but I don't think I could if I tried."

She looked up at Rita. "Ask me another question," she said. "Just get me going. Ask me something."

Rita shifted in her chair, taking a measured breath. "What did you tell your parents?"

"Nothing at first. I kept it general. I said Erik and I had a fight, we needed some space. I was exhausted and wanted to collapse and be alone. Something like that. The thing is, even when I wanted to talk, something was wrong with me. I mean physically wrong. I thought I had broken my mind because I couldn't speak."

"You couldn't speak. At all?"

"I would want to say something and the sentence would be in my head. The words all lined up in my mouth ready to go. But I would have this delay. I could count the seconds between the time I wanted to talk and the actual spoken words. The same thing happened with movement. I'd be in a chair and want to stand up. My brain would say *stand up, let's go, stand up now.* My legs got the message but with this strange delay."

"Did you tell anyone?"

"No. I guess if I hadn't been so tired and distraught I would've been more upset about it but..."

"Psychomotor retardation."

"Pardon?"

"Psychomotor retardation," Rita said, sternly. "It's a common side effect of drug withdrawal."

"Oh," Daisy said, uncomfortable.

"Were you still using cocaine or anything else?"

"No," she said, a small shiver of revulsion at the back of her neck. "Even if I wanted to, I wouldn't have known where to get it. But the thought of getting high and going back into the dark alone... No. I quit."

"Cold turkey."

"Yes."

"That could have been dangerous. Cocaine withdrawal is no joke."

Daisy opened her mouth to defend herself and realized she had no defense. "In all honesty," she said slowly, "I didn't care what happened to me."

A corner of Rita's mouth lifted as she nodded. "Fair point. I imagine you didn't."

"It stopped after a while and then I could talk about it."

"How much did you tell them?"

"My parents?" Daisy said. "Everything."

A SAPPER'S DAUGHTER

SHE SAT AT THE KITCHEN table with her father and told him the simplest and most truthful story she could. Then she sat in his silence, staring at her chewed-off fingernails. Her body quivered like a racehorse at the gate, ready to flee down the track. As the moments ticked by she shrank further and further into herself until she could bear it no longer.

"Excuse me," she whispered, and darted from her chair, toppling it sideways as she ran out of the kitchen. Through the living room and the front hall, bursting out the screen door onto the porch. A cry wrenched from her chest as she looked across the garden to the carriage house.

Do you ever think of marrying me?

She crumpled down on the steps, buried her face in her hands and wept.

The sun and wind dried her tears. Her head hurt. Her eyes burned. She could sleep forever. She would lie down and never get up if she could.

The screen door opened and shut behind her. Footsteps on the wide, scuffed planks, then the quick click of a lighter and the smell of cigarette smoke.

"You must face him," Joe said. A creak of wicker as he sank into one of the chairs. Daisy stayed on the steps, curled tight with her head against one of the uprights, her mouth on her knees.

"The longer you wait, the harder it will be," Joe said.

"I know."

"It's going to be terrible."

"I know. I'm so sorry, Dad."

"I know you are. We all make mistakes. I've made mistakes, you know this."

A hot wind blew a cloud of dried apple blossoms past the porch. Bees buzzed in the lavender buds.

"Face him, Dézi. He may not forgive you. He may not speak to you. But he should know and see your regret."

Her throat scorching and aching, Daisy nodded against her knees.

"You're a sapper's daughter," Joe said. "We put together what's broken. We blaze a road, find a way. We snuff the fuses and dismantle the bombs."

Marching orders in fist, she got up and smoothed her skirt over her knees. Joe caught her hand as she passed and held it to his cheek. "And we come back from war changed, Dézi."

She nodded through the tears puddling her eyes, damming her lips against the next flood of weeping. She let her fingers nestle against Joe's goatee, let his love soothe her a moment. Then she went inside to call Erik.

Again.

"I can't force him," Christine said. Her voice was soft but chilly. She knew. Her allegiance was plain. She stood at the door of her son's grief and didn't forbid Daisy to pass, but she didn't step aside, either.

"I'm sorry," Daisy said. "I know this is awkward, I don't mean to put you in the middle. I just need to talk to him."

"I know. But I can't force him to come to the phone. Anyway he's sleeping now. I'll tell him you called."

She hung up.

You're excused.

OVER AND OVER SHE replayed the day and imagined walking out of David's apartment at the critical moment. That's all it would have taken. Get high, walk out. Just walk out, walk away and none of this would have happened.

You stupid, stupid bitch.

It's all yours. Deal with it. You made this bed. Lie down and deal. Own it. You did this. You only have yourself to blame. Stop crying and own it. It's yours.

"I wish you'd been more trouble as a child," Francine said into the tangle of Daisy's hair. "You were always so good. I feared when you fell it would be such a long fall."

"I'm sorry," Daisy said, muffled with weeping. "I ruined everything."

"It's fixable," Francine said. "Everything can be fixed. You just have to find the right glue. Now, look at me. Stop crying. Separate the emotion and tell me what's true."

Daisy dragged hands over her wet, swollen face. "I love him."

"And he loves you. He will always love you. You're a young couple but your love isn't childish."

"This was my fault."

"You made a choice, yes. A poor one. But we all make mistakes, sweetheart."

"I want to die."

"No, darling. That's emotion, not fact. Anyone can lay there and die after they fall down. You're a dancer. You get up, figure out what you did wrong and try again. You keep going. It's everything you've trained for. And you go fight for your love because if I know Erique at all, I know he needs to see how much you're willing to do."

Daisy called again.

And again.

She couldn't get through to him.

"Then go to class," Francine said. One of life's great answers to tough questions. Daisy put her pointe shoes on and went. She and Will were both in the summer intensive program at the Pennsylvania Ballet. The recital in August would be attended by scouts from ballet companies all over the country. This was the doorway to opportunity. She could not fuck this up.

She became a ruthless perfectionist in class, permitting herself no mistakes. It kept her grounded: the world was in shambles but first position was always first position. Her technique was envied by all, but no amount of praise or attention could get her to smile. She knew the soul had gone out of her dancing, but she could not allow emotion into what had become her sanctuary. It had to stay separated from the factual steps.

AWKWARD EXCHANGES with Christine ended when Erik got his own phone line. He almost never picked up. Daisy left countless messages on his machine which weren't returned. Once or twice, she caught him live and he refused to speak to her. No amount of apology, encouragement, coaxing or goading could get him to break his silence. She couldn't recognize him, couldn't grasp how he was so ruthlessly and completely disconnecting.

How can he? she thought. *Isn't it killing him? Doesn't he miss me? Doesn't he need to know where I am?*

"He does," Will said. "He can't breathe without you. But you have to give him time."

Will was her motivation and her rock. Will was affectionate physical contact and constant reassurance that all would work itself out. He, too, was calling Erik night and day and getting the same unrelenting void. Daisy didn't understand. Will did nothing wrong. How could Erik be distancing the one person who could comfort him?

Days piled up on days. Every morning a mountain she had to drag her bones over.

Lucky was job hunting in physical therapy. Offers were dry in Philadelphia and she began to look further afield in New Jersey and New York, moving away from Will. Their relationship grew strained. Everything around Daisy was stretched tight and thin, trembling under the pressure. One pizzicato pluck too many and something was going to snap. Crack back through the air and tear it open.

Daisy drove her body harder on less and less food and more and more cigarettes. She walked through a cloud of ash. Even her skin was grey and sick. Her eyes went flat blue. Her hands and her heart shook. At night, she burned with fever as she reached hands into the darkness to a body that wasn't there.

She'd been sleeping next to him since she was on the cusp of eighteen. Three years with practically no break from Erik's body next to hers in the night. His back pressed to her front, her hand over his heart. The smell of his skin and his hair. The length of his legs, the planes of his shoulder blades. The clink the charms made on his necklace when he rolled or shifted. The sounds he made at peace and the noises he made when he was worked up. Now Daisy threw herself from one side of the mattress to the other, a vast desert with only one body occupying her bed. She rolled and wept, gripped in a physical desire she felt would tear her in two.

Never again. He'll never touch me again. He'll never speak to me again.

He doesn't care where I am anymore.

You ruined it. You did this.

You stupid bitch.

She woke to haul herself over another mountain, somehow got up and went back to class. To the off-tune thump of the rehearsal piano and the whisper of seventy-five slippered feet against the floor, she did tendu after perfect tendu to the cadence in her head.

I'm sorry (you're so stupid). I'm sorry (you're so stupid). Sorry (stupid)...

"We're done," Will said one morning before class. His eyes were red-rimmed and circled with sleeplessness. Angry misery etched every line of his body.

"Who?" Daisy said. "What's done?"

"Me and Fish. I had it out with him on the phone last night and it's done. Forget about him, Dais. He's gone."

"What are you talking about?"

"He's not coming back. For any of us. I'm not calling him anymore and I don't want to talk about him anymore."

"Will..." She tried to touch him and he shied away, his jaw clenched. "He can't—"

"He can. I'm not going into details, but the shit he said last night... It's not just you, Dais. He's throwing it all overboard. We're dead to him. He's gone. His heart's a fucking stone now and you'll never chisel your way back in. Spare yourself the conversation I had to go through and move on."

"Will," she said, the loss of a great friendship fitting around her shoulders like a yoke. "I'm so sorry."

"Yeah, so am I," he said. He walked away and for the first time, didn't do barrework next to her.

The rest of the summer blurred into a watercolor wash of confusion. Will apologized for being harsh, but remained distant and reticent. He and Lucky fought constantly and Daisy stood in the middle, a child of divorce, barely knowing what was going on. The only way to survive was to shut down and dance.

The recital came and went and the Pennsylvania Ballet offered Daisy a corps contract. Will got an offer from the National Ballet of Canada and accepted. He was going home. Lucky took a job offer in the Bronx and she was staying.

"I think we're through," Lucky said. "And I swear, Dais, I'm numb. I can't deal with him. He's become so toxic. He's like a ball of barbed wire, angry and miserable, I don't even recognize him anymore."

"I really fucked it all up," Daisy said.

"Not everything is about you," Lucky said. After a moment her face softened and she reached a hand to pat Daisy. "But I can see how you'd feel you put it all into motion."

"Didn't I, though?"

"I'm starting to think it was only a matter of time," Lucky said. "If not what you did, it would've been something or someone else."

Holding hands, they rested their heads together and went still and silent, two lost little girls staring at the rubble and ruin of their youthful dreams.

DAISY GOT A LITTLE APARTMENT in Philly and went to work. She fell into a mindless rhythm of company class, rehearsal, performance. Company class, rehearsal, performance. She honed her already impeccable technique into something preternatural. Digging deep into her imagination, she created an alternate universe where everything was fine and Erik still loved her. He was simply away right now and she had to be brave about it. This vague explanation crafted enough plausible illusion for her to find both her smile and her stage presence.

She elaborated the daydream, placing Erik in a faraway war, fighting for them and unable to communicate for fear of capture. It shored up the façade and gave her strength. A bit of hopeful optimism infused itself into her dancing, and she began to get short, flattering mentions in reviews. Praise for her breathtaking footwork, her effortless turns and sparkling presence. Word on the street was she was going to be PB's next big star.

But the accolades were bits of rhinestone pasted on a shell of loathing. Nobody knew the effort it took for Daisy to show up. No one could see the guilt and chagrin coating her like an invisible film. The daily pain that was an axe blade to her heart, a noose around her neck, slivers under her fingernails.

Get up. You've got to get up...

The pretense got harder and harder to maintain as the shame ate her insides like cancer. She tried to starve it out, to equate the pain with the sharp pangs in her stomach. She tried to smoke it out, to char and burn it away, layer tobacco and tar on top of it to tamp it down forever. She starved and smoked. She destroyed her own health trying to keep the façade intact. With no sustenance, it slowly began to disintegrate. She showed up, but the sparkle faded. The effort showed and she wasn't distinguishable anymore. She was merely filler. And when the company didn't renew her contract after a year, she didn't have the strength to cry about it. She cleaned out her locker and her dressing table and left.

She didn't tell her parents. She stayed in Philadelphia, going to dance classes with the last of her money and trying to make a plan.

What will I do?

This is killing me.

Isn't it killing him?

Through the past year, she had continued to call Erik, following him from Rochester to a new number in Geneseo, where, she guessed, he was attending the state university and finishing his degree. She could only guess because all her calls continued to be met with stony silence.

"Erik, please, I'm so sorry, please talk to me," she said. Baring her heart into the void, showing him her throat, wishing he would take a bite already.

Not a word. Not even, "Don't call me. Fuck you. Go to hell. I never want to see you again."

She didn't give up. His stubbornness only fueled her own determination. She wouldn't quit until he said something.

"I can't believe you're giving up," she said one night, primed with a couple glasses of wine and frustrated enough to switch tactics. Maybe she'd been going about this the wrong way.

Maybe he wanted a fight.

"I fucked up but I'm here trying to make it right," she said, pacing and drinking. "You won't even... Jesus, Erik, one stupid mistake and you're just walking away without a word. Like it never happened. Like *we* never happened."

He was silent but she thought she could hear a choppiness in his breathing. It was a reaction and she pounced on it.

"Say something," she cried. "Yell at me. Curse at me. Say you hate me. Jesus Christ, you're like your fucking brother going electively mute. He's deaf, you don't have that excuse. Now *say* something."

"There's nothing to say," he said.

As her mind fumbled to grasp the sound of his voice, the line went dead in her hand. With a cry of rage she fired the wine glass the length of the tiny galley kitchen. A shattering explosion, a sprawl of dark red across the far wall and she was on her knees. Doubled over, her hands threaded through her hair, pulling hard. Teeth clenched against the screaming in her throat. The brittle pain of Erik's words in her ears. She was free-falling in a nearly psychedelic terror, as if she had inadvertently yanked out some crucial circuit in her brain.

It took a long time for her to come down.

She stopped calling and began to write him instead. The letters weren't returned, so she continued to pen them. Breathing herself onto the paper at first, then bleeding onto it with apology and entreaty. Soaking the paper with her sorrow until it became embarrassing, even to herself. She got a leash on her emotions, made them heel and behave. She began to talk gently to him about everyday things. Like a visitor would speak to a vegetative patient, filling the silence with this and that. Because he still needed to know where she was.

Didn't he?

And then the pain jumped the leash and went running off into the night, leaving her empty-handed. After three years of living a conjoined life, he was lost to her.

"I promised you," she cried, to the walls, to the pillows, to her hands. "I promised you I wouldn't disappear. We promised. Each would always know where the other was..."

She never dreamed he was capable of such finality.

"Such unforgiveness," Francine said, sighing over the phone. "I don't understand. Who has he become?"

A sweet boy with a bitter palate, Daisy thought.

"I don't know what to make of it," Joe said. "I gave him a medal and I meant it. I will carry what he did that day in my heart forever. But to be so ruthless and stubborn over a foolish mistake? To make such a stone of his own heart and not even give you a chance to explain yourself? I don't know, Dézi. Maybe at the end of the day...he's not the boy for you."

No, Daisy thought, eyes wide with denial. *No, he's the one for me. I was born for him. He was born for me. He's mine.*

This is my fault.

She didn't know where he was.

And he didn't care where she was.

WITHIN A MONTH OF LOSING her job she weighed eighty-nine pounds. She was a starved, smoked out hull of a boat. But somewhere in the hold, down in the ballast, was a last ounce of sensibility. A single nut left in the storage room that once stockpiled all her pragmatism. She took it carefully between her palms.

What will you do?

Waiting for the water to warm up in the shower she stared at her naked body in the mirror on the back of the door. Shadowed eyes and hollowed cheeks. Bones and sinewy muscle showed under dry skin. Yellow fingertips and scarred legs.

I was beautiful once.

She stretched a leg out in tendu, her foot arching like a crescent moon. The faintest stirring of pleasure made the corners of her mouth flick. She still had her feet.

Her fingertips moved down the concave curve of her abdomen, trailed over her hip bone. The little red fish lettered there.

I have my feet. And I have my fish. He lives here. He lives on my body.

And he needs me to stay alive.

She got in the shower, repeating the words to a drumbeat cadence. *He lives on my body. He needs me to stay alive.*

Her chest began to loosen. She inhaled carefully. A bit of light began to move through her head.

What are the facts? Separate the emotion and tell me what's true.

She loved him.

If you love him then you must live.

He was inked into her skin.

And he will stay there forever. No one can take it away. Unless you die.

She wasn't the girl he loved anymore.

Then get her back. Get up. Put your pointe shoes on and live. He fell in love with a dancer. Go back and dance. Be who you were. Stay alive for him.

The hands washing her hair grew brisk and efficient. She imagined Lucky breezing around on the other side of the curtain, making decisions. Soaping up a sponge, she washed herself roughly then became more gentle. She looked at her body—the only thing she had left.

This was yours before you met him. It's still yours. And it's all you have. Dancing relies on your body. You've got to get it back. Without it, you're nothing. Take care of yourself. You have to be here when he comes back.

She squinted through the steam, daring anything to retort with "if he comes back."

"When," she said, her voice echoing off the tiles. "When he comes back. I will be here."

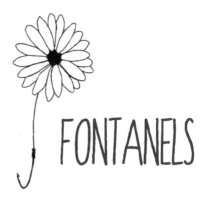

FONTANELS

SHE WENT NORTH WITH the last of her money. She slept on the couch in Lucky's Fort Lee apartment and went every day to Manhattan, taking class and auditioning for any company that was hiring. Not many were.

The Metropolitan Opera Ballet certainly wasn't the crowning achievement of her dreams. The resident corps de ballet suffered a perpetual identity crisis, never sure if they were pretty filler for the grand operas or artists in their own right. But it was a guaranteed season with health insurance—she'd be a fool not to take it and use it as a foothold for the next thing. She signed a contract, and was humbly grateful when her father offered to co-sign the lease on the one-bedroom apartment on West 86th Street.

Don't you fucking fuck this up.

She moved in and wrapped herself in work. Company class every weekday at ten, in the studio on C-level, three floors beneath the Metropolitan Opera House's vast stage. Class was followed by rehearsal: two months to learn new productions, but only three intense weeks to learn the revival operas. Sometimes she could hop the subway home for a nap and quick dinner before heading back to Lincoln Center for the performance. Other times, she had to bolt a salad and snatch forty winks in an empty dressing room or the lounge.

She danced between three and five nights a week. Some operas, she was onstage in a myriad of roles with frantic backstage costume changes. For other works, she arrived to dance twenty minutes and go home. In some of the longer productions, she didn't dance until the third or fourth act. She often found herself warming up at ten o'clock at night and stepping onstage at eleven-thirty. Once when a crucial piece of scenery broke down, pausing the performance until the stagehands could fix it, she didn't make an entrance until quarter past midnight.

One week her schedule was relaxed and manageable, the next was a seven-day panic attack. The lack of routine left her no wiggle room to make plans. She didn't mind—she had nowhere to go. The company gave standing room tickets to all the artists for their off nights and Daisy always used hers. She watched and absorbed. As she wrapped her mind around not only choreography, but music and libretto and language, she found she loved it. From Bizet to Mozart to Verdi, she began to learn and appreciate the great operas, as her capacious memory cataloged the stage action.

Every role in every opera had a "track," a roadmap of exits and entrances. For every three dancers, the Met assigned one cover—a dancer who learned all the tracks, ready to go on wherever and whenever they were needed. The pressure of learning multiple tracks cold was tremendous. Once an opera was in production, its studio rehearsals ceased.

Daisy became a cover and gained a reputation for being the one to call when the shit went down. As she discovered one day when she found herself in the elevator with Maestro James Levine himself.

"Miss Bianco," he said with his elfin smile. "Our steel trap."

She stared at him a moment. "I'm sorry, you are...?"

His halo of frizzy hair shook as he threw back his head laughing. "I'm the new janitor."

"Of course."

They kept up a running gag of her pretending to forget his name and ask if he could unclog the toilet in the ladies' room. And whenever Levine caught her eye from the podium, he winked.

She relaxed into her work.

She started being nicer to herself.

She'd been denying everything she loved. But one day, she passed a store window with a sale on cashmere sweaters and couldn't resist their siren call. She stopped and backtracked, gazed at the luscious softness and shimmering colors. She imagined one on her skin and how it would hug her. She bought it.

She sliced her cigarette habit in half and put the extra dollars and cents in a mason jar. She dipped into it to go for a massage or a mani-cure. The latter was an almost silly waste of money—she wasn't allowed to wear nail polish in performance. Really she just liked someone holding her hands.

She started putting thought and effort into food. Growing up at Fran-cine's elbow, she knew her way around the kitchen. Despite anxious nausea being a constant companion, she began to eat again. Like a grownup.

You must stay alive for him.

She coaxed her body back into its optimal shape. She ate well, stayed hydrated, took her vitamins and supplements. If she wasn't perform-ing, she was in bed early. Sleep was up for grabs but her body was put down to rest without exception. She cheated some nights with Tylenol PM but a friend warned she would fuck her liver up if she did it too often.

She did have friends. Her reticence about herself made her a beacon for other people's troubles and woes. She didn't dispense much advice but she knew how to listen and validate people's feelings. People wanted her, sought her out and included her. They were there to have lunch with and go to class with and occasionally meet for a Sunday movie or museum walk.

Whether in company or not, Daisy hit the city streets in her off time, avoiding idleness like it was jury duty. Sitting home alone only gave her time to think and dwell. She dipped into her mason jar and went on little adventures, riding the subway from Battery Park to Morningside Heights. She hit every museum, every gallery, every tourist trap. If she wasn't flush, she walked, plugging herself into her music and criss-crossing the grid of Manhattan.

Her closest friend in the company was Julie Valente, who mentioned one day she was a volunteer cuddler at New York Methodist Hospital, holding premature babies.

"I go on Sundays, instead of church. I find it more meaningful."

Daisy was fascinated. "You just go and...hold them?"

Julie nodded. "The physical contact is therapeutic. It helps them thrive. Their parents can't always be there twenty-four-seven, so the hospital created this volunteer group to cuddle."

Daisy applied, went through a background check and started giving her Sunday hours as well.

She had never gravitated toward babies. She'd held a few in her time and while they were darling as hell, none ever made her melt or coo or mentally start knitting blankets.

The first time the NICU nurses brought her a preemie, translucent and fragile, she was petrified. How was she supposed to hold this bundle of tubes and wires, a knitted cap at one end, out of which emerged a nose and mouth no bigger than her fingernail? How could her arms cuddle when it seemed her mere breath would shatter the poor thing into pieces?

The smell of the hospital was making her feel a little sick.

"You all right?" Julie said, composed and confident in a rocking chair, her thumb stroking the pale, porcelain skin of her baby's foot.

Daisy managed to nod and lift the corners of her mouth as the nurse got the baby settled, neatly coiling the tubes out of the way and draping a blanket. The infant was a boy, Sam, born eight weeks early.

Daisy's throat grew warm at the sight of his tiny hand resting motionless on her chest. After a few stiff moments, she dared to nestle her pinky into his palm. His fingers widened then slowly collapsed, as if he was going to take hold of her. But they stopped halfway.

"You did great," Daisy said. "Good boy. You're so strong."

Little by little her shoulders relaxed and her hands became surer. A sense of purpose crept over her. A desire to do a good job. Between the hypnotic humming and beeping of the nursery's machines and monitors, and the deflection of her thoughts away from herself to another, Daisy fell into a lucid trance. Her head was empty, chest open, stomach calm.

Her arms were full.

"It was like prayer," she said to Julie on the bus later. "You're right, it is like church."

She went every Sunday. As she grew more confident, she began to take more notice of the NICU. Specifically, a glassed-in room set apart where a single volunteer cuddler worked. This woman didn't sit with her charges. She paced.

"Why are some babies alone in there?" Daisy asked Louise, the head nurse.

"Oh, honey," Louise said. "They're the ones born to drug addicts. They're all in withdrawal. They need to be held the worst, but not many volunteers can handle them."

Daisy moved closer to the glass which, she realized, was soundproof. Now she could see the baby held in the volunteer's arms was not a preemie. It was full-term, chubby and solid. And it cried and fought against being cuddled. The body didn't curl. The limbs splayed, the spine twisted. The little fingers hooked into claws. It didn't want to be soothed or comforted. It wanted something it couldn't explain. It wanted a feeling. It wanted the way it was before.

It wants what it can't have.

"Louise." She turned from the window. "Let me go in."

Arms crossed, the nurse looked Daisy up and down then shrugged. "You're the last one I figured, but all right. Try fifteen minutes. Annie probably needs a break anyway. If you need to come out, catch my eye."

Daisy's courage faltered on the threshold and she fought not to show it. Other babies were in here and all of them were crying. Screaming like nothing Daisy had ever heard before.

Except inside her own head.

"This here is Job," Annie, the volunteer, said, carefully handing off the shrieking baby. "It's not his real name. His mother didn't name him.

I call him Job because it sure seems like the Lord is throwing everything He can think of at him."

Daisy could barely speak. As Louise and Annie left the room, they shut the door and sealed Daisy off from the rest of the ward. Her arms tightened around Job's angry body.

"I know," she managed to whisper. "Oh, I know..."

She stayed an hour. Every Sunday after, she went straight into the glassed-in room. It was where she was needed.

"How can you bear it?" Julie asked. "That kind of crying cuts my heart in two. It's torture."

"It's hard to explain," Daisy said. "But I feel like I understand them."

She didn't want the passive, docile preemies. She wanted the ones who were turned inside-out with pain and want. They were her grief manifested a thousand-fold. She gathered them into her arms. She sang and crooned and consoled, the way she craved to be atoned. She whispered to their delicate whorled ears and spoke to herself.

"You cry," she said, pressing one screaming infant to her breast and cupping its pulsing fontanels. "You go ahead and cry as much as you want. Nobody understands how much it hurts. I know. It hurts so much. You want it so bad. The wanting will just kill you. You're so brave..."

CERTAIN SACRIFICES

SHE WAS SIGNING into Nina Popova's master ballet class at Steps Over Broadway one Saturday morning, when a man's voice filled with hesitation called her name. She looked up. Her breath caught in her throat as her eyes blurred with sudden tears. Her mouth formed an O all ready to be spoken when he pointed a finger and said, "Don't you fucking call me Opie."

"John," she cried, flinging away the pen in her hand and throwing herself into his arms. Her feet left the floor as he pulled her hard to his chest. She crossed her wrists behind his head, buried her face in his shoulder and exhaled.

"Oh, John," she said.

"I love conversations that start this way," he said.

She couldn't answer, just held on tight.

"It's terrible to see you," he said, one of his hands moving to the back of her head. His laughter floated through his chest into hers. He kissed her temple as he let her feet find the floor but he didn't let go. His warm, lean strength against her body was a balm.

"Oh, John," she said again. "I haven't seen you in..."

"Two years," he said. "Two years and five months. And twenty-eight days. Give or take an hour."

He let go then, held her away from him and swept his eyes up and down. She looked him over as well. His red hair was artfully tousled. The dimple flashed in a scruffy cheek and his dark brown eyes were filled with pleasure.

"Are you taking this class?" she asked.

"No," he said, holding a fold of her coat in his fingers and moving her away from the desk. "I'm buying you a cup of coffee and asking a thousand questions."

Like a cavalier, he led her downstairs, steered her across the street to a coffee shop and into a booth.

"Tea, right?" he said. "Tea's your drink."

"Coffee's fine," she said.

John looked at her a long, probing moment. "What the fuck happened?" he said softly. "Where's Fish?"

She shook her head. "Not with me. What did you hear?"

"Not a damn thing. You stopped coming to class, then Will disappeared. Kees wouldn't tell me anything. I went by Colby Street and it was empty. I went by Jay Street and it was closed up too. I went to find David—he was a strung-out mess and looked like he'd been in a fight. He shut the door in my face. Everyone disappeared, nobody said goodbye, nothing."

"I slept with David."

John sat back, slack-jawed. She stared into his eyes. No excuses, no reasons, no requests for pity or understanding.

John shook his head a little and he took a long sip of coffee. "So, you're..." His eyebrows knitted. "Are you with him now?"

She shook her head and had to smile, laughing a little into her cup. "No, I'm alone."

"Where's Fish?"

"He's up in Geneseo. Finishing his degree at SUNY, I guess. I haven't actually talked to him. I mean, I call him every few months, listen to him breathe thirty seconds before he hangs up on me. Mostly I write him. The letters don't come back but it doesn't mean he reads them."

John shook his head again. "This makes no sense. So he left and it's over and that's it? You don't talk?"

"No." She shrugged. "I fucked up."

"Yeah, no way to sugar coat that." He ran a hand through his hair, exhaling heavily. "For what it's worth, I never trusted David."

Daisy rolled one of her shoulders again. "He's not to blame. I went over there. I got high with him. I got into a situation I could've walked out of. *Should have* walked out of. But I didn't." She picked up her coffee, held its strong scent and warm steam to her nose.

John's hand navigated plates and balled-up napkins and took hers. "Don't beat yourself up, Dais. You did a shitty thing but you're not a shitty person. Anyone can see you're sorry as hell about it."

She nodded over her mug. Pulled in a long, fortifying breath and tried to believe him. Across the table, he smiled at her, the dimple indenting his cheek and his eyes crinkling at the corners.

"Where's Will?" he asked. "And Lucky?"

"Will got into the corps of National Ballet of Canada," she said. "He did two seasons and then got an offer from the Frankfurt Ballet, so he's in Germany. Lucky lives in Fort Lee and she's working at a physical rehab center in the Bronx."

"I take it they're not together then."

"No, about a year after graduation they split."

John's fingers slowly shredded a napkin. "This is heartbreaking."

"Lucky's seeing someone. Edward. He works on Wall Street. Young, rich workaholic. Catholic. Republican. Her mother's wet dream."

John laughed.

"I haven't asked a thing about you," she said. "What are you up to?"

"Dancing and starving," he said. "What else is there?"

"Are you in a company?"

"I did a season with the Joffrey Ballet but they've relocated to Chicago." He rubbed the back of his neck, his mouth twisting. "I was not invited to come along."

"Ouch."

"I auditioned for Finis Jhung's Chamber Ballet last week and I have a callback tomorrow. If I don't get this gig, I may have to start turning tricks for rent money."

"Callback tomorrow?" she said. "You shouldn't be cutting class."

He shrugged. "When the girl you were in love with in college appears out of nowhere and throws herself in your arms, you have to make certain sacrifices. Will you give me your phone number? So I can call you when I'm evicted?"

Something about how his mouth stayed in a slightly parted smile made a warmth flicker through her chest. A prickle of curiosity. A cue begging to be picked up. Her own smile widened, muscles she hadn't used in months. When was the last time she smiled enough to show her teeth and scrunch up her eyes?

"It's good to see you," she said.

"I'm so glad I found you," he said. "I always wondered where you were."

Such joy in knowing someone was wondering about her. Someone was glad to see her and didn't think she was a horrible person. She breathed it in. Took a small, careful taste. And wrote down her number.

"Call me tomorrow," she said. "Let me know how it went."

He carefully folded the slip of paper. "I'll call you tonight."

IT WAS THE WINDOW

JOHN DIDN'T GET INTO Chamber Ballet but he got a tip to go audition for the revival of *Carousel* at the Vivian Beaumont Theater. He was cast as the ruffian boy in the dream ballet sequence, the role Jacques d'Amboise made famous in the film version.

"Damn, I had visions of you as the next American gigolo," Daisy said.

"It's always an option," John said.

Fall swept over New York. The days shortened and the air grew crisp and thin. Both John and Daisy were working within the Lincoln Center complex and they began spending all their free time together. Their early mornings were free to go to class: they met for breakfast and took turns picking a venue. They hooked up for lunch when they could, and if their respective performances ended at the same hour, they grabbed a late supper and John walked her home before hopping the subway to his tiny place in Washington Heights.

"New boyfriend?" Julie Valente said, running interested eyes over John as he waited at the stage door of the Met, chatting with the security guard.

"Old friend," Daisy said.

She found herself looking forward to supported adagio class where John was an excellent partner. He was strong and perceptive and his hands were confident. They felt good on her. He led when she needed him to, and followed when it was warranted. Not with the wordless instinct that marked her partnership with Will, but she liked talking to John while dancing. Liked how they narrated their way through mechanics and choreography, joking and laughing and learning together.

They laughed a lot. In the long hours together, John's demeanor stayed easy and neutral. He hugged her hello and goodbye, held doors, helped her with her coat, touched her casually. Her curiosity continued to prickle whenever his ginger handsomeness caught her by surprise. When he threw or caught or crushed her against him in class, she found herself thinking about their dance turned horizontally: imagining John's strength, perception and confidence in bed and wondering what kind of lover he was.

Winter threw a tantrum and began blanketing the city in relentless snowstorms. The novelty of Manhattan being brought to its knees was cause for a wild celebration. The streets, free of traffic, became a playground. Crowds walked the fluffy byways, flocking to Central Park to sled and build snowmen.

One snowy Sunday evening Daisy walked with John over the Brooklyn Bridge. She kept stopping and looking back to Manhattan, charmed at how the falling snow softened the skyline into dreamy, sparkling shadows.

"It's like living in a snow globe," she said. "I always wanted to when I was little. I made my mother take one apart once, so I could see. And I was crushed to discover no magic was in there, no little people living in the tiny house."

John took her gloved hand in his. "I wish I'd known you when you were little."

"Why?"

He smiled straight ahead, flakes collecting along the ribs of his wool watch cap and sticking in his lashes. "You could've been the girl I knew since kindergarten," he said. "I could've cut my teeth crushing on you. Maybe gotten a head start on all those other guys."

"What other guys," she said, laughing.

On the Brooklyn side they found a diner and ordered omelets and cheese fries. They passed plates and ketchup, talking around mouthfuls. Daisy watched John eat. Watched how his fingers worked a fork or wrapped around his coffee cup. Noticed the tendons in his neck flexing as he chewed. The skin was smooth across his collarbones beneath the opening of a Henley T-shirt, inviting the caress of fingertips. The dimple winked in and out of his cheek and she was struck with an impulse to kiss it.

I'm attracted to him.

Chewing on the revelation, she toyed with the idea of asking him to come home with her. She hadn't had sex in over two years. She'd never had sex with anyone but Erik. David was a five-minute grapple. Only Erik knew her body, where to put his mouth and slide his fingers and how she liked to be kissed. Only his hands unbuttoning or unzipping her clothes, pushing them off. Only his body on top of hers in the night. Or beneath hers. Or behind hers.

I don't know how to make love with anyone else.

Jesus, what if I suck in bed?

"You look thoughtful," John said, wiping his mouth and smiling at her, his dimple appearing, smoothing, then appearing again. She imagined his face in her hands, tilted up to meet her mouth. Imagined her fingers taking hold of his shirt and drawing it up his back and over his head. His skin over his muscles and bones, his body in her hands.

Maybe I can let go now. Maybe it's time to let go.

Begin again.

She put down her cup, feeling a little afraid. She hadn't quite given herself permission to want this yet. A roaring was in her ears. A Doppler rush of rumbling sound, coming closer.

"I was just—" she said, but then a shattering of glass.

(The center window of the lighting booth melts away in pieces. Then the one next to it. Then the next. Winking, twinkling slivers and shards imploding and exploding. Up on her elbow, twisted around she watches the last window disintegrate and she falls back, her arm unfolding to reach where Erik is in the booth. The booth with its shot out windows and the black-clad man in the aisle raising the gun again.)

"—hurt? Dais? *Dais...*"

The scrape of chairs. The clang and clatter of falling dishes and silverware, just as it sounded in her kitchen at Jay Street. Daisy drew herself into a ball under the table, threaded her hair tight through her hands and pulled it hard. She curled and pulled and she screamed and screamed.

(Erik Erik Erik Erik Erik Erik Erik Erik.)

"Daisy." John had her by the wrists, pushing against the pulling, holding her still. "Sweep some of this glass away. Let me get her out of here."

"Do we need an ambulance?"

"I don't see blood," John said. "Just let me get her out. Daisy. Daisy, come on, it's all right. Come here."

She shied from his hands, twisting away from the past.

(Fat peppering cracks echo through her head. Will is on the floor, his shirt red with blood and the blood starting to spread around him. She pushes up on her elbow—she can still make her upper body work. She twists and looks back to where Erik was. The black-clad man in the aisle raising his arm and the glass is breaking.)

The staff cleared a path, stepping on dishes and shards. Daisy was split open, eviscerated onto the cold hard floor of her kitchen, down in the blood again with the broken crockery and flung cutlery. The veins on Will's arms popping as he bear-hugged Erik. Erik kicking and writhing, his boots scraping on the floor as Will pulled him out, dragged him out of the house, letting the door slam. And Daisy never saw him again.

(The windows explode, one by one. Erik is gone. She can't see him.)

Now Daisy kicked and writhed as John pulled her out from under the table, pulled her into his grip, murmuring to her all the while. "Come on, it's all right. Don't be afraid. Are you hurt?"

(Her legs are gone. The windows are gone. Erik is gone.)

"Sit down, honey," John said, getting Daisy off the floor and into a chair. He pulled a chair and sat, too, facing her, his hands on her upper arms. "Are you hurt? Did you get cut?"

"The glass," she whispered. Her brain was a whirling snowstorm of sharp-edged snowflakes.

(Erik Erik Erik.)

"It was a snowplow," the proprietor of the diner said, wringing his fat hands. "It threw all the snow against the front of the building."

"It was the window, Dais," John said. "The window broke."

"He shot the glass," she said. "He shot the glass out..."

John seemed to rear back a little, his eyebrows drawn down. His hands tightened on her arms and then softened. He leaned back in and his face fell into a calm understanding.

"I see," he said. His hands slid on either side of her face and he held her forehead to his.

"He shot the glass," Daisy said, weeping.

John nodded. "I know. I know what happened, Dais. I know."

He put his arms around her, held her tight. His hand pressed the back of her head. He gathered up all her trembling, shattered pieces and put them in his pockets.

"I'm taking you home."

SNOW GLOBE

"THIS IS US, DAIS," John said.

She lifted up her head, startled from a thin sleep.

"It's our stop. Come on, honey."

Her feet stumbled and skittered on the snow-covered subway steps. She was so tired.

"Almost there," John said. "You can do it."

Her shaking hands dropped her keys twice. Finally he opened the door of her apartment himself and bolted it behind them. She shivered as he unbuttoned her coat, drew it off her and hung it away. She wanted her bed.

"Go," John said. "I'll make you some tea."

But instead he brought a glass of water. "You don't have any tea," he said.

The mattress sagged as he sat and pulled the covers up to Daisy's chin. "You're not allowed to have tea, are you?" he said softly. "I bet you don't eat Swedish Fish anymore, either. Anything and everything that reminds you of him, you're not allowed to want or have."

"It hurts too much," she said.

"Go to sleep."

He stayed by her side until she did.

In her dreams she stood at the window of the lighting booth, gazing not at the theater but on snow-shrouded streets. New York in an ermine coat. A snow princess, gentle and clean.

I always wanted to live in a snow globe.

The far-away sound of a single gunshot.

Breaking glass.

Snow and blood.

Another gun went off, followed by the baying moan of a wolf. Paw prints appeared in the snow.

She put her hands over her ears, trying to block out the shots and the shattering and the howling. Her heart pounded against her eardrums. An ominous throbbing cadence.

She opened her eyes and sat up. As her heart quieted, the silence of the apartment pressed on her ears. Through it emerged another repetitive noise, thin and metallic. Slowly she looked at her night table, John's watch set by the lamp. Deliberately arranged, like a calling card. She set her fingers on it.

Don't leave him there. Don't leave him alone.

Don't you fuck this up again.

On cushioned feet she went out to the living room and perched on the edge of the couch. Fully clothed, John slept with one arm thrown over his head, profile outlined against his bicep. Daisy laid her hand on his chest. Felt the steady beat of his life. The implacable rise and fall of his ribs.

"John," she whispered, feeling his name in her mouth.

The whites of his eyes glowed in the dimness as he looked up at her. She slid her hand up to his throat, out over his shoulder and down his arm, curling her fingers around his.

His smile unfolded. "Hey," he said softly.

She stood up. John swung his feet to the floor and followed her back to her bed. There, she curled into his arms, pressing her face to his chest. His hand moved along the length of her hair. He held her like a lover and she let him, feeling his long slow breaths and the underlying patience beneath his touch.

He tilted her chin up. His kiss felt good. Not Erik's, but nothing and nobody ever would. John's mouth was soft. His tongue tasted of snow, of a man's desire and a boy's hope.

"Go to sleep," he said. "I won't let anything hurt you."

Daisy relaxed her fingers. She let go.

And she believed him.

GLASS

SHE BEGAN TO COURT happiness and found it a coy, elusive lover. Her tentative joy was studded with the sharp edges of broken glass and her dreams began to twinkle with it.

She went from the black cavern of oppressive nothingness to a hall of mirrors and windows. In dreams she beat her head and hands against the panes. Beat and beat and beat until the glass broke and the blood spattered, and then another transparent wall appeared.

Sometimes she was in the theater of Mallory Hall, approaching the lighting booth. Either walking up the aisle like a normal human or descending from the ceiling like an international spy. But always, Erik was in the booth, looking through the glass. Sometimes straight through her, his face pinched with hatred. Other times, he looked right at her with the same hatred as she pounded her fists bloody against the booth windows. The glass didn't break. Not until Erik, his cognac-colored eyes murderous, put out a single finger, touched it to the pane and made it explode.

To the sound of breaking glass, Daisy would wake up, soaked with sweat and gasping. Sometimes she screamed into the night, even as her lower belly contracted down in waves of wicked pleasure.

A strange compulsion wove its way into her days. She trailed her fingertips over windows and mirrors. She stared countless minutes at a water glass before finally filling it. At restaurants she stroked tumblers and goblets as if they were human limbs. Smooth, pretty glass. Prettier when it was cracked and shattered and flung across the ground in a glittering mess. Whenever she came across a mosaic of broken glass on the sidewalk or street, she halted in her tracks, gazing as though transfixed by a work of art.

John squired her around Manhattan which, in early December, was full of romance: ice skating at Rockefeller Center beneath the mammoth Christmas tree. The decorated store windows. The season spectacular at Radio City and Balanchine's *Nutcracker* at the New York State Theater. They went up to the Bronx to see the train show at the Botanical Gardens and down to the Village for a staged reading of *A Christmas Carol.*

I have a new boyfriend, Daisy thought, trying it on for size.

"I met someone," she told her mother. "Met again, actually."

"I'm kind of seeing John," she told Lucky.

"Kind of?" Lucky said, smiling. "What, you have one eye closed?"

"This is my girlfriend, Daisy," John said, introducing her to his brother.

I told you he'd make a nice prince someday, Will wrote from Germany.

She often got the feeling they were acting in a play. This jacket didn't quite fit her. It was worst when she and John went out with Lucky and her boyfriend, Ed. Their relationship struck Daisy as bizarre. They lived to argue about *everything* and treated it as a huge joke. And then they argued about how funny it was or wasn't. Ed got sullen if the other three talked about Lancaster. He often made rude cracks about John being a dancer, which gave Lucky a legitimate excuse to light into him.

The double-dates were either jaw-achingly boring or excruciatingly awkward. Even lunch dates alone with Lucky felt artificial and forced to Daisy. As they talked about Ed and John, elephants named Erik and Will lounged beneath the table.

She and John hadn't made love yet. He stayed over a few nights a week and in her bed they took it slow, kissing and touching like teenagers. When she plummeted out of glassy nightmares, his soothing hands and voice caught her. He coaxed her to tell him about the dreams but she was embarrassed. She clung to him, hungry for physical contact, but every time she thought she was ready for sex, anxiety took hold of her and shook her senseless.

"I'm sorry," she said, trembling and nauseous. On more than one occasion, she sent John home so she could throw up in peace.

"Stop apologizing," he said. "If I were only interested in getting laid, I'd be gone by now."

"I feel so stupid."

"Then let me stay," he said against her head, his arms a strong circle around her. "Don't be alone and stupid. Be stupid in company, it's much nicer."

SHE WONDERED IF ERIK had found someone else. The breath left her lungs in a gasp of despair and she was certain he had a new girl-friend. Daisy saw her: a California blonde, healthy and athletic. Patty. Debbie. Beth.

Cynthia.

She played basketball in high school, maybe even ran track. She was getting her master's in education because she loved kids—she'd be that sunny first-grade teacher everyone wanted. Or she'd be the cool, high school drama club advisor. Erik would bring her coffee at rehearsal and help her kids build sets. She was smart, outgoing and cool. She was ten kinds of fun.

She had pretty feet.

Daisy clutched the edge of her kitchen counter, shoulders heaving in a jealous rage over this girl's feet. Smooth-heeled and flawless, the nails perfectly shaped and painted red. No, pink. Pale pink. Beauti-ful pristine feet. Erik was holding them in his lap, marveling that a woman's toenails could be so enticing.

"My ex-girlfriend," he was saying. "That dancer chick I told you about, the one who fucked me over? Man, her feet were ugly. They didn't even look human."

And that blonde bitch—Tori? Liz? Ashley?—was smiling at him, holding out her suntanned, muscular arms, pulling Erik down on her. Wrapping legs around his waist and resting those pretty feet on the small of his back. She had him now. She had his body and his mouth and she was a balm for all the damage Daisy had caused. She was sliding an expert hand between their bodies, unzipping Erik's jeans, intent on making him forget. Perhaps he'd already forgotten. He was kissing this girl and sliding his hands up her shirt like he didn't remember anything. Daisy saw the inside of his left wrist, a blurred pink network of scar tissue where a daisy had been tattooed.

He got rid of me.

He cut me out.

The sound of breaking glass shattered the vision. Daisy looked down into the sink and the wine bottle she had smashed against the steel. She picked up one of the green shards, wet with red wine and glistening with promise. Her head swelled, her body expanded. She was going to explode. If only she could forget the way Erik did. If only she could laser him out of her memory. Cut him out of her skin.

She pressed the point of the glass into the rope of scar tissue on the inside of her calf. Tears sprang to her eyes and she bit down hard on her lower lip. Her skin resisted but finally she drew blood. Four round rubies bubbled up to the surface and then ran together. She let her breath out, panting as the drops converged into one thin river, then forked and branched down her calf to her ankle. She blinked hard, looking around the apartment. Everything seemed clearer. Brighter. Sharply outlined and focused. The breath she pulled through her nose was clean and bracing. She felt full of a tingling energy. This was the answer all along. So simple.

And so stupid. The Met's wardrobe mistress clucked her tongue in irritation at the hunk of gauze beneath Daisy's tights. It was too conspicuous. She didn't think it through.

After that, she cut herself where it couldn't be seen. A ritual developed. She lit a candle and passed the shard of green glass through the flame, charring it black and wiping it clean with an alcohol-soaked cotton ball. Pass. Wipe. Pass. Wipe.

Then she cut.

Staying away from her arms and legs and any skin visible in a leotard, she first made lines between every rib. Then radiated them out to her waist and toward the small of her back. She didn't ruthlessly slash, but concentrated on making the cuts pretty and came to admire her skill in drawing the precise amount of blood she wanted. The cuts stung like hell when she got sweaty. In partnering class when John held her waist or supported her back in a lift, the gashes screamed in a near ecstatic release.

She started to worship the patterned, punishing web of lines girdling her body, holding her in place as it let out the dark, one slice at a time. One anxious night, she was careless and leaned too hard on the glass. Alarmed at the amount of blood, she seized the cotton ball to staunch it. The sting of the alcohol made her cry out. It burned like fire, crawling up her side like a swarm of red ants, a hundred bee stings.

It felt good.

The alcohol, decanted into a pretty bottle with a cork, took its place with the glass. Soon a second little bottle with vodka joined it. A small tub of menthol, anti-itch lotion. A wooden box of salt was a satisfying metaphor. Lemon juice made her cry for ten minutes straight. Night after night, she cut and rubbed anything that stung into her wounds.

Then she could sleep.

CHOCOLATE

THE STARS ALIGNED to give Daisy and John the same night off. She invited him to dinner and choreographed a feast: two Cornish hens each, with roasted Brussels sprouts and red grapes lashed with truffle oil. John wrinkled his nose, saying he didn't like sprouts. Halfway through the meal, they were dueling with forks over the bowl, fighting to the death for the last caramelized leaves. They killed a bottle of wine and opened another. John twisted a candle into the empty bottle's neck and lit it while Daisy stacked dishes and began melting squares of bittersweet chocolate for fondue.

"I'm a little drunk," she said, smiling as she dragged the spatula in figure eights through the bubbling sauce. She was a lot drunk. She hadn't tied one on like this in years. Her thoughts wheeled around like giddy seagulls, tumbling and giggling through her buzzing head.

"You still have this?" John asked, crouched down at her bookshelf and holding up the battered copy of *The Eyes of the Dragon,* which he had brought to her in the hospital after the shooting.

"Read it three times," she said. "It's one of my favorites. Did I ever thank you?"

"Not yet," he said, coming to lean on the counter and watching her slice strawberries and bananas. His body was relaxed and sexy, his teeth curled a bit over his bottom lip.

"Thank you for the book," she said. Her lips tingled as the words slipped through them. She fed him a strawberry, watched it disappear into his mouth and wanted to follow.

He dipped a banana slice in chocolate and fed her. "You're welcome."

She dipped her finger and offered it against his lip. He licked the chocolate off, then took her wrist, pulled it up around his neck as his other hand slid into the back pocket of her jeans. Then they were kissing and grappling up against the refrigerator door. A greedy need for skin swept through her, redolent with singed sugar.

"It's burning, Dais," he said.

"I know," she whispered.

"The chocolate," he said, laughing.

Daisy reached to turn off the burner and pushed the pot off it, shaking with a bald wanting and the sensation of being desirable. A man's body, hard with the need to be inside her. Strong male hands running along her limbs and curves with a fevered knowledge.

"You're killing me," he said, turning with her and pressing her up against the door of the fridge.

She wound her arms tight around him. Her mouth open and hungry in his, sucking gently on his tongue, making him moan. Her heartbeat enormous in her ears. Her own little, whimpering noises in her chest. Her body melting, drunk on wine and lust. Spreading and arching as John's palms swept from her shoulders down over her breasts and stomach.

"I don't want to stop," he said against her mouth. "Please let's not stop. I want to make love to you so bad."

He tugged her shirt free from the waist of her jeans and drew it up over her head. As the cool air swept her bare skin she froze. And remembered.

Now filled with panic, her body contorted. She jerked her arms tight to stop him but it was too late. His eyes widened. His mouth parted in shock. She turned her face away, buried it in the fabric around her neck, tried to break free but his hands held her tight.

"Dais," he said.

"Let me go."

His hands tightened. "Hold still."

"John, please."

A rush of air through his teeth made a soothing hush. "Let me see."

"No."

"I'm not going to say anything," he said. "I'm just going to look."

She was crying then. "Please don't."

He shushed her again. "Let me look." His hands were gentle but firm as he guided first one arm, then the other out of her sleeves. She stood shaking in her bra as he touched the angry red lines on her ribs. Sobbed into her hands as he slowly turned her around and looked at her back. Breath through his teeth again but in an agonized hiss.

"Honey..." His fingertips touched two particularly deep cuts—one at the bottom edge of her shoulder blade, the other lower down at the base of her spine. She made those on a bad night. Torqued her hand behind her back and slashed blindly with the glass, not caring if the cuts were pretty or part of the design. She couldn't see them, couldn't reach to tend to them and they weren't healing properly. She didn't want them to.

John turned her to face him again. Shame, that old friend, sat on the couch in Daisy's heart and asked what she had to say for herself.

His hands slid up her shoulders, peeled her own hands away from her face. He held her head and put his brow against hers.

"Do you trust me?" he said.

"John, go," she said, trying to twist away. "Go now before I do trust you. Go find a girl who's normal, a girl with pretty feet and not all this baggage."

"I don't want pretty f— Dais, you don't know the first thing about what I feel for you and what I want."

"I *know* I'm only going to hurt you," she said, the crown of her head against his chest. "You don't want this. You love a dream, you love a girl you put on a pedestal and crushed on in college. I'm not her anymore. You won't love who I am now."

"Look at me." His thumbs were under her chin, making her head tilt up to his unsmiling face. "Do you trust me," he said again, more slowly.

She gazed into his eyes. It wasn't like it was with Erik. No sense of falling slow-motion into another time and space. John's being stayed separate from hers but his gaze was that of a danseur noble giving hand: *Come here. Come dance with me. Let my strength be your strength.*

She felt him with her, felt her feet solid on the floor. This wasn't a pedestal.

"Yes," she said.

"Then I want you to show me," he said. "Show me what you use to cut yourself."

Her body tensed, and his hands moved soothingly at the back of her neck and her shoulders.

"It hates to be talked about," he said. "That's how it keeps you a prisoner. But if you tell someone, if you show someone, you take away its power. That's how you start to stop. Show me, Dais."

Her heart blocking her throat, she led him into her bedroom. On her windowsill, on a piece of black marble, she had made an altar. John looked at it a long time. Looked at the candle and the little bottles and the single piece of green glass at the center. He listened as she told how it started after the window broke in the diner and evolved into a ritual. He didn't laugh or dismiss it. He nodded as if it all made sense.

"It seems logical," he said, picking up the large shard of glass. "In a twisted way. To hurt yourself as much as you hurt him."

A sob burst from Daisy's throat and she buried her face in her hands.

"This isn't the way, Dais. It won't bring him back and it won't make you feel better. All it will do is make you bleed. And eventually it'll kill you..."

She nodded into her palms, sinking onto the bed. She could hear the tiny clink as John set the glass back down on the marble. Then he knelt between her feet, slid his arms around her. "I don't want you to die."

She took her hands from her face as his fingers glided down the straps of her bra and along the lace edges of the cups. She stared down at her untouched, uncut skin as if it belonged to someone else.

He kissed her mouth, still tasting like chocolate and fruit. She shivered in pleasure and fear.

"I still want you," he said.

"No you d—"

"Hey," he said sharply. "Don't tell me what I want. I'm not a kid and I don't love a dream. I don't cling to some stupid notion you're something to be idolized and can do no wrong. You're fucked up right now, but I don't define you as this, Dais. This isn't *you*. This is just a place."

With each powerful word John seemed to grow bigger. Wider. His shoulders touching opposite walls, unfolding like wings. Filling the dim room with his conviction. As she gazed up at him, Daisy's eyes squinted, as if looking into the sun. A swarm in her chest like a cloud of bees. Deep within, a warm pulse began to beat. She inhaled him, took in his scent, his light and his words.

"Tell me to go and I'll go," he said against her mouth. "But don't tell me not to love you. It's too late."

His kiss on hers again, the sweetness of it mixing with her tears. Strawberry and chocolate eclipsing salt. Snow melting in the sun's warmth.

"Stay," she whispered.

They carried the piece of marble out to the kitchen and tilted everything on it into the garbage. Back in the bedroom, John became her lover. He was strong and skilled and her body opened to his. As he peeled the rest of her clothes off, he kissed every scar. Before his tongue glided where she was wet and aching, he promised he'd help make it go away. She trusted him. As she unbuttoned and unzipped his jeans, she caught some of his light and began to burn even brighter. She remembered sex, remembered the musky smell of a man and the vulnerability of the first touch. The tender taut skin and the jerking impatience. She took him first into her hands, then into the wet behind her teeth and he gave a soft howl into the dark.

"*God,* I wanted this…"

She was off the pill and hadn't bought condoms in years. She had no need.

"I don't have anything," she said.

"I do." His silhouette was beautiful in the dark. Long sculpted muscles in his legs flexing as he knelt down, digging through the pockets of his jeans for his wallet.

"Let me," she said, tearing the foil open, shaking with need.

"Marguerite," he whispered, rolling onto her, sliding up her body. The unfamiliar sound of her own name was a revelation. She caught him in her hand, guided him in. He pressed down hard, pushed deep and she gave him her own howl, gave him her tongue, the beauty of her pain and her flawed passion. Gave him her name and her scarred, female power.

"I love you," he said. "I always loved you."

Being his dream come true bore her up on courageous wings. She flew with him through the night until John unleashed one last moan and buried his brow in the curve of her neck. His fists curled tight around her hair but he didn't pull.

"You're mine now," he said. "I swear to God I'll keep you safe, Dais."

"No, say my real name," she said.

"You're safe, Marguerite. You're safe with me."

She fell asleep in his arms and dreamed Erik was behind her. He bent her over and pulled her pants down but then he left her like that, vulnerable and exposed, waiting to be spanked or fucked because she was so bad. Left her worked up, moody and humiliated.

She woke filled with an anxious nausea. Her room full of wolves snarling and hungry. They sniffed at John's sleeping body and growled their disgust.

Dawn was easing through the windows as she crawled to the bathroom. She buried her face in a bath towel and cried carefully so John wouldn't hear. She was sick for a long time, fighting with the minutes not to cut herself, but she lost. She had to get it out of her. She didn't dare rustle in the kitchen garbage for her glass shard or in a drawer for a knife. Her shaking hands couldn't get the right angle out of her disposable razor.

Finally, she broke the kohl-caked blade out of her eye pencil sharpener and cut line after sloppy line into her skin until the shaking stopped. She put her head on the edge of the tub and closed her eyes, exhausted and half-smiling.

She woke as one arm slid beneath her knees and another under her shoulders. John picked her up and carried her back to the bedroom. Spots of red bloomed first on his T-shirt, then on her sheets. He tucked her in and then picked up the phone and dialed. A slice of Daisy's brain turned white with alarm.

No. No don't. Don't tell. I'll be good, I promise...

Then it all faded to dull grey. Fuck everything. He could tell, he could call. She didn't care anymore. She wasn't getting up anymore. Not for herself. Not for anyone.

"Mom, it's me," John said.

A beat of silence.

"I need help..."

SUICIDAL IDEATION

STATEMENT OF ADMISSION, Westfall Hospital
Cross River, New York
December 8, 1995
Attending physician: Dr. Herbert Montgomery, MD, Psy.D.
Admission referral: Dr. Janet Quillis, Psy.D.
Patient name: Bianco, Marguerite C., DOB 12/15/71

Patient is a single white female, age 24. Patient lives alone in New York City, currently employed by the Metropolitan Opera Ballet. Patient was brought to the hospital by her parents after her boyfriend alerted them to increased symptoms of depression including self-injurious behaviors. Patient presents as alert and oriented X 3.

Both open and healed lacerations are evident on patient's arms, legs, torso and back, two requiring sutures at this time with antibiotic treatment and tetanus booster. Some scars present on left leg are unrelated (see below).

Patient reports self-injurious behavior began six weeks prior. Patient reports a recent history of increased cutting behavior with glass. Other presenting symptoms include *hopelessness, helplessness and anhedonia. Patient reports passive suicidal ideation with no defined plan.*

Patient reports persistent nausea, difficulty falling asleep and staying asleep and decreased appetite. Patient also reports a history of nightmares and flashbacks related to her experience in the 1992 shootings at Lancaster University. Patient suffered gunshot wound to the left leg with subsequent complications from compartment syndrome. Full recovery of vascular and motor function.

Patient is assigned an Axis I diagnosis of Major Depressive Disorder, single episode, severe, without psychotic features and a rule out of PTSD.

Patient states she is in agreement with admission at this time.

IT DOESN'T MAKE
YOU A MYSTERY

YOUR FINEST HOUR

DECEMBER 13, 1995

Dear Lucky,

Hey darling girl. Thanks so much for the flowers and X-rated birthday card. You know how to make a girl feel special in the loony bin.

I shouldn't call it that. It's not a bad place. Food kind of sucks but I'm not hungry these days.

So welcome to rock bottom. May I take your order?

Anyway...

I've been sitting five minutes thinking of what to write. I feel embarrassed. I feel stupid. I feel so much and it hurts like hell and I tried to make it stop and it got out of control. John did the right thing by calling my parents. They headed straight for New York while John's parents, who are both psychologists, made some phone calls. My mom was pretty adamant about me not being in a hospital in the city, not sure why. She must have some preconceived notions about Bellevue or something. Anyway, they found this place up in Westchester County. Pop's gone back home but Mamou is staying in a *hotel nearby and she comes every day. Only family is allowed so John hasn't been able to see me. We don't have phones in our rooms and it's hard to have an intimate conversation on the payphone in the hall. But he writes the sweetest little notes and cuts the comics out of the newspapers for me, too.*

Pop's going to run out of medals to pin on these heroic boys I fall for.

A cardinal just flew by the window and now it's sitting in the snow-covered bush outside. Pretty.

I've been here five days now. Not sure when I'll be leaving. Sucks to spend my birthday in this place but hopefully I'll get out for Christmas. I'm on antibiotics because the two cuts on my back are pretty badly infected. Tetanus shot for the stunt I pulled with my pencil sharpener...

God, I feel like an idiot. Like I took everything great that's ever happened to me and just shit on it.

They started me on anti-depressants. I don't feel much different yet. Holding out hope I will. I'm really tired. The days are filled up with one-on-one therapy and group therapy and art therapy and therapeutic therapy, blah blah. Other activities where you have to show your face. A gym is on the premises and I try to get in there every day and stretch and do some resistance training. Don't worry, I remember— low weight, high reps. I do my barrework in my room every morning. There's enough space to swing a leg. My roommate doesn't seem to mind. Her name's April. She's a cutter, too. Except she cut her face.

Not much more I can say about that.

I was just about to write "I'm all right" so you wouldn't worry. But I know you're already worried and obviously I'm not all right. I go between feeling numb and feeling like I want to claw my skin off. Jonesing all the time for something. With-drawing from everything. Cigarettes. Caffeine. Sugar. Class.

Cutting.

(sorry)

I don't know what to do with myself. Or I can't get away from myself. Either bored out of my mind or trying to escape all the shit that's in my mind. I suppose that's the point. They say the first couple weeks of treatment are more about not doing than doing. I am supposed to not cut. Nothing else. Eat, sleep, go to therapy and not cut.

So I'm not. For four days and eleven hours and (checking my watch) twenty-six minutes. Yay, me.

The therapy is going all right. Actually it sucks. It's a lot of silence. I know I have a lot to say but it's stuck. Or I'm stuck. I don't know if it's the meds or me or the therapists. I've seen two separate ones but I can't seem to make a connection, so I'm not exactly spilling my guts yet.

I don't know how it came to this, Luck. I'm going to be twenty-four in two days and what am I doing blowing out candles here?

John said the sweetest thing: "It feels like your darkest time. But I think it's going to be your finest hour."

I hope he's right.

I miss you, darling girl. The other night I couldn't sleep and I was thinking about that god-awful horrible night at Jay Street after I slept with David. When you crawled right in bed with me and got me through it. I swore the sun wouldn't come up the next day but it did. I'm trying to remember that.

Write me a lot. I need it.

Love,
Dais

P.S. I really will be all right.
P.P.S. Won't I?

SLIGHTLY STARVING

THE SKIES WERE WHITE. The Hudson river churned in milk-crested hills of grey. The Palisades thrust up vertical stripes of brown and slate. From the Henry Hudson Bridge, Daisy pressed her fingers against the passenger window and thought she'd never seen the gateway to Manhattan look so beautiful.

"Wish it were a nicer day," John said.

She turned her smile to him. "I'm going home."

He squeezed her hand, brought it up to his mouth a moment, then let go as he slowed to pay the toll.

"You sure you don't want to drive down to Pennsylvania tonight? I don't mind."

"I want my bed," she said. "I want a giant roast beef sandwich and then I want my bed and all the pillows and a decent night's sleep. We can go tomorrow."

The George Washington Bridge loomed ahead, geometric and majestic. Daisy craned her neck, hoping for a glimpse of the little red lighthouse at its base. But it was best seen from the New Jersey side.

"Do you have to check in with anyone? You know. At..." John jerked his head at the highway behind them.

"At the place?"

He smiled. "The thing?"

"A counselor will be on-call between Christmas and New Year's. I can call if I need to. First week of January, I'm supposed to check back in with Dr. Montgomery with the name of a new therapist. Or at least show I'm trying to find one."

"Which one was Montgomery?"

"The milquetoast guy with the beard."

"Right. Didn't get to first name basis with him."

"No. Dr. Reilly was at least Mary."

"You didn't dig her, either."

"Eh?" Daisy looked out the window, uncomfortable. She felt the therapy sessions with both Montgomery and Reilly were unproductive and somehow it was her fault. She didn't have any profound, promising breakthroughs to share and it was embarrassing.

John had stayed at her apartment while she was in the hospital and everything was neat and shining.

"Oh my God, did you dust?" she said, sliding out of her coat. "I never dust."

"I don't either," he said, setting down her bag. "Julie Valente came over and cleaned. She told me to tell you the babies at Methodist Hospital miss you."

"I miss them too. Hope Jules didn't find anything embarrassing while she was cleaning."

"I hid your vibrator."

Daisy swatted him then went around touching things. Home. The relief of it. She pressed her face sideways to the window and looked west down 86th Street. She could glimpse a sliver of the river between two buildings.

John's arms slid around her waist and he buried his face in her neck. "I missed you so much."

She patted his wrists with a small noise of appreciation and her shoulders stiffened slightly. She knew he'd been missing and worrying and thinking about her for two weeks, knew he'd want to make love. And she had zero interest.

He moved her hair and kissed her neck, pulling her back tight against him. Carefully, she turned in the circle of his arms and put her face against his chest.

"I know you're dying," she said. "And we will. Just let me...be home a little while." She turned her head up to him. "All right?"

"I'm not dying," he said, running his hands along her spine. "Slightly starving. But not dying."

She hugged him hard. "Later. Promise. I'm tired right now."

The phone rang.

John kissed her head. "I got it. Go lie down."

Touched at how he was keeping a barrier between her and the world, Daisy kicked off her shoes, ripped open the duvet and slid in between the sheets. With a luxurious groan she rolled face-down in the pillows, inhaling fresh clean familiarity. She ignored the twin wolves of guilt and worry parked on the rug.

It's not my fault we only got to make love once and I ended up hospitalized twenty-four hours later.

One wolf turned its head with a disgusted look in its yellow eyes.

All right, fine. You're right. It was my doing. I'm sorry.

She closed her eyes, exhaling heavily.

Sexual drive was first out and last in, she was told. Dr. Montgomery said it. Dr. Reilly said it. Everyone said it.

"They put you on Prozac?" April, her roommate at the hospital said. "Welcome to the zero libido club, kid. Kiss your orgasms goodbye. And wait until the night sweats kick in, it's a blast."

Kid set Daisy's teeth on edge, along with the gleeful warnings. She'd just been admitted to a psychiatric hospital—sex was the furthest thing from her mind. But as the days accumulated, she was alarmed at how distant a dream sex became. How utterly uninteresting. Even her trusty go-to reenactments of lovemaking with Erik only brought a dull warmth, blurred and dim, as if behind dirty sunglasses.

"It will all come back," Montgomery said. "It's not your body's priority right now."

She kept asking her body if it was sure. On restless, anxious nights when she touched herself to bring on sleep, nothing would work. She kept grinding the key in the ignition but the engine wouldn't turn.

"Give it time," Reilly said. "Try not to think about it too much."

Daisy rolled onto her side, wondering if thinking about how much she didn't think about sex qualified as thinking about sex.

With another explosive sigh, she rolled the other way, tucking her cold hands between her knees. *Let it be,* she thought. *You're home. You're in your bed. Now is now, later is later. Be honest with him and do what you can. Tomorrow you'll be at La Tarasque.*

Her eyes opened.

Her mother would probably put her and John in the carriage house. *Do you ever think of marrying me?*

The bedroom door creaked open. "You asleep?"

"Not yet."

He lay down next to her, holding a scrap of paper. "That was my mom. She had a few numbers for you. Therapists on the West Side you could try."

"Oh." She freed a hand and took the slip. Scanned the four names without interest and twisted to set it down on her night stand. John's hand smoothed her hair as she faced him again and burrowed into the covers.

"I'm so glad you're home," he said.

He looked adorable, stretched out on his side, his head pillowed on one bent arm. His use of "home" was relaxed and unassuming, asking nothing of her but her company. She slid her hand around the back of his neck, filled with a true and tender gratitude for everything he'd done for her. Pulling up close to him, she whispered against his forehead, "Thanks for coming to get me."

GETTING LAID PROPERLY

DAISY RAN HER FINGERS over the cap of her left shoulder. Nearly three months after she cut herself with the pencil sharpener, the scars were barely perceptible. "These are almost gone. The ones around my waist and back are taking longer to fade." She pulled her T-shirt sleeve down and drew up the lapel of her cardigan.

"How do you feel about them fading?" Rita said.

Daisy smiled. "You always know what to ask."

"It's my job."

She picked at the rough edge of her fingernail. "Is it weird to say I miss them? That I feel almost mournful when I notice how they're disappearing?"

"Not at all," Rita said. "Cutting has two aspects. One is to release pain and the other is to have a physical, or rather visual, manifestation of pain."

"It's about the scar."

"Yes. And it can often be difficult when the scars fade."

Daisy nodded and drew in a breath. "Which is why I'm here with you."

Rita smiled as she drew off her glasses and cleaned them with one of her cuffs. "I'm curious what made you choose me from the list John's mother gave."

"Do you know her?"

"We have mutual colleagues. I know who she is but I don't know her personally. Would it bother you if I did?"

"Yes," Daisy said. "And to answer your original question, I picked you because you were a four-block walk from my apartment."

Laughing, Rita put her glasses back on. "Convenience first."

The silence shuffled around, getting comfortable.

"So I'm back at work," Daisy said.

"What's that like?"

"I'm a little out of shape but everyone's being nice to me. And it's a relief that class is still my friend. I mean it seems no matter what happens, dancing is still a constant. First position is always first position. I put my hand on the barre and put my feet in first and two pliés later, everything goes away. I guess I need to find the equivalent for when I'm not in class or onstage."

"What do you like to do?"

"Read. I started knitting again. I did it a little in college—Taylor Revell taught me. But I never got into it as a hobby. I remembered it while I was in the hospital and my mom brought me some yarn and a pair of needles. Big fat ones, it's like knitting Fisher Price style. I find working with my hands to be relaxing. Something meditative about it and I don't much care about the end product." She smiled. "I sound like David. Get there but not be there. I like to knit but not to have knitted something. Anyway..."

"How do you feel, physically? Are the meds giving you any issues?"

"No. Yes. I mean, I feel better, no question. I don't have that constant anxiety. The daily road of life isn't filled with sudden sinkholes. I'm eating and I'm sleeping."

"Are you having disturbing dreams?"

"Not disturbing, but vivid. Vivid and weird. And the night sweats, oh my God."

"Yes, unfortunately it's one of the adverse effects."

"It's so gross. It's not even a clean sweat but that really slimy post-workout drench. I'm killing four pairs of sheets a week and for no fun reason."

"How is your sex drive?"

"Out to lunch. Every now and then I'll feel like it but it's always a passive thing. Like I can have sex because I can tolerate it. Like I know John wants to and I think *yeah, all right, I can do it for him, I can accept him into me tonight and find something in it.* But I never feel spontaneously sexy. I'm never...horny. I'm never fully connected. I don't lose myself in it and I can't have an orgasm to save my life. And frankly, that sucks. I've never come with John. I tell him not to feel bad about it because I can barely make myself come."

Rita flipped the pages of her notebook. "You're on the Prozac alone, correct?"

"Yeah."

"I'm going to write you a scrip for Wellbutrin. It's shown to be effective in treating SSRI-induced sexual dysfunction. We may have to fiddle around with the dosage but let's give this a try."

"All right."

"This isn't the most professional of observations but life is so much easier to deal with when you're getting laid properly."

Daisy worried her teeth at her thumbnail as Rita was writing, her throat dry around unspoken words. Poised on the edge of a secret, caught between hiding and telling. Why was hiding so much easier?

"Funny," she said, and cleared her throat. "The one thing that always turns me on is when John touches my scars."

Rita finished writing, tore the slip off her pad and handed it to Daisy. "Can you tell me more?"

Tears sprang to her eyes and she pressed her lips tight, shaking her head. "I don't know."

"You're safe here," Rita said.

"I don't know what it is. He runs his fingers over them... The ones on my back. The two deep ones that won't ever fade. He touches them and I love it. I'm glad they won't fade. In a sick, twisted way I'm proud of them. God, I'm such a coward."

She thought Rita was unsurprisable but for the first time in two months of sessions, Rita's face registered true shock. "You're a coward?" she said. "Why do you say that?"

"They're on my back," Daisy said. She was crying now. "I cut the deepest on my back where I wouldn't have to see. He has to look at them. And he runs his fingers over them and he hates them, but I love it. Sometimes it's the only intimate touch I love." She yanked a tissue from the box and held it to her eyes. "I cut where I couldn't see. It's so passive-aggressive."

Her shoulders went limp as she blew her nose. A euphoria existed in unburdening her heart. She felt a little sick inside, yet the buzz beneath the skin of her face was almost pleasant.

"You set so little value on your own strength," Rita said.

"Because I feel like I'm weak. And stupid."

"You toughed it out after the shooting. Worked your ass off to make a comeback only a year later. You toughed it out through drug withdrawal. You're still toughing out a cruel emotional desertion by your lover. Where most people would bottom out, you quickly regrouped after you lost your job, came to one of the hardest cities in the world to make a living as an artist and found work. On your own. You have little free time, yet volunteer to comfort infants who are detoxing from *heroin*. You're one of a handful of cuddlers with the stomach and the strength to hold that kind of screaming. These are not small feats, Daisy, nor accomplishments made by idiots. On one hand, I'm aghast at what you suffered alone. On the other hand, I don't often encounter your kind of resiliency and it's not something to be dismissed."

Before Daisy could process the speech, maybe preen a little, Rita went on.

"Why do you tough everything out alone? What happened to the courage to be a mess?"

Open-mouthed, spent and stunned, Daisy could only shake her head. "I don't know what happened to me."

Rita's eyes flicked to her watch and she smiled. "Something to think about for next week."

But Daisy still sat frozen, turning Rita's words over in her mind. "Do you really believe," she said, "what Erik's been doing to me is cruel?"

It took Rita a moment to answer. Daisy could see her mind's gears turning, measuring words and weighing their objectivity.

"I don't know him," Rita said. "But I believe what you did hurt him terribly. And I also believe he could have made better or different choices to deal with it. I sometimes wonder why he chose such total disconnection."

"I wonder, too," Daisy said. "Every day I wonder."

THERAPY LEFT HER SO emotionally shredded, she tried to schedule her appointments on the days when she wasn't performing. After a late afternoon session, she had just enough energy to stumble the four blocks home and trudge up the two flights of stairs to her apartment.

John was already there. At her parents' insistence, she'd given him a key.

"I want him to be able to get to you," Joe said, in a tone that brooked no discussion.

John didn't abuse the privilege, and always let her know when he'd be letting himself in on his off nights, which he tried to schedule with hers whenever he could.

He was napping. Daisy tiptoed and heeled off her shoes as quietly as possible. Without opening his eyes he put out an arm and folded back the quilt for her. She slid beneath, moved into the warm nest he made.

She sighed. Of all the simple pleasures in life, lying down was in the top five.

His arm with the quilt closed over her, tucking her in. "Get beat up?" he whispered.

"Bruised."

He cuddled closer, his mouth against her temple. "Poor thing."

"So tired."

"Shh. Go to sleep." He held her tight, his arm heavy and protective across her chest, one of his calves over hers. It took five minutes for her ears to sort out the ambient sounds of the city outside and weave them with the ocean waves of John's breathing. Her thoughts slowly dissolved and she fell into a deep, motionless rest. When she woke up, the room had gone dark and John's hands were on her with a different heaviness.

It was easiest when she was still wreathed in sleep. Her body more open to sex when she was slightly lethargic. It wasn't bad. It was *sex*— it didn't suck. But she was always conscious of how she made love *to* John, not *with* him. How she surfed the waves of his pleasure, knowing how happy it made him when she responded to his overtures. Even happier when she extended them—slid a hand down his pants while he was cooking, climbed on top of him in bed or stepped into the tub while he was showering.

Seeing him happy filled her with a genuine joy. It was a lot like the joy of daily barre work: Daisy loved being in class but she often hated *going to* class. Getting up and dressed and motivated was a drag. But the only way to be there was to go. In the same way, she made herself initiate sex, knowing some kind of pleasure was usually waiting for her. Even if it was only feeling John's smile against her mouth. She loved his smile.

She sighed.

"I love conversations that start with sighing," he said. He was curled up naked behind her, their hands twined between her breasts.

"Rita gave me a new prescription," she said. "Something called Wellbutrin. It's supposed to help with the lack of sex drive."

The chuckles in his chest vibrated against her back. "You have such charming pillow talk."

She squeezed her eyes. "I'm sorry."

His arm tightened around her. "I'm teasing. I'm all about whatever makes you feel better."

"You're so sweet to me," she said.

"I'm not sweet, I'm greedy," he said, curving a hand around her breast.

She knew he was. Greedy for the tsunami of her own passion to crash over him for once. To see her crumbling under the weight of desire. Undone and uninhibited in the dark.

"You're sighing again," he said. "Is this angst or afterglow?"

"I detect some sass here."

"I'm sorry, what? You respect my ass, dear?"

She grabbed a throw pillow and whacked it over her shoulder. "Cute."

He put his face in the curve of her neck and shoulder and pulled her close. He was adorable. Sweet, sympathetic and attentive. And patient.

"Like a polar bear," Daisy said to Lucky at lunch the next day. "Waiting for the seal to poke through the ice."

"You could do worse," Lucky said. "And he dances."

"True." It was the one arena where John left Erik in the dust. Any night off they could coordinate together, they went out dancing. Clubbing. Or Swing 46. Ballroom, square dancing, country line dancing, a polka night at the Polish-American Club. Nothing was beyond them, beneath them or too hokey.

("Greek Orthodox liturgical dance workshop," Daisy said, reading from *The Village Voice.*

"Bring it," he said.)

Lucky stirred her ice tea and tapped the spoon on the rim of the glass. "How is Opie in bed? I always wondered."

"You did?"

"No, just making girl talk."

"He's fine. I mean, he's great. I'm the boring one."

"Oh, come on, I know you have chops. I've heard you in the dark, remember."

Daisy threw her napkin across the table. Lucky laughed and deflected it.

"Was it weird, you think?" Daisy asked. "The four of us so uninhibited in the night?"

Lucky shrugged. "I found it kind of comforting, actually. Beat the alternative. Will always said, 'I'd rather overhear them making love than fighting.' Not that you guys fought."

"We spared you, right until the end," Daisy said over the rim of her coffee cup.

"I would've welcomed that screaming match, to be honest," Lucky said quietly.

"So how's Ed in bed?" Daisy wasn't particularly interested to know, but girl talk made a convenient subject change.

"Ed? He's predictable."

"How so?"

"I can set the calendar to it. Twice during the week. Always on Saturday night. Sunday is iffy, depends on the football game." Lucky ran her hand over her head and scrunched her curls. "And he talks too much."

Daisy laughed. "Talks about what?"

"He just *talks*. Not even dirty. I mean, good Lord, Will and I would have our goofy nights, sure. But they were the exception to the rule. Ed's home base seems to be goofball. He doesn't get... I don't want to say serious. What do I want to say?"

"Passionate? Intense?"

"Intense, yes. He doesn't get that way unless he's stoned. And he's never indulgent about going to bed, like lying around naked for an entire Sunday would be out of the question. Staying in bed to screw and talk and then fall asleep and wake up to touch and make love again. Calling in sick to work so you can go back to bed. I don't know, Dais, we have a good time, we laugh, we joke. He's not a bad lover but..."

"He's not Will."

Lucky raised her glass. "Fuckin' A."

"Did we get ruined?"

"I hope not." Lucky took a long drink then set her glass down. "Do you talk to Opie about what goes on in therapy?"

"Rarely. Why?"

"I just wondered. I mean, how much of a ghost is Erik?"

Daisy smiled. "Too much. And it's hard. John says he's open to whatever I want to tell him but..."

Lucky rolled her eyes. "Oh, sure, talk about whatever you want. Except Erik."

"Which is pretty much all I talk about in therapy," she said. "You know, it's hard to be in a relationship when you're working out your shit with your ex-boyfriend."

"You think?" Lucky said.

"Between you and me and the pickles, I spend way too much time worrying about how it's going to end. How I can possibly get out of this without breaking John's heart."

"You won't," Lucky said, smiling.

God, don't let me.

Don't let me be that girl again. I won't cheat. I'll slit my wrists before I do that again. But please, don't let me kill him. Let it end amicably. Let him leave first.

After sex, night after night, she lay awake in the circle of John's arms. He slept behind her, spooning her, and she couldn't deal. Couldn't drift off with him leaning on her back, the breeze of his breathing irritating the nape of her neck. She lay wide-eyed and trapped, watching the numbers on the digital clock. Twenty minutes was her quota then she gently eased him off her and rolled flat on her back.

"No spoons?" he said.

"I like holding hands when I sleep," she said, taking his. And some truth was in that: lying on her back next to him, hand-in-hand, sleep finally came to her.

You sleep differently with different boyfriends, she argued with herself. *Don't make such a big deal about it. Don't compare everything to Erik. It's boring.*

It was impossible not to.

TINY INSIGHTS

"I'D LIKE TO GO BACK to something you said earlier," Rita said. "In fact, now that we've caught the past up to the present, I have a few things tagged I'd like to explore. How does that sound?"

"All right," Daisy said. Her eyes were mesmerized by the pages Rita was thumbing through. Chunks of handwriting. No words discernible from where she sat, but she could see colors. Highlighted sections in neon pink, orange and blue. Tiny post-it flags. One paragraph flashed by and seemed to be circled several times.

She never doubted the woman was listening to her. She watched Rita take notes at every session. But what lay in her lap now went beyond notes. It might be her salvation. Or her undoing. And Daisy felt smack between wanting to curl up in bed and read it, and wanting to seize the fucking thing and fling it out the window.

"I might be talking more than I usually do," Rita said.

Daisy picked up her coffee cup. "I might enjoy that." She took a sip and burned her mouth. "Dammit..."

"You said people at work were being nice to you."

Wiping her chin, Daisy raised her eyebrows.

"Have you told anyone what happened to you?"

She sat back. "You mean the cutting?"

"Any of it. Lancaster. How do you explain your scars?"

"I cut where nobody could see. I didn't have to."

"I mean the scars on your leg."

"Oh. Shark attack."

Rita laughed. A real guffaw, not a polite and precipitating chuckle. A laugh that slowly faded as she took in Daisy's bland expression.

"Oh," she said. "You're serious?"

"Yeah. Actually. It does the trick."

"What trick?"

"Well...it sends the message that no, obviously, it wasn't a shark attack but it's not something I talk about."

"Why is that?"

"It's private."

"Why? Let me stop a minute. I'm going to be saying the word 'why' a lot. It's not confrontational. And it's not invalidating the answer. It's digging into it. Like a two-year-old would. Except with a Ph.D."

Now Daisy laughed. "All right."

"It might be difficult to fight the kneejerk 'because' and allow yourself to tease it out a little. Try to lean into the why and let yourself talk. Don't worry about being coherent or eloquent."

"Kneejerk the other way. All right. Which 'why' were we at?"

"Why is it private?"

"It's not a short story. I don't know how to tell a condensed version. And it also... I mean, I imagine it would bring all conversation to a grinding halt. I'm not sure what I mean." She blew her breath out. "What do I mean? Which scars are we talking about?"

Rita seemed to rear back a little. "Do you treat them differently?"

"No. Yes."

"This is interesting. Are you more willing to talk about one set than the other?"

Daisy opened her mouth then closed it. Nodded slowly as her chest grew tight. "The scars from the shooting are private," she said. She drew her favorite pillow into her lap. "This got hard all of a sudden."

"I know."

"Those scars are private."

"Are they worthy?"

"Worthy? I don't understand."

"Are they worthy of sympathy?" Rita looked uncertain as she touched her fingertips to her temple. Her voice was hesitant as it followed her own train of thought. Daisy found it comforting to see her fumble. It felt collaborative.

"Is your story touching?" Rita said, her cadence slowly picking up. "Moving? Would people have compassion for your ordeal? Would they admire your courage and your bravery? Would they understand your battle with post-traumatic stress disorder and your experience with self-harming?"

Daisy stared, not recognizing herself in all of that.

"Or," Rita said. "Would they only see the girl who cheated on her boyfriend? Is that how you define it all? So in essence, if you shared your story, it would be boring at best and repugnant at worst."

Clutching the pillow, Daisy looked around, unable to recognize anything. She was in the dark, lost in that black, dimensionless cavern whose vastness could kill her.

"Your professional life is about other people's entertainment," Rita said. "Why do you make your personal life about it as well?"

"What do you mean?"

"Always presenting a pleasant exterior. Hiding your weaknesses because nobody would be interested or sympathetic. Or possibly because they might find it terribly upsetting."

She felt sick. "I don't know," she said. "I don't know what happened."

"All that time in rehab," Rita said. "Working with your trainer. What were you doing? Don't think, just answer."

Daisy's eyebrows twisted at the stupid question. "Recovering?"

"From what?"

"My leg," she said.

"What happened to your leg?"

"I was shot."

Rita's eyes bored into her. "Say it again."

"I was shot."

"Again."

"I was shot." Her throat was on fire. A flame ignited through the center of her chest, as if it were a piece of paper. Scorching brown, then the edges charring and curling before blue and gold flames licked through.

"James shot me," she said.

She felt hot. Her mouth was dry.

"You were shot," Rita said. Each word chiseled from the air. "It's a fact. Not a dramatic ploy for attention or a way to monopolize conversation. You had nothing to do with the scars on your leg. You were shot. Not by a random stranger but by someone you knew. He was your partner. You connected with him as a sister. In your own words, you gave him your time and your trust. You brought water to his desert. And he shot you and killed your friends."

"I'm cold," Daisy said, reaching for the throw blanket draped over the arm of the couch. Her teeth chattered as she drew it around her. "This is crazy," she said. "Why does this seem so obvious and yet at the same time it's like it's never occurred to me?"

"I was wondering that myself. It's as if you downplayed your entire role in this. And made Erik's experience of the shooting a much more terrible thing."

"Wasn't it? He tried to talk a gunman down. He watched James blow his head off."

"And you were shot in the leg and lying on the stage floor, all but bleeding to death next to your partner. And watching as James shot the windows of the booth where Erik was. You were bedridden for a month with a horrible injury. You nearly lost your life's dream. Wasn't that terrible as well?"

"It was. But..."

Rita was still.

"I don't know where I was going with that," Daisy said. Her skull was a vacuum. No train of thought, not even the tracks.

"A traumatic event like this is tantamount to being in war, Daisy. Tell me again what your father said to you."

"We come back from war changed," she whispered.

"Yes. Spiritually and emotionally changed but also neurologically. Trauma like this literally rearranges your brain's neural pathways. I've read studies about how traumatized youths have trouble regulating their body temperature or judging external temperature. Something I think about every week when I see you dressed inappropriately for the weather or burning your mouth on your coffee."

Flashing hot and cold, Daisy stared, thinking of all the singed tongues. All the times she misjudged how hot the water was in the shower and how it was always colder outside than she thought.

"You have a strong sense of responsibility, Daisy. You don't shy from ownership of your actions, which is admirable. But at the same time, sometimes a legitimate reason exists for poor judgement. I'd like to see you recognize the things beyond your control and acknowledge one or two of the truly shitty things that happened to you. And maybe even accept how being shot severely disabled your ability to take the temperature of a situation and make good decisions."

"I was shot," she said, shivering inside her burning skin.

"LUCKY SAID YOU held it all together," Rita said at the next session. "She pulled you out of bed, saying you had to get up or everyone else would fall down. Why would she say that?"

"I don't know. It was something dramatic to shock me back on track, I guess."

"Or was it true? Did you feel like you held it all together?"

Her thoughts rolled their eyes but she moved past them, looking for how she felt.

"Sort of," she said, blinking hard as she remembered the teary-eyed applause the first day she walked back into the dance studios. The hands reaching to touch, hold, hug and squeeze her. Support was in their touch but also a desperation: *Thank God. Our captain. Our leader. You're here.*

Will's pained eyes leaping from his shorn head as he learned to partner her again. Lucky fussing over her with the royal we. Kees embracing her at the end of the day, saying as long as she showed up, he'd show up. And Erik, who wanted her as close to him as possible, whenever possible. Pulling her into his lap or pushing his shoulders up against her chest in bed.

As long as you're all right, I'm all right. I just need you. Nothing else. Get up, Dais.

You have to get up. If you don't get up, we all fall down.

"You did get out of bed." Rita said. "You found it in you to get up."

"Erik needed me."

"You needed him, too."

"I... You know, after I got out of the hospital last December, and John and I drove down to my parents' house, I overheard him and my father talking. John said, 'I'm sorry I didn't call you sooner.' Pop kind of laughed a little and said, 'The time to call us was two years ago. And you didn't have our number.'"

Rita nodded.

"Nobody called for help," Daisy said. "Was that youth or ignorance?"

"I think youth certainly played a part. When you're full of adolescent resilience, you feel nothing can permanently hurt you."

"I was hurt," Daisy said softly. "But I was lucky. Other people I knew were killed. I was still alive. And it's not like I..."

Rita leaned forward a fraction. "Not like you...?"

A long, liquid moment where Daisy stared, mouth open. Pressing, reaching, groping for the tantalizing revelation just beyond her mind's reach. Finding and pushing the words out was like trying to string beads on the end of an unraveled and frayed string.

"I don't know," she said.

"Try."

Her brain dug deep, scrabbled in the barren dirt and came up empty-handed. Except for, of all things, Christine Fiskare's face. When she was sitting on the edge of the hospital bed, and she and Daisy were discussing what to do about the man they loved.

I need to talk to you as a mother. He's breaking down... He wouldn't get out of the car after the last funeral. David almost had to carry him. He can't eat. I've never seen him not be able to eat.

"He was sick. He'd been through so much..."

"And you hadn't?"

"I had but..." Her breathing was growing choppy.

"But what?"

"But it was different."

"How?"

The words were sharp, cutting the inside of her mouth. "It wasn't as bad."

"Why?"

"Because I... Because... I can't, I don't know, I don't know what's wrong with me."

"Try this on," Rita said. "And don't be afraid to say it doesn't fit. But within your circle of friends, the friends who survived the shooting, something made you feel your pain didn't measure up to theirs. You didn't hurt as much. You weren't quite in the same club."

Daisy felt her eyes bulge. Tears spilled over and down her face. "Yes."

"Especially Erik."

"No." She shook her head in vehement denial. "He never implied he had it worse."

"It's not what he did. It's what you *felt*. What you believed to be true. You downplayed your part and thought his was the worse experience."

"But it... It was. Because I didn't remember."

"You didn't remember the shooting."

"Yes..."

"Why did that make you different? Tell me."

"They all remembered. Erik could tell a story. David, Lucky and John, even Will had tangible memories. I had nothing. I got plucked out of that place and woke up in the hospital and missed everything. Their dreams had imagery and context and mine were a black cavern of nothingness. I was scared of nothing."

"Go on."

"Erik went to the funerals. I was safe in the hospital while he went to four funerals in three days."

"You were bedridden."

"I know but... I know now. Now that you're pointing it out to me, but why... What does all this mean? I don't understand." She hammered her fists on her knees, confused and frustrated as her memories were dissected and twisted.

"What do I do with this? I didn't consciously think 'Oh, I had it easy. I shouldn't complain.' I only know that I..."

"That you what?"

She was frantic to be understood. "I loved him."

"But you couldn't let him hear you scream. Just like you couldn't let your father hear you scream."

Anger swept through her and she seized it. "Don't give me any childhood psychobabble bullshit. Don't you blame my father for this. I *love* my father."

"Of course you do. And you kept him safe."

"I told you what happened. Hearing me scream would kill him."

"He's a grown man. And he's your father. I think he could have handled it. You were lying in a hospital bed with your leg shot and your calf sliced open, yet you thought about your father's needs first. That's incredibly selfless, but it also might have been damaging."

"I screamed on Erik. I screamed then. I threw up in front of him. I threw up *on* him."

"In the hospital."

"Yes."

"But ever again?"

"I...I don't remember. No."

"So just the once you flayed your own self open and let him see you weak. Shattered and broken."

"Like glass," she whispered.

"And what happened shortly after?"

Daisy stared, confused. "He went home?"

"Before that?"

"He broke down. He collapsed."

Rita nodded.

Daisy clicked her tongue in contempt. "You're saying those two things are joined? Connected in my mind? I let him see me wrecked and helpless and shortly after he broke down and left. And I tied those things together and thought *whoa, better not do that again.* Who thinks like that?"

"Nobody actively thinks like that," Rita said. "But certain primitive parts of your brain *only* know how to think like that."

Daisy crossed her arms. "I'm not entirely on board with this, but I'm not entirely dismissing it, either."

"It's all food for thought. And not all of it will taste good."

DAISY ALMOST CANCELLED her next session, weary of self-introspection and dreading what would be the next thing to emerge from the dirt. At the same time, she was fascinated by the process. And, she had to admit, she was feeling a shift deep within. Not a window shade snapping up to flood her with clarity, but a slow dawn made up of tiny insights. Things were shifting around in her head and heart and gut. Lining up. Matching edges. Nodding and thinking, *Yes. I see. This feels strange but it makes sense.*

She gathered her courage and her coffee and she went.

"Let's talk about your dreams," Rita said.

"Which ones?"

She turned a few pages. "Your dreams were of black nothingness. Or else you were vaginally consuming Erik to save him."

Even the mention of the dream made Daisy squirm. "And?"

"When was the last time you had the black dream?"

"A long time ago, I guess."

"When exactly, do you remember?"

She had to think hard. "I don't think I've had it since the window broke."

"When the window broke in the diner."

"Yes."

"And what happened?"

"I remembered watching James shoot the glass of the booth."

From far away, the sound of smashing glass.

"Where you had just been," Rita said.

Another window shattered. Closer.

"Yes."

"What were you doing in there?"

Her fingers pulled at the fringe on the pillows. "I was with Erik."

"What were you doing?"

"We were talking about the way we'd had sex the night before. Talking about love and us and everything. What are you getting at?" With a wooly snap, a strand of yarn pulled free in her fingers. She tucked it in a guilty fist.

"What did you tell him you wanted to do?"

Fuck him? she thought, and flinched. No. Something else. She'd been sitting in his lap. Straddling his lap, in fact. He had half an erection and his eyes were dripping lust. The previous night's memories clung like perfume to her skin and all she wanted was to...

"I wanted to ditch the rehearsal and leave," she said. "I wanted to go back to bed with him."

Behind her head the window exploded. A roar of icy wind and a tempest of snowflakes from inside the shattered globe.

"Oh my God," she said. Her hands flew to her mouth. Through the blizzard her mind screamed the impossible.

"It's impossible," she said, but even as the impassioned words left her, her body was telling another story. She was shaking now. Her bones rattled.

I left him.

A splintering sound in her head.

"What happened in the booth, Daisy?"

"I wanted to take him out," she said. "But then I left..."

A slow motion cracking. Daisy threaded her hands through her hair and started to pull.

"I left him in there," she said, her voice rising up shrill. Of its own accord her head turned, twisting back over her shoulder.

James raised his arm and shot the glass.

(Erik Erik Erik Erik Erik Erik.)

"I left him in there. I left him and then I watched James shoot out the windows."

"Did you think he had been killed?" Rita asked. "Do you remember thinking anything when you saw the windows breaking?"

Her head tipped back and forth. "I could have saved him," she said. "I could have saved us. All I had to do was... If only I had gone with that impulse. I... We would have been out of the theater. Far away from it all and I wouldn't have been shot and I wouldn't have broken..."

But she did break. Broke and shattered into a thousand razor shards. Erik didn't even look back after she aimed, fired and blew their love to smithereens.

He just left.

"No, I left him," she said. "I left him first." She dissolved into weeping, endless tears streaming from her eyes and mouth and nose. Endless. It was endless. She would sit on this couch and cry for the rest of her life.

"It wasn't your fault," Rita said softly. "You had no control over what happened that day."

"But what about the other days," she cried. "Those belong to me, those are mine and I can't do this anymore."

"Can't do what?"

"I walked away from Erik when I should've stayed. And I stayed with David when I should've walked away. That's my big revelation, now what am I supposed to do with it? Tell me. What does it change? Nothing. I can't stand this, Rita. It was easier to cut myself. It was sick, yes, but it *accomplished* something. Cutting into how I feel, digging into the psychological dirt doesn't *do* anything. Nothing's changed. It still hurts so much and I still need him to know I'm sorry."

"Of course," Rita said. "It's difficult to be unresolved."

"I would do anything, anything but... What am I supposed to do? I was stupid and weak and I cracked. I let him down. I never let anyone down in my life. I've always been there, I've always been strong. But I was shot."

She cried hard, terrible sobs from her knees into her palms. Tears from the years gone by. Tears from future years she had yet to get through. The pores of her skin wept with her, wailed and pleaded to be torn and rent with grief, to let the blood flow with her tears.

"I hate what I did. I hate myself for what I did. I fucked up, I admit it. I'm not denying it or hiding it or making excuses. I'm trying to face him but he won't open the door. I was shot and I fell apart and I fucked up and I'm *sorry.*"

She slumped, tattered and wrecked, a dozen balled-up clumps of tissue at her feet.

"It makes no difference how sorry I am," she said. "That's what kills me. It makes no difference. I can't do anything about what I did except be sorry and want him to come back. Every day I whisper it inside my head or out loud when no one is listening. It's what I chant inside when I want to cut myself. Every day I wake up with a man who loves me, and yet I'm reaching out to Erik and thinking, *Come back to me, please come back...*"

A LITTLE FEVER

AS USUAL, JOHN WAS at the apartment when she got home. Curled up under the quilt, napping. And as usual, his arm folded it back for her.

She sat on the bed. Her eyes ached. Her heart pulsed with a pain she didn't think was possible to feel, let alone endure.

I can't do this anymore.

You have to. If you don't get up, everyone else falls down.

No. I don't have to. I don't have to get up at all. For anyone. Erik doesn't care. Why should I?

"Honey," John whispered.

A single sob cracked out of her chest, bounced off the walls as her mouth clamped down tight.

A creak of bedsprings as he scooted over and curved his body around hers at the edge of the bed. His hand soft on her back.

"I know it sucks," he said. "I know how bad it hurts."

You know nothing, she thought, trembling with the effort not to cry. She was angry he was there and hated herself for it. Because he cared more than Erik did.

"Tell me, Dais," he said, stroking her back. "Tell me what happened."

"It's hard," she said. "It's hard having so little to give you. Feeling like I have nothing but the scraps of myself on my best days. And then coming home from my sessions so shredded and raw. And you want me to tell you, but it's nothing but him. It's *him*, John. And Lancaster. And glass. In my bones and my skin and I can't get it out. I don't know how you can stay here and watch this. Day after day, you give me your heart and your soul and get next to nothing in return. I honestly don't know how or why you stay."

She sank her face into her hands, curved and curled like an ampersand of misery.

"If I want to leave, you'll be the first to know, Dais. And we'll have something called a conversation about it."

"I'm sorry," she said to her palms. "I'm...lost and flailing and if you weren't here I'd probably be slicing my skin right now. I'm sorry. You wanted to know and that's how I feel. I'm sorry. I'm no better than I was a couple months ago. But I'm glad you're here. And...I'm sorry."

"I'll get you some water," he said. "Be right back. Take your shoes off."

Face still buried, she heeled off her shoes. Then she drank the water John brought, icy and numbing against her battered, abused throat.

"I go around with either a lump in my throat or a knot in my chest," she said. "Like my heart is slowly being ripped out of my ribcage. Sometimes I wonder if I have cancer... Or if I'll end up with cancer. This perpetual hurting. How much damage is it doing, how many years am I taking off my life with this kind of constant stress?"

"It's poison," he said, curled around her again. "It hurts coming out. The hardest thing to do is let it hurt. Let it get worse before it gets better."

She forced her eyes not to roll as she set the glass on the bedside table. One more platitude of recovery and she would scream the building down to its girders.

"Tell me what you dug up today," he said. "Show me. Same way you showed me the glass once. You take away its power, remember?"

She took a deep breath and tried to pick out the salient points and string them together. The guilty responsibility implanted in her subconscious as she watched James shoot out the windows of the booth. Thinking if only she had acted on a spontaneous, sexual impulse, she and Erik wouldn't have been in the theater. How the thought had been suppressed and buried for all these years, save for an inexplicable need to save Erik while they were making love. How the broken diner window had somehow unleashed it all again.

"It's crazy," she said. "On one hand, I don't believe it. I can't wrap my mind around the idea. It makes no sense, it seems too convenient. Too pat and contrived. And yet, when Rita and I put it all together, I couldn't stop crying. Part of me recognizes it as the truth. It's what happened and I believe it. God, you must think I'm nuts."

John's hand had kept up a steady stroke along her back. Winding his wrist around the length of her hair and letting it fall through his fingers. He listened like an expert—not interrupting or interjecting, only humming to show he was with her.

A long moment of exhausted silence then. Outside, the city sang its incessant song. The clang of tires driving across metal plates, the trumpet of car horns and the dull, rumbling roar underneath it all. Daisy slowly became aware of the apartment being a single hexagon cell in the hive of her building. And the building being one of dozens in her block. Hundreds in her neighborhood. Millions of windows looking down on the noisy streets. Millions of stories behind those windows all making a collective rumble.

How you could feel so lonely and misunderstood in the midst of all those buzzing lives.

"Hey," John said.

She looked down at him. His handsome, loving gaze staring up at her. He hadn't laughed or dismissed her. Or tried to put his own spin on her pain. She laid her hand on his face.

"I love you," she said. "I'm sorry I'm so out of my mind."

His hand circled her wrist. "Can I tell you something now? Come here, honey. Lie down."

She fell onto her side, pushed her shoulders up against his chest. Let him cover her up and hold her.

"Do you remember," he said. "After James dropped you in rehearsal? The day I ran into you and him on the stairs?"

She nodded.

"And I threw my dick around a little and got him in that armlock against the wall?"

"Did Will teach you how to do that?"

"No, Erik did."

She turned her head back a little. "He did?"

"Yeah. I don't think you knew about the secret army of brothers keeping an eye on you after the incident. Will and David, naturally, but Neil Martinez, too. And me. Fish talked to each of us, asking to keep an eye out for trouble. He didn't want James anywhere near you. When he talked to me, he said something like, 'I don't care what you do. Rough him up if you need to.' And I was like, 'Dude, he's a freakin' *dancer,* not a street thug. Jesus, artists don't get violent, we get dramatic. Anyway, I don't know the first thing about roughing people up. What, you want me to grand jeté into his face?'

"So he showed me a couple moves, taught me how to punch. I remember wondering who taught him that kind of shit if he didn't have a father."

"Will," Daisy said. "He went to taekwondo classes with Will."

"Ah. Anyway, I figured I'd never need it. But then I did. Or rather, I didn't need to do what I did but I... I was just..."

She rolled over to face him. "Tell me."

"I was in love with you," he said. "At the same time I loved Fish like a brother. My own brother always kept his distance from me. I know my being a dancer embarrassed him. It was nothing like the abuse James suffered but still. I never felt like Tom had my back when I was taking crap from the jocks at school. He sure as shit never took the time to show me how to fight. So when Erik, someone I admired, took me aside and gave me, one, his trust with the thing he loved most and two, the means to fight for you if I had to... It meant a lot. It felt big-brotherish. It soothed my ego. It helped me reconcile being a dancer with being a man or whatever. Anyway, when I came across you and James on the stairs, I didn't have to do what I did. It wasn't necessary. He wasn't going to hurt you. He was such a sorry-ass mess by that point. But it was you. And it was the job Fish gave me. And to be honest, it felt really fucking good."

The tiniest trembling was coming from under his clothes. She put her cheek against his chest and listened to the hard beat under his ribs.

"So after you left..."

"What happened?"

"Well he kind of shoved me off, shrugged his jacket and his pride back into place. He was like Judd Nelson in *The Breakfast Club.* He said, 'Check out little Opie. I think I might actually have a hard-on.' I was high on testosterone by then, I can't remember what I said. He was like, 'She's out of your league, kid. It was a nice rescue attempt but you'll never fuck her.' Then he was trying to get under my skin, implying he had an idea of what you were like in bed."

"What...?"

"Oh, stupid shit. 'You know I slept a couple nights at Jay Street. Holy shit, you should hear how Fish makes her scream. She's a handful in the sack, bet she gets her legs around him in ways you can't imagine.'"

"He never slept at Jay Street," she said.

"He was just trying to get his pride back," he said. "I see it now. I could've helped."

"No, you couldn't," she whispered.

"Maybe not help, but I could've been decent. Been the bigger man. I could've walked away, I could've done the right thing. Instead I got up in his face and said 'At least I didn't piss my art away.' Then of course I had to twist the knife a little. 'Where do you think you'll go with this on your transcript? Think Marie or Kees will write you a glowing letter of recommendation? I'll be dancing your role in *Who Cares?* in a couple of weeks. You'll be applying to community college back in Pittsburgh. Won't that be fun? Living at home, dodging your old man and taking care of your poor, drunk mother...'"

He sighed, his heart kicking up under Daisy's face. "That's the shit I had to wrestle out of my soul in therapy. Feeling like I'd helped put James over the edge. Like I'd driven a couple of nails into the coffin of what he'd done to his life and I had a part in what happened next. Because when the shots went off and I was in the wing with Lucky... I had her tight under me and I looked out across the stage and saw you lying there in the blood. This frozen second where James was standing over you with the gun in his hand. And then he looked at me..."

"John," she whispered.

"I thought he killed you. He looked at me and all I could think was *I'm sorry, Fish. You trusted me. I wasn't supposed to let this happen, I was supposed to be guarding her. Instead I made her a target and now she's dead.*"

She was crying then. A relieved river of validation pouring out of her eyes and nose and throat. She wound her arms up around his neck, pulled herself into him and clung hard.

"You need to know it makes sense to me," he said, holding her tight, pressing her head to his shoulder. "What you're doing and what you're feeling and pulling out of your guts. It makes *sense* to me. I can deal with you thinking it makes you unlovable because I'm going to love you anyway. But you have to know, please know it doesn't make you a mystery to me. Don't be afraid to tell me how you think you could have done something to keep it from happening because I get it. You have no idea how much I get it."

He held her. Rocked her until she quieted. His hands ran cool over her flushed face and dry, burning eyes.

"Feels like you have a little fever," he said. "Want me to get you some Tylenol?"

"No. Hold me. Don't go away."

He gathered her close.

"Thank you," she said. "For being here when I got home tonight."

"I'll be wherever you need me to be."

And it was clear to her then, how John was always where she needed him. Stepping in to dance when James left her partnerless. Showing up to protect her on the stairs. Coming out of nowhere to call her name on a random day. Waiting at the stage door of the Met to see her home. Pulling her out from under a table. Forcing her sliced skin into the light. And having the guts to call for help.

She held his head. His air filled her with peace. "I love you."

His mouth shaped a smile as it grazed hers. "James was wrong about that, wasn't he?"

They kissed again, longer. Her hands came up and undid a button on her shirt. Then the next one. And quickly the rest, then the clasp of her bra. Peeling open to him, her skin on fire. His cool hands slid to cup her breasts and his mouth fell open under hers.

"He was wrong," she said.

They rolled, pulled and yanked at their clothes, slid together and understood each other. The windows buzzed, a single cell in a hive now dripping honey and telling the sweetest of stories.

"I HAD NO IDEA JOHN carried a piece of James around with him," Daisy said. "It makes me wonder if everyone who was in the theater that day thinks they could have changed it. If only they had done or said one thing differently..."

"James was coming into the theater no matter what you did," Rita said. "And the shooting would have irrevocably changed your life whether you were in the theater or not. Will or Lucky could've been killed and it would have been just as devastating for you. A different kind of guilt and responsibility to carry around."

"I didn't think of it that way."

"Nothing you did or didn't do could have changed the outcome, Daisy. James came into the theater and certain parts of your life were no longer under your control. "

"I tried so hard to be strong."

"And maybe you did hold it all together," Rita said. "I don't doubt you were a bastion for your friends. A rock. Maybe even a mascot. The symbol of survival. And when you cracked and fucked up, it seemed everything and everyone scattered. That's a terrible emotional burden to carry."

"More than ever," Daisy said absently. "I wish I could talk to Erik. Just to tell him about some of these things. I feel like I could explain it so much better now. Make a better apology."

"Not being able to atone is a trial," Rita said. "For Erik to cut you off and disconnect with no closure, without giving you a chance to show your remorse is a terrible burden to carry."

"But I fucked up."

"Not admirable, no, not your finest moment. It was a thoughtless and cruel thing to do. An egregious error of judgment when your judgment was badly impaired. We've already gone through what happened that day and dug into what may have driven you to it, so let's take it in the other direction now. You're full of guilt and remorse and shame and self-punishment. We need to channel that away from your body to somewhere else. Somewhere safe until Erik turns around again. You are beating your head and fists against a closed door—"

"A glass door," Daisy said. "Glass and windows. It's all I think of."

"And closed. You cannot resolve your regret until the door, or the window opens. And that's the unfortunate unknown. Will it ever open? I don't know, Daisy. But what can we do with this remorse and regret? How can we get you to evolve even though you are not resolved?"

"I keep thinking about James. When he was out in the yard, looking up at Will's window."

"Why?"

"He wanted Will. He was in love and he was out in the dark and the cold, looking up at the one thing he wanted. And I'm him now. I'm James. Out in the yard in the cold. Looking up at the window, wanting what I love to look out and see me. To come down and talk to me and give me a chance."

"Yes," Rita said, nodding. "I can see that."

"I'm looking up at Erik's window. He went down to talk to James but he won't come down for me."

"You both broke each other's hearts."

"I changed." She exhaled heavy and dark. "Erik was... He liked when things behaved the way he expected them to."

"And people."

"Well, sure."

"Including you."

Especially her. But she had fallen apart. Smashed like a window and scattered in pieces. She hadn't behaved the way he expected.

And he left.

"But it was my fault," she said, and noticed the words didn't cut quite as deeply as before.

"You were shot," Rita said quietly. "The girl he expected and the behavior he expected were shot."

"It doesn't excuse it."

"But it helps explain it."

Daisy closed her eyes and reached soft hands to touch the things which had been beyond her control.

She had to agree.

FARFAR OCH FARMOR

THE COMPANY WAS IN the final rehearsals for the season premiere of *Aïda*. In a week, Daisy would be bare-legged on the stage of the Metropolitan Opera House. Scars out in the open. To explore the options of covering them, she knocked on the tiny office door of Vincent Callegro, the new head of the Met's makeup department.

He was eating a sandwich and doing the crossword and didn't look thrilled by the interruption. He had a reputation for being intolerant of divas, fools or drama. She introduced herself and got to the point.

"I'll be quick," she said, rolling up the left leg of her sweat pants. "Can we do anything about these? Or do you think anyone will even notice?"

Vincent's face was expressionless as he stared at her leg and finished chewing and swallowing.

"I'm interrupting your lunch, I'll come back," she said.

Vincent wiped his mouth and looked up at her with hooded, unreadable eyes. "Two things," he said. "First, you're the little girl who went on in *La Gioconda* last week."

She nodded, her face filling with warm pride. The Met always hired stars from American Ballet Theater to lead the famous *Dance of the Hours* ballet in *Gioconda*'s third act. Just before curtain, Matilda Schenke tripped on a loose cable and sprained her ankle. Next thing Daisy knew, she was being sewn into Matilda's $15,000 red tutu while

Igor Koslov—one of ABT's Russian superstars and now her partner—was shaking her hand.

They had exactly twenty minutes of rehearsal and then she was onstage, unannounced and anonymous in front of a full Saturday night subscription house. Dancing half the steps from memory and the rest from Igor's whispered cues. She blanked out on the choreography for her solo in the coda, so she whipped out double and triple fouetté turns until the audience was screaming. She and Igor took four bows and the *Times* threw her a posy in the Sunday "Arts" section.

Matilda Schenke took an unfortunate fall before the third act. An unidentified understudy took over the role and took home the audience's heart as well. Hopefully, we'll see this mystery ballerina again while Schenke is on the mend.

"Second," Vincent said, and bent over to raise the leg of his pressed trousers. Above his argyle sock, the scar was unmistakable.

"Wow, that's a beauty," Daisy said, her stomach doing a small flip. "I ordered the matching set."

She twisted her leg so he could see the other side.

He nodded, a smile lifting up his mouth and a bit of his stiff reserve slipping off his shoulders. "Quite a thing to wake up to. I took one look at my flesh bulging out and they had to sedate me again."

"I screamed for about five minutes and then I threw up. Then they sedated me."

"Well, well," he said, rolling his pant leg down again. "It's not often I'm surprised this way, Miss...Bianco?"

"Daisy. What happened to you?" she asked, heart thumping a little stronger.

"To strangers I say a freak accident. To you I will confess to screwing around with fireworks. One exploded near a bucket of nuts and bolts. I turned just in time to take it in the leg. Then an infection set in. Next thing I know, I'm auditioning for *Silence of the Lambs*."

Daisy laughed.

He cleared a space on his desk. "Put your foot up here, dear."

Still holding her pant leg out of the way, she set her foot carefully between sketchbooks, watercolor sets and papers. Vincent put on his reading glasses and peered. "This looks like a gunshot wound," he said, pointing to her thigh.

"It is. The bullet severed the artery. My leg didn't take kindly to the graft and the pressure started building up. You know the rest."

"Tell me, how does a ballerina find herself in the line of fire?"

"When she goes to school at Lancaster University."

A silence shimmied between them.

"I see," he said, setting a warm, respectful hand on her shin. "Then these cannot be your only scars."

She shook her head.

"I'm sorry," he said. "I have no other words."

"You know," she said. "Believe it or not, this is the first time I've thrown the topic out to someone casually. I mean voluntarily." She smiled, letting her eyes and nose wrinkle. "I'm only just learning how to talk about it. And truthfully, I don't know what we're supposed to say now."

"Well then, we'll go back to the matter at hand. Will anyone notice? The question is, my dear, will you mind if people notice? Because my job is to either transform you into someone else or make you feel beautiful as you are. If you need help with either, I'm your man."

Daisy's throat grew warm. Partly with gratitude. Partly because his Italian accent was so reminiscent of Marie del'Amici.

"For opening night, I mind," she said. "Maybe in time I won't."

"Come early at dress rehearsal then," he said. "You can watch me do it, learn how. And in time you can cover them yourself as you see fit."

"All right. Thank you."

"No, Miss Bianco," he said, shaking her hand and laying his other one on top. "Thank you."

The encounter gave her courage, as did finding a bearer of the same war flag. And a week later, when she stood on a table in the dressing room and Vincent explained to his assistants various techniques for covering the scars, she felt almost blasé. People passing through stopped and stared, openly curious. Some asked questions, making exclamations of shock, disbelief or concern at her answers. Whenever she started feeling self-conscious, she looked down at Vincent, who winked over the rims of his glasses or smiled at her.

It was a novelty for a few weeks. As telling the story became more and more natural, it became ordinary. A line on her resume, not the caption on her headshot.

"You can make your remorse ordinary, you know," Rita said.

Daisy was skeptical. It seemed remorse had taken permanent possession and put down roots too deep to yank out.

"Let's just accept it," Rita said. "You will always be sorry for what you did to Erik. It matters. Deeply. But you can let your sorrow accompany you on the road of life without letting it be the road itself. Without letting it define the rest of your life. You don't have to walk around with a scarlet A on your chest."

It could be part of everything.

"I'm sorry, I will always be sorry," Daisy said slowly. "I love you, I will always love you. But—"

"No," Rita said, holding up a finger. "Not but. *And.*"

"And?" Daisy said.

"And," Rita said.

"I love you, I will always love you," Daisy said. "And I am... And I am moving on."

"You can do both at the same time."

"And," Daisy said, staring.

"What else?" Rita said.

"I love you and I'm letting go."

"What else?"

"I'm sorry, I will always be sorry. I love you, I will always love you. And..." Daisy drew in her breath. "And I'm forgiving myself."

IT BECAME HER MANTRA. Changing *but* to *and.* Whispering or thinking "I'm sorry, I love you *and* I forgive myself" when the sorrow threatened to drown her in the night. Trusting she could do all things simultaneously. Channeling the regret into a section of her being, not letting it become her entire being.

She picked at the tight stitches on her invisible scarlet letter and gradually let it fall free. It belonged in a keepsake box of learned lessons, not on her chest as a constant, shaming reminder. As if she could forget.

Spring came. She went around bare-legged, letting the air and sun touch her scars. Trees and flowers bloomed in the park and space bloomed in her apartment. She shoved things aside in closets and dressers to make room for John.

"I just realized the date," he said, setting down an armload of boxes. "Tomorrow is April nineteenth."

"It is? You're right. I lost track of time."

"Four years," he said.

She touched his face. "Seems a good day to make a beginning."

He hummed agreement but his eyes were off to the side. She followed their gaze to the cardboard box where she kept the things Erik left at Jay Street. She'd have to get creative if it was going to go back in her closet.

Or maybe it was time to accept she had no room for it anymore.

She wasn't onstage that night. After John left for work, she unpacked the box. Jeans and three shirts. Erik's pocket knives and Allen wrenches. Guitar picks, strings and a capo. His book of Swedish folk tales. The rest were the pictures, cards and notes she pulled out of his wastepaper basket.

She held the clothes to her nose but they only smelled of cardboard. Her fingers dipped into the front pocket of the jeans, pulled out a crumpled dollar bill, a dime and four pennies and some lint. The other front pocket had a couple of small screws and washers and a guitar pick. And more lint. She searched the other pockets, then gazed down at the small pile.

"Honestly," she said.

She gathered John's bag of dirty laundry along with the contents of the bathroom hamper, added Erik's clothes and took it all to the washing machines in the basement.

Enjoy the threesome, she thought, slamming the lid and giving the dial a vicious spin.

Back upstairs, she fished from a hidden compartment in her jewelry box a small scotch-taped lock of Erik's hair. She put it into an envelope and added the pocket finds and the lint. From another hidden place she pulled the packet of love notes, cards, pictures, the empty bag of Swedish Fish and all the other keepsakes. Everything went into an accordion folder on her closet shelf, behind her bank statements and tax returns. She wasn't ready to throw the mementos away, probably she never would. But she could handle assembling them in one unemotional place, up high and out of sight.

She sank onto the bed and opened the book of folk tales. She couldn't remember how it had gotten into her room at Jay Street. Part of the invisible migration of objects back and forth.

The text was entirely in Swedish. Peppered with umlauts, slashed Os and ringed As. Erik couldn't read it but he loved the pictures. Every other page was a full-color illustration. Giants, trolls and werewolves. Golden queens and princesses in glass mountains. Roosters, lame dogs and hornet swarms.

The inside flyleaf was inscribed in neat, looped handwriting. A Christmas dedication to a grandson: *Till Byron Erik. Med kärlek vid jul. Farfar och Farmor.*

Swedes had different terms for maternal and paternal grandparents, Daisy remembered. Farfar was father's father. Farmor was father's mother.

On the back flyleaf, in careful, childish print: *Erik Fiskare. 307 Hugunin Street. Clayton, NY.*

She fetched the laundry, folded Erik's clothes, smoothing them square and trim. She packed the other possessions tight around them and put the book on top. She let it go with a sighing regret, not a crippling grief. The box was just a box now, not a shrine. The religion had gone out of his belongings.

The next day, after John left to run some errands, she squared her shoulders and dialed Erik's number. One more time. She didn't go in crawling, but standing on her feet, head on his level. He'd ignored her for three years. Rita said his statute of limitations was over. It bolstered Daisy's courage, having the tiny bit of reassurance that Erik, perhaps, was slightly in the wrong now as well.

The same hollow silence on the other end of the line, although he did manage, "Hi."

"It's the nineteenth," she said. "I was thinking about you."

"That's right." His voice was tight, as usual. Like he was threading words through a needle. And yet her ear thought it detected the tiniest bit of hesitation, as if he weren't fully committed to this strategy anymore. A flickering flame of conciliation. She let her breath hover over it, fighting the urge to pile on tinder and kindling.

"How are you?" she said.

"I'm fine and I have to go." The flame snuffed itself out, leaving only a wisp of smoke. "I'm late for a game."

"Erik, please. It's been three years." She kept her voice low and gentle. The voice she used with the drug-addicted babies.

I know. I know it hurts. Please know that I know, Erik.

"Are we ever going to talk about this?"

Silence.

She closed her eyes. *Please let's talk about it. It doesn't have to mean reconciliation but it's been three years. We're older, we're wiser. Can't we have a conversation?*

He hung up.

Daisy opened her eyes. They were dry as she put the phone down.

She tore a piece of paper in half and wrote one last note to say she was sorry, he would never know how much. She would love him until she died. And she was done now. She taped the note to the inside of the box and taped the flaps shut.

Before leaving the apartment she wrote a second note, letting John know she was going to the post office.

It was important her boyfriend know where she was.

NOT BAD, MARGE

JULIE VALENTE CONVINCED HER to go to Chicago where they were holding non-union auditions for *Phantom of the Opera*.

"I don't sing," Daisy said.

"You're auditioning for the ballerinas," Julie said. "You don't have to sing. And anyway, you have a sweet little voice."

"I do not."

"You know, when I don't hear you talking to yourself—"

"Those are private conversations."

"—I hear you singing to yourself. You're right on pitch. Probably with regular voice lessons you could have some decent game."

The idea of a girls' weekend away was more appealing than the audition. And in Chicago, where Daisy had never been.

"It'll be fabulous," Julie said. "My girlfriend practically lives on top of Wrigley Park. We can watch a ballgame from her roof. We'll have the quintessential Windy City tour."

"Go," John said. "Have a good time."

With Julie's help, Daisy put her resume in order. Starting with the training at the Gladwyne Academy of Dance. Her acceptance into the junior company of the Philadelphia Youth Ballet when she was only twelve. Lancaster Conservatory awarding her the Brighton Scholarship.

Her roles and her degree. The year in the corps of the Pennsylvania Ballet. Ending with her present employment at the Metropolitan Opera.

Not bad, she thought. *Considering I got shot and had a bit of a mental breakdown along the way.*

"You're talking to yourself again," Julie said.

"Private conversation," Daisy said. "Do you mind?"

"I MISS YOU," John said on the phone.

Daisy lay on her back in the nest of the hotel bed. The ceiling swayed slightly. "I'm a little lit," she said.

"It's not even nine o'clock."

"I know. Drinking beer in the sun at the ballgame. Then I don't know how many bottles of wine at dinner. I'm going to be hurting on the plane tomorrow."

"How did the audition go?"

"I didn't get kicked or put."

"Didn't get what?"

She tried again. "Picked or cut."

"Oh my God, you are lit."

"I made it to the third round. Got singled out a lot. Six of us were left by the end and we had to sing. But they don't tell you if you got a role. They'll keep your name, headshot and resume on file and if they need someone on the tour, they'll call."

"I see. Well, it's good experience."

She turned on her side, curling up to the phone. "What did you do today?"

"Worked out, got my ass kicked. Took master class with Danilo Fuertes, got my ass kicked. Stage fighting workshop—we learned the street scene from *Romeo and Juliet.* I nearly got impaled with a sword. Came home tired and horny to an empty apartment. Poor me."

Daisy giggled. "Poor you."

"Took a shower and thought about my gorgeous girlfriend's hot body."

"Talk slower."

"Rubbed...one...out...."

"What was I doing?"

"Helping."

"Then what did you do?"

"Cuddled with myself and fell asleep. Got up, made something to eat. Puttered around. My brother called wanting to go out. Trying to decide if I'll go or stay here and be horny."

"Again?"

"Again. It's a chronic condition."

"What's the cure?"

"Your ass back in New York where it belongs."

"Tomorrow."

"Drink a lot of water. I'll be on you whether you're hungover or not."

"Promise?"

"I'm putting the 'come' in 'homecoming.'"

She smiled against the phone. "Night, Opie. I love you."

"I love you," he said. "And don't fucking call me Opie."

SHE AND JULIE shared a cab from LaGuardia. It dropped Daisy on 110th Street where she could pick up a cross-town bus to the West Side.

"See you at the slave pens," Julie said, blowing a kiss out the window.

"You're my favorite." Daisy blew a kiss back and waved.

The late August afternoon was glorious. The humidity had calmed. A lengthening in the sun's shadows hinted at fall. On one side of the street, storefronts announced back-to-school sales. On the other, Central Park reared up yellow and green. Daisy gazed out the bus window at her city.

She realized she was happy.

Her chest was open. Her stomach was calm. She stood out at a musical theater audition and made the final cut. Possibly she could get a job out of it. But she already had a job. She was making it. She was paying her way, doing what she loved. In the Big Apple. Warm and gold on an August evening. She was home.

She had done it.

Not bad, she thought again, smiling at her reflection. *Not bad at all, Marge.*

She transferred to the Columbus Avenue bus and rode smiling to 86th Street, where she pulled the bell and alighted into the soft air. The skies over New Jersey were turning pink and orange. Maybe she and John could take a walk over to Riverside Park tonight, go out to eat.

After homecoming, of course.

"Where's Johnny?" she called in the front hall.

Silence.

She set her keys down and heeled off her shoes. "The mistress of the house hath returned."

More silence. She wondered if he was sleeping.

Bag still on her shoulder, she rifled through the mail. Bills and the latest *Dance Magazine.* And an airmail envelope with Will's address. "What's up, asshole," she said happily.

"Hi."

She looked up. John stood in the hall. He did not look happy to see her. To the point where Daisy ran a quick moral inventory, wondering what she could have possibly done.

"What's wrong?" she said.

He crossed his arms and leaned against the wall. "Erik called."

For a crystal second, the universe ceased. Then Daisy's heart gave a lurch and dropped a load of adrenaline from her chest into her stomach.

Careful, her mind warned her. *Be extremely careful right now, Marguerite.*

"When?" she said.

"Last night."

She stared at him. Sweat trickled from armpit to elbow as her heart kicked her breastbone with thick, audible thuds.

"Oh," she said. She let her bag slide off her shoulder to the floor. "What did he want?" she asked. Her voice was steady but her body had gone numb. She was nothing but air and stomach and that pounding, thudding heart.

"He was looking for something."

Her throat tightened up. *Don't cry,* she thought. *Don't you fucking start crying.*

"Looking for what?" It would help if John would be a little less elusive.

"His necklace. The gold one he used to wear. You know."

Now tears prickled her eyes. "He lost it?"

"That's what he said."

"Oh." She swallowed hard. "Well, that sucks. It was an heirloom. All the men in his family wore–"

"I know what it was, Dais. Where is it?"

"I don't know." The accusation should have filled her with outrage. Instead, the clamp around her throat tightened with something that felt like guilt. "I don't have it," she said, feeling on trial. "Everything I had of his went back to him in that box."

"Are you sure you didn't keep it back as bait?"

"Are you seriously doing this?" she asked. "Springing this on me the second I walk in the door. Hinting I have something to do with him calling?"

"How did he get our number?"

She held out her hands. "Maybe he called my parents. Maybe he called directory assistance. It's not like I'm in hiding."

"Do you have his necklace?"

"I do not have it. I don't have anything of his. I sent it all back. I moved on."

They glared at each other, prickling and defensive.

"Did he say anything else?" Daisy asked. She meant to be conversational but it came out reeking of desperation.

Oh, what did he want? What? Tell me what he said. How did he sound, what did he want?

Something was smug in John's narrowed eyes, as if he hoped she would ask. "He asked how you were," he said. "And I said you were fine now. Told him it was bad before. He asked how and I said you'd been cutting yourself."

"You told him that?"

"You're goddamn right I did."

Her face numb, she opened her mouth and closed it a couple times. "Well," she said. "That was my story to tell but—"

"Oh *your* story," he said, his voice raising. "Sure. I have nothing to do with it. I'm just the guy who found you bleeding in the bathroom. That makes me a bit player in this drama?"

"It does not. John, you—"

"Good. Then as your live-in boyfriend, I told him I'd appreciate if he wouldn't make a habit of calling," John said. "I was pretty nice about it. Not that I think he deserves it. And not that anyone gives a shit what I think."

Grabbing his keys, he pushed past her, heading for the door and muttering under his breath. "Son of a bitch couldn't make a fucking phone call when you were in a death spiral three years ago. Now he finds the stones to call and he gets me. Little ol' Opie." He looked back at her with a cruel expression she barely recognized. "It was fucking beautiful, Dais. I enjoyed hearing him squirm. I relished it. *Relish,* was the word."

"John, stop it. Don't leave, I'm just—"

The door slammed.

"Surprised. *Fuck.*" With a groan of frustration she slid down the wall to sit on the floor, face in her hands. "You called," she said. "Now you call me? Now? What, you think I didn't mean it all those other times? I send your stuff back and *then* you decide?"

She was crying. Half in exhausted despair, half in primal triumph.

He called.

He didn't have my number. He had my address but he didn't have my number. He had to go looking for it.

He came looking for me.

He wanted me.

"No," she said, getting up, mopping her face. "No, this is not fair. You do not get to do this to me. You had a chance. You had three years. You missed it. You're too late."

He called me.

He came looking for me.

Erik, Erik, why did you, where are you, how could you...?

She lay on the couch, filled with anger and crushed with sorrow. She was so happy five minutes ago. Now a bomb had gone off and everything she worked for, all her achievements were worthless again.

I missed him. I wasn't here. My back was turned. He called and I wasn't here. It's not fair.

"You can't," she said. "I have worked too hard, Erik. You can't do this."

His necklace was lost.

Was it really, or was it an excuse he made up? That necklace meant the world to him. It was his history and she added herself to it: the tiny pair of gold scissors had been her gift to him. One of their first private jokes when she thought, upon first hearing his surname, that it meant "scissors."

Lost.

"I'm sorry," she whispered. "If it's lost, I feel terrible. It was your treasure. But I don't have it, I don't have anything anymore, Erik. I'm sorry. I have nothing for you."

He called, her heart sang, ignoring her. *He called, he called. I knew he would. I knew he'd come back.*

"Shut up," she said. She pulled a pillow over her head, clamped it to her ear, as if that could shut out the cacophony of emotion. "Shut up," she said. A manic laugh poked through the weeping. "And stop talking to yourself."

She was losing her mind. This was it, she was certifiable now.

"Someone kill me," she said, laughing and crying. "Please. What the fuck?"

He called me.

He came looking for me.

He came back.

AT THE SOUND of the door closing, she woke up.

The apartment was dark. And cold. The air conditioning was up too high. She was curled tight against the crease between the bottom cushions and the top, her feet tucked within.

John turned on a lamp, filling the living room with gold. He took the blanket off the rocking chair and came to her, shaking it out. Tucked it around her. Then he sat cross-legged on the floor. Elbows on knees, hands folded up around his mouth.

"I figure I had a dozen ways to handle that situation," he said. "I wanted to go with the worst so I picked territorial asshole. How was it?"

"Epic," she said.

"Jealous douche was my second choice."

"I could leave and come in again. You could give jealous douche a try."

"Then I wouldn't have the element of surprise."

"True. A lot depended on me."

"It does." One of his hands dropped lightly on her head, smoothing her hair. "I'm sorry," he said.

She put her hand on his, fingers intertwining. "Thank you."

"I was just...a jealous, territorial lunatic and I had to pee on what was mine."

She chuckled under her breath.

"It threw me off when he called. So springing it on you made me feel back in control. I'm sorry."

"I'm glad I wasn't here when he called."

"Are you?"

"I don't have anything of his. I don't have anything for him."

She put her hand on John's face. Snugged his jaw into her palm and ran her thumb along his cheekbone. He turned his mouth into her and exhaled.

"I need to say something and I just want you to listen to me."

She nodded.

"I love you. You know that. But I don't think you know how fiercely protective I feel of everything you've worked so hard to get back. You nearly killed yourself over him. You gave up the things you loved and you starved yourself. Cut open your old scars and cut new ones in your skin. And I feel protective about my role in this story. It's mine to tell, too, because I found your scars, Dais. I was the one you showed the glass to. I was the one who called for help."

"John—"

"Me, Dais." He shied from her caressing hand and his eyes narrowed. "I watched you fight back to this place. Watched you come home from therapy like a broken doll and then get up the next day and go back out to fight again. Watched you bleed and cry and hurt and... *Fuck* him if he thinks..."

His head dropped back into his hands. "I'm sorry," he said. "I know he was hurt and I know he's not a malicious person at heart. But I only had to hear his voice on the phone to think I was going to lose you."

"You won't." She ran gentle fingers through his hair but he still seemed wary of her touch. She took her hand away and let him be.

"Fuck him, Dais," he said. "He had his chance. Three years of making it crystal clear he couldn't have cared less if you lived or died. Three years when he couldn't give you the time of his fucking day. He's out of chances. He doesn't get to pick and choose. He doesn't get to dictate your state of mind anymore. I live here now and I am not going to step aside, invite him in and watch him destroy you again."

"He won't. Honey..." She pushed the blanket aside, slid off the couch into his lap. She wrapped both legs and arms around him. "He won't," she said, rocking their bodies. "He was looking for something and I don't have it. And if he was looking for me, I'm not her anymore."

She held him tight, rocked with him until a trembling shook his shoulders and his arms went around her waist.

"I missed you," he said along her neck.

"I'm home." She took his head and set her eyebrows on his. "So are you. You're more than just the guy who picked up the pieces. You live here. I came home to you."

THAT'S IT, TOO

"I GOT THE JOB," Daisy said. "The *Phantom* touring company called a few nights ago, wanting me to play Meg Giry starting in January."

"Wow," Rita said. "Congratulations."

"I went for my wig fitting, it was a scream. I fly to Chicago after New Year's for rehearsals and then join up with the tour in Michigan."

"How exciting."

"John got a job offer too, from the Boston Ballet. It's a soloist contract and a really great opportunity."

"Is he going to take it?"

"He'd be crazy not to."

"What about your apartment?"

"Well, all these pieces seem to be falling into place. Lucky and Ed broke up over Thanksgiving. She moved out and she's been living with her mother in Rockland County and commuting into the city. It's a horribly stressful situation. So we asked if she wanted to sub-let from us and she couldn't pack up fast enough."

"It all came together."

Daisy nodded. "As for John and I... It won't be easy, we're not kidding ourselves about it. We'll have to wait and see what happens."

"And communicate. Often."

Daisy sighed. "It's been a little tense since Erik called."

"How so?"

"The phone rings and John narrows his eyes. I don't think he realizes he does it but it's like he's braced." She spread her hands. "And I'm human. I'm a *girl*. The compulsion to know what your ex-boyfriend wanted when he called out of the blue... I still have moments when I want to grab John and shake him and squeal like he's one of my girlfriends, 'Oh my God, tell me everything, what did he say?'"

Rita smiled. "Perfectly human."

"But I can't," she said. "I can't ask him for the play-by-play. I mean, I can but I won't. And he could tell me but he won't. It's like this little power play. This tiny elephant on the bedside table or a ghost dragging around two pathetic links of a chain. Not enough to haunt but enough to be. And I find we're bickering over the stupidest things. Like we can't fight about Erik so we'll fight about who last bought toilet paper or who ate all the leftover Chinese food."

Daisy pulled on her ear, chewing on the silence. "What if I need you? While I'm on the road?"

"Excellent question. If you get me a list of cities where you will be, I'll see if I can locate any colleagues in the area. But certainly if you are in a crisis, you can call me and I hope you will. I don't consider this relationship terminated because you are no longer seeing me on a regular basis."

Daisy exhaled in relief. "Thank you."

"Were you worried?"

"I just didn't know what the rules were."

"You can call me. If you want, drop me a letter every now and then. I can't counsel you by mail or be your pen-pal, but I would love to know what's going on."

"I'll feel so much better knowing I can do that. I'm more than a little nervous, mostly because it's the unknown."

"Do you need refills on any of your scripts?"

Daisy drummed fingertips on her mouth. "The Xanax is a little low."

"I'll write you one before you leave. How often are you taking it these days?"

"Funny, not all that often, but I sure like knowing it's there."

"We call that the Back Pocket Effect."

Daisy smiled. They sat in silence a minute.

"It's occurred to me," Daisy said. "It's been three years since I've seen Erik. Four in April. I've now been away from him for as long as I knew him."

She held out her hands, palms up, like scales. "It's even now. We were together three years, we've been apart three years."

Slowly she tilted the balance, raising one hand higher.

"And now the time away from him is going to start outweighing the togetherness."

"How does that—"

"Make you feel?" Daisy said, grinning. "I feel like time really is an amazing thing. People tell you time heals all wounds, all things heal in time. All that shit your mother says while you want to scream. But I mailed back the box of Erik's things and I couldn't believe how calm I was. I felt sadness, but it wasn't overwhelming. It wasn't in my veins or splitting my chest open. I talk about strong emotions being like a jacket I wear. This was a brooch on a jacket, not the entire garment."

Rita nodded. "This is huge. Considering your state when you first came in to see me." Her fingers fluttered in calculation. "It's November. Ten months you've been working. Not even a year."

"I thought my heart was literally broken. The way my chest felt like it was going to split open. I thought I was dying."

"And yet here you are."

"Alive."

"And coping. Quite well, I might add."

"I had a funny dream about Matryoshka," Daisy said. "Russian nesting dolls. I collect them. I was here with you and I was opening one, but it was like an infinite doll. I kept opening them and opening them. It got cartoonish, with piles of doll halves falling off the couch and building up on the floor."

Rita's head tilted. "Interesting. And then what happened?"

"I got to the end, to the last doll, and it was this microscopic speck." Daisy held out a cupped palm. "Right there, this piece of invisible something in my hand. I held it up to you and said, 'Is this it?' And you said, 'Yep. That's it.' I got really insistent. 'Really? You're sure? This... *This* is it?' And you kept nodding, yes, yes. Then I pointed around the room, to this unbelievable mess of doll halves and I said, 'Then what the hell is all that?'"

Rita laughed. "What did I say?"

"You said, 'Well, that's it, too.'"

Rita brushed one hand against the other. "And now I retire."

Daisy laughed. "It wasn't hard to interpret." She held up her palm again. "This is it. And the mess you make getting to this is part of it too."

OUT OF
THE ASHES

A LESSON IN BLEAK

JANUARY 27, 1997

Dear Rita,

I have the dubious honor of kicking off my gypsy lifestyle in Michigan. In the middle of winter.

Pray for me.

Before I joined, the tour just finished up their stop in East Lansing which, I hear, is beautiful. We now occupy the Masonic Temple in Detroit for the next four months. The theater is beautiful. Detroit is not.

Detroit in winter is a lesson in bleak. A study in neutral tones. Everything is grey, brown and white. And flat. Frankly it's depressing. But if I can get through this leg of the tour and not expire from Seasonal Affectation Disorder, then I think it's safe to say I can live pretty much anywhere.

I'm settling into the routine. We're put up at a pretty good hotel with extended-stay accommodations. Meaning we have access to a kitchen and I've become an unofficial cast cook.

As long as someone else is willing to food shop, I don't mind whipping up something that can be heated up after curtain.

We get our own rooms, although a lot of cast members buddy up in order to bank half the per diem. I might do that eventually but for the moment I'm being selfish and solitary about my personal space. I'm reading a ton. The amount of books lying around the green room and the dressing rooms is not to be believed. And puzzles and board games, too. Backstage looks like a combination of a Red Cross knitting circle and a nursing home rec room.

Tuesday through Friday, we do only one evening show so my days are free until around four in the afternoon. I've acquired a GBF, a Gay Best Friend. His name is Gabriel Ostin and he is fabulous. He's an amazing dancer with a fearless ability to hustle. Like he knows how to work his inner agent. He walked right into the offices of the Detroit Ballet School, dragging me behind. He introduced himself and got us both enrolled in professional-level classes. And he's organizing a small group to perform with Detroit City Dance Festival next month (as long as it doesn't interfere with the tour's rehearsals or shows, we're allowed outside engagements). This is all fantastic because I was worried my ballet technique would suffer while I was on the road. Now I see being in different cities is actually a huge opportunity to study. I just follow Gabriel and let him do the talking.

Weekends are intense with two shows on Saturdays and Sundays. Mondays we have off and I use that day to get a massage or a manicure, go shopping or do something nice for myself.

John and I are managing. A lot of phone calls and letters, but the separation is taking a toll. Our schedules simply don't coincide and trying to coordinate time to see each other is proving both a logistical and financial challenge. I feel sad. Not heartbroken but... He's been so good to me and I do love him. He's dear to me. And I'll always want to know where he *is. If this ends, I don't want to be totally disconnected or have things be unfinished.*

Anyway, that's where things stand. Now I bundle up and head off to the theater.

I hope you're well. Take good care.

Daisy

THE LETTERS DWINDLED to notes. The phone calls became more and more infrequent and the conversations grew more and more like small talk.

It was over by March.

"I didn't want to do this over the phone," John said.

"We're seven hundred miles and a time zone apart," Daisy said. "It was kind of unavoidable."

"Breaking up?"

"No, the phone part."

"Right."

A long aching silence, edged with static. "Fuck," he said. "How do you do this without all the stupid clichés?"

"It's not you, it's me," she said.

"It is me," he said. "To be honest, I... God, I don't know how to say this."

Another wedge of silence. Then the mental clouds parted and Daisy felt her eyes widen. "Holy shit," she said. "Did you meet someone?"

Of all the ways he could have reacted, she didn't expect him to start crying.

"Honey, don't," she said. "John, it's all right."

As if it were storyboarded in front of her, she knew exactly what happened. He met a girl and connected with her. She liked him. Openly, spontaneously and freely. No shadows from the past lurked over their shoulders, no eggshells underfoot to brush aside or topics of conversation to avoid. No scars under their fingertips when they touched. He liked her. She liked him. End of story. Whether it was an affair of the heart or a sexfest, it was no doubt refreshingly mindless and simple and healthy. And accessible. John probably wanted to stuff his face with it and collapse into a stupor of contentment.

"I'm sorry," he said. "It was the last thing I expected."

Me too, she thought. "Is she in the company?"

"She's in the orchestra." After a beat he added, "She plays viola," as if it explained everything.

"I see."

"I'm sorry, Dais," he said. "I'm all torn up and I can't keep doing this. It makes my stomach hurt and it's not fair to you or Kelly."

Kelly was an ice-water splash of reality. A name made it real. Daisy closed her eyes, feeling hurt and confused and with no right to either.

Let him go, she thought. *You wanted it this way, after all. You got the breakup you hoped for.*

She opened her eyes and told him he deserved to get all the love he wanted to give. He deserved his passion reciprocated, deserved what she couldn't...

"Fucking clichés," she said.

"I hate conversations like this."

"I love you," she said. "I wouldn't be here...anywhere if it weren't for you. It's the truth and it's what I'll take with me for the rest of my life."

"I'd do it again," he said. "I wouldn't change anything. I'll always love you, Dais, it's just..."

"I know."

You're worthy of more, she thought. *You want to be loved completely. Right now. Today.*

They lingered on the line, each clearly feeling more should be said. Their breakup deserved more time.

"Stay in touch," she said. "Please don't disappear."

A tiny chuckle. "I'm not Erik."

Tears came to her eyes. "No, you're not. You're a prince."

He let out his breath. "I need to go now, honey," he said.

She let him go, and in the weeks following she battled a low-grade emotional flu. Confused by a phone that didn't ring when she expected it to. Blinking at the box office manager's apologetic expression when her mailbox was empty. Sideswiped by visions of John lying around in bed with this Kelly person and her damn viola.

Then Daisy got pissed. A little. Her skin flared up hot, then she shivered with cold. Her heart moped and slammed a few doors, but it felt half-assed and phony. Sulking because it was the thing to do. She didn't know what else to do. All the emotion was ill-fitting, as if it belonged to someone else's breakup.

You're pissed because you're lonely, she counseled herself. *And John isn't. You're jealous. Just feel it. Let it sit in your lap a while. If it has something to say, it will. Or else it will get up and leave.*

It did leave, only to be replaced by an intense craving for physical contact, which she assuaged by sleeping with Gabriel Ostin.

"This won't get you kicked out of the gay boys' club, will it?" she said.

"You'd be surprised how many gay boys like cuddling up with girls for a good night's sleep."

"Really?"

"Really. You're soft, you're smooth, you fit nice in my arms, you don't snore and you smell amazing. None of that gets me hard. Analyze it however you want, just don't wake me up."

He was the only boy who could successfully spoon Daisy for an entire night. None of her customary wide-eyed claustrophobia rose up when he wrapped his arms around her from behind. In fact, the first time, she went into such a deep sleep, she awoke in the exact same position, her bottom arm completely numb.

"This is outstanding," she said. "Pillow talk and snuggles with no hassle or drama."

"Or wet spot," Gabriel said, yawning.

"Why didn't I think of this years ago?"

"You were in a psychiatric hospital years ago, if I remember correctly."

She pummeled him hard with a pillow. "Asshole."

"I'm sorry, that was cheap. Lie back down. I'll play with your hair."

"This is the weirdest thing I've ever heard," Lucky said over the phone.

"Listening to myself tell you about it, I agree, it's beyond weird," Daisy said. "On the other hand, I sleep great, I'm not lonely and he's the world's most perfect back-scratcher. So what the hell?"

"I may resort to this," Lucky said sourly. "I'm so horny I'm rubbing against the furniture."

"Any dates?"

"None I could rub against. By the way, you know the sex toy shop over on Amsterdam Avenue? They closed. Not another shop in ten square blocks. I have to head down to the Village this weekend and look for a bedside table boyfriend."

"Yeah, speaking of which, I need batteries..."

THE REPORT OF GUNFIRE

APRIL 22, 1997
The Cleveland Plain Dealer
Arts & Entertainment
"Old Works and Fresh Faces: Cleveland Dance Movement
Presents Emerging Artists"
By Dilys Silverman

The Museum of Art was an exhibition of unparalleled gener-
osity Monday night. Established community artists provided
those lesser-known a chance to shine in a collaborative, gala
performance. Together with Cleveland Choral Arts Society, the
Chamber Symphony and Cleveland Dance Movement, young
composers, vocalists and dancers took to the stage in both
original works and classics.

The apex of the evening came with the Lacrimosa of Mozart's
requiem mass. Set against the gorgeous, haunting music and
the equally breathtaking talent of the chorus, was a pas de
deux of such delicate emotion, I couldn't decide if it were
heartbreaking or triumphant. Perhaps the beauty lay in its
juxtaposition of both. The pas de deux was choreographed
by Marguerite Bianco, who plays the role of Meg Giry in the

touring production of Phantom of the Opera *(currently running at Playhouse Square). When not performing or rehearsing, she and her partner Gabriel Ostin teach and coach for Cleveland Dance Movement and other local schools.*

Bianco is an astonishing dancer who, for four minutes, made the spacious atrium of the museum into an intimate and timeless space. The audience was filled with longing by the time the chorale "Amen" shook the windows—longing to see it from the beginning so we could dissect what, exactly we had just seen.

It was mournful but enlightened. Grief-stricken yet courageous. Joyful but with a dark edge. Dark but with a wash of golden light. With stunning phrasing and interpretation, Bianco and Ostin wrung the score into its extremes of heaven and hell.

But how?

What did we see?

Bianco, who hails from Philadelphia, is a graduate of Lancaster University.

Sunday, the nineteenth of April, was the fifth anniversary of the Lancaster shootings.

It was the report of gunfire echoing in the choreography. The grief for friends in her endless extension and the mourning of dreams in her phrasing. The triumph of a twenty-year-old girl shot down and left to die, only to live and be told she might not walk again.

What five hundred people in the museum saw on Monday night was not a requiem mass, but a eulogy. And an enduring love story of the highest order.

"MORE COFFEE, miss?"

Daisy looked up from the paper, checked her watch. "No thanks."

She read the article again while the waitress wrote up her check. Dilys Silverman, the *Plain Dealer's* art critic, was a humorless commentator who was known to skewer young, unknown artists alive.

Daisy's heart had been in her throat when she first folded back the newspaper, expecting the worst at best and crucifixion at worst. Now her chest caved in with a triumphant relief that slowly rose up pink and warm into her face.

An astonishing dancer.

She secured some bills under the ketchup bottle, shrugged on her jacket and left the coffee shop, heading over to Playhouse Square. Her stride was a strut and her head floated above the column of her spine.

Mike, the security guard at the stage door, looked up and smiled as she signed in. "How are you today?"

"Astonishing," Daisy said. "Any mail for me?"

Mike whistled the tune of "Daisy Bell" as he fetched the contents of her box. Letters from her mother and Lucky. A postcard from Will (*Having a wonderful time, wish you were her*).

She found Gabriel in the green room, surrounded by his posse, each with a copy of the *Plain Dealer*. They applauded as she came in and Gabriel scooped her up in a spinning hug.

"Dilys has a soul," he said. "Hallelujah."

"We *wrung* the score into heaven and hell," she said, planting kisses on his face. "How was the reception after?"

Gabriel set her down and picked up his newspaper. "You should've come."

"I had to ice my ankle. What did I miss?"

"Oh. Nothing." His face was bland. Too bland. Daisy's eyes narrowed.

"Gabriel," she said, a warning note in her voice.

His eyes on the page, he reached into his shirt pocket and brought out a business card. He snapped it with a flourish through his fingers as he handed it to Daisy. "For you, Madame."

C. Harland Kent, III
Production Assistant
Cleveland Art Museum

A phone number was underneath, underlined twice in pen.

"Who is he?" Daisy said.

"Well, from what I understand, a museum production assistant sets up the galleries for exhibitions. And also sets up the stage when the museum presents a... Hold on, let me find it. *An exhibition of unparalleled generosity.*"

Daisy closed her eyes. "A stagehand," she said. "Of course."

"He was quite taken with you."

Daisy opened her eyes. "Oh?"

Gabriel nodded.

"Nice guy?"

"*The grief for friends in her endless extension and the mourning of dreams in her phrasing.* Not bad. It's a little unctuous but it is Dilys after all."

"Gabe, don't toy with me."

"*The report of gunfire echoing in the choreography.* Not sound but *report.* This dame knows her way around the English language. I'm sorry, did you say something?"

"You're going to make me beg, aren't you?"

"Yes."

She sighed. "Is he cute? Please tell me."

"No," he said. "Seedy dresser and a definitive lives-with-mom air. Needs to find a new barber pronto. However..." Gabriel held up a finger. "Superb sense of humor and smart as fuck. And you being a museum junkie, he could probably give you an amazing private tour. I'd definitely go and have a cup of coffee."

"All right," she said, looking over the business card. She shrugged. "Maybe I'll get dinner out of it."

"Or laid."

She smiled. "I don't need to get laid. I have you."

"Glorified cuddling with your gay roommate is not getting laid."

"If you'd let me grind against you occasionally it would be."

Gabriel eyed her a long moment. "You need to get laid."

"You secretly want me. I could totally turn you with my endless extension."

"Ugh, the report of traumatized pussy in my bed, just what I want."

"It's the best kind," she cried, throwing her arms around him.

He laughed against her head, one hand sliding down her back. "You have a nice ass," he said, giving it a caress and a squeeze. "I'll give you that much."

APRIL 26, 1997

Dear Lucky,

Hello darling girl. We gypsies are hitting the road again. I'm writing this in the airport, on the way to Washington D.C. for the next leg. Sending you a clip from the Cleveland Plain Dealer. *Lacrimosa was well-received and the Arts critic, as you can see, did a bit of homework. In fact I think she did more homework than me. I swear I never consciously set out to choreograph Lacrimosa as my "I am a survivor" piece. I just loved the music and it made me see movement and steps and patterns. And Gabriel of course helped make it come to life.*
     But maybe all along...
     I'm now listening to the other sections of the Requiem thinking I have more to say. Or rather, I'm thinking the structure of the piece is telling a story. Perhaps my story. All of which has me dancing around the hotel room at odd hours and scribbling like mad in notebooks. We shall see what comes to pass.
     By the way, funny story, one of the dancers got all flustered and embarrassed when she read the review. "The piece is called Requiem?" *she said. "I thought it was Rakewind."*
     Of course, the official name of the ballet is now Rakewind.
     Anyway, let me tell you about one C. Harland Kent III. You have to say his name with your teeth clenched and your jaw thrust out. (You just did it, didn't you?) He's a production assis-

tant at the Cleveland Art Museum. He chatted Gabe up at the reception after the performance (I was back at the hotel icing my ankle. It's been acting up). And he passed along his business card to give to me. A conquest, ladies and gentlemen.

Gabe gave me a "not cute, but a great personality" description. But my inner geek was interested in knowing someone who works at an art museum, so I called him and suggested meeting for coffee and corn flakes after the show.

(No, this does not end well.)

C. Harland Kent is instantly-cream-yourself gorgeous. Like if Will and Erik had a love child. Dark hair, beautiful eyes, killer smile, insane body. Check, check and check. And I show up at the coffee shop in post-performance loungewear with my wig-crushed hair and eyelashes still greasy with baby oil. I thought I would KILL Gabriel. Looking like shit, I had to rely solely on my witty, sparkling conversation.

For the record, the C is for Christopher. And his friends call him Trey. Because his grandfather is Ace and his father is Deuce. Get it?

(You're not amused. Hold on, it gets worse.)

Also for the record, in the presence of impossibly handsome men called Trey, I have no witty, sparkling conversation. So I talked about Erik.

(Let me lie down so you can stomp me to a pulp.)

In my defense, let me say that while the conversation wasn't sparkling, it wasn't superficial either. He's a superb listener. And my God, these amazing chocolate-brown eyes and... What was I saying? Oh yeah, he kept me talking about myself. And I wasn't bawling all over the table about Erik, I was just telling my story. And for the first time I felt like I was telling a cohesive, coherent story. Not all over the place and going off on ridiculous tangents. I finally put it all together with things I've learned in therapy and...

I can see you're getting bored. No, I did not sleep with him. Feel free to stop reading, I'll just keep babbling.

He did end up giving me a killer private tour of the museum on my day off, and bought me lunch. He's twenty-seven. Went to John Carroll University. Art History major with a minor in (don't kill me) technical theater arts (it's my type, what do you want from me?) He's getting his master's from Case Western Reserve and... You're bored again. I didn't sleep with him. God, he was hot though, fucking hurt to look at him.

I need to get laid, don't I?

We're getting ready to board. I'll post this when we reach D.C. Miss you, darling girl.

Love, love, love,
Dais

P.S. You're disgusted with me, aren't you?

IN PARTE DEXTRA

THE BETHESDA REVIEW
July 19, 1997

CityDance Conservatory welcomes guest artists Marguerite Bianco and Gabriel Ostin who are currently touring with the national production of Phantom of the Opera *(at the Kennedy Center through October). Bianco and Ostin will teach ballet and contemporary classes during their residency. Bianco will also stage her work-in-progress* Rakewind, *set to Mozart's requiem mass, for the Professional Artist Series at the Strathmore Music Center at the end of August.*

AS A PEN-PAL, Trey made no demands save one: he insisted Daisy join the twentieth century and get an email address.

I know how much you love your quaint letters, he wrote. *But I have atrocious handwriting. And no patience.*

He called her nearly every Monday, her day off. Either in the morning to hear what she had planned or in the late evening to hear what she had done. Their conversations—written or spoken—were long and interesting but never flirtatious. Trey was open about his social life, but didn't mention a girlfriend.

"Or a boyfriend, for that matter," Daisy said to Gabriel one night.

"For fuck's sake, he lives in Ohio," Gabriel said drowsily. "You couldn't be much more than a long-distance booty call. Too expensive. Take the friendship."

"You're right. He's good company."

"Bet he wouldn't scratch your back the way I do."

"Who could? My feet are cold. Can I put them on you?"

"Shit, no. Get those frigid claws away from me."

"We bicker like an old married couple. Isn't it adorable?"

"Woman, you put those feet near me and I will shiv you."

Daisy finished the section of *Rakewind* set to the Confutatis Maledictis. She wondered if anyone would guess it was her interpretation of a pot-and-ecstasy high roll. First the violins boiled in vigorous ostinattos under the male vocal, then melted into fluid, lilting arpeggios under the female voices. Chaos melting into a murmur. Her dancers clustered center stage, shifting and morphing in sculptural lifts and lyrical falls to the floor. Slow-motion embraces on the middle plane. Constantly evolving shapes, bodies passed hand to hand, giving and receiving weight. The combined chorus built up like clouds which then rolled over, yawning. The strings seemed to drop away, as if the stage were falling asleep. Perfect silence. Out of which would arise the Lacrimosa.

Now she was faced with the Rex Tremendae Majistatis, which had to come first. And she was stuck. So she called Trey to procrastinate.

He sounded tired, but jubilant. "Did I tell you I applied for an internship at the British Museum?"

"You did not," she said. "What kind of internship?"

"Curatorial support and assisting with cataloging and care of drawings and watercolors. Seventeenth to nineteenth century, in case it interests you."

"I'm more a sixteenth century kind of girl."

"Dammit."

"Anyway, did you get it?"

"I got it. I'm in."

"Trey," she cried. "You're in."

"This is me. In."

"Congratulations."

"Thank you, thank you. I'd like to say it was a team effort but it wasn't."

"When does it start?"

"Second week of September."

"Exciting."

"What's going on with you? How's construction?" Trey asked.

"Awful."

"Still? Don't worry, you'll think of something."

"I got five weeks left, I better."

"Do you have to do the Rex, are you committed to it? Could you stick to the Confutatis?"

"I could, I guess," she said. "But I think, musically speaking, it would sound weird. The Confutatis is definitely the middle of a thought, not the start of one."

"Good point."

She tapped her pencil on her notes, frowning at the Latin text she'd copied from a book at the library.

"Confutatis maledictis," she said. "What does that even mean?"

"When the confounded are accused."

She sat up. "You know Latin?"

"Twelve years of parochial school and a Jesuit college degree, ding-dong. Of course I know Latin."

"Oh my God. Help me."

"I'll try." He let out a groan, with accompanying noises that sounded like a body collapsing. "God, I'm tired," he said, yawning. "I've been riding this crest of anticipation for so long. I read the acceptance letter and the bottom fell out."

"We don't have to do this now."

"No, I want to help you. C'mon. Speak Latin to me."

"Rex tremendae majestatis," she said. "I know Rex is king. Tremendous majestical king?"

His soft laugh curled into her ear. "King of tremendous majesty."

"I was close."

"I think I'll have it put on my business card."

"You should," she said, smiling. "How about quantus tremor est futurus."

"I'm sorry I didn't kiss you when I had the chance."

She looked up as if he were in the room. "Is that the literal translation?"

"Loose."

Her fingers wrapped tight around the pencil and a smug triumph coiled up in her chest. "I didn't know you wanted to."

"Oh, I wanted. Bad." His voice was pitched low, husky with an indolent fatigue. It seemed to caress her. Or want to be caressed.

"You wanted to kiss me bad?" she said. "Or you wanted to kiss me well, you just wanted it badly?"

"Bad," he said. "Cro-Magnon bad. Me you kiss. Ungh."

She laughed. "Why didn't you?"

"I thought about it when I was giving you that tour at the museum," he said. "But every time it seemed the time... I don't know, I guess I was feeling shy. Which is the nice way of saying I chickened out."

She curled into his words. "No, you were shy."

"If I ever see you again, I'm kissing you immediately."

"I hope you'll say hello first."

"Hello. Can I kiss you? Me you kiss? Ungh."

"You don't have to ask," she said, smiling. "Just the hello."

"Got it. More Latin, please."

"Quantus tremor est futurus."

"Est," he said. "I know the French part of you wants to drop the T. Latin isn't devious that way. Just say it the way you see it."

She repeated the phrase, pronouncing all the letters.

"Great trembling will come," he said.

"Doesn't coming always involve trembling?"

"Always with me. You?"

"Sometimes my teeth chatter."

"Thanks for the visual..."

"Ad te omnis care veniet," she said, and then closed her eyes.

"To you all flesh shall come."

"And tremble?"

"Mm-hm."

She opened her eyes. "Quaerens me, sedisti lassus."

"Faint and weary you have sought me."

"Are you weary?" She imagined his profile in sleep, head nestled against her. His hair falling through her fingers.

"No."

The single syllable was both confident and vulnerable. In her daydream his head lifted. He was awake. Eyes filled with lust. Her mouth was dry. Then all at once, it was wet. Then everything was wet. She pressed her thighs together.

"Ingemisco, tamquam reus."

"I moan as one who is guilty."

"I kind of want you," she whispered, nearly soundless.

A swallowed pause. "I kind of want you too," he said. "Bad."

The pencil rolled out of her fingers. She slid to lie down as her heart sat up, beating slow and deep, squinting at the unfolding scene with keen, interested eyes.

"Statuens in parte dextra."

"Guiding me to your right hand."

Her breath thick and hot in her chest as she pretended him taking her hand, guiding it to the fly of his jeans.

"Don't stop," he said.

Her mind pulled an imaginary zipper. "Oro supplex et acclinis..."

"I kneel with submissive heart... God, I want to taste you."

Her reply stumbled, words piling up in her throat. She heard him inhale and exhale. His sigh stroked a single, deliberate finger down her stomach.

"I want that, too," she said. "Bad." She drew her forearm over her face, blocking out the light, blocking out everything but his voice. She was flayed open, exposed to the tight, trembling core of frustrated vulnerability. Her body was clutching at his voice. Clutching at the want.

I want him.

"This is crazy," Trey said softly.

"I've never done anything like this," she said. "Have you?"

"Couple times. But I felt like an idiot."

"How do you feel now?"

"Like I want to eat your voice. Like I want to tear the phone apart to get to you."

She pushed her papers off the bed, turned off the lamp and lay down, curled into the dark and rolled into him. "Trey..."

"I'm so fucking hard for you."

"Ungh," she said.

SEVERED

SEPTEMBER 7, 1997

Dear Luck,

So... Jesus, I'm blushing before I even start. So Trey came down to D.C. for the performance last weekend. Oh wait, let me get the performance out of the way. It went great. Review clipping enclosed. Skim it politely. Done? Good, back to the matter at hand. Curtain came down and I took Trey back to the hotel room and had my way with him all night long.

Oh my fucking god. Or rather, oh god my fucking.

It was fantastic. The whole business was so frank and unabashed and unapologetic. After a month of intense phone sex, describing in no uncertain terms what we wanted to do with each other, when we finally met up after the show... It was like a five-second decision. If that. You want to get coffee or go back to the r— We're going back to the room, right, who are we kidding?

I loved it. It felt so fucking good to WANT. I haven't had that pure streak of sexual itch in such a long time. And I was really scared I would never feel it again. Seriously, like Erik ruined me for anyone else. He not only pulled the plug on our relationship but yanked out a few circuits in my libido switch-board for good measure.

The switchboard, darling girl, is alive and well. It was beyond hot. And it could've been a total bust, right? Big buildup and then crash and burn and disappointment. Nope. Nuh-uh. Came my brains out. Housekeeping pretty much scraped us off the ceiling the next morning. We made a spectacular Walk of Shame to a diner and had one of those warrior's break-fasts. Grinning like morons.

We did get a little sappy saying goodbye. Breaks all the rules of a one-night stand but it's not like he was a total stranger. Sniff. If only we had just one more night. Clutch. Kiss. I'll miss you. Sigh. Sniff.

Bittersweet, was the word.

Yeah.

(Pause...stare into space)

Anyway, he's safely arrived in London and in a few weeks I'll be heading out to Los Angeles. I'm excited to see the West Coast. We're supposed to get a half-dozen new cast members. Thank God because the company is getting on each other's nerves. We're all bickering like siblings. We need some fresh air and some fresh meat.

(Pause...stare into space...)

Got a letter from John, he's doing really well in Boston. Got some outstanding reviews when he played Mercutio in their staging of Romeo and Juliet. He has a new girlfriend, Paola.

Will called me last week. He's also doing great things in Frankfurt. He asked how you were and said to say hi to you. No really, he did. So this is me, as Will, saying hi to you.

Hi. Please take your clothes off.

Come on, you laughed. I know you did.

Anyway, got to go now. I love and miss you.

Put your damn clothes on.

Dais

OCTOBER 10, *1997*

Dear Rita,

Have you read The Golden Compass? *I met this guy, Trey, and he said a lot of my story reminded me of the book. He gave me a copy to read on the flight to L.A. I'd never heard of it. Now I can't un-hear it. I devoured it on the plane, cover-to-cover without stopping. It's possibly the most beautiful thing I've ever read. I want a daemon. I love the idea of having your soul manifest itself as a live animal companion you can hold and hug and talk to. A constant counselor and helpmate. I find it somewhat offensive this does not exist. Why isn't this real?*

I wonder what my daemon would be.

Anyway, I'm not sure you know the plot, but briefly: it involves a sinister plan to separate children from their daemons because doing so releases a great deal of energy. The child usually dies as a result, or else wanders as a soulless outcast because not having a daemon is horrifying—equivalent to someone not having a face.

Trey wrote me a note inside the book's cover, "When you read about daemons, I think you will find the word you've been looking for to describe Erik leaving you."

He was right. The word is sever.

A child without a daemon is called a severed child.

When I read that, I actually put the book down in my lap and stared out the window a good twenty minutes. Repeating 'severed' over and over in my head. This notion of severing, disconnecting two soul mates, releasing an immeasurable amount of energy, enough to rip a hole in the sky. My head was whirling. It all seemed to make sense. When Erik severed himself from me, all the released energy had to go somewhere.

It went back into me.

A bullet severed my artery. Its energy caused compartment syndrome and they had to cut to release it.

My lover severed his heart from mine. My entire body developed compartment syndrome and I had to cut to release it.

This is quite a thing to realize at 33,000 feet.

So here I am in La-La Land, playing the Pantages Theater until April. It's the longest leg so far. We'll be here six months. But I cannot complain because the weather, in a word, is spectacular. After the cold winters in the Great Lakes and the disgusting summer in Foggy Bottom, I cannot get enough of perfect 72-degree day after perfect 72-degree day. And so much to do.

All my free time has been a slugfest compared to the action-packed hours we cram in before curtain. Disneyland and Universal Studios and the beach and Hollywood and tours and this attraction, the other attraction.

Plus this is Gabriel's home turf. Our reputation and his hustle precede us and we have a guest artist spot with the Anaheim Ballet School starting in January. I'm grateful for the delay and looking forward to working just one job for a couple of months. I'm exhausted after the Washington leg. On a whole lot of levels. But it's good.

I feel good.

Take care and I'll talk to you soon.
Daisy

NATIVE SON MAKES GOOD

DECEMBER 25, 1997

Dear Trey,

I thought I would be blue being on the road during the holidays, but it's actually been one of the most festive seasons I've had in a long time. The company takes excellent care of its own and nobody is left alone or out in the cold. We had an epic Thanksgiving dinner at Melisse and last night's post-show supper was a total bacchanal, being both the first night of Hanukkah and Christmas Eve.

Your package arrived at the theater about a week ago, but I held off opening it until today. How did you know I would love a copy of The Subtle Knife? *You shouldn't have. But I'm awful glad you did. Can't wait to crack the spine and fall into the next part of* Golden Compass. *Funny, I've waited so long to read this and I know I'll tear through it in two days. Books can break your heart that way.*

Looking ahead, Gabe and I start our guest artist stint with Anaheim Ballet School after New Year's. The plan is to stage Rakewind for their spring recital. Phantom will load out in April and then it's back to Chicago. I'm getting a little tired and wondering if it's time to bow out. I feel homesick but in a confused way, like I'm not quite sure which home I mean. New York? Philly? A new home?

Anyway, the theater is dark and the company is hosting another dinner tonight. Much booze and caroling and unveiling of Secret Santas. I hope you've had a merry little everything, king of tremendous majesty, and may the New Year bring much coming and trembling. (Not necessarily in that order.)

Love and ungh,
Dais

DAISY CLOSED THE CARD and slid it into its envelope. Trey preferred email but it was Christmas, he'd get a card and be happy.

She stood up and went to the window, drew back the heavy drape to look out at the bowl of Los Angeles. Strange to see the silhouette of palm trees at Christmas, a desert vista instead of snowdrifts. The holiday décor seemed so tatty and out of context.

Her CD player whirred and changed discs. Nat King Cole began crooning "The Christmas Song."

Loneliness laid gentle hands on her shoulders. From a bookcase in her heart, she took down a photo album and thumbed through old snapshots of La Tarasque. Decorating the tree, handing up ornaments to Erik who hung them on the highest branches. The memory wreathed in the scent of wood smoke and pine and orange-spice cookies.

Do you ever think of marrying me?

She put her hand on the window pane and looked through her reflection to the city outside. Time and accomplishment had dulled the pain to an ache. Yet rare were the days when Erik didn't float through her mind for one reason or another.

Where are you?

She didn't often let herself lean into it. But now she pressed her forehead against the glass. Her breath drained from her lungs, fogging the sparkling clump of lights.

I'm lonely tonight.

I'm thinking of you.

It still matters. I'm still sorry. And I still love you.

"Come back," she whispered. "Come back to me..."

THE LOS ANGELES TIMES
February 15, 1998
"An Evening with the Anaheim Ballet"

The program ended with Rakewind, *the work of guest artist Marguerite Bianco. Set to Mozart's haunting* Requiem Mass, *the ballet is a tribute to the victims of the 1992 shooting at Lancaster University, where Bianco did her undergraduate work.*

The ballet opens with the Introitus *with Bianco center stage in the circle of a single spotlight. The stage then explodes with the* Dies Irae, *a rolling boil of non-stop movement and emotion through which Bianco slices, sometimes like a sword, other times like a ribbon.*

Rex Tremendae Majestatis *features six dancers—one for each of the dead at Lancaster shootings—and Gabriel Ostin, who dances the same choreography but with his back to the audience. One might think this was done in ostracism. Or perhaps to see through the eyes of a disturbed and marginalized youth driven to the unthinkable.*

Confutatis Maledictis *juxtaposes euphoria against dark-ness, community against outcasts. A clump of undulating bodies keeping Bianco and Ostin separated. The clump dissi-pates and silence is broken by the tentative notes of the* Lac-rimosa. *The climactic pas de deux starts as a duet in unison and evolves into Bianco and Ostin's breathtaking partner work against the corps carrying candles. At the final amen, the combined company constructs a multi-tiered cathedral of bodies, under which the couple embrace.*

Bianco's choreography is fierce but never maudlin. She dances with the honesty of a storyteller. The ballet's goal is not to garner pity but to create understanding. And this young artist triumphs on both fronts.

MARCH 10, 1998

Dear Dais,

Was ist los, du Arschloch? So glad my customary greeting doesn't get lost in translation.

Dude, I bawled like a girl reading the review of Rakewind. *Did anyone videotape it? Seriously, I cannot live much longer without seeing this piece. I feel like I've been with you the whole time it was being choreographed. Over the space of a year and across four cities. Now I'm dying to see it live. And hopefully a greater chance exists because starting April I'll be on the same continent as you.*

Let me back up. Last November, my dad had to have heart surgery. I came home a couple weeks and long story short he's doing well with good prognosis but it's been hard on my mom. You know I got one sister out in Vancouver and the other in Oregon. Maurice and the Pompatus are pretty well entrenched in the Moncton community, but let's face it: they move in circles their age and nobody's getting younger. Still, it's not their plan to move out West yet. If ever.

Cue problem of What's A Good Son To Do? And enter solution in the form of Andre Mejia, my old teacher from Ballet Canadiens. He now heads New Brunswick Ballet Theater and is seriously feeling my shit up. He's offered me a guest artist spot for the spring and summer, with a possible principal contract for the fall season. Native son makes good and comes home. I'm not going to think it to death. It's the perfect solution for the problem du jour and I'm ready to leave Europe anyway. My work here is done on a lot of levels and I know that's cryptic and annoying, but one day I'll explain it better. Or write my autobiography.

Anyway. Enough about me. Dais, I'm so fucking proud of you. Everything you've done and everywhere you've been and your whole evolution into the artist I always know you were... The only thing that sucks is I'm not closer to see it. And in case I've been stupid enough to not mention it, I've danced in three companies in three countries and have yet to find a partner like you. We need to dance together again. Someday soon.

Love and shit,
Will

ORCHORALE

SEPTEMBER 6, 1998

Dear Rita,

Thanks again for finding time to see me before you left New York. Isn't life ironic? I hang up my gypsy shoes and come home to the Big Apple and now you've pulled up roots and headed to the good life in Vermont. I hope it's everything you wish for and more. And I hope you don't mind me still writing. Even though you don't answer back, it feels like you're listening as I sort stuff out on paper.

Gabriel left the Phantom tour as well. He's living with a friend down in SoHo while I'm back at my place on West 86th. Squeezed in with Lucky, but she's looking around for new digs. And she's lovely to squeeze with. I missed her.

Gabriel is still full of nerve and hustle, and I follow him from class to audition to workshop to class to audition. Pounding the pavement in New York is a thankless business, especially as the balance in the bank account steadily dwindles.

Last week, we auditioned for a relatively new company. They're called Ballet Orchorale, only in their fifth year and just starting to pick up speed. They choreograph primarily to chamber music and have an affiliated string ensemble. The company has about thirty members right now. They just secured a huge grant from the Shubert Foundation and signed a lease on a beautiful studio space in Harlem. They do a month-long season at City Center, and then tour a lot of venues in the New York Metropolitan area.

Gabe and I have been to see Orchorale in performance twice now and I love their range. They do some short works from the classical repertory, but their original ballets set to the string ensemble are amazing. Brilliant and breathless choreography. I can barely sit still when I watch. And when I was at the audition class in their new space, I had this strong, unexplainable sensation of being home. To the point where I'm jumping when the phone rings. I want to dance with this company.

So say a little prayer for me that the phone rings soon with some kind of work. Until then, it's off to class I go.

Hope all is well in your new life. Take good care.
Daisy

THE VILLAGE VOICE
November 16, 1998
"Ballet Orchorale at City Center"

The second half of the evening was devoted to the premiere of Primo Vere, *Ballet Orchorale's tribute to springtime, when a young man's fancy inevitably turns to thoughts of love.*

The ballet is set to the first section of Carl Orff's chorale masterpiece, Carmina Burana. The opening sequence, "Fortune Plango Vulnera," sets the tone of celebration and joy, anchored by the flying leaps and turns of Tunisian-born Anouar Bourjini.

"Veris Leta Facies" heralds the entrance of Orchorale's newest artist, the mesmerizing Marguerite Bianco. Formerly with the Metropolitan Opera Ballet, Bianco is by far the finest dancer to be seen at Orchorale, and clearly the company displays her as the greatest of its treasures. Bianco has a sinewy grace and frank sensuality, both qualities perfectly framed within her stunning technique. In tiny, skillful mannerisms—a slight overextension on her arms, a tiny arch of the back, and most of all, the remarkable use of her eyes—she subtlely reveals her prowess. Chipping away Bourjini's resolve until he can do nothing but take her in his arms, which he does in "Omnia Sol Temperat," a tender but chemical pas de deux.

Primo Vere is an uplifting work, full of innovative choreography and inherent emotion. Anchored by Bianco and Bourjini, the result is a glorious tribute to love.

FIRE, FLOOD OR APOCALYPSE

APRIL 19, 1999

Dear Rita,

I haven't written in a while but for a good reason. Amazing things have been happening.

Last fall, I entered Rakewind in Capezio's A.C.E. competition (Award for Choreographic Excellence). In February, the fifteen finalists were announced and Rakewind was chosen. At the end of March we presented at the Dance Teacher Summit and holy shit, I WON. It's a $10,000 prize but the recognition that comes with it has been priceless. Now the phone is ringing with people wanting me to come teach and do workshops and stage choreography. I still can't believe it. It is, to date, the most incredible thing ever to happen to me professionally.

The night itself was pure magic on so many levels. We performed at the Brooklyn Academy of Music. My parents came. Lucky of course was there. And best of all, Will was able to come. He joined New Brunswick Ballet Theater last fall and he arranged to take the time off and finally see this piece I've been telling him about for so long in letters and emails.

Well, after the performance and the awards, it took me forever to get from backstage out into the house. My parents went ahead to secure dinner reservations (and a case of champagne), so I came out into the lobby myself. And off to the side, I saw Lucky and Will. They hadn't seen each other in six years. I hadn't seen them together in six years. They were hugging...

DAISY PUT HER PEN DOWN and rubbed her cold hands, smiling back at the memory of her two best friends caught up tight in each other's arms. Lucky had wormed her hands between the lapels of Will's jacket, slid them around and up between his shoulder blades. Curved over her, he looked hunchbacked. His hand was at the back of her head, buried in her curls. They rocked and swayed gently within the embrace but their stance was immutable. Only fire, flood or apocalypse could move them.

Or Daisy. Who shamelessly wormed her way between them like a demanding child, gathering them into her arms and kissing each tear-streaked face.

"I totally planned this," she said.

"Well planned," Will said, dragging the heel of his hand across his eyes.

It took a good half-hour for them to let go of each other, mop up and make their way to the restaurant. All through the late supper with the Biancos, Will and Lucky kept glancing sideways at each other with bright, emotion-ringed eyes. Daisy didn't need to drop her napkin to know their legs were probably cozied up beneath the table. Outside the restaurant, she kissed and hugged them, suggested brunch the next morning.

"But whatever you want. Call me. Whenever."

And she walked off with her parents, leaving Will and Lucky to sort the rest of the evening out on their own.

She picked up her pen and went back to writing.

The upshot is Lucky has gone to Canada four times in the past two months and although I haven't seen any of their reconciliation personally, I can feel it when I hang out with her. She's all lit up inside but her feet are still planted on the ground. I want to cry at the thought of them back together. It gives me hope that

Her cell phone rang. Followed by her regular phone.

"It's me," Lucky said on her cell. "Have you—"

"Hold on," Daisy said, and yanked the house phone from its cradle. "Hello?"

"It's me," Gabriel said. "Have you seen the TV?"

"What?" Daisy said. "Hold on." She switched phones. "Hey, I have Gabe on the other line, let me—"

"Turn on the TV," Lucky said. "I'm coming over."

She hung up. Daisy wrinkled her eyebrows at the dead screen then turned her ear back to Gabriel. "What's going on?"

"Turn on the TV."

"What channel?"

"Any channel."

"Did someone die?" She clicked the remote. The screen flamed to life and centered on the NBC news desk. The anchor's earnest face filled the screen. To the right a graphic of the state of Colorado. Denver next to a star. A smaller dot beneath it, slightly to the left with the word Littleton.

Across the top of the graphic flashed two words: *School shooting.*

"I'm coming over," Gabriel said.

Daisy's hand with the phone lowered into her lap. She stared at the screen, the news exploding from the open wound that was Columbine High School, spraying in green glass shards onto her living room floor.

Lucky stayed all day. They ordered in and parked in chairs and on the couch, watching the news.

"We should take a break," one of them would say occasionally. They walked down to Riverside Park and back or over to Lincoln Center. Picked up ice cream or cigarettes and went back to the apartment.

The phone rang and rang.

"Are you all right, darling?" Francine said. "It's so terrible."

"I'm not sure what I am," Daisy said.

"Don't be alone. Is Lulu there with you?"

"I'm practically sitting in her lap," Lucky said loudly. "I'm not leaving."

"Call us," Joe said. "Four in the morning, don't worry. Wake us up. Come home if you need to."

"I will," Daisy said and hung up, only to answer another ring minutes later.

"Oh, Dais," John said.

"I feel sick."

"I hate conversations that start this way," he said.

"Are you alone?"

"I'm at the theater of all places. Oddly, I feel safest here. Who's with you?"

"Lucky."

"Stay together tonight. Don't be alone."

"I will. You be safe too. Call me."

Colleagues from both the Metropolitan Opera and Orchorale called, wanting to know if she was all right. Friends she made on the *Phantom* tour. Calls came in from Cleveland, D.C. and Los Angeles.

"Are you all right?"

"I'm watching the news, I thought of you. It's so terrible."

"I'm thinking about you."

"It must be like reliving it. Are you all right?"

A crackling, delayed voice from across the ocean. "God, Dais," Trey said. "Your heart must be torn apart."

How quickly her mouth formed *I'm okay* and wanted to push it out and not be a bother. She let it dissolve and looked for something more truthful as she leaned into their concern.

"I feel terrible," she said.

Lucky paced from kitchen to bedroom and back, talking to Will on her cell. She passed him to Daisy after Trey hung up.

"I wish I were there," Will said. "I need to be with both of you."

"I know," she said. "Oh, Will. Nothing is going to be the same for them."

Her heart waxed and waned like the moon. First it was dark and numb, shielding its face. Then a sliver of feeling broke through. Curved and stretched and expanded as she took in the children being shepherded by police across lawns and parking lots, their hands on their heads. The cutaways to witnesses. The uncertainty and chaos a palpable film across the television screen. Until her heart was wide open and wailing, tearing its hair and rending its garment, raising a voice filled with agony—*how? why?*—to the ends of the universe. Then it sank to its knees, retreated within. Curled down into a crescent then hid again.

"Enough," Lucky said. "No more TV. It's the same damn thing over and over again."

Daisy lit candles and put on some classical music.

"Is this good?" Lucky said, pulling Daisy's much-worn copy of *The Golden Compass* from the shelves.

"More than good, it's my life."

Bach soothed Daisy's crackling nerves. She found the hole in her own book and tumbled into it, grateful to leave the world behind. Lucky, however, seemed to grow more agitated. Sighing frequently, casting murderous looks at the phone until finally she tossed the book aside and fired a throw pillow across the room.

"Ring, dammit," she cried. "Call, motherfucker, what the fuck is *wrong* with you?"

"Jesus," Daisy said. "What's the matter?"

"I can't believe he won't call you today." Lucky smacked her feet down on the floor and began pacing again.

"Who won't call?"

Lucky whirled around, her curls snapping like they were filled with electric rage. "Fish."

Daisy stared.

"Jesus Christ, he can't let down his veil of stubborn *pride* and call you in the wake of another shooting? Can he stop being your cuckolded ex for ten seconds and just be a human being, a fellow survivor?"

"Luck," Daisy said.

But Lucky was unleashed now. "Is he that heartless? What the fuck, Dais? I don't understand and it pisses me off. I'm so angry with him."

"It's all right."

"No it's not all right. You had sex with another guy. It was shitty and hurtful but for crying out loud, you didn't murder his mother. This relentless silent treatment is *bullshit.*"

Spent and deflated, Lucky sank back into her chair, viciously gnawing at her thumbnail. "Who the fuck does he think he is?"

"A sweet boy with a bitter palate," Daisy said, staring at the darkening windows. She closed her eyes and the tender core of her heart unfolded and reached soft tendrils into the coming night, where wolves were lurking. Hungry for the kill.

Erik, where are you, she thought. *Are you safe?*

A hound's snarling exhale replied. She raised her chin a little, refused to be afraid.

You don't have to answer, Erik. Just be safe.

Behind her closed eyelids, her mind's edges began to soften. Her palms, of their own volition, rolled upward in her lap. She came in peace.

Sweet boy, be safe.

APRIL 23, 1999

I was interrupted before by the news from Columbine. It took over everything for a little while, as you can imagine. I'm not all right. I'm heartbroken and haunted but and I'm letting myself feel it. And reaching out to talk about it. So many people called me the day of, wanting to know if I was okay. They wouldn't have if I hadn't let Lancaster become an ordinary part of my history. If I hadn't learned to share my scars and my story. I see that now. It's easy to see so many things now.

A candlelight vigil and service was held in Damrosch Park. Orchorale performed Rakewind *at the band shell. At the end of the Lacrimosa, when the corps filled up the stage with their candles, and I looked out over the sea of candle flames filling up the park, I felt such a sense of serenity. Peace caught me up under my ribcage and lifted me out of myself. I was float-ing, rising over the park and New York and the world. Remem-bering how Trey translated the text for me. Lux aeterna luceat eis. Lux perpetua luceat eis. Let eternal light shine on them. Let perpetual light shine on them.*

And qua resurget ex favilla: from the ashes shall rise again.

I'm thinking of having it tattooed over one of my scars.

Next time Lucky goes up to Canada, I'm going with her. I want to see Will, and I was also invited to audition for New Brunswick Ballet Theater. Maybe it's time for a change. I can't lie and say the thought of dancing with Will again has no appeal. The daydream of him, Lucky and me being together in one place makes me feel incredibly happy, too. But I'm getting ahead of myself. I'll go up there and audition and see what comes of it.

I'm not quite all right. But I'm mostly right. I hope you are too. Talk to you soon.

Daisy

ROOM 473

THE SAINT JOHN Telegraph Journal
September 26, 1999
"New Brunswick Ballet Theater: Goodies From Oldies"

The debut of New Brunswick Ballet Theater's nostalgia ballet
Standard *Saturday night was the feel-good sensation of the*
year. A joyful night around the radio with songs from the
golden age of Big Band to highlights of the Grand Ol' Opry.
Ballet met ballroom and NBBT's dancers stretched both their
styles and their hearts to create a celebration of music, lyrics
and movement.

Dinah Shore's "Shoo Fly Pie," The Andrews Sisters' "Bei Mir
Bist Du Schoen," Tommy Dorsey's "Opus One," and Nat King
Cole's "L-O-V-E" are a few of the gems embedded in the neck-
lace of this delightful ballet.

William Kaeger's rollicking, caffeinated solo to Frank Sina-
tra's "The Coffee Song" is not to be missed. Neither is Rose-
mary Clooney's "Come On-A My House," danced by NBBT's
newest principal, Marguerite Bianco. If you don't walk out of
the theater in love with this blue-eyed American ballerina, you
have no pulse. Kaeger and Bianco together in Patsy Cline's

"Crazy" is nothing less than magic. They have known each other since college and their offstage friendship lends itself to an onstage partnership of the highest order.

The ballet ends with Louis Prima's "Buona Sera." The company goes from tango to swing and blows the roof off the Imperial Theater. The audience is left crackling with infectious joy and a bittersweet longing for the good ol' days.

MONCTON TIMES & Transcript
April 10, 2000
"Kaeger and Dare Joined in Marriage"

William Maurice Kaeger and Lucia Grace Dare were joined in marriage on April 8, at the Algonquin Resort in St. Andrews By-The-Sea.

The groom is the son of Maurice and Ségolène Kaeger of Moncton. The bride is the daughter of Thomas Dare of Riverside, California, and Judith Dare Millerton of Pearl River, New York.

The best man was the father of the groom. The bride was attended by her close friend, Marguerite Bianco.

Both Dare and Kaeger are graduates of Lancaster University in Pennsylvania. Kaeger was a Brighton Scholarship winner in 1988 and holds a Bachelor of Fine Arts in dance. He was a corps member with the National Ballet of Canada and a soloist with the Frankfort Ballet. He joined the London Festival Ballet for a year before returning to his native Canada and becoming a principal dancer with the New Brunswick Ballet Theater.

Dare holds a master's degree in physical therapy and works in a private practice in Saint John.

By request, the couple stayed in the resort's infamous Room 473 which, according to legend, is haunted by a jilted bride who died there in the early 1900s. They plan to honeymoon in the Caribbean.

AGAINST YOUR DOOR

APRIL 11, 2002

Dear Rita,

I'm going back to Lancaster this weekend. It's the ten-year anniversary of the shooting and the university planned a memorial ceremony. They're re-dedicating the auditorium to my ballet teacher, Marie. The conservatory invited Will and I to perform, so we contacted the Balanchine Trust and asked permission to dance "The Man I Love." They not only gave it to us but one of the trustees told us anytime and anyplace we wanted to dance it, we may. A beautiful gesture, but as we've been rehearsing the past few weeks, Will and I pretty much agree this will probably be the last time. It's too much.

But never say never, right? After all I am going back and I swore I never would.

"How does that feel?" I can hear you say.

I am, honestly, a little bit of a wreck. Like refill-the-Xanax wreck. I don't know who will be there. Translation: I don't know if Erik will be there. He might. Or he might not. And I don't know which would be more difficult, frankly. Of course

I want to see him. But if he's there and he's cold or distant or avoids me or...(Be brave, Dais. Say it out loud.) If he's married...

Ugh.

Then again, there's something to be said for finding out. If he's cold, he's cold. If he's married, he is. If I know, then I know and I can go from there. It's best I go in with the expectation of being aloof-ly avoided at worst, or introduced to his beautiful wife at best.

Actually, reverse those.

Cause of death: ugh.

On the positive side, it's not like I'm walking in there alone. I'm flying down with Will and Lucky on Thursday. John is coming as well, from Boston. And I'm beside myself knowing I'll see my old teacher, Kees Justi. I've talked to him on the phone a few times, making arrangements, and he's the same wonderful, wonderful soul. So full of love and energy. A total emotional hamburger with fries on the side. I can't wait to see him.

Another exciting thing is that National Public Radio is covering the ceremony. The segment will run on their show "Moments in Time." I'll give you a heads-up when I find out the date.

So off I go to war. If it's bad, I will divert the return trip through Vermont and throw myself against your office door. I'll warn you by phone first, promise.

Take good care and I'll talk to you soon.
Daisy

FIRST THE VOICE, THEN THE HEART

ARMS DROPPED TO HER SIDES, Daisy stood in wings of the theater, letting the waves of sensory nostalgia crash onto her head. The distinctive backstage odor of sweat, sawdust, musty velvet curtains and damp concrete walls engulfed her. Taped-down cables were underfoot and the catwalk was overhead. The disorderly order of everything hadn't changed. The same haphazard stacks of sets, the cubicles for quick costume changes, the stage manager's station. And the memories. Everywhere. Waving wildly, rushing up to throw arms around her neck, bury their heads in her shoulder and sob, "Remember me? Remember me?"

Daisy held them. Patted and caressed them. *Of course I remember. Of course.*

She ran her hand along the two freestanding barres where she warmed up countless times over the course of four years. She put her feet in a loose first position and closed her eyes, breathed in again, her heart pounding. She knew it would be hard. *Just let it be hard,* she thought. *It's hard. It's sad. It's emotional. Let it be what it is.*

Leaving the barre, she walked over to a wall of wooden pigeon-holes, each little compartment labeled with a name. Daisy reverently touched the fourth cubby from the left, third row, now labeled Browning but once upon a time, Bianco.

This was mine. I lived here. I danced here. I loved here.

I was shot here.

A rectangle of white had been painted on the wall above the mailboxes. The memorial plaques for the shooting victims would be hung here on Sunday. At dinner last night, Kees said some disagreement between the families and the school surrounded the placement. Administration wanted them hung in the lobby. The families insisted their fallen loved ones would have wanted them here, in the thick of production. Not alone and isolated in the cold, formal lobby. Their lives and passions had been backstage, where they died doing what they loved.

I lived here. I died here.

She crossed to the stage left wings. The Mylar floor hadn't yet been rolled out and the heels of her boots were loud and hollow on the wood planks. Will and Lucky were crouched in the curtains, in silent reflection together.

Five shot dead here. Eyewitness accounts from survivors differed slightly but one was undisputed: Trevor King, the assistant stage manager, was first to fall.

"When he has a squad in his crosshairs, a sniper almost always shoots the communications man first," Joe Bianco once told his daughter. "He takes out the voice. Then he'll go for the smallest man in the squad because, psychologically, the other men view him as the baby. No matter his age, rank, strength or personality—the shortest man is the kid brother. Shoot him, and you shoot the heart of the squad. So first the voice. Then the heart."

James Dow, whose sister was a soldier, took out Trevor, who died still wearing his headset. Then James turned and shot Manuel Sabena, five feet, five inches tall.

Allison Pierce, one of the stagehands, fell next. Then Taylor Revell, with her knitting stuffed down the front of her shirt. And last, Aisha Johnson.

One by one they fell to the scuffed planks. And just like in the movies, the police outlined them in tape. The bodies were taken away. The tape stayed. And in the days after the shooting, the students crept back into the theater and began to fill in the white outlines with signatures and messages. When the tape was pulled up, five bodies remained memorialized on the floor. The custodial staff varnished over them every year. Dancers, actors and musicians gathered around them before performance.

"And still do," Kees said at dinner. "Ten years later, when nobody who was there is here. It's legend. It's lore. They pick a shrine and pray to it."

Kees was forty-seven now. His eyebrows were shot through with grey. His eyes were circled but they still sparkled with an undefeatable spirit. And his hands couldn't get enough of them. Over and across the table at the restaurant they darted and swooped. Patting Lucky's five-month pregnant belly, rubbing circles on Will's back and sandwiching Daisy's own trembling fingers.

"So good to see you," he kept saying. "God, you're beautiful. Look at you. I'm so glad you're here."

"I'm here," Daisy whispered now, crouching down by Taylor's outlined body. Tracing a finger, she found her own farewell words: *K1, P2—Don't 4get ILU.*

Lucky knelt beside her, silently passing a tissue.

"Jesus." Daisy mumbled thanks.

"My hormones can't take this," Lucky said.

Daisy stood up, her knees popping. Wiping her eyes, she went back onto the stage and exhaled heavily as she finally looked the maw of the theater in the face. Cavernous and solemn. Stretching up high and wide. Lanterns lined up like soldiers along the bars, their cables neatly coiled and taped. Industrial. Productive. Yet the rows of seats curved toward her like arms, making the space intimate. Draped in soft curtains. Two worlds meeting to create a third universe where magical things happened.

Like me and Erik, she thought, looking toward the lighting booth. Its windows shining and intact, but dark and empty within.

Isn't it time? Can't we talk about it?

He was either coming or he wasn't. And she'd wait and look for him until he showed up or until she went home. If only she could know, then she could stop surfing this awful wave of anticipation.

Even now, her heart lurched sideways as a man who certainly wasn't Erik came into the theater, looking left and right. Hands stuffed into the pockets of his jacket. His gaze stopped on Daisy. Then his hands pulled free, his arms flung wide. Like a hero he came running down the aisle. Daisy's face turned warm with pleasure, pulling wide toward her ears. Without thinking she ran to the edge of the apron and jumped.

John caught her. Crushed her to his chest and spun in a circle.

"Oh, John," she said against his neck.

"I love conversations that start this way."

"Thank God you're here."

"It's terrible to see you."

She laughed, rubbing her wet face on his shoulder. "This is brutal."

"Tell me about it. I parked my car and started crying."

He set her down and stepped back, hands on hips. His copper eyes looked her up and down, a corner of his mouth twisting. "I think we should set some ground rules. Are you dating anyone? Because if not, I'm going to be shamelessly clutching you all weekend."

She wrapped herself in his handsome appeal, letting it be what it was. "Fuck rules. Clutchez-moi."

His arms scooped her up again and hugged her tight. She pressed her lips against his jaw. Over his shoulder, she saw another man had come into the theater. Standing in much the same way, hands in pockets, looking up and down as well as left and right. He wore a black watch cap pulled low. Daisy's heart didn't bother with a lurch. This man's build was far too slight and lean. Still, something about him made her tilt her head and squint, the hair on the back of her neck stirring.

"Who's that?" she said.

John turned, still holding her. His arms loosened and Daisy's feet touched the carpet.

"Dave?" John said.

The air reared back in Daisy's throat. She pulled from John's embrace and started walking up the aisle. It couldn't be. David was a burly and solid bear. Not this rail-thin, stoop-shouldered person with jeans that bagged in the legs. As she drew nearer, the facial features coalesced. It was David, and yet not. As if he'd been disassembled and put back together backward. A David avatar. Something was almost alien about his features. She couldn't put her finger on it. Not until she was five feet away and he reached up and slowly drew off the watch cap.

His hairless pate shone under the lights. A bit of stubble was growing in his sideburns and it sparkled silver. As the gap between them closed, she realized what was so disturbing about his face. He had no eyebrows or eyelashes.

"David," she said. "Qu'est-ce qu'il y a?"

He smiled. "It looks worse than it is," he said. "And it's better than it was."

"Oh my God," she said under her breath, and put her arms around him.

He seemed to jump in his skin. Laughed as if her embrace surprised him.

"Marge," he said. "Goddammit, you're still the prettiest thing I ever saw in my life." And finally he hugged her back.

A stampede of footsteps behind Daisy. John was there. And Lucky and Will. They piled on in the aisle, arms weaving around and through in a wreath of welcome.

"Opie, you prince," David said. "Look at you, all grown up. And Lulu. Holy shit, you're knocked up. Who got lucky with Lucky?"

"Get your hands off my wife," Will said, kissing David's bald crown.

"Get your hands off my ass."

Lucky ran her palm over David's face. "What happened to you?"

"I'm fine, I'm fine," he said. "Life kicked me in the kidneys but I'm all right."

"Cancer?" Daisy said.

David nodded. "What a bitch, huh?" He looked around and sniffed. "I survive cancer only to be killed by this place. Jesus, it's the same. It's all here."

"Still here," Will said.

"What, am I the only stagehand representation?" David asked. "No other rats came?"

A voice boomed from the lobby doors. "This rat came."

He's here, Daisy thought, although she knew it wasn't Erik. The voice was wrong.

David broke from the group and loped up the aisle, into the arms of Neil Martinez. They swayed and rocked side to side, slapping and pummeling. The others moved up toward them. Neil reached past David to grab and touch the men, to kiss Daisy and Lucky.

"Holy beefcake, dude," John said, punching Neil's massive shoulders.

Neil laughed. He was always handsome in a Latin lover way, but now he was twice the size. Like a bodybuilder. Smooth, dark skin with twin dimples. A nearly hairless head and a trim, salt-and-pepper beard.

"You look like Hector Elizondo," Lucky said, holding his face between her palms.

"I'm telling you, bald is hot," David said. "You haven't lived until you've felt a woman's inner thighs on your naked pate. Right, Neil?"

Neil grinned, but within Lucky's hands his eyes were brimming and they darted about the theater in a nervous volley.

The day of the shooting Neil had been sick. Dedicated, he'd dragged himself in late, slightly feverish and muffling a cough into a fist. He'd been behind the Manhattan skyline set with David when James walked in. Together they hit the floor and through a crack between two faux buildings they watched it all. And Neil had never been the same after. Like a bottle of soda left open, he'd gone flat.

Big as a pile of boulders, Neil hugged David again now. His hands still patting and thumping, but gradually they grew still. The fingers curled into fists, clutching David's jacket. The brawny shoulders shivered. How his massive frame crumpled against David's slight one tore at Daisy's heart.

"It's all right, man," David said. He pulled up tall and seemed to expand. "We're going to get through this together. You and me. Okay?"

The others exchanged sympathetic glances and quietly stepped away. Daisy noticed a woman at the back of the theater, one hand on the handle of a stroller and the other clasping a little girl's fingers. Daisy smiled at them as she walked up the aisle and introduced herself.

"Maribel," the woman said, and pushed aside the proffered hand to hug instead. "I'm sorry," she said, sniffing. "I'm hugging everyone this weekend."

"Not a problem," Daisy said. "That's my strategy, too. This is Lucky. And Will. And John."

Maribel hugged them all. The little girl had retreated behind her mother's legs.

"This is our daughter, Rosie. And the baby is Carlito."

Lucky crouched by the stroller, already intent on seduction by peek-a-boo.

"Are you all…" Maribel shook her head, searching for words as her hand crept around Daisy's sleeve. "Were you there? Here, I mean. When it happened?"

"We were all here," Will said, sliding an easy arm around Maribel, as if they'd been friends for years.

Lips turned in, Maribel kept shaking her head. Her gaze followed Neil and David who, arm-in-arm, had walked down the aisle to the apron of the stage.

"I didn't know if he was going to come today," she said. "He kept changing his mind. Yes. No. I can go. I can't go. I have to go. Don't make me."

"I changed my mind a hundred times, too," John said. "Including when I drove onto campus. I almost drove off again."

"He talks about it," Maribel said, looking around the group. "It's like I was right there with him, he tells the story so vividly. But he…" She drew her breath in a ragged sigh. "He's haunted. Even after all these years, it haunts him, especially when he gets sick. He was sick that day, you know."

"We know," Will said. "He almost didn't come in."

"Whenever he starts to get a cold or a flu, it's like he comes down with a virus in his head. He's equated the two things together."

"We all have a trigger," Daisy said. "It's the sound of breaking glass for me."

"For me it's Gershwin," John said. "Because all through the shooting and after, the music kept playing. Nobody turned it off. Do you remember? It was surreal. We're down in the blood and the carnage, police and paramedics everywhere. And over our heads 'I'll Build A Stairway To Paradise' is coming out of the speakers."

Will looked at him, eyebrows wrinkled. "It was? I don't remember that at all."

"Oh yeah," John said, nodding as he stared out over the rows of seats. "Like the musicians playing while the *Titanic* was going down."

"Who is Fish?" Maribel asked. "Neil always talks about this friend called Fish. Is he here?"

Daisy kept her eyes fixed on Neil and David, now on the stage, pointing up at the lanterns and catwalk as if strategizing a focus session.

"No," Will said. "At least not yet."

Daisy closed her eyes, wishing she could know.

HOPEFULLY EVER AFTER

"SANTA," ROSIE MARTINEZ cried when Leo Graham entered the theater.

A whoop of laughter followed. Leo was indeed snowy-white now, both hair and beard like fine grizzled cotton around his round-rimmed glasses, his belly bulging like the earth under a Grateful Dead T-shirt.

He opened his arms and gathered David and Neil close, holding his prodigal sons in an enormous hug. Within minutes, they were his devoted slaves again. Neil was running, fetching and hauling as if he were a freshman. David was six inches from Leo's shoulder, frantically scribbling notes on a clipboard.

Meanwhile Kees was assembling the dancers.

"Jesus, they're infants," Will muttered.

Daisy's eyes were just as wide at the fresh faces. "Were we that young? We couldn't be."

Kees laid out the arc of the ceremony. He had choreographed a piece for his students. Will and Daisy would dance "The Man I Love" and John had his solo piece from his senior concert ready. To go with the live performances, the communications department had combed through the conservatory's archived videos and spliced together a montage. All the footage they could find of Taylor, Manuel and Aisha over the years, interspersed with pictures of Trevor and Allison their families had unearthed and sent. Since the sound quality of the old tapes was so abominable, the student orchestra would play under the presentation.

"Please God, no Gershwin," John said.

Through it all, the journalist from NPR was shadowing them. Interviewing and recording, or simply gathering the ambient sounds of the production coming together.

"Do you think you'll talk about the cutting?" Lucky asked Daisy.

"I don't know," Daisy said, stretching on the floor by the piano. "I'm ready to talk about how hard it was but I don't know how detailed I'll get."

She sat back against the piano's leg and drank her water. If she glanced out the corner of her eye, she could imagine Erik sitting at the keys, picking through a Bach prelude for her. Telling her secrets. Holding her eyes.

Little fingers touched her pointe shoes. Daisy smiled at Rosie, who had also been shadowing her all day. Putting down her water bottle she opened her arms and the child sat in her lap.

"Is she bothering you?" Maribel called from the front row.

"Not at all," Daisy said, inhaling baby shampoo and spring air from the little girl's head.

"She loves her ballet lessons," Maribel said.

"Point your toes like I'm doing. Let me see." Daisy looked up at Maribel. "She's got good feet."

Camberley Jones, from NPR, beckoned Daisy over to where she and Will were sitting. Daisy set Rosie aside with a last little hug, then got up, wrapping her black shawl around her shoulders. Sliding into the seat next to Will, she took his hand. Their cold fingers slid together, lined up and pressed down.

"My memory is full of holes," Will was saying. "Some parts are clear, others are blank. He came onstage at the part of the pas de deux where Daisy does this really difficult lift on my back..."

He went on telling what he remembered and Daisy turned within, assembling her thoughts. Did she want to talk about the broken glass? The cutting? She didn't know how to touch on it a little bit. It felt like an all-or-nothing topic and once she started, she might go on for hour after vulnerable hour. Already she felt skinless, bones and nerves exposed to the air, quivering and flinching at everything.

Will's fingers squeezed. She realized silence was filling her ears. Her eyes flicked over to see both Camberley and Will looking at her.

"My last clear memory is walking down the aisle," she said. "Right over there. I had been in the lighting booth with my boyfriend then I walked down the aisle to go to the stage and... It splinters apart after that. I don't even remember starting the dance."

"He didn't come in until three-quarters of the way through," Will said.

"I know," Daisy said. "But I have no memory of it. Everything stops there in the aisle, when I turned around to wave at my boyfriend. And then it's a black hole, until I woke up in the hospital and I still didn't know what happened."

She was talking to Erik. She had reached acceptance he wasn't coming and she tried to imagine her voice surfing the radio waves into the future. Hoping that somehow, he would hear the piece when it aired. But her voice was big, loud and obvious in her ears. *My boyfriend* felt clumsy and passive-aggressive in her mouth. A fidgety, fretful desperation clutched her, certain this was her one last chance to fix things and she was botching it right out of the gate.

Don't you fuck this up again...

John joined the group, sliding into the seat behind Daisy's as Camberley began to nudge them toward the post-shooting spiral into the dark.

"I was a mess," Daisy said.

"Her scars are crazy," John said to Camberley.

"Being shot nearly destroyed me," Daisy said, and she imagined Rita Temple nodding approval.

You were shot. Your life changed. It's a fact, not a dramatic ploy for attention.

"This is all I've done, all I've been since I was five. And then I wake up in a hospital bed with my leg sliced open and I had no idea what happened. The randomness, the senselessness of it... I truly became two people afterward. I had the me who worked like hell, trained and fought and never looked back. And then this other me who was just... dark. Angry and depressed and constantly anxious. Things I had never been before. Feelings I had never entertained, let alone been consumed by. I didn't know how to express them. A lot of times, I didn't have words for what I was experiencing."

"What got you through it?" Camberley asked.

Erik, Daisy thought. But steel bands wrapped tight around her throat and chest. All at once, she couldn't get the syllables of his name to come up.

He wasn't part of the getting through.

"Take your time," John said. From the seat behind hers, his arms came around to hold her. "You all right?"

She nodded as both John and the truth wrapped her in an undeniable embrace and pressed her into stillness.

I didn't get through it. Not then. I got through it years later. And Erik wasn't there.

She drew her breath in. "John got me through," she said. "John was the one who got me into therapy and got me on track to... Back to myself. I got through it but..." Her voice broke. Her conviction was absolute, still she felt like a traitor.

I love you. I will always love you. I will always be sorry. And when I finally faced it, you were gone.

John was holding her hands tight. His forehead touched the curve of her neck and shoulder.

"It's all right," he said.

Camberley Jones's mouth mirrored the words. She nodded in encouragement, her eyes brimming.

"I got through it," Daisy said, "but I don't think I ever got over it. I can't... I lost things I'll never get back... Sorry, this is hard. It's... In a lot of ways I'm still two people. Part of me has moved on and evolved, yet part of me is still haunted."

Oh I love you, I will always love you, where are you? Erik, sweet boy, where are you...

"The shooting changed me," she said. She didn't know what she was saying. She stared at the aisle, at the last place she remembered feeling happy and complete, before everything changed forever. Warm wet spilled over down her face. Like a wild stallion, the remembered pain of the days spent in a crucible of self-hatred reared up.

You stupid bitch, you stupid, stupid, stupid...

Green glass cutting into her skin. The bracing, clean breath of release as her blood welled up. The terrible beauty that lay in scarring herself. Hurting and destroying her skin as she had so thoughtlessly hurt and destroyed the one thing she loved more than dancing.

I just want to ditch this place and go back to bed with you...

"It changed who I was," she said. "And for a long time I didn't like... her." She put her face in her hands. "I'm sorry."

"Come on," John said, standing up. "Let's take a break. Get some water."

He led her away to the side of the stage, held her tight in his arms. "You did great," he said, rubbing her back.

Shaking to her bones, Daisy blew her breath out, pressing the backs of her hands into her eyes. Tiny hexagons of orange and yellow swirled behind her lids. "Jesus, I wasn't expecting that."

"It took guts. I'm proud of you. It wasn't easy."

"I couldn't get it out. God, I sounded so stupid."

"No," he said. "It was your story and it was genuine. Not stupid. I promise."

Boots scuffing toward the edge of the stage by her back. David's voice soft on her head. "You all right, Marge?"

"She's good," John said.

Daisy took her hands away from her eyes. Golden blobs swam past as she smiled up at David's face, sleek and lashless like a rabbit's. "Small exorcism."

"Dave, come here," Leo called.

"I'm coming, you old fart," David said, something he never would have ten years ago.

Maribel approached with a sleeping Carlito in her arms. "Here," she said to Daisy. "Hold the baby. It's calming."

So Daisy sat with the baby snugged on her chest, her cheek nestled against the soft head. One finger closed up in a tiny fist and John's arm around the back of her seat. When the stage manager called her and

Will to rehearse, she was calm, but physically wrung-out, limp with emotion and catharsis. In such a state, she thought hearing "The Man I Love" would be the end of her. Instead, the music poured into the well of her aching heart and filled it with a thick joy. She let her legs and feet take over. Let the past flow through her. Turning in the circle of Will's strong arms, she gazed up at him and made her fingers trail along his face before falling backward in his grasp.

"Jesus fuck," Will murmured, bringing her up and into his chest. "I'm never going to get through this."

"I'll get you through," she said. "Hold onto me."

As they neared the section of the dance where they had been shot, Daisy saw the tension rise up in Will's face. She was about to run and leap onto his shoulders. He would catch her physically but emotionally, he was falling into her arms.

Will's eyes reached to her and she realized it must be just past three in the afternoon on April nineteenth. In her peripheral, she spotted John and Lucky in the wing where they had been that day, holding each other tight. David and Neil were together—standing now, not sprawled on the floor with their arms over their heads. Kees watched from the front row, not the back row. Their eyes were on her skin. Their thoughts were hers as they all pulled tight and remembered.

I lived here.

I danced here.

It happened. Here.

Brave and beautiful, she ran down the diagonal. Ran to Will. Caught his hand, threw her leg. Rolled over his back and caught him safe.

She came to a stop, poised in arabesque on his shoulder. Waited to hear a shot ring out.

Only applause.

WITH A FINE-TIPPED Sharpie Daisy signed the boxes of her pointe shoes and gave them to Rosie.

"They're a little stinky," she said, capping the pen.

"What do you say?" Neil said, nuzzling his nose against his daughter's cheek.

"Thank you," Rosie whispered, clutching her prize tight.

"Thank you," Maribel said, hugging Daisy. "I didn't think he would stay for the vigil tonight, but he says he's going to."

"Let him do what he can," Daisy said. "Even this much is wonderful."

"Dais, we're going back to crash," Will called. "You coming?"

"I don't know yet. I'll meet you back here tonight."

"I need a nap, too," John said, shrugging on his jacket. "I just hit the wall."

"I might walk around," Daisy said.

"I'll see you later." He kissed her cheek and left.

Dressed and packed up, Daisy went slowly up the aisle, approaching the lighting booth. As she had done in so many dreams, she put her fingertips against the glass, picturing Erik inside, looking daggers at her. She stepped in carefully. Looking for some proof of their love she knew wasn't there. No initials carved in wood or secret, scribbled graffiti.

"You talk to him?"

She looked back. David was in the doorway, a foot up on the step but going no further.

"No," she said.

"At all?"

"No."

He leaned a shoulder against the jamb. "I really ruined your life good, didn't I?"

She turned full around and smiled at him. "It wasn't your fault. And I'm all right."

He nodded, arms crossed tight. "We're all right."

"What are you doing with yourself now?" she said. "I got so caught up in the moment, I didn't even ask. Where are you living?"

"Virginia Beach."

"Why there?"

A shy smile unfolded above his chin. "I followed a girl."

"David," she said, teasing. "What is this sappy look I see?"

His face grew pink and he dragged a toe through the dust of the floor, kicking at a cable. "It happens to the worst of us."

"What does she do?"

"She's a nurse. Came in handy while I was sick. She..." He rolled his lips in and out, passed a brisk hand across his face. "What can I say? It's your everyday love story. I gave her my heart and she gave me a kidney. What can you do but live happily ever after?"

"Not much else," she said. She went to him and gently kissed his smooth face. "I'm so glad you're all right."

His mouth flickered in a smile. "For real?"

"For real."

"It was hairy for a while but... What about you? Opie said you had a tough time."

"I got through it. No happily ever after yet but I have to believe someone is out there for me."

"Sometimes hopefully ever after is enough." David dug his fists by his neck, stretching his elbows high to the ceiling and yawning. "You going back to the hotel?"

"I think I'm going to wander around a little. Overdose on nostalgia."

"You're braver than I, Marge." He stepped down into the aisle and Daisy followed. In silence they left the theater, walking out through the lobby and into the slanting rays of late afternoon sun.

"I'll see you back here for the vigil?"

David drew on a pair of sunglasses. "Yeah, I'm going to sleep a bit."

Daisy didn't wander far. She only reached the end of the mall before it became too much. Too emotional to be walking the old campus, with the budding dogwoods postcard-pretty among brick buildings. Too wistful to be passing through groups of laughing, chattering kids and hand-holding couples. Too hard for them to be kids and in love while she was chasing down thirty-one and alone.

She went back to the hotel and called her mother to share some of the afternoon. Then fell into an exhausted and dreamless nap.

NOBLER THINGS

IT WAS AFTER SUNSET. The sky was a bowl of indigo blue, banded with gold at the horizon. They gathered in the courtyard of Mallory Hall. Each hand held its unlit candle. Free hands joined.

The president of the university began to speak. His voice was weak with emotion. From where she stood with her friends, Daisy could only catch every third word.

From behind, John crossed his arms over her collarbones. She leaned back against him, staring out over the sea of heads. Leo and his wife swam into focus and then blurred into the crowd. Over in her peripheral, Kees and his long-time lover, Anton. Neil, Will and Lucky were a little bit behind her. David slightly in front.

The president finished speaking. Clumsy one-handed applause. The rap of the music director's baton on the podium and the string ensemble unfolded: violins to shoulders, bows at attention.

"Please, no Gershwin," John said.

Smiling, Daisy shushed him, rubbing the back of her head into his shoulder. She closed her eyes and sighed into the aching bittersweet. When she opened them, a galaxy of flames was starting to spread through the crowd.

The musicians began the Allegretto from Beethoven's seventh symphony. The bass viols deep and solemn in the hauntingly simply two-note theme.

Leo passed his flame to Kees's candle. Kees lit John's, who lit Daisy's. She turned and touched her wick to Will. Kissed him. Then kissed Lucky and brought her flame to life. Turning back toward the courtyard, she saw David, still standing alone, holding his now-lit taper.

Daisy stared as the cellos picked up the theme, weaving with the bass like a braid. Point and counterpoint.

A string of beauties hand-in-hand.

David's parents had played the Seventh for their little boy. Now he stood alone in the crowd, the nape of his neck exposed and vulnerable beneath the cuff of his watch cap. The hairless ridge of his brow. The unfamiliar jut of his cheekbones. How his jeans bagged in the ass and his smart tweed jacket hung on his narrow shoulders.

Daisy cracked a long-bolted door in her heart and reached within, pushed aside chemical squalor and shame. Other things were in here. Better, nobler things. Like opening her eyes in the hospital to find David reading by her bed. The touch of his fingertip to her nose.

Being told David held her hands when she was lying shot on the stage floor.

David had watched over Erik in the hotel room that night, and barely left his side in the days after the shooting.

"Will you do something for me?" she had asked.

"Anything," David said. "It's done."

The comforting smell of burnt sugar essence as a fish was inked into her skin. A strong hand holding hers, wanting to be useful.

She's the brave one. I'm just the chauffeur.

David forever passing her his headphones, his eyes dreamy with classical music and its stories. "Here, Marge. Listen to this."

David in front of the fireplace at her parents' house while they decorated the Christmas tree. Holding a candy cane like a microphone. A satirical serenade.

Roast nuts chesting on an open fire. Nipfrost jacking off your nose. Yuletide Carol being laid by the choir...

The joyful, singing smile on his face morphed into the lift of his cheekbones in her hands, when his body was over hers in his bed. She had made him smile. She remembered now.

I hate you.

"You all right?" John said.

Everyone hates me.

"I need to stand by Dave," she said.

She went to him so swiftly, her candle blew itself out. She slipped her hand into the crook of his elbow. He jumped in his shoes, his head turning as if he were being attacked. Eyes wide like a deer. A hundred flickering flames in the pupils.

"Seulement moi," she said, laying the backs of her fingers on his cheek. Their gazes held as the violins came in, adding another layer to the growing sound.

"Je suis désolé," he whispered.

She slid her hand around the back of his neck, slid her fingers under his cap. His pulse beat on her fingertips as she put her forehead to his.

"I'm sorry too," she said. "I'm so sorry, David."

Taking his arm again, she held her flame to his, relighting it, merging the wicks together.

John stepped in, put his arm around David from the other side and put his flame with theirs. Will and Lucky came to the circle and added their candles. Then Neil squeezed in. They huddled around the tiny pyramid of fire, their faces splashed with gold.

"It's not right," David said. "Fish should be here."

"Fish is safe," Lucky said, closing her eyes.

"The journalist asked me where he was. It's not right none of us know. Did anyone even try to find him?"

They pulled closer. "It's okay, Dave," John said.

"He should be here."

"He's where he needs to be," Will said.

"We're here," Daisy said.

"We're here," Neil said. The taper in his hands trembled. Wax dripped onto the stones.

They held each other tight in the candlelight. Their lifeboat bobbing on the open seas.

And the musicians played on.

ELEVATOR

THE ELEVATOR GAVE a sedate chime.

"Ever notice," Daisy said behind a yawn, "The more cushy the hotel, the more dignified the elevator bell?"

John smiled at her but the smile was disconnected from his eyes. He seemed preoccupied with something as they stood aside to let the elevator occupants come out. He ushered her in. The doors purred shut.

She reached and pressed nine, moved to the back wall. He reached then, and his hand hovered over the number buttons, index finger extended. One beat of silence. Another. His head turned and he looked at her. Nothing playful in his expression, nothing teasing in his finger hovering over the buttons. Rather something deadly serious, almost dire in his eyes and their single, simple question.

The doors had closed and they were rising now. She had the sensation of moving not up but forward, at a clip, afloat on a fast-moving river, heading straight for an intentional precipice. The elevator chimed past the fourth floor. She reached and folded his pointing finger back into his palm, brought his hand back to his side with hers in it. Fifth floor. Their fingers squeezed.

"When you told her I was the one who got you through," he said. "It meant the world to me."

She rolled her brow against his arm. "I told the truth."

A sixth ding. He put his hand on her head, let it trail down the length of her hair and her back. Seven. She put her arms up around his neck. Eighth floor. He pulled her mouth into his. She remembered his taste at the ninth and last bell.

Down the long corridor, dim peachy light layered with oblique flashes from the mirrors on either side. A deep hum resonating from within the belly of the building. Do Not Disturb signs dangled from doors, shut tight as secrets. Her door clicked behind them and they became another undisturbed cog in the furtive, nighttime machinery of the hotel.

"Get me through tonight," he said.

All night long, in the light of a single candle flame, their bodies came together. Aching and passionate. Driven by the primal need to connect at the most elemental level. To validate their survival. Giving death the finger with the ultimate act of life.

With breath and touch and fingers and mouths they disappeared in each other. They slept and woke and reached for each other again.

"I need you," she said, lips open and straining against his skin.

"I'm here." His voice hoarse with desire.

"Come here," they said in the dark. "Come with me. I need you."

"I'm here."

"I'm here, Dais."

We're here.

"Sleep," she said, and he did.

"Wake up," he said, and she did.

No needless explanations or justifications.

"It feels so good to hold you," he said, hands buried in her hair.

"I'm so glad you're here."

"I needed this. I remember this."

"Hold me. Come inside me again."

"I'm here. Be with me."

"Here."

"Here, Dais. Right here."

LUKEWARM AND CREMATE

"WELL," WILL SAID, LOOKING around the table. "Are we going or not?"

John folded his napkin and tossed it into the center of the table, narrowly missing one of the nine empty Bloody Mary glasses. "Fuck it, I'm in." Under the table his calf rested against Daisy's, weary and sated.

"I think we've had enough liquid courage," Daisy said. She ached pleasantly all over.

"I'd kill for a cigarette," David said. "All right, bitches. Let's go before I change my mind."

They sorted out the check then pushed back from the table, gathering bags and jackets. They stepped into the bright sunshine and started walking toward the old neighborhood. Daisy took Lucky's arm, anticipation thick in her chest.

"Maybe nobody will be home," Lucky said. "We can just peek in the windows and that'll be it."

But it was Sunday and everyone was home, nursing hangovers or sleeping them off. An appliance truck was parked outside the apartment on Jay Street. On the front steps sat two girls, painting their toenails.

"Infants," Will said again. "Who are these children they let into college these days?"

Lucky and Daisy approached, smiling.

"We used to live here," they said to the girls, who were sweet and welcoming. Hobbling around with their pedicures they got up, shook hands and invited them in.

"The delivery men are here," one said. "We're getting a new stove."

"You should've seen the one we had," Lucky said, laughing. "Vintage Whirlpool, avocado green. The oven had two settings: lukewarm and cremate."

The girls exchanged glances. "That's the one they're taking out."

"No," Daisy said. Lucky turned back to the boys.

"Guys, the *stove* is still here," she said.

"No," the boys said together.

They came up the porch stairs, but at the last second David wouldn't go in. "It's too much," he said and sat on the front steps. His fingers patted his jacket as if to take out a cigarette, but he only came up with some gum.

Daisy and Lucky held hands tight as they stepped into their old living room.

"It's so small," Lucky said.

Daisy didn't fight the instant wave of emotion. With liquid eyes and a tight throat, she squeezed Lucky's fingers and looked the rooms full in the face.

I lived here.

I loved here.

Erik was everywhere and it helped to have the memory of John still on her skin—a thin veneer of distance between her and the memories waving from the couch. Grinning from the floor. Winking from the stairs.

I loved here.

And here.

And God, remember the time over there?

"Is it how you remembered?" one of the girls asked.

"Exactly the same," Daisy said.

Still holding hands, she and Lucky went into the kitchen. The workmen had disconnected the gas line and were getting ready to heave the stove out.

"Farewell, soldier," Lucky said, saluting. "Go and fight no more."

But the appliance, in a decade-old rut, refused to budge. The men rocked and coaxed it. Will stepped in to help. They dug, braced and cursed and finally pried it free.

John held the screen door as the three manhandled the stove onto the back porch. Daisy glanced at the wall by the basement door, a poorly-spackled patch in the sheetrock by the light switch. Painted over and slightly bulging from the surface. But unless you were in the know, you wouldn't guess the hole was created by someone's head.

You like fucking her? Did it feel good?

She looked down at the square of blackened dust and grease on the linoleum floor. Bits of foil, cardboard and cellophane. Rubber bands and bottle caps.

And a dull glitter of gold.

Her heart knew what she was seeing before her brain could form words.

"Oh my God," she whispered.

She crouched down, picking it up with careful fingertips. The clasp was still joined, but one of the jump rings holding it to the chain had broken. She coiled it into her palm, closed it up safe and pressed her fist against her mouth.

"Dais, what's wrong?" Lucky said.

Daisy held her hand out.

"Holy shit," Lucky said. "Will, come here. Quick."

Daisy closed her fist around the chain and charms again, held it at the base of her throat. The full weight of the day pressing on her back. She knew what happened. It broke while he was fighting David. It broke and fell off him, got kicked under the stove in the scuffle. And he was so upset and shocked, so destroyed, he didn't even notice.

Will crouched down by her. "Qu'est-ce qui se passe?"

John hunkered down, too, his hand on Daisy's neck. She opened her palm to them.

"I'll be fucked," Will said slowly. "He's been here this whole time."

"Waiting for us to find him," Lucky said, with a sad tiny laugh.

John's hand tightened on Daisy's nape as he pulled her head to his chest.

"I'm sorry," he said. "I really thought you had it all this time."

Will cupped his palms and Daisy gave him the necklace. He held it up, touching each charm in silent inventory. The gold fish. The boat. The St. Birgitta medal.

The scissors were missing.

I fell down.

And then I fell off.

Daisy looked up at Will. Through the links of gold he met her eyes. He made to give it back to her and she shook her head.

"No," she said. "No, you do it."

"Are you sure?"

She glanced at John, then back at Will. "He wouldn't believe me. It should come from you."

Will put it carefully into his shirt pocket and they all stood up.

"Luck and I are going upstairs," he said.

Daisy wiped her face and managed a laugh. "No, thank you. I'm done."

"Will you go over to your place after?" John asked, tilting his head toward Colby Street.

"No," Will said, heading into the living room. "I don't need to see where I slept with James."

Silence in his wake. John and Daisy flicked wide eyes to each other.

"I'll check on Dave," John said, and with a last squeeze on Daisy's neck he headed out.

Alone in the kitchen, she walked about, touching drawer handles and the sink fixtures in a stupid and transfixed state. She brushed her hand over the patch in the wall. The floor was clear, but her feet remembered the crunch and rattle of broken dishes.

Her hand went to her throat, felt for a charm that had never hung there.

Commotion on the back porch, the workers were bringing the new stove in. Quickly Daisy started picking around in the dirt and dust, heart pounding. Fingers flicking and pushing. Loose pennies. Crumbs and wrappers. A petrified French fry. It had to be here.

Please.

A flash of gold. Her fingertips darted and she had them. Relief washed over her as she stood up and carefully blew the last bits of grime off the tiny scissors. She tucked them in the inside pocket of her purse, and with a last look around the kitchen she went out to meet the boys on the porch.

"WILL YOU DO something for me?"

"Anything," Daisy said, picking a loose thread off David's watch cap. "It's done."

He wanted to go downtown and see if Omar's tattoo parlor was still there.

"Are you getting ink?" she said.

"I might," he said. His chin lifted and his closed-mouth grin was a wry challenge.

On the drive over, she thought she might too. Have the bit of Latin from the Requiem put on top of one of her scars—qua resurget ex favilla. From the ashes shall rise.

But as they walked down the street, they saw the parlor was no more. The West Indian grocery store was still open, but next door was now a hair salon. Disappointment flooded Daisy's mouth, unexpected and bitter. They stood outside the door a few minutes, lost and forlorn.

"Do you want to try somewhere else?" she finally said.

"No." David looked so tired. "No, I wanted to come here. Can we sit down a minute?"

Alarmed, she put her hand on his arm. "Are you all right?"

He shrugged her off. "I'm fine. I'm tired and my hopes are dashed and I just want to sit down, Marge. Don't have a baby."

The grocery store had a few little tables. They got coffee and sat in the window. Daisy's eyes kept darting around, looking for Omar or Camille. Where did they go? What happened?

"A tattoo parlor used to be next door," she said to the girl who refilled their cups. "When we were in college ten years ago. Do you know what became of it?"

The girl apologized, saying she'd only been working there a week.

David's hands trembled as he picked up his cup. Daisy was about to chide him for drinking coffee but bit her tongue. He was a grown man. And not hers to fuss over.

"Can I see your ring?" she asked. He pulled the puzzling band off his index finger and handed it over.

"Funny," he said as he watched her play with it. "That day..."

She smiled. "The day. Capital D."

"If I could go back and do it over, Marge. I swear I would."

"I know," she said. "Me too."

"Irony is such a bitch," he said, smiling into his cup. "I don't remember a damn thing about...you know...being in bed with you. For however long it was. Five minutes. The one thing I wanted in the world, you'd think it would sear itself into my brain. No. A little glimmer of skin here and there but otherwise, nothing."

"I remember the shape your smile made in my hands," she said.

"You do?"

She nodded.

He shook his head. "I got nothing. The memory of you throwing up afterward is crystal clear, though."

"Great."

"You're gorgeous when you're puking, Marge."

"Bite me."

They went quiet a few minutes, their heads moving in unconscious rhythm to the reggae playing over the speakers.

"I don't remember much from the fight either." David said. "Two things really. Three. One, being shocked Erik had that kind of fight in him. I'd never seen him touch anyone, male or female, with anything but kindness or love or respect. The strength of his rage... Jesus, I didn't know who he was."

"Me neither."

"And I let him. That's the second thing. I didn't fight back. I just tried to shield my most breakable parts and let him have at it. Mostly because I deserved it. Partly because..." His voice broke apart and he looked off to the side, tears tracking down his face.

Daisy put the ring down and reached to squeeze his fingers.

"Because I didn't want him taking it out on you. When you... You tried to grab him and he pushed you off and you went flying back on the floor. I thought *my God, he's gonna kill her, too.* And I hit him then. To get him to refocus on me."

She put her other hand on the pile of their fingers.

"What's the third thing?" she asked softly.

David took a long swallow of coffee. "He was punching the shit out of me and he said something. Like, 'She's the last good thing you're going to feel in your life.'"

"I remember."

"And for a long time, he was right. It was like he cursed me. Nothing and no one felt good for..." A small chuckle in his chest. "Many moons."

"Me too," she said. "I almost envied you getting beat up like that. I had to beat myself up. For too many moons."

He freed one of his hands and pushed a strand of hair out of her face. "We made it, though."

"We did."

"Wherever he is and whatever he's doing, Dais... I know he still loves you."

She shrugged and looked out the window.

"Trust me. If I still love you, he still loves you. If I go, we all go. I got my hands on the curtain rope, remember? Nothing happens until I pull."

She laughed and picked up the puzzle ring again. "You love the last moment. You just want to get there, not be there."

He smiled. "Over the years, I've learned to make friends with the destination."

"I'm glad." Teeth clamped on her tongue, eyebrows wrinkled, she shifted and slid the silver bands around, still trying to solve the arrangement.

David clicked his tongue. "Give me that. Jesus, you're dumb." He took the ring, assembled it swiftly and slid it onto his finger.

She set her chin on the heel of her hand. "When will your hair start growing back?"

His shoulders raised and dropped. "Whenever it feels like it, I guess." He drained the dregs of his coffee and then glanced sideways at her. "Pubes are growing back already."

"I really didn't need to know that."

"Want to see?"

"No, I have the visual, thank you."

Grinning, he jerked his head toward the door. "Let's go. Opie doesn't trust me with you."

"Opie's not my bodyguard."

"Yeah, but I bet he throws a hell of a punch."

Their stride down the sidewalk was companionable. David gave her a stick of gum and took one for himself. As they walked, their clasped hands swung between them, easy and unaffected.

"I'm glad I came," David said. "And don't take me the wrong way, but this might be the nicest date we ever went on."

"It is," Daisy said.

"Can I kiss you?"

"No."

YOUR SKIN IS THE BRAVEST
THING I'VE EVER SEEN

SEDUCED AND ABANDONED

"I FOUND HIM," Will said. "He's in Brockport. Adjunct professor of technical theater. A little Leo..."

As if it might combust at her touch, Daisy took the sheet of printer paper. An article out of SUNY Brockport's newsletter. "Fiskare receives accolade from United States Institute of Theater Technology." A conference in New Orleans and a picture of the eight recipients. Erik in the back row, unmistakable. Her breath caught in her throat as her eyes took him in. She hadn't looked at him in nine years and her finger couldn't help coming up to touch his image, handsome in suit and tie. He was wearing his hair shorter but the sweet smile was the same. Her beautiful boy now a thirty-one-year-old man.

"He looks the same," she said. Her heart pounded fast within her ribs.

"Wasn't hard to find an address. I mailed the necklace back this morning. Along with a charming letter."

"What did you say?"

Arms crossed, Will shrugged. "I kept it light. Talked about the memorial and caught him up. Told the story of how we found it. Made a lot of cocksucking jokes because they never grow old and, you know, it's such unfinished business."

She laughed.

"So on and so forth. Yours truly in Christ, William. And P.S. Don't fucking call me."

She folded the paper, handed it back and smiled at him. "I guess we'll see if he still has a sense of humor."

Will shrugged again, staring at her neck. She'd threaded the jump ring of the tiny scissors onto a simple gold chain. The charm rolled and glided at her throat and she believed it connected her to Erik.

The belief was flimsy. Both Will and Lucky glanced at the jewelry with identical expressions of concern but said nothing. Daisy ignored them and the unease at the back of her own heart, tinged with a small guilt. It was a game. A silly one. And the scissors weren't hers. They had been a gift. She was keeping them as bait.

She was only fooling herself.

Will invited her for coffee a week later. And once they were ensconced in a booth, he slid yet another folded piece of paper across the table to her.

"Love note?" she said, smiling.

"Sort of."

April 28, 2002

What's up, asshole? I heard the radio show yesterday. Then arrived home to find your letter and my necklace. Mind blown. If you delivered it in person, you would've been blown as well. But it's allergy season and I can barely breathe through my nose. So it's for the best.

Seriously. I'm an overwhelmed and sloppy mess from this. But I wanted to let you know I got it. And thank you. Thank you for being the kind of guy to step in and help lug a stove out. Thank you for being the kind of guy to hunt me down and send back the thing that means the world to me. I don't have words to tell you how much I appreciate it. (Other than "suck" and "cock," of course.)

    I'm taking care of my ass. It's not as high and tight as it used to be, but it's in one piece. And it is sorry...

I won't fucking call you. But I fucking thank you.
E

Daisy folded the note. Unfolded it.

I heard the radio show yesterday...

The impassioned, unstructured lament that had come pouring out of her mouth on the air. He had heard it. Confirmation in her hands. He knew.

She felt a little sick.

Her fingertip touched the words. Erik's long-lost voice emerging from the void. The same handwriting, slightly slanted to the left. Ink from a pen he had held. A sepia splatter by his signed initial—he had been drinking tea while writing this. Two bags steeped a long time to bring out the tannins, with a lot of milk and barely any sugar.

A sweet boy with a bitter palate.

Daisy imagined his fingers wrapped around the cup, his mouth taking a scalding sip. His lost treasure glinting out the top of his collar. A drip from the cup as he took his mouth away and now molecules of Erik embedded in the paper, touching her skin.

She looked up at Will, who was lighting a cigarette. The diner waitress set a plate down in front of Daisy with a blueberry muffin. She refilled their coffee cups, tossed a handful of creamers on the table and retreated.

"Wow," Daisy said. It was the best she could do.

Will's eyes flicked to the ceiling as he exhaled a ribbon of smoke.

"What do you think?" she said, setting the paper down and peeling the wrapper off her muffin.

"I keep reading it," he said. "And reading it. And reading it. And looking between the words and between the lines. I don't know what I'm looking for. I don't know why it's made me upset but it has."

"He thanks you," she said. "He's humble. Genuine. He makes a few cracks. Volleys back the cocksucking jokes. He's still a player. He sort of tells you he's doing all right."

Will's finger pressed down on the second-to-last line.

And it is sorry...

"The fuck is that," he said. "His ass is sorry? Or he's sorry?"

"He is," she said. "Not for nothing, but I knew him pretty well. This is him saying he's sorry but not knowing where to go from there."

His finger tapped again. "I love the E. Real subtle. No name, no Fish. Just E."

"Bare minimum."

Will crushed his cigarette out. "So what the hell is my problem, Dais? I mean, what was I expecting?"

"More than you got."

"He said thank you. Clearly he was moved and grateful. He's doing all right. He's alive. His sense of humor is intact. What else is there?"

"I miss you," she said softly. "I'm sorry and I miss you. I think about you all the time. I was an idiot. Maybe we could get together. It's been long enough, what the fuck was I fighting with y—"

"Knock it off," he said, sinking his forehead into a palm. "Jesus Christ, I fucking *swear.*"

She reached for his hand, threaded his three fingers between her five.

"I guess neither of us got over him," she said.

Flushed and wet-eyed, Will tapped out another cigarette and lit it. "You knew, didn't you?"

"I knew what you felt for him had no name."

He sat back, mouth parted. "It didn't," he said.

Daisy nodded with a smile and let go his hand.

"It had no name," Will said. "Because it was a way I'd never felt about a guy before. Men to me were... It was always a physical thing. Another dimension of sex I occasionally dug. It's just part of me. You know this."

"I know this."

"With Erik though... In the beginning, I wasn't attracted to him that way at all. Didn't suck to look at him but it wasn't a thing. The friendship came first. How it was so easy to be myself with him. All my selves.

The way the compatibility kept evolving and surprising me. Thinking something and hearing him say it a second later. Talking about everything, feeling flattered when he'd come to me with a problem. And the way we'd crack each other up. God, I'd get an ab workout laughing with him. And then watching him fall in love with you was a big part of it. It was him but it was also you and I was falling for Lucky at the same time. So it became the four of us. One big tangled mess of love and friendship and the physical attraction bloomed out of it."

"When?"

Will took a long breath through his nose. "Right at the start of senior year. When along comes James..."

Daisy's heart began to thump and she felt her eyes widen a hair.

"James had it figured out in thirty seconds. He smelled the air at Colby Street and said, 'You always been in love with Fish or is this something new?' And Jesus fuck, it threw me. He wedged his foot in the closet door and found the one skeleton I kept hidden away. He didn't go broadcasting it around Mallory, but when we were alone, he loved to bring it out and play with it."

"How?"

"He'd say out loud what I only secretly thought. 'Damn, Fish is hot when he's concentrating. He gets that look on his face and bites on his bottom lip. Hurts to look at him. Man, if he were my roommate, I'd never get anything done, I'd just be jerking off all the time.'"

"I know the feeling," Daisy said under her breath.

"One time he said, 'You ever see Fish naked? You know, pass by his bedroom door when he's getting dressed?' And I laughed it off when the truth was that same morning, I'd walked by Fish's room and son of a bitch, he was getting dressed. I froze up for a few seconds, watching through the crack in the door with a hard-on for my best friend.

"It was shit like that. Being outed and busted, over and over. James constantly caught me in the act. Like he had a sixth sense for when I was distracted and confused by thoughts of Erik. So I took all that turmoil and... I mean I'd be..." He glanced up at Daisy, his eyes vulnerable and cautious.

"Go on," she said.

"I'd take James to bed and take it out on him. Use him, if you want to be brutal about it. And he wasn't an idiot. He knew. 'You're pretending I'm him, aren't you? You're dying to yell his name out, aren't you? Go on. Give it to me like you would him. I don't mind.' Twisted shit but it turned me on like crazy. It was addictive. James made me mine this vein of psychological darkness in my sexuality. He pushed me to pretend and finally I thought *fuck it* and I pushed back. We fed off each other. Fed on each other. Ultimately, I thrived on it and it slowly ate him alive. He told me he was in love with me and I had to end it. I'd been playing a game and he'd been playing for keeps. Not that I'd ever lied to him about what the situation was but..."

He set the heel of his hand against his eyebrows, rubbed it a moment. "After the shooting, when I was lying in the hospital, feeling like I'd lost control of everything and people were dead because of it... Erik came into my room. I could barely look him in the eye. I promised him I wouldn't let you get in the middle of my shit but when James raised the gun, you were right there. Smack between us. I thought Erik had come to rip my other hand off. Say he'd want nothing more to do with me, tell me to get out of his life and never go near you again. Instead, he put his arms around me and held onto me. Told me it wasn't my fault, told me he'd stand by me forever. And I broke down. I was crying like a baby in his chest and I was done pretending. I loved him. I loved him and I wanted him and it made no difference if I'd never have him either way. I loved him without a purpose. I wanted without needing to have. It was one of the purest feelings I'd ever known."

"I had no idea," Daisy said. "About any of this."

"Because I didn't tell you. Nor did I tell you what Erik said to me that last phone call. How he did a complete one-eighty and blamed me for everything. Said I strung James along and then tossed him aside. Chewed him up and spit him out. I was no better than David. And it all went back to me. I brought it down. James came into the theater looking for me and everyone else was an innocent bystander. And Erik was done being one of my casualties."

She took his hand and held still.

"Nothing I hadn't already accused myself of," Will said. "It just hurt like hell coming from him."

"He was angry," she said. "Angry and lashing out. Needing to make everything and everyone else hurt as much as him. I don't think he meant it. I can't believe he meant it."

"Yeah, well..."

"You ever go talk to anyone about it?" Daisy asked, taking a cigarette from the pack.

Will lit it for her, then put the Zippo down and began spinning it on the table top. "No. I ate it. Choked it down in a spectacular feast of self-loathing. Threw it up in Lucky's lap and broke her heart. Because I suck, so fuck everything. Moved an ocean away, thinking that would help. Then I got into big trouble in Germany. This is something else I never told you."

"What happened?"

"You mean *who* happened. His name was Seb. Short for Sebastian." Will reached in his back pocket and brought out his wallet. "Can't believe I still carry this around."

He dug in the tight fold behind credit cards and drew out a tattered piece of glossy paper, something cut from a magazine or brochure. Daisy took it. And once more her chin dropped.

"Jesus," she said. "He looks just like Erik."

"Right? But taller. And he could dance."

Daisy smiled. "You must've been a head case."

"I pursued Seb with an aggression I barely recognized. I was used to it coming to me, know what I mean? This was the first time I went actively hunting for a male lover."

"And? Did you kill and drag him back to the cave?"

His eyes far away, Will nodded. "Yeah."

"How was it?"

"Like living a fantasy. Except he left the next morning, said 'I'll call you.' And never did." Will spread his hands out. "I was had. Hugely had. Seduced and abandoned. And targeted. He turned out to be one mean motherfucker."

Daisy stubbed out her cigarette. "And you tanked?"

"Completely. It was like losing Erik all over again. More than that, it was like going through the shooting again. Or rather, the weeks before the shooting. Except I was James. Begging and vying for this guy's attention. Following him home on the streetcar. Stalking his friends."

"Oh God, honey," she said.

"And hating myself every fucking second."

"I wish you'd told me. Why didn't you... Oh, never mind, I know better than to ask. I was the queen of not telling."

"I almost told you. I called you and I got Opie. And he told me you were in the hospital."

She closed her eyes. "Shit."

"I couldn't tell you. Not then. You were fighting your own war and I couldn't unload more on you. The only other person who would understand was Lucky, and I'd shit all over that relationship. But I sucked it up hard and called her mother, who took great pleasure in telling me Lucky was on vacation with her rich boyfriend in the Bahamas."

"Jesus. What did you do?"

Will smiled. "Kept sucking it up. Seb left Frankfurt and went to the Dutch National Ballet, which put an end to the daily torture of seeing him. But I knew something else was wrong. Something deeper and Seb was the catalyst. A can of snakes was open and I couldn't close it. In a way I didn't want to close it, like I'd deserved what happened. You know?"

"You were James, out in the yard," she said. "Staring up at Seb's window. Wanting him to come down."

He nodded. "Everything kept getting darker, colder and more depressing. And when I reached the point where I didn't even want to get up and go to class anymore, I guess I knew then it was time to do something or die."

"You were so far from home. Were you terrified?"

He started to shake his head, then closed his eyes with a faint smile. "Yeah. It was bad."

"How did you find help in Germany?"

"I knew this girl in the corps. Beatrice. She was American and I knew she'd had trouble with anorexia when she first joined the company but had gotten a handle on it. I figured she might know where to get some help. And she was awesome, she helped me find a shrink and... Well, you know what it's like. It gets a whole lot fucking worse before it gets better."

They drank their coffee in silence for a moment.

"I wonder," Daisy said. "We all have our horror story now. Me. You. John and David. And Neil, look how messed up he still is."

He pressed a finger into the muffin crumbs on her plate and ate them. "What of it?"

"Do you think Erik ever... I just wonder if he tanked at some point, too."

"Maybe that's what I was looking for in here." Will flicked Erik's note. "Or maybe you put it better. I wanted, 'Hey, great to hear from you. I miss you, asshole. Call me. Let's cut the bullshit, we're too fucking old for it now.'"

"But what would it be like seeing him? Honestly?"

Will swallowed, slowly shaking his head. "I miss my friend," he said. "I love Lucky. I don't have to tell you. She makes my life so sweet. I love being married to her and I can't wait for this kid to be born. I'm in a place now that's so precious, Dais. I wouldn't fuck around with it if you paid me. But I miss my friend. Every time I look up at the catwalk over the stage, I'm looking for him. I got a problem, I talk to him in my head, working it out. Eight times a day, I want to tell him something funny and crack my ribs open laughing. It's crazy he wasn't at my wedding. It's bullshit I can't call him when Lucky has the baby. I miss the four of us. I want it back. I'm sorry, it must kill you to hear it and I'm a shit for even say—"

"I want it back, too," she said. "I'd settle for a close facsimile."

Will sighed. He reached for Daisy's hand and held it to his lips a moment. "Thanks for listening."

"Thanks for telling me."

Over her knuckles his eyes crinkled at her. Then he let go her hand and checked his watch. "We should get back."

They reached for jackets and bags, threw some bills on the table. Will picked up the picture of Seb and regarded it a minute, then crumpled it in a fist and tossed it into his coffee cup. He seemed about to do the same with Erik's note but Daisy stilled his hand.

"Keep it," she said.

"Why?"

"Because you returned his treasure and he was grateful. Even if he didn't make any other overtures, you can tell he was thankful. And he made jokes. It's a start. Keep it for hope, Will. You did nothing wrong. You did nothing but love him."

Will set his hand on her crown, leaned and kissed her forehead.

"Sometimes I forget who my true best friend is," he said.

SHRINE

SHE DREAMED ABOUT ERIK that night. She couldn't see him but knew he was there. Below her. His arms locked around the back of her neck, giving her his dead weight. Hanging onto her.

She woke up with a stiff neck and the truth: it wasn't a good idea to have Erik literally hanging around.

She came to the theater a little early the next evening, sat at her dressing table and turned on the mirror lights, revealing her shrine. All around the frame, newspaper clippings and memorabilia were tucked—from the Met Opera, from *Phantom* and Orchorale. Pictures of her friends and colleagues. Her parents and her cat, Sovereign. Small bouquets of dried roses hung from the top of the mirror along with the first pair of pointe shoes she wore when she was twelve. From a white ribbon hung Taylor Revell's knitting needle.

Knit one, purl two. Don't forget, I love you.

On the table top were her Matryoshka dolls, un-nested and lined up in size order. She'd collected them since she was a child and had several sets at her apartment. This set stayed at the theater. Erik gave them to her for her eighteenth birthday. Every dressing room from Philly to New York to California, she had unpacked and arranged them, and they watched her dress and make up.

Why had it taken her so long to realize all of her mementos of Erik belonged here?

She slid the jump ring of the scissors off the gold chain and put them into the littlest doll. The lock of his hair went into the next doll. All the pocket finds—spare change, guitar picks, screws and washers and the ridiculous clump of lint—were put carefully away. Almost immediately she felt better.

He was off of her neck and out of her closet. Away from her living space and behind the scenes, backstage in the middle of creative production. Exactly where he should be because it was the place he loved best.

RAY FLOWERS

EDWINA MEAGHER, the company's senior rehearsal accompanist, was turning sixty and throwing a bash. Daisy looked forward to the party all week, but after Saturday's matinee, she was tired to her bones and had a splitting headache. Two aspirin and a quick catnap didn't help much. For Edwina's sake, she gritted her teeth and got into the shower. She'd go and show her face, have a drink and hit the road. She could be back in bed with a book in a couple of hours. As enticement, she straightened the covers and plumped the pillows high, laid out her pajamas all ready to fall into. Sovereign jumped up and curled herself into a purring ball against the bolster.

"Be home soon, lover," Daisy said, putting in her earrings. "Don't start without me."

At least it was warm out. After weeks of sulking, spring had finally decided to make an appearance, and the soft June evening felt good on Daisy's shoulders. She rolled down the windows and sang as she drove along Chelsey Drive toward Indiantown, north of the city.

Fifteen people were the minimum required to secure the double-long picnic table on the porch of Michael's Crab House. When Daisy arrived, Edwina's guests had taken raucous possession of the veranda. Daisy loped up the scuffed steps in the wake of a sturdy waitress confidently bearing two pitchers of beer in each fist.

Drink in hand and engaged in conversation, Daisy felt herself perk up. Without realizing it she was soon caught in the shuffle of everyone taking seats, maneuvering their legs under the picnic table and arranging their phones and beers on top.

Daisy squeezed in, got one leg under the table. To pull the other one in, she practically had to lean back into the lap of the man sitting next to her.

"Hello," she said. "Sorry."

"No problem," he said, moving over a little.

She smelled him before she got a good look at him. A tiny top note of cologne or aftershave. Barely there. Underneath it was a deeper note. Something much more elemental and male. Skin. A waft of confidence. Maturity. And subtle sexuality. All of it cozied up into Daisy's nose and smoothed away the last bit of ache between her brows.

She was seated properly now, stowing her bag under her feet and feeling the man's eyes on her as she shrugged out of her blazer. Underneath, she wore a black sleeveless top. Her many silver bangles jingled from wrist to forearm as she brushed her hair back. The man's face was set straight ahead, but his swiveled gaze was still on her. Sideways and a little shy. She offered him her hand. "Daisy. Hi."

His shake was warm and strong. "Ray. Nice to meet you."

His short, thick hair was salt-and-pepper, definitely easing into silver. Underneath dark brows, his eyes were denim blue. He smiled at her. His expression seemed to slide an invisible arm around her shoulders.

"Are you a friend of Edwina's?" he asked.

She nodded. "I'm in the company. And you?"

Ray set down his empty beer bottle. "You know Daria, Edwina's daughter? She works for me."

"She just started a job at an art gallery, that's right. Are you the owner?"

"I am."

That was all the small-talk allowed before the food arrived. Service was immediate at the menu-less Michael's: crabs and beer. Period. Three waiters burst out of the main restaurant with bus tubs held high over their heads, trailing steam and the strong, briny smell of the ocean behind them.

"Oh boy," Ray said to no one, looking like a child looks at a birthday cake. People moved glasses and bottles aside in anticipation. The long table was covered with layers of newspaper and brown butcher paper, and down its center marched old mason jars with crackers, mallets and picks, and rolls of paper towels on wooden spindles.

Women were taking the plastic bibs kept in a basket on the table, unfolding and spreading them carefully across their nice blouses or white jeans. Daisy's only precaution was to slide an elastic off her wrist and pull her hair back in a ponytail.

Ray smiled at her. "I see you equate eating well with a good sporting event."

Daisy grinned back at him, toes curling in her shoes as the evening took on a whole new flavor. Then, without ceremony, the waiters dumped their cargo on the table in a magnificent sprawl. Hands lunged in all directions, tearing off legs and ripping off claws. Hammering, cracking, picking. Dunking bits in butter and eating with their fingers. The cross-talk and laughter got louder, the beer was flowing and everyone was being a glorious slob.

Daisy felt her petals unfold in the sunshine of Ray's attention. He wasn't leering at her, but she could feel his frequent glances as she licked butter and Old Bay spice off her fingers, or used one clean knuckle to tuck a wayward strand of hair behind her ear. She talked equally to him and the people sitting across from her. Ray made friendly conversation around as well.

But at some point the balance tipped, and their bodies began to angle further and further in toward each other. Beneath the table their calves bumped. Bumped again. Then agreed to stay still and get acquainted. And then it was just the two of them, chattering away in a bubble, sharing one mallet and one pick and one clump of paper towels. One of their many exchanged glances snagged and caught. And held.

"I'm sure you hear this all the time," Ray said. "But..."

She blinked. Waited for him to say something about her eyes.

"You have beautiful posture."

She drew her neck up, holding his gaze. Trying to keep the smile from exploding through her mouth and failing.

"Your shoulders are lovely," he said.

Her hands were fully engaged in dismantling the body of a crab, all ten fingers in. As she looked down, laughing, that strand of hair came untucked and went sliding across her temple. Ray reached a finger and stopped it, moved it back behind her ear.

"I'd like to see you again," he said, his voice a low confidence.

She finished chewing, swallowed and said in the same low tone, "You will."

They were the last ones sitting at the table. The busboys cleaned around them as they exchanged cards over coffee and chocolate cake, the restaurant's single dessert offering.

"Daisy," Ray said. "Short for Marguerite."

She looked down at his card. *Gallerie 247, Ltd. Jean-Raymond Bonloup, owner. Québec City. Montréal. Saint John.*

"Bonloup," she said, touching the word. "Good wolf."

He tilted his head, corners of his eyes crinkling over the rim of his coffee cup.

"Usually the wolves come for me at four in the morning," she said in French.

He put his cup down. "Did you know," he said, also in French. "That the head of a daisy is made up of several smaller flowers called 'ray flowers'?"

He reached a hand and helped her on with her jacket. They extricated themselves from the bench seats and Ray walked her out to the porch. They shook hands and pressed cheeks three times.

"I almost didn't come tonight," Daisy said.

He tucked her hair behind her ear. "That would have been a tragedy."

"Will you call me?"

"Will you answer?"

She laughed, and her hand, of its own accord, brushed his cheek. Ran out along his shoulder, down his arm, and squeezed his fingers. "Goodnight."

She had only turned onto the main road when her cell phone rang.

"I don't know if you remember me, but we met tonight?"

Her face stretched with pleasure. "Where are you?"

"Still standing on the porch. Watching you drive away."

Her eyes flicked to the rearview mirror but she'd rounded a bend and the cove was out of sight. "Aren't you supposed to wait something like three days before you call a girl?"

"Three days to call a girl. If it's a woman like you, call immediately."

"I see."

"I was thinking of going to the Hopper exhibit at the arts center tomorrow," he said.

"Alone?"

"That was my plan. Would you like to go with me?"

"I'd love to."

"Will you have breakfast with me first?"

"I'd love that, too."

"What else do you love?"

She laughed. "I don't love talking on the phone while I'm driving so I'm going to hang up now."

"Will you call me when you get home or do you have to wait three days?"

"I can call when I get home. If you want."

"I want. Your French is beautiful. You were either raised in the Rhône-Alpes or by someone who was."

"My mother is from Lyon. You have a good ear."

"You have beautiful eyes."

"I'll call you in a few minutes."

"All right, Daisy. Drive safely."

"A bientôt, bon loup."

YOUR KIND OF FIGHT

SHE SUGGESTED KATE'S BAKERY for breakfast, and declined to be picked up. "I'll meet you there."

Through the glass front doors, she saw him sitting on the wooden bench in the vestibule, elbows on knees, feet tapping a tattoo on the terracotta floor. His face lit up when she walked in. He stood, his tall frame unfolding until it seemed to fill the small space with joy.

"Good morning," he said. Something in his voice and eyes reminded Daisy of Kees Justi. How Kees could call your name and say hello as if only you existed for him.

"Sleep well?" he asked after they were seated. He shrugged his leather jacket off and onto the chair back. Under it, he wore a handsome button-down shirt, navy blue with a raised, textured pattern. His hair looked damp and his face gleamed freshly-shaved.

"I did," she said, sliding her own jacket off.

"I feel bad I kept you up so late talking."

"I don't feel bad at all," she said, smiling.

The waitress appeared and poured water into their glasses. "Can I bring anyone coffee?"

"Yes," Ray said, and glanced at Daisy. "For you?"

She nodded, digging in her purse for a hair elastic. "No, actually... Make it tea," she said.

Because I'm sorry and I'll always be sorry and I think I can have a cup of goddamn tea now.

"I love when you do that," Ray said.

"What? Talk to myself?"

He laughed. "I meant pull your hair back when you sit down to eat. But the mumbling is adorable, too."

"Get used to it," she said, opening the menu.

She ordered the eggs Florentine and he got the French toast. By unspoken arrangement, halfway through their meals, they switched plates. Conversation flowed like syrup, puddling comfortably around their ankles.

"What did your wife do," Daisy asked. From last night's conversation she knew Ray was widowed ten years before, leaving him with a sixteen-year-old daughter, Arielle.

Ray smiled as he ran a bit of toast around the last of the egg yolk on the plate. "She came from a long line of book binders," he said. "She lived for books. Loved nothing more than an afternoon in a library or a dusty secondhand bookstore, looking for treasure. If she wasn't reading, she was writing."

"Did she publish anything?"

"No. After the baby was born, well... You know how it is. Dreams get put on hold during those years. Too little time. Too little energy. She thought about going back to school, but never put a plan together. She worked with her father, but as it suited her." Ray's soft laugh was affectionate as he looked out the window. "Noelle had no end of dreams and ideas, but so little drive to make them come alive."

"She liked to be there, not get there," Daisy said.

Ray's head tilted. "Yes. Exactly."

"I have a friend who's the opposite. Go on, though."

"I would draw these funny pictures for Arielle. Little people." Ray wiped his mouth and his long fingers began folding his napkin. "We'd make up names for them, group them into families and create life stories. Noelle had an idea to write a series of children's books based on them. I thought it was a spectacular idea. A husband and wife collaboration. I churned out a hundred drawings. But she was still working on the story when she died. Ah, thank you," he said to the waitress, who brought the check. "Do you want to drive over to the Arts Center?"

"No, it's beautiful out," Daisy said. "Let's walk."

After three hours at the Hopper exhibit they went to lunch—a long one in a sunny window at the Wharf Tavern.

"You look sleepy," Ray said, chin resting on the heels of his hands.

"A little," she said. "After lunch is usually when I nap."

"I love to nap," he said, sighing. "And I'm so good at it."

She laughed and was genuinely disappointed when he checked his watch and sighed again. He was due back in Quebec City for an opening and needed to get to the airport.

While the conversation was non-stop, they hadn't been particularly touchy-feely during the day. Only now, on the walk downtown, did Ray take her hand.

"I'll call you when I land."

"Yes, let me know you got there safe."

A strange sadness came over her as they neared the building where he was renting a studio apartment. She was filled with a thick longing.

"I feel so emotional," Ray said. "I'm not sure why."

"I do too." Her hand hesitated then reached up. She glided her thumb across one of his eyebrows. He leaned and kissed her mouth. Soft, like a promise. His scent filled her head.

"Come back soon, good wolf," she whispered.

"I will." He kissed her again. A corner of his bottom lip curled under his teeth. He tried to smile through it, but ended up shaking his head and touching her cheek with the backs of his fingers. "Go," he said. "Or I won't."

With an effort, she walked away, turning back twice to wave. Once at home, she called Lucky.

"I met someone."

"Who?" Lucky said. "Another zygote?"

"Oh my God, are you ever going to let that go? Seriously, it was six months ago."

"Let go of you having a fling with the nineteen-year-old behind the deli counter? Not anytime soon."

"He was twenty. And he served a certain purpose."

"Served it all night, I bet."

Daisy laughed. "He didn't know what he was doing, but he could do it all night. Anyway, this guy isn't a zygote. He's forty-six."

"Forty s— Hold on, I need both ears for this. Will. William. Man the fort, I have to talk to Dais. She met someone."

Through the receiver, Daisy could hear Will give a bark of laughter. "Another zygote?"

The sound of a closing door and the domestic cacophony was silenced. "All right, my dear. Say again, he's how old?"

"Forty-six."

"Holy shit," Lucky said. "You met a *man*." She sang the word with relish.

"A man," Daisy said, echoing the high note.

They sang it together. "A man. She met a man."

"Not a boy but a man," Lucky said. "And what line of work is this man in?"

"He owns an art gallery in—"

"He's gay."

"Goddammit, don't say— Now you ruined it."

"And we were doing so well."

"Fuck," Daisy said.

"Well, we won't jump to conclusions. Let Will meet him. Out of all of us, he's got the superior gaydar."

"I do want you to meet him. He's coming back next weekend. We have tickets for the Symphonie New Brunswick."

"I insist on meeting him. Let's go for drinks. Or brunch. Hey, not for nothing, Dais, but it's been a while since you had that goofy tone in your voice…"

"IT'S SO NICE TO meet you," Lucky said, shaking Ray's hand. As he turned to greet Will, she widened her eyes at Daisy.

"Silver fox," she mouthed.

Daisy's returned smile was smug.

They chatted through a first round of drinks. Daisy excused herself to the ladies' room and coming back, met up with Will buying a second round at the bar.

"Un régal pour l'oeil," he said.

"He is easy on the eyes, yes. And he also speaks French, so behave."

Will smiled and put his arm around her. "I meant you look beautiful, dumbass."

Daisy felt beautiful. Her dress was new—pearly grey brocade with a halter top and a swingy skirt.

"I'm not getting a gay vibe," Will said.

"From me?"

He lightly swatted the back of her head. "He's a good guy."

"I like him," Daisy said. "We've talked every night this week until the wee hours. My phone bill is going to be a scream."

"He's how old?"

"Forty-six." She drew in her breath. "He's going to be a grandfather soon."

Will's eyebrows flew up. "What, did he get married when he was twelve?"

"Almost. Got his girlfriend pregnant when he was eighteen."

"Well. I guess no wondering if he's a decent guy. Did they end up divorcing?"

"She passed away ten years ago. Their daughter is having a baby any week now."

"Making Ray the hottest grandpa in town."

Daisy smiled.

"Age doesn't mean anything. Let it unfold." Will laid his hand on her cheek. "I like seeing you happy."

She hesitated. "He comes from money."

"What kind of money?"

"Montreal banking money."

"Patron of the arts money?"

She nodded.

Will gave her a little push toward the table. "Go fuck him before I do."

DINNER WAS BOTH EASY and relaxed, smoldering and chemical. At the symphony concert Daisy sat with her arm looped through Ray's, her hand in his, buzzed with both wine and attention. Luxuriantly content in her skin. Slightly bored.

Ray brought her hand up to his mouth a moment. Then tilted his head toward her. "I'm bored out of my mind," he whispered. "Let's get out of here."

She suppressed a giggle. "And go where?"

"Dancing."

"As if I didn't like you enough."

In the coughing pause between pieces, they took flight, skulking down the aisle and not making eye contact with the ushers. They dashed like bank robbers down the wide front steps. As he peeled out of the parking lot, Ray's laughter filled the car. "Stupid," he said, shifting gears. "But I always wanted to abscond with a beautiful female and lay rubber as I drove away."

"Am I your first abscondment?"

"You are. Did you make that word up?"

"I did."

Ray shifted gears again, a delicious smile around his face. "Make up another."

"Absconce."

"Sounds like a lighting fixture."

"A stolen lighting fixture."

"Oh, fuck this," he said. He downshifted and brought the car to a stop on the shoulder.

"Did you see a cop?" Daisy said, turning in her seat to look out the back. Then Ray's hands were on her face and he was drawing her to him over the console. The warm smell of him. His inhale catching her exhale. "Come here," he said, just before his mouth took hers.

She melted into his kiss, running a hand up the back of his head. A rush of air in her ears, layered with the click of the hazard lights. The jingle of Ray's keys as his knee set them swinging from the ignition. A sigh first in her chest, then in his.

"Where," he said, his forehead against hers. "Where have you been?"

"Right here," she said, and kissed him again.

I'M SO HAPPY, she thought later, caught up in Ray's arms as the band played "Can't Help Falling in Love."

"I'm so glad you dance," she said.

"Not all that well, I'm afraid," he said. Which was untrue, but typical of Ray's self-effacing manner.

"I don't care that a man can't dance," she said. "I care that he won't dance."

She laid her head on his shoulder. He was warm and solid beneath her. She felt both powerful and protected in his embrace.

During all the late-night phone conversations of the past week, her stories had easily flowed from her heart to his ears. Erik. The shooting. The cutting. Therapy. Life on the road and her career. Ray listened, gathering her tales in his hands, examining them and asking thoughtful questions. Peeling her open.

"I want to hear more," he always said before they hung up. "I can't wait to talk again."

She couldn't wait either. She woke up thinking about him. Fell asleep with his voice lingering in her ear. His inviting manner made her want to share herself. Folded in his strong arms, swaying to the music, she was enveloped in a multi-layered attraction she hadn't felt in years.

Are you the one? she wondered, tilting her head to smile up at him again.

"You're so beautiful I want to die," Ray said. He took her hand and put it up behind his neck, then slid both his palms against the small of her back.

The band modulated and segued into another song. The female vocalist stepped up to the mic and began singing "The Man I Love" in a throaty alto.

Daisy sighed.

Someday he'll come along.... The man I love... And he'll be big and strong...

"This was your song," Ray said.

"Yes."

"Does it bother you to hear it?"

"No," she said against his neck. "But I'm bored out of my mind. Let's get out of here."

HER BEDROOM GOLD with candlelight, a dozen votives melted into clear liquid around sputtering flames. Her dress was in a silvery heap on the floor, the sleeve of Ray's flung shirt across it protectively. One of his shoes was spooning one of her sling-backs. A constellation of loose change twinkled on the rug.

On the bed, Ray sprawled on his stomach, his expression intent as he stroked her left leg, fingertips touching her scars.

"You were only twenty," he said.

"Just."

"Turn over."

She rolled away and showed him her back. His fingers were curious but gentle. They touched the one deep scar by the base of her spine. Its companion beneath her shoulder blade.

"Can you see any others?" she asked.

His breath floated warm over her back as he peered.

"Yes," he said, touching the curve of her waist. "They're there if you look close. And know what you're looking for."

"I wondered."

"You cut where you couldn't see," he said.

"It was a dark time."

He kissed the back of her neck.

"I'm thinking I might tattoo over them," she said, nestling a cheek into the pillow.

"Don't." His hands were turning her again. "Leave your skin alone."

She toppled onto her back and her hand went to his head, playing with his hair. Both his hands were at her hip bones, his mouth on her stomach. He was majestic in her bed. King of the wolves.

"Rex tremendae majestatis," she said.

"Pardon?"

"Does Raymond mean king?"

"Protector," he said. "Or counselor."

The behind-the-scenes man, she thought.

His thumb ran a circle around the little red fish by her hip bone. Stretching her skin taut then letting it go.

"It's what you do when you're twenty," she said. "Ink a boyfriend into your skin. Because forever is only as far as you can see."

"You do these things when you're in love," Ray said. He laid his cheek on her belly, his warm palm sliding over the fish, almost reverently. "You do these things when someone tries to shoot down that love. It's what you do to survive. Maybe the lover goes away but what you do for love stays with you forever." His arms slid up her sides and he held her. "Maybe you did one terrible thing to him. But everything else you did *for* him, Daisy, was beautiful."

She breathed in the truth of that, making Ray's head rise. Slowly she exhaled him down then opened her arms.

"Come here."

He slid up her body, crushing her with his warm strong weight and his heady scent. Hard shoulders and arms. Soft hair on his chest. Her head in his hands.

"What do you want from me," he whispered, kissing around her mouth. His voice caressed the words. They were an offering, not a lament.

"Your time," she said, touching the neat edge of his sideburn. "Your attention."

He kissed her, slow and gorgeous. His eyes open and staring into hers.

"Your secrets," she said, her chest thick with desire.

"I don't have secrets."

"Everyone has one secret."

He looked off to the side a moment then gave a resigned sigh. "My name isn't Raymond," he said. "It's George."

"Shut up," she said, laughing.

He dodged the swat of her hand, grabbed it in his and pressed it against his smile.

"You're a lovely man," she said.

His eyes closed. "Say that again."

She kissed him. "You're a lovely man."

His body shifted. She felt him hard on her inner thigh, and then pushing into her.

"What do you want," she said, wrapping her limbs about him. He rocked back, then moved deeper in her. All up in her legs and hips, his arms holding her tight. Soft like the coat of a wolf. Wild and commanding inside her. Beautiful.

"I want to take care of you," he said. "Not because I think you're helpless. Helpless women don't fight your kind of fight and win. It's because of your strength that I want to take care of you."

She rolled and rose up over him, planting her knees on either side of his heaving chest. The ball of his shoulder in her palm, his hands twining up into her hair. She slid along the length of him, delicate and precise, as his hips pushed up hard.

"I want to fall in love with you," he said. "Don't stop me."

She let him fall, tumbling right alongside. Her heart was free. She was in. She felt beautiful and glorious. A daisy made up of ray flowers.

THE HEAD WON
ON A BET

AT FIRST DAISY THOUGHT the illustrated notes Ray left on her pillow were darling. Little flowers, faces and figures punctuated his loving and funny words. She tucked the slips of paper into the mirror frame at her dressing table. Collaged them on the refrigerator door and used them as bookmarks.

Little by little, she noticed when his hands had nothing to do, they reached for a pen. And he never went anywhere without scraps of paper tucked in his inside pocket.

"Why not carry a notebook?" she asked once.

"If I have a notebook with me, I don't feel like drawing," he said. "It seems to be only when it's inconvenient to draw that it strikes me."

Ray liked to make swift decisions and not be second-guessed by others or himself. He did the crossword with a pen. He drew only in ink. "I like having one chance at some things," he said.

As if, Daisy thought, he had missed a crucial chance once and was forever drilling and rehearsing not to miss again.

Without the safety net of eraser he drew creatures with large eyes and no mouths. Their bodies were roly-poly and too small for their large heads. But as the weeks with Daisy passed and Ray spent short hours observing her in performance, and longer hours running his hands over her in bed, his little beings began to change shape on paper. Their figures grew elongated and slender. They began to leap over flowers instead of sitting upon them.

"Hold still," Ray would often say, catching Daisy in the middle of stretching up to retrieve something off a shelf, or bending to pick something off the floor. She was a dancer. When she did such mundane things, one leg or arm unconsciously went up in an accompanying pose. She didn't even think about it.

"Don't move," Ray said around the cap of his pen held in his teeth. His dark eyebrows furrowed as he pinned the lines of her body to the paper.

"They're silly," he said, shrugging. He capped the pen and slid the paper across to her.

"I love them," she said.

As a serious joke, she bought a pack of washable magic markers and slid it under the pillow on his side of the bed. (They had been together a little over a month, and he had a definitive side.)

Ray laughed and bopped her lightly on the head with them, but she could tell he was pleased. And after loving her, he made a mural on her back. Little fey with wings of gold, coral, azure and violet. Fluttering up her spine and nestling beneath her shoulder blades. Sprinkling petals on her shoulders. They smeared rainbows from her skin to his when they made love again, color melting into the sheets. Enchantresses bubbled away down the shower drain the next morning.

"I love you," Ray said, washing her back. Under the spray of water he began to sing softly. "Daisy, Daisy... Give me your answer, do."

"True," she said.

"What?"

"It's give me your answer true."

"No, it's not. It's *do.*"

"Excuse me, it's my song. It's true."

"Excuse me, I'm more than a decade older than you and I know what the lyrics are."

"My father sang me the damn song. It's *true.*"

"He sang it wrong. You are absolutely wrong."

She reached and turned off the taps. "I'm right."

Ray snapped a towel off the rack and threw it at her then took one for himself. "Would you care to make a small wager on this, darling?"

"You will lose, darling."

"I'm giving you the chance to capitulate with dignity."

"Never."

Wrapped in towels, leaving damp footprints on the floor, they marched to Daisy's desk.

"If I'm right you're buying me shoes," she said.

"You're wrong and I'm getting a blow job."

"Why do men always wager that?" She typed *Daisy Bell lyrics* into the search box and hit the enter key. "Shoes last longer."

"The sweetest head is given voluntarily. The next sweetest is the head won on a bet."

"What about the head you have to beg for?"

"Not as sweet but definitely not sour. Well?"

"Fuck," Daisy muttered, staring at the screen. "You're right."

"Oh, I love 'you're right.' Say it again."

"You're right. I'm wrong. It's do."

With a flourish, Ray whipped the towel from his waist and tossed it away, narrowly missing Sovereign, who mewed indignantly.

"I've been singing it wrong for thirty years," she said.

"It's never too late to fix these things."

"I have to rearrange my entire childhood."

Ray cleared his throat. "I do have a flight to catch."

Still staring at the screen, Daisy reached and closed him up in her fingers. "I can't believe it," she said.

"I'll never tell."

She sighed with a shrug. Then got up and went back to the bedroom, leading Ray behind her. Not by the hand.

"You're a lady of your word," he said happily.

GIVE ME YOUR ANSWER TRUE

THE JACQUES CARTIER BRIDGE spanned Montreal Harbor and averaged ten suicides a year. On a rainy spring evening, Noelle Bonloup became one of 1992's statistics.

"Her heart was broken," Ray said, as he and Daisy lay in bed at his apartment in Montreal. "Arielle wasn't our only child. Sandrine came a year later. But we lost her to cancer and Noelle...was never the same."

Daisy squeezed her eyes shut, involuntarily turning her head from the image of a woman poised on the rail of a bridge. Poised on the edge of a life no longer worth living.

When asked, Ray went out to the living room and came back with some photos. He showed Daisy the girls as babies, then as toddlers: a pair of gorgeous redheads, like flame under sunshine. Daisy smiled and exclaimed as her fingers turned the years over. In the last shot, the sisters were perhaps five and six, sitting with Ray at a table crowded with paper, brushes and paints. In the background, slightly blurred, Noelle loaded the dishwasher. A beautiful portrait of a loving family. Except...

"God," Daisy whispered, reaching with a fingertip to touch the image. Arielle's hair fell long and lush down her back, but Sandrine was bald, veins showing through the porcelain skin stretched over her skull. From her free hand snaked tubes to the IV pole behind her chair. "Oh, Ray..."

Ray turned the photo toward him. His smile wobbled, but it was filled with a fierce affection. "She was tough," he said. "So brave, right until the end."

"How old?"

"Nearly seven."

"I'm so sorry."

He showed her the collection of little people he drew for his daughters over the years, now bound into a half-dozen miniature books.

"Did your wife bind these?" Daisy asked, examining the cloth and leather covers with an almost reverent awe, admiring the meticulous craftsmanship. The pages' deckle edges were luxuriantly thick against her fingertips.

"No, my father-in-law," he said. "I asked him to after Noelle... I wanted them bound for Arielle. I feel the pictures belong to her. But she's never come to claim them or bring them to live with her. I thought maybe when she had the baby..."

Daisy set the books carefully on the nightstand and turned to put arms around him. "I'm sorry."

His fingers pushed into her hair, carefully tugged their way down and out. His body felt so serene and peaceful under her hands and she didn't understand how. Something about his peace was upsetting her.

She pushed the sheets aside, got up on one elbow as her eyes followed the path of her palm over his chest and shoulders. Her touch trailed down and up his arms in a confused search.

"What?" he said.

"Roll over..."

He gave her a puzzled look and turned onto his stomach. The skin was softest on his back, freckled over his shoulder blades and solid further down, like tea with a splash of milk. Her eyes and hands kept sweeping him, searching, moving down the strong muscles of his legs to his feet. He shivered as she touched the hollows of heels and the secret place behind his knees.

"What are you looking for," he said.

She surfed up his body and stretched out on his back, curving her arms around his arms. Beneath the pillow, she wove their fingers together.

"You had to explain to your child she was going to die," she whispered against his head. "You buried your daughter. Then you had to go claim Noelle. You got the call and you had to go... Did you go to the bridge?"

"The morgue," he said, his fingers curling around hers.

"And you had to tell Arielle what happened. Twice you had to tell her."

"Yes."

She swallowed. "Did you feel to blame? For Noelle? Wonder if you could have done something differently?"

"Of course. I tore my soul to shreds wondering what I could have done to stop her. And I bore the brunt of Arielle's grief as well. She was young and needed justification, something or someone to blame for the loss of her sister and her mother. I know our relationship suffered because I was her whipping boy when she needed a father. For years, it seemed everywhere I looked, including the mirror, I only saw incriminating eyes."

"And yet..." She slid off him again and set her palm in the center of his back. "You don't have a mark on you." Tears blurred her vision as she gazed upon the whole, unmarred and intact surface of his skin. "Not one cut, not one scar, not even a tattoo. You felt no need to make the blame visible on your body."

He rolled to his side. "No, I didn't."

His fingertips gently touched her wet face as her hand moved along his arm. "This is hard to explain," she said. "But it's like your skin is the bravest thing I've ever seen."

He looked up at her, bewilderment in his expression but understanding as well. "Thank you," he said.

SHE WOKE UP ALONE in bed the next morning, which was typical. Ray didn't sleep in—up at dawn no matter what day of week. He never disturbed her rest, although he insisted she get up by ten for practical purposes.

"You must get up," he would say, opening the drapes. "Or you won't nap properly later."

She gathered the sheet around herself and went down the hall, trailing 500-threadcount Egyptian cotton like a bride. The apartment smelled of fresh coffee. Ray had a fire going and Chopin on the stereo. He sat at his drafting table wearing the textured, navy blue shirt she loved. The sun through the window making a halo around his head. His quiet, rugged handsomeness making Daisy's heart press against the wall of her chest.

Are you the one?

He looked up. Took off his glasses and smiled at her.

"Can this be mine," he said, opening his arms.

She went to him, wriggled between his knees between the high stool and the drafting table, which he preferred to a desk. She snuggled back against him as his arms circled her and went on drawing.

"I'm so happy," she said.

He put his forehead down on her shoulder, kissed her neck. His hand, she noticed, was covering up his work.

"What are you up to?"

"Just a bit of an idea."

"What?"

"It's stupid."

"Show me."

He shuffled drawings around and brought to the top a sheet where he'd written the lyrics of "Daisy Bell."

Daisy, Daisy give me your answer true.

"True?" she asked.

"True," he said, kissing the side of her face. "From now on it will always be true."

I'm half-crazy all for the love of you
It won't be a stylish marriage
I can't afford a carriage
But you'll look sweet upon the seat
Of a bicycle built for two.

Surrounding the words was a bower of daisies. And beneath it, a couple on a tandem bicycle. Ray's distinctive creatures made human. The same button eyes and mouthless faces but they were definitively people, not fairies. A mid-century feel was in the illustration. A bygone time rendered soft with watercolor and detailed with India ink.

"Did you make this for me?" she said.

He turned over another page. "Here's where it gets stupid."

A skyscape now, going from pastel day in the bottom left to indigo twilight in the top right. A hot air balloon piloted by a man in cap and goggles. His passenger a blonde lady, a long white scarf waving floating behind her like a banner. Out the back of the basket dropped tiny purple flowers, drifting down and about the page, circling another verse:

Violet, Violet, give me your answer true.
I'll be a pilot and fly away with you
On top of the clouds we'll tarry
Among the stars we'll marry
And songs we'll sing upon the wings
Of an air balloon built for two.

Every page a woman's floral name, a made up verse and an illustration.

"Ray," she said again, completely drawn in. "It's..."

She couldn't think of a word to do the illustrations justice. Charming. Precious. Breathtakingly simple and innocent.

"I want to live in them," she said. The sweet, lullaby tune filled her head. Her finger touched a scene of a couple on a back porch, cozied on a glider swing. Beneath the railings was drawn the sword-like foliage of irises.

> *Iris, Iris, give me your answer true.*
> *I'll blow one kiss across the lawn to you*
> *You'll catch it on your finger*
> *And through the day 'twill linger*
> *'Til fireflies dance and hold us entranced*
> *On a back porch built for two.*

"If I were a little girl, I would want a book like this on my shelf," she said. "I'm a big girl and I want it."

"It's yours." His warm hands ran up and down her back, gently pushing the sheet open and away, turning her to face him. "And so am I," he said.

Ray was well-connected, and friends and colleagues were more than happy to help him get it published. Within a month he'd finished the verses and drawings. Pitched the book and sold it and partnered with a children's charity to donate all the proceeds.

He arrived in Saint John one weekend and brought Daisy one of the first printed copies. He drew her into his lap and opened the book to the dedication page.

> *For Daisy.*
> *Because you do these things when you're in love.*

PARTNER IN A NEW WAY

THE SAINT JOHN HERALD
December 15, 2003
"Nutcracker Brings Endings and Beginnings For New Bruns-
wick Ballet Theater"

Saturday evening's performance of the second act of Nutcracker *was a charming and heartfelt farewell for Margue-*
rite Bianco and William Kaeger, who are retiring as principal
dancers with the company and taking up reins as co-artistic
directors in January.

Since 1999, this partnership has been bringing a magical
joy to NBBT's repertory. But the roots of Kaeger and Bian-
co's affinity stretch back another decade, to when they met
at Lancaster University in 1989.

"Our teacher put us together in partnering class," Kaeger
says. "I don't know if it was a random choice or she had an

idea we'd dance well together. But within ten minutes we had a connection."

"It was magic," Bianco says. "I don't typically believe in magic but right away dancing with Will was extraordinary."

"We're not alike," Kaeger says. "She's a much more cerebral dancer than me. She's pragmatic and thoughtful and I do everything on impulse. But somehow it worked. She made me think a little more."

"He made me let go a little more."

"And then we were partners."

Partners and friends through Lancaster's 1992 tragedy, when a fellow dance student came into the theater with a gun and opened fire, killing five students and a professor before turning the gun on himself. Kaeger was shot once in the side and again in the left hand, losing two of his fingers. Bianco was shot through the leg and did not dance for a year. When she did come back to the studio, she and Kaeger had to learn to partner in a new way, working around their injuries.

"We were even closer then," Bianco says. "The trust and the love were so much stronger between us. I've never had with any other partner what I have with Will. And I feel so fortunate I was able to be in a company with him for four years. And now taking over as artistic directors. There's no one else I'd want to do with this with."

"No one who'd want to do it with me," Kaeger says. "She's the only one crazy enough."

Both Kaeger and Bianco are accomplished choreographers. Bianco's memorial ballet Rakewind won Capezio's coveted A.C.E. award and has been staged for the Anaheim Ballet, Charlotte Ballet Theater and Miami Civic Ballet. Kaeger's Powaqqatsi, set to music by Philip Glass, was featured at the Jacob's Pillow Dance Festival this summer. Both ballets are planned for NBBT's coming season, as well as other works in progress.

Their final performance as Sugar Plum and Cavalier in Nut- cracker *brought the Imperial Theater to its feet Saturday night. Kaeger and Bianco danced not as storybook charac- ters but as dear, human friends. And as they took their right- fully-deserved multiple curtain calls, one can only see this finale as an overture.*

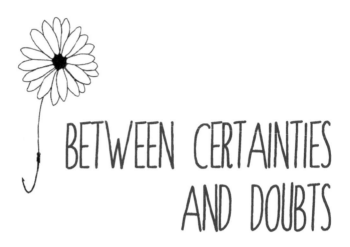

BETWEEN CERTAINTIES AND DOUBTS

JUNE 17, 2004

Dear Rita,

It's been an exhausting, exciting time. I feel like I've reached a creative apex in my career and I feel so happy. So complete.

"And?" I can hear you say.

Ray and I hit our first major pothole a few months ago, when Daisy, Daisy *was released. His daughter Arielle called on the phone screaming at me. Screaming at him. How dare he take the pictures he drew for her and her sister, publish them and dedicate them to another woman?*

I'd never been on the receiving end of such an ugly scene. And I have to say, even though they weren't exactly the pictures he drew for them, I could understand how she felt. In her mind it was her mother's unfinished project, now finished and given to someone else. I was shocked Ray hadn't told her about the book. It seemed so thoughtless and out of character for him.

The situation has cooled down but so has the air between Arielle and me, which was never warm and fuzzy to begin with.

Meanwhile, Ray and I have been talking about getting married. Oh God, I don't know. I love Ray, but his family dynamic is so strange. His parents are stiff and formal and one of his brothers is a real misogynistic prick. Do I want to marry into this? Furthermore, do I want to bring a child into this?

Which raises another issue: Ray had a vasectomy years ago. It didn't matter when we started dating. Now that our eyes are turning further down the road, I'm feeling like it's going to start mattering. I am not getting the feeling he wants to have a family with me. I think he wants just us.

God, the crossroads suck. In a way, Ray has been the perfect boyfriend for me. He's elbow-deep in his own ventures and he isn't possessive of me or my time. So our affair continues along with neither of us making demands or making plans. It stays in the present. Ray goes from Montreal to Quebec City to Saint John to Halifax. And he's toying with the idea of opening a gallery in Toronto.

And me, I'm racking up the frequent flier miles as well. Will and I go here and there to give master classes or workshops, stage ballets on other companies. Ray and I simply arrange our time so it works. We're here. We're there. And in between, we're together as much as possible.

His is certainly a style of life I could get used to. He doesn't throw his money around but he cherishes me. Gifts. Weekends to Paris. Concerts and shows and museum openings. Black tie events. Any time I'm homesick, he puts me on a plane. Or gives my parents the keys to his apartment.

"And...?"

I love him. Yet on the Sunday nights when my apartment door closes behind him, or when I'm buckled into my seat on the plane, it's the tiniest frisson of luxuriant relief. Not that I *want to escape him. But I look forward to my solitude again. Home in my little apartment with only Sovereign's company.*

I miss Ray when we're apart, but not enough to die over it. Certainly not enough to change my life for it.

And it kind of bothers me.

Anyway, between life's accomplishments and struggles, between certainties and doubts, I'm hanging in the middle doing all right. I hope you are too.

Daisy

SOVEREIGN

RAY'S HAND WAS ALMOST rough as it turned Daisy's face to him. "I want to marry you."

Tears sprung to her eyes, but not from joy.

"Will you marry me, Daisy?"

To shake her head would be cruel, as cruel as saying no. But she had no words. She bowed her forehead into his palm and did nothing.

"Give me your answer true," he said.

A smile tried to break through her mouth and failed. She slid her arms around his waist, taking handfuls of his shirt as she lifted her head. "I will want to have children, Ray. This won't change. I need to know if it's part of your vision. Do you want a family with me? Or do you want to be just a couple?"

His hands gripped her shoulders. "I want to be your husband."

"And that's all? Don't tell me what you think I want to hear. Give me your answer."

"I don't want to lose you. I love you more than I ever..." The bravery of speaking the truth made his voice crack open. Knowing the truth could cost him.

"I want you and me," he said. "I want you to myself. I have no doubt you'd be a wonderful mother but... Being a father at twenty and being a father at fifty are two completely different things."

"Honey, this isn't about your age," she said.

"Of *course* it's not," he said, breaking away. "You want the ugly, selfish truth? That I'm afraid to have a child with you? Afraid at best I won't be the sole recipient of your attention and at worst, to see the light sucked out of your eyes if God forbid, something should happen? Will hearing it make you feel better?"

Deflated, one of his hands dropped onto the back of a chair, the other dragged across his face.

"I'm sorry," he said.

Her heart tore down the center as she went into his arms. She understood how he kept love at a distance all those years, understood the extent of the risk he took loving her after he lost Noelle. But the risk of having another child, the risk of losing that child and watching another wife go mad with grief? Ray's soul would never make such a gamble again. He'd drawn this decision long ago in ink.

But... And *I can't erase my dreams to keep him safe.*

"I want children," she said. "I want a family with the man I marry."

In the grey Canadian twilight, he looked old. A broken-legged wolf. His blue eyes swam with tears. "I can't."

"I'm sorry," she said through a throat of iron while the marrow in her bones felt all too much like glass.

They crept through the rest of the evening, speaking softly, touching each other as if they were burned and bruised. Ray pulled into the solitude of a book. Daisy sought distraction in work, sitting down at her desk with notes for a new ballet she and Will were working on. She played the music softly and sketched out an idea for the set design, using the beautiful colored pencils Ray bought for her.

"You have no idea," he said, "what a thrill it is for me to see a woman chase down a dream like a hunter."

He got up from the couch and came over to her. "You get an idea for a ballet and three months later, I sit in the theater and see it manifested. You want your bathroom a new color and the next day you're putting down newspapers and opening cans of paint. You don't wait for someone to come along and do it for you. You roll up your sleeves and get to work. I love that. I love you, Daisy."

He crouched down by her chair and set his forehead against her side. She ran her hand through his hair.

"Ray, I do love you. And—"

His fingers touched her mouth. "Come to bed with me," he said. "Please no more words tonight. Just come be with me."

She followed him to bed where he made a hard and desperate love to her, like a hunter chasing down a dream. A last stand. No words or tears spilled between their grave, urgent bodies, and afterward Daisy surprised herself by falling into a sated and dreamless sleep.

In the thin grey of morning, Ray shook her awake.

"Daisy. Wake up, Daisy."

She batted his hand away. "Stop."

"Wake up, sweetheart."

His face was drawn up and grim. He looked even older than the night before.

"What's wrong?"

"Something's happened."

"What?"

He took her hand, led her into the foyer where he threw his wool overcoat around her shoulders.

It seemed a dream. "Ray, what is it?"

He led her out on the porch and gestured toward the small front yard of her apartment. She followed his pointing finger to a lump of black fur in the frosty grass. She squinted then looked back at Ray, noticing he had a towel in his hands.

She turned back to the yard and took a step down. "Sovereign?"

His hand checked her. "Don't. I'll get her."

Her legs buckled and she sat on the steps.

"Sové," she said, louder. "Come here, honey. Come here, Sovereign."

Ray was wrapping the cat in the towel. He came back to her, the bundle cradled in his arms. A trickle of dried blood trailed from one black ear. The topaz eyes stared at nothing.

"Oh, honey, no," she whispered, reaching. Carefully, Ray put Sovereign in her lap.

"She must have been hit," he said, sitting down. He put his hand over the cat's empty gaze. His other hand spread wide on Daisy's head.

"I'm so sorry."

She leaned on him, weeping, clutching her darling.

Ray held her tight and said nothing.

PHANTOM PAIN

DAISY WRAPPED HERSELF in work after she and Ray broke up. Her job remained a constant source of joy. She could get up in the morning and look forward to the day. First position was always first position. She was a gifted choreographer, a sought-after teacher. She and Will were coaxing the flowers of New Brunswick Ballet Theater into bloom and great things were happening.

But she was lonely.

It intensified when the Kaegers' second baby, Sara, was born. Daisy helped Will and Lucky by taking two-year-old Jack off their hands whenever she could. She fell hard for her honorary nephew, who seemed just as smitten with Aunt Daisy. He slept over every Sunday night, snuggled up close in her bed, thumb in his mouth and the other hand holding to a lock of her hair.

Watching him sleep, something in her heart contracted. A cold, fuzzy unease took shape in her stomach as she balanced on a contemplative edge.

I'm going to grow old. Alone. I'm going to live alone and die alone.

Anxiety, which had made itself scarce for many years, came calling. Mean wolves snarling in the wee hours, making her take flight from bed and go digging for Xanax. She paced her apartment, thoughts undulating like a murmur of birds, wheeling and turning. The ominous, prickling heat down her limbs even as she shivered. She breathed deep against the growing knot in her heart. She needed to find the hook, the platitude or mantra that became a shelf she could lay her mind down on. But the beasts kept laughing at her from the shadows.

I'm alone, this is my life. This is what it's come to.

I gave up a man who loved me for a dream that might not ever come true now.

I'll never be that woman standing on the porch, waving to her children.

"You all right, honey?" Will said when she dropped Jack off one Monday evening. He was lying on the couch in front of the fire, Sara asleep on his chest.

Daisy sat on the floor, tracing Sara's pink earlobe with her fingertip.

"Wolves," she said. "I don't know why they're showing up lately."

Will's hand rested on her crown a moment, then went back to Sara's head. As Daisy watched him caress his sleeping daughter, her own fingertips cried out for soft, plump skin and milk-sweet breath. Her chest pounded fists and stamped feet, wanting the weight of an infant as she lounged on the couch in front of her own fireplace.

I'm alone.

Oh, Erik, what the hell happened to it all?

I wish I could talk to you.

"Talk to me," Will said softly.

"All these years," she said. "I date the nicest guys. But everything comes back around to Erik eventually. And it still hurts."

"Phantom pain," Will said, holding up his maimed hand. "They're gone. But they hurt."

Daisy reached to touch the scar tissue.

"I didn't get to say goodbye to those fingers. Or grow unattached to them. They were here one minute, gone the next. I never saw them again. Same with Erik. He was blown off you the same way my fingers were blown off. Part of you still feels him. Part of you will always be in love with him. Because you never detached. You never fell out of love."

"Sometimes I feel like a strand of Christmas lights with one bulb burnt out. I'm happy, Will. But not the way I was when I was with him. Will I ever be that happy again—completely, with all the lights on? Was it a dream, a once-in-a-lifetime feat that can't ever be replicated? I don't know."

"I wonder if he ever replicated it," Will said, his hand spreading wide across Sara's back.

Daisy pushed the thought away. Always, she tried to impose some kind of discipline on her thoughts of Erik. Not to dwell on the scenario of him with another woman.

Was he married?

Probably. With kids. She had to accept the possibility.

"I think about him every day," she said.

Will's eyes closed. "So do I, Dais."

Lucky's voice came into the room. "You ever think of calling him?"

Will's hand went up to stroke his wife as she passed by the couch, a towel-wrapped Jack on her hip. Daisy turned and stretched her legs out long, holding out her arms. Lucky dumped her damp son off and plopped into the easy chair.

"I could," Daisy said, drying Jack's toes with a corner of the towel. "At the same time, I've worked so hard to get here, Luck. I couldn't take it if he were cold or dismissive. Silence is preferable to either of those."

I don't know him anymore, I only know what he was.

"I love who he was," she said. "Is he still that person?"

"And is it worth the risk of finding out," Lucky said.

"Better to be here with the love I knew."

"The man you loved," Will said.

"I see what you did there." Smiling, Daisy wrapped her arms around Jack, whose eyes were drooping. Thumb in mouth, he pushed his forehead against her sternum a moment, then put his cheek against her and sighed. She kissed his head.

"I don't think you make bad choices in partners," Lucky said. "You pick nice guys."

"She picks princes," Will said.

"But you also pick them safe. Trey went off to London. The zygote was too young. Ray was too old. You don't pick anyone with promise. Because you're still waiting for Erik."

Her tone wasn't accusatory, nor did Daisy take it that way. It was the truth only a friend could tell.

"Want to stay here tonight?" Will said.

She smiled into Jack's hair. "No, I should go home," she said. "Face the wolves."

"Why wolves?" Lucky said. "What made you choose them as the enemy?"

Daisy looked right and left, thinking. "I don't know," she said. "I came up with that expression years ago. Four A.M. when the wolves come. Why?"

"It's got me thinking about *The Golden Compass.* And daemons. And how wolves are vicious and brutal hunters, true. But they mate for life."

Daisy stared at her friend, who smiled back.

"You always say you want a daemon," Lucky said. "Maybe it's not a pack of wolves coming for you in the night. Maybe it's just one. And it's not coming to kill you. It's coming because it needs you."

Come to me.

Come dance with me.

Let's have a conversation.

Daisy closed her eyes as her chest unfolded in sudden understanding. Behind her lids she saw a wolf. Its fur wasn't black but silver and sugar-white. It glistened as it circled three times and lay down beside her, nose on paws. A whine in the back of its throat as she put her hand on the soft fur and stroked with and against the nap. Slid her fingers into the juncture between arm and body, curled into the warmth and felt the great heartbeat under the fur. Beating as hard and fast as her own.

You're not my enemy. You come here because you need me.

"I like that," she said. Her fingers dug into ruff at the imaginary wolf's neck. *You're with me. You* are *me. My soul manifested. A helpmate and confidant. And you will never sever yourself from me.*

"I really like that," she said.

From above, Will's hand fell soft on the crown of her head.

"You're not meant to be alone," he said.

YOUR WAR IS OVER, DÉZI

GUARDED BY AN UGLY FRENCH MYTH

BARBEGAZI
Stevens Road
Saint John
October 24, 2005

Dear Rita,

Aren't I subtle with the new address? Yes, I now officially have equity. I wasn't looking to buy a house at all, but over the summer our rehearsal accompanist Edwina Meagher retired. And she and her husband asked if I'd like to buy their place on Grand Bay.

I'd been there a bunch of times—for tea, for knitting club, for no reason—and it's a miniature La Tarasque. A sweet little farmhouse with a wraparound porch and pretty gardens. The clincher was its name: Barbegazi. They're legendary winter gnomes in Swiss and French folklore, and Edwina had a dozen statues of them around the property. They're hideous but darling. Most she took with her but she left me a few to keep watch through winter, she said. So I'm now perfectly at home in a pretty house guarded by an ugly French myth.

I have a live-in lover. Don't get excited—it's of the four-legged variety. Another instance of serendipity: I was having lunch in the Wharf Tavern one afternoon when the bartender Nick asked if I'd help him get a cat out of their dumpster. It was an unfortunately disgusting rescue, but we pulled out this pathetic scrap of a kitten. Skin and bones with one pierced ear—badly infected. Its eyes were powder blue and I recognized it as a Russian Blue which, by the way, cost a bloody fortune. Who buys a Russian Blue, pierces its ear and then throws it away? Honestly, sometimes I hate people.

We wrapped it in a bar towel and left it at a local shelter. But after going unclaimed for two weeks, I adopted it, or her as it was discovered. I call her Bastet, after the Egyptian cat goddess with earrings. Pardon me while I show off my liberal arts education.

Tons more to tell, where do I start? NBBT is busy getting ready for our first full-length Nutcracker. The stress is unbelievable but the excitement is addictive. We have a double cast of children for the party scene and (wait for it) a growing Christmas tree for the battle scene. A monumental and expensive feat of engineering, but also the kind of spectacle that sells tickets.

A reporter from Dance Magazine came to do a feature story on us. Let me say that again: Dance Magazine. I felt like Linda Richman when Barbra Streisand walked on the set. "I can die now. That's all the time we have this week. I have to go die now."

The most exciting news? About a month ago, I went home for a few days. We're lounging around one night and the phone rings. And it's my father's son, Michel, calling out of the blue. Hi Dad.

My poor old man almost collapsed. He got so emotional, he handed the phone to ME. Like I'm helpful in this surreal situation. "Um...Hello. Nice to meet you...?"

I admire my mother so much. After five minutes of my shrill small talk, she, the freakin' ambassador, takes the phone and starts chatting away like it's her favorite nephew. "Come see us. Oh, absolutely, darling, we'd love to meet you in New York."

Meanwhile, Pop is crying and I'm staring like an idiot.

Michel is a chef and has come to the States on a year-long work visa, bringing his wife Anya and a three-year-old daughter, Dominique (Kiki). The first meeting in New York was Michel and Pop alone. Which they needed to be. Then Michel brought Anya and Kiki to Philadelphia for a weekend and they met my parents for dinner. It's going along cautiously but it feels really positive. Mamou invited them for Thanksgiving so I will get to meet him in a few weeks. I'm excited. And so happy for Pop that he's gotten this chance to resolve and rebuild a relationship with his son.

I'm kind of jealous, actually.

And on that cry-for-help note, I am off to rehearsal.

Take care and talk to you soon,
Daisy

CHILL OF THE REFRIGERATOR DOOR

"THIS IS YOUR BROTHER," Joe said, his voice gruff.

Daisy burst out laughing, as did Michel.

They had the same eyes.

"But you knew this," Joe said.

"No," Daisy said, as she and Michel pressed cheeks three times. "How would I know?"

"From his pictures in my study."

"They're in black and white. I honestly had no idea he had the eyes."

"The eyes," Michel said to his wife, Anya. "See? I'm not a changeling."

Anya raised her eyebrows and made a zipping motion across her lips. Behind her leg lurked Kiki. Green eyes like celery and blonde hair in two stubby pigtails atop her head.

"Come into the kitchen, darlings," Francine called. "Look at my present."

Anya, whose family hailed from Switzerland, had gifted a cuckoo clock to the Biancos. Francine was beside herself, making everyone hush at each quarter hour to see the little bird emerge.

"I love it," she said over and over. "It makes me so happy."

They lived in the kitchen for the next three days. Francine was in her element and with Michel co-piloting, each meal outdid the next. Joe sat at the long farmhouse table, alternating between sous-chef chores and watching his son with thoughtful, misty eyes. Anya was exhausted from her post-doc work and spent a lot of time napping, which left Kiki for Daisy to eat up with a spoon. In childish French, they played with old toys and games Daisy brought down from the attic. Daisy gave her a bath in the evenings and read stories—including all the verses from *Daisy, Daisy*. They cut paper snowflakes, gathered eggs and baked cookies.

"You sure she's not a bother?" Anya said, poking her head into Daisy's bedroom to say goodnight.

Daisy looked up from her book, then down at the sleeping child next to her. "We're good," she said smiling.

"Fantastic," Anya said. "I'm going to get laid."

"I've been laid in the carriage house many times," Daisy said. "You'll love it."

Francine never made turkey on Thanksgiving. Instead, dinner was a perfectly rare beef tenderloin with roasted vegetables and creamed spinach. Apple pie and homemade rum ice cream. They sat around and talked until the butter went soft and the candlewicks were fighting to stay alive in pools of liquid wax.

Michel and Daisy cleaned up the kitchen together while everyone else drifted off to their beds, talking easily as they crammed the dishwasher and packed up the leftovers.

She liked him. She was still feeling out their connection, deciding it was best, for the moment, to think of him as someone she'd like to know better. She imagined he was doing the same with Joe.

Michel told stories of his difficult stepfather and being forced to keep Joe at a secretive distance. Daisy rolled up the leg of her jeans and told him about Lancaster. Then, popping the lids onto Tupperware containers, she confided in him some of her worries about getting older. Not having anyone. Wishing she could give her mother a grandchild.

"So have a baby," Michel said, drying the last copper saucepan. "You always have the option. Maybe it's not conventional or exactly what

you envisioned. But even the best dreams have something askew."
He reached and hooked the loop of the handle onto the pot rack. He
looked at home.

"You're right," she said. The solution was simple, but only when
someone pointed it out. She could. If it came to that.

"You're only thirty-three, Dézi," Michel said, smiling. "Christ was
just getting his start at that age."

She laughed.

"Anya had Kiki when she was thirty-seven. She wants another. What
do Americans say—it ain't over 'til it's over?"

"Or until the fat lady sings."

"Forget it, I'm not saying that to Anya."

She looked at him a long time. At the eyes they both inherited from
Joe.

"I like you," she said.

He tossed the dishtowel at her. "As far as sisters go, you're not bad."

She took the compost tin and walked Michel back to the carriage
house. After saying goodnight she headed to the chicken coop, warmed
from the conversation. Almost regretting her plans to go home the
next day instead of staying to cut down the Christmas tree.

But sometimes it was better to leave the party when you were
having a good time.

She dumped out the tin of vegetable scraps in the chicken run
and made sure the doors of the coop were securely fastened. A fat
three-quarter moon shone, streaked with silver clouds. The air was
laced with wood smoke. Daisy stopped and looked around the land,
held still a moment and leaned into it.

Thank you, she thought. *I had a good time tonight.*

She showered, turned down her bed and plumped all the pillows
high. She was going to start her third trip through *The Golden Compass*
and decided a piece of pie would go well with the journey.

She went downstairs. Pattering through the living room, the phone
rang, startling the sleepy house. She ran for the kitchen extension,
seizing it up with a breathless "Hello?"

A man's voice. "Francine?"

"No, it's Daisy." She tucked the receiver in her shoulder and opened the fridge.

"Daisy?"

"Yes, it's Daisy, who is this?" She took out the pie and knocked a Tupperware container off the shelf just as the man spoke.

"Rick."

Annoyed, she tucked the phone tighter in her shoulder, picked up the Tupperware, crammed it back in. "Who?"

"Erik."

Her chest pulled backward through her shoulder blades. She stood in the chill of the refrigerator door, clutching a pie plate in one hand, the phone in the other, open-mouthed and stunned.

It's today? she thought.

"Hello?"

"Fish?" she said, her heart pounding.

"It's me."

It's you.

"Hi," she said. Touching the word the way she would touch a burn.

"Hi," he said. The word was a quick exhalation of sound but she heard the trembling in it.

She blinked, trying to shape a reply. "And holy shit."

She closed the refrigerator door and put the pie down. She felt dizzy. And more than a little sick.

"Yeah," he said. She heard him blow out his breath, a load of steeled courage within it. This wasn't a whim.

The walls and surroundings of the kitchen swam back into focus. Now she was confused. She was at her parents' house. Why was he calling her here?

"How did you know I was here?"

"I didn't. I was calling your mother to find you. It didn't occur to me you'd be there."

"I'm right here..."

I'm here.

And he came looking for me.

The cuckoo clock whirred and its doors popped open. The little red bird emerged for a single two-tone chirp then retreated.

It was nine-thirty on Thanksgiving night.

He came back...

A DIFFERENT US

DECEMBER 13, 2005

Dear Rita,

Erik called me on Thanksgiving.

I can hear you now. "And how did that feel?"

Frankly, I almost threw up. Because you think about someday and prepare mentally for someday. But someday is never today.

But he called. He called my mother's house, actually, looking to get my number from my parents. Not thinking I would pick up the phone myself. At least Fate was kind enough to throw us both off guard and level the playing field.

He sounded just as shaky and vulnerable as I felt, which was a surprise. I mean, all the ways I envisioned a conversation happening, I always had him somewhat distant. Definitely defensive. But that was with me calling him. He looked for me. So he was open. Bringing a lot of leftover hurt but wanting to be an adult about it. It was a conversation, not a confrontation. And though it wasn't blithely picking up where we left off as if no time had passed, it felt like the conversation was waiting for us. Two chairs set in front of a fire-

place, reserved for this moment. Come on, it's time. Sit down. It was only about five minutes of shaky chit-chat before we got right into it.

We talked about two hours. It was brutal. Holy shit, it was tough. I can't remember the last time I had that kind of adrenaline level. Probably in your office. Erik likened it to an exorcism. I don't disagree. I never doubted it would be a hard talk in terms of subject matter. Plus every ten seconds I was trying to grasp I was actually hearing his voice. Getting my mind wrapped around how he called me. Came looking for me. Wanting to talk.

I can't describe the relief. I keep thinking up words like cleansing and baptismal and rebirth. Makes it sound like a religious experience but...I guess it was. The ultimate confession. "What happened, Dais?" he asked and I told him the story. Let it unfold in its honest, bare-bones version and I told him, finally, how sorry I was. How it had never stopped mattering to me.

Part of me still can't believe it.

By the way, I'm insanely proud of getting through the entire exchange, including the crying, without a cigarette during or a Xanax afterward.

Erik asked if he could come see me and nothing I want more exists in this world. Nothing. We've been talking on the phone nearly every night these past two weeks. It's not easy. Actually, let me rephrase that. It's still easy to talk to him. We go at it until we're hoarse. One topic leads to five others. We finish each other's sentences and definitely still have a rapport. But the stories we have to tell hurt like hell. Like finding out he was married. They separated more than a year ago and I believe him when he says he didn't entertain the idea of reaching out to me until the divorce was final. But he was married. He met a woman and he loved her and married her. I had to swallow that and... God, you think you're prepared but you're never prepared. He was somebody's husband. It just twisted me inside-out and I cried hard. And he let me. He lets me and I let him and we mop up and keep talking.

Sometimes after I hang up with him, I think, "fuck everything, I'm his. I'm still his, who are we kidding? We'll pick up where we left off and it'll be fine." Other times I step carefully out of the conversation, almost not daring to want what I want. Trying to go as far as I can see, which is tomorrow. When he'll be here.

He'll be here tomorrow.

Rita, he's coming to see me. I couldn't tell you what's going to happen. But everything in the past couple weeks has been more than I dared wish for. And

The timer on the oven dinged. As she had been writing, the kitchen filled with a warm, spicy scent. Out of the oven, Daisy pulled two trays of cookies and anxiously inspected them. Their edges had browned nicely but the centers looked soft. They were supposed to be crisp.

She called her mother.

"They don't look crisp."

"They'll harden as they cool. Do you have them on a rack?"

"Yes."

"Leave them alone, then. Don't push on the centers for at least ten minutes."

"You're sure?"

"It's the exact same recipe for pepparkakor I used before. It comes right out of that Swedish holiday book, word for word. I promise, darling, they'll be perfect."

"All right, I trust you."

"How are you? Excited?"

"Yes."

"Terrified?"

Daisy laughed. "Slightly."

A pause, then Francine asked, "Happy?"

"Oh, Mamou. It's still not real to me."

"Darling, don't misunderstand me. But if it doesn't work out, call me right away. Or just come home. We'll be here."

"Mamou, if it doesn't work out, I'll be all right. I know I will."

"I know but..."

"It's already worked out, Ma. It's already more than I ever wished for. And I'm fine. I'm perfectly happy right now."

"I'm so glad, darling. Oh, there goes the timer on my cookies, I have to fly now."

They kissed their ends of the phone line and hung up.

A glass of wine in hand, Daisy looked around her kitchen. The garland of pine greens and white lights on her windowsill. Her paper snow-flakes dangling on invisible threads against the dark, frosty panes. The candles burning on countertops and the cookies cooling on the wire rack. Christmas music floating over like a light layer of powdered sugar, all the vintage old-school favorites from a CD her father burned for her.

Gingerly she touched the center of one of the pepparkakor. It was still soft. She broke it in half for a taste test. She'd attempted to put her own twist on the recipe by adding a little burnt sugar essence, and using white pepper instead of black. Closing her eyes as she carefully chewed, she was pleased by the combination of orange and spice, singed and sweet with just the right amount of heat. Perfect with the dry red wine, too.

Brushing off her fingers, she took her glass back to the table and returned to her letter writing. Bastet rubbed against her ankles, walking in figure eights. Daisy reached down to smooth the silver head as she looked up at the lights and decorations. Looked up at her home. Looked up at her life.

Right now, I'm just grateful, she wrote.

> *Grateful and happy with where I am and who I am. I can believe he will forgive me and even if he doesn't, I still forgive me. I'm still the girl he knew yet I'm different. He's different, too, but still familiar to me. Our journeys mirror in so many ways. I believe he truly regrets disappearing and leaving it unfinished for so long. And yet, I can also believe we're better*

people for it somehow. And if there is still an "us" to be found in all this, it will be a new us. A different us. Even a better us. And somehow that makes everything that came before necessary to get to this one moment.

And now you retire, right?

I'm sure I'll be writing again soon. Until then, have a wonderful holiday and be well.

Daisy

P.S. Thank you.

WHAT I THREW AWAY

HER CHEST WAS ON FIRE, throwing lightning bolts down her arms and legs. Threatening to throw her stomach up into the stratosphere.

Don't let me throw up, she thought. *Fainting is fine. Don't let me throw up...*

She stepped onto the white-lettered Bienvenue on the hotel doormat and the doors purred open. She slid her sunglasses off, looking around the busy lobby. The people meshed into a clump of humanity. She couldn't distinguish anyone. Maybe she wouldn't recognize him. Maybe he changed his mind. Maybe...

From the easy chair by the fireplace a figure unfolded and stood up.

"Oh God," she whispered around her breath.

It's you.

She pressed her lips tight as he came closer and pushed her hands deep in her pockets to hide their shaking. He was coming to her. Jeans and a blue V-neck sweater under his jacket. A plaid scarf hanging on either side. Hands in his pockets. His hair cut short and spiked every which-way. A little grey in his sideburns. His face pale and beautiful. His eyes wide and nervous. His smile not sure if it should stay or go.

He stood in front of her then, close enough to touch. She could feel him trembling.

"Welcome to Canada," she said.

"My new favorite place on Earth."

They both took their hands out of their pockets. Started. Stopped. Started again and moved into each other's arms.

His last touch was him bucking and throwing her off his back onto the floor. Tossing her away from him. Now his arms gathered her to his chest and held her close.

She took a breath. Took it in.

It's you.

THE FIRE HAD DIED DOWN to orange jewels. Weak, tired steam rose from the mugs of tea on the table between their chairs. The tin of pepparkakor was nearly empty. Lights twinkled from the garland on the mantle and Bastet made a continuous, purring thrum as she slept in a ball in Erik's lap.

He went through Daisy's two dance scrapbooks, looking at the pictures and reading articles and reviews.

"I can't believe I missed all this," he said. "I missed seeing you dance with Will in a real company. I missed your entire stage career. All these ballets, all the collaboration and all your success... I missed it."

Sighing, he put the scrapbooks aside and picked up the envelope of memories Daisy had also brought down.

"Oh, no," he said, laughter in his voice. "You have these?"

One at a time he went through each card, note and picture, letting them fall to a neat pile by the leg of his chair. Piece by piece, finishing with the empty wrapper of Swedish Fish, the love note and the condom wrapper. Then, empty-handed, he looked at the fire, his expression blank.

Watching him, Daisy peeled and ate clementines, throwing the orange scraps onto the fire as she went. She was quiet and still, letting him think.

"I left this behind," he said, gesturing to the pile on the floor. "All of this. I packed up my room that night and I was in an insane rage. I took everything of yours, of ours, and I chucked it."

"I know, I dug it out of the garbage," she said.

"Why?"

"I couldn't blame you for leaving it behind. But I fucked up so I had to pick up the pieces."

He stared at the undulating, scented flames, his hand making long strokes along Bastet's body.

"Thank you for saving what I threw away," he said.

"I threw it away," she said.

"You dug through the garbage to get it," he said. "You picked through the pockets of my clothes because it was in there and it meant something. You kicked aside dust and grease under the stove to look for it and find it and keep it. What did I do but bury it in the backyard and walk away?"

"Because I hurt you."

"And I punished you for more than a decade."

"And you're here now."

"Here I am," he said, running his hands over his face and back through his hair.

"What made you do it?" she asked. "Finally pick up the phone and call?"

He exhaled roughly. His finger reached up and started playing with the charms on his necklace. "It wasn't any one thing," he said. "But lots of little things building up. I think it started when I heard you speaking on the radio show. I knew you were talking about me, but you didn't say my name. Not once. It really bothered me. And I felt stupid about it bothering me because what the fuck—here's this chick I slammed the door on, how dare she not publicly acknowledge me as the number one asshole in her life. What, do I not mean anything anymore?"

Daisy covered her mouth, laughing around oranges.

"So that was in the back of my mind. Then the day we signed divorce papers, my ex-wife told me the entire last month she was living at home, I was calling your name out in my sleep."

"You were not."

"According to her, I was. And then my friend Miles... I told you about him, right?"

She nodded. "Friend, mentor, substitute father figure."

"Right. After my divorce, we were running in the park one day and I expressed surprise...not surprise but puzzlement that Melanie wanted to keep in touch with me as a friend. Miles said it was puzzling because I didn't have any experience with relationships ending in a healthy manner and by the way, I did to you what my father did to me."

Her mouth fell open and she stared.

He nodded back. "My head exploded. Even as I'm self-righteously sputtering 'what the fuck are you talking about,' I saw it all laid out before me. Black and white. His tree. My apple. Have a nice day."

He drank some of his tea and shifted around in his chair, trying not to disturb Bastet. "But really what clinched it was when I started thinking about my mom. Not as my mother, but as a woman. I'd never let myself do that before. I had this intense vision where I saw her sitting alone somewhere. In a room that was dark except for one lamp on a table, and under the lamp was a phone. She was looking at the phone. Staring at it. Willing it to ring. And the phone was never ringing."

Daisy blinked and swallowed hard as she gathered up orange peels and threw them on the fire.

"It made me feel sick," Erik said. "And I hated him. God, I *hated* him for doing that to her, leaving her so unfinished and unresolved. Then I went and did the same fucking thing to you. The exact same thing. Walked out and left you sitting alone and cut off with no answers. And for what? Pride? A point? As I'm sitting in the dark with my failed marriage and no more able to breathe without you than I was twelve years ago? Nice point.

"A couple weeks later I went down to Lancaster. Because it was time. And I ended up sitting in a bar having beers with Kees, and he looked me up and down and said it best: 'You're better than this.' He was right. I am better than this. I *have* to be better than this..."

He looked over at Daisy and began to raise his fingers. "So first your voice. Then Miles pointing out my genetic predisposition for being a prick. Kees seeing through my bullshit. And last, the undeniable fact that I don't stop thinking about you. I never stopped thinking about you. It was no more finished for me than it was for you."

Holding her eyes, he let his fingers fall in a loose fist. "And I'm sorry," he said softly. "I'm sorry I couldn't get past it. Couldn't find the stones to face it. To even just talk about it. Give you a chance a week later. Give you some closure a year later. I wasn't sorry then because I wasn't letting myself feel anything. But right now, looking back...I'm so sorry, Dais."

She couldn't answer him. She wasn't crying. Not actively sobbing. But the tears tracked down her face and she let them go unchecked. "I need a second," she said.

"Take as long as you want," he said. "God knows I did."

"This is just more than I ever hoped for," she said. "All these years, I only wanted to tell you I was sorry. I never really imagined you saying it to me. Or wanting to hear my side of it."

"I owe you a huge apology. And I want you to tell me what it was like for you. I need to know what those years were like. It doesn't have to be tonight. Whenever you're ready. Or whenever it comes to you. I just want you to know I'm going to listen this time."

"You wouldn't talk to me," she said, her throat swelling up hard and hot. "I did a terrible thing to you. I wasn't expecting you to want to speak to me for a while but the days turned into weeks. And weeks kept piling up. I couldn't understand. Couldn't...recognize you."

"I knew I was doing it," he said. "Even when I would ask myself, *what the fuck are you doing? Enough already.* It was just...I don't know. I couldn't pull out of the spin."

"Do you remember," she said. "The time I was gone all day. I had shut myself up in the library and didn't tell you where I was. And you found me and you were upset and I had the big epiphany that you needed to know where I was."

"I remember."

"I promised you. I told you I would never disappear. And when you were gone... It was so bewildering. Not knowing where you were made me feel I didn't know where I was. Like looking in the mirror and not seeing a reflection."

"I shut down," he said. "I warned myself if I kept it up, I was cutting off my chances for ever opening up again. But I kept doing it. Just pulling inside and slamming doors in my head and heart. Literally trying to erase it. Like I had no other options. And Jesus, I had so many other ways to deal with it. I wish I had a brilliant theory for why I didn't chose any of them. A reason for why I chose to walk out instead of fight. Something to make you feel better..."

She pulled her breath hard through her nose, held it suspended in her chest and let it soothe what it could. "We're here now," she said. "And it feels so much better."

"It feels," he said. "Everything feels to my bones. It's like I have no skin."

As if cued, she slumped in her chair, her head foggy and eyes aching. "I just hit the wall."

He looked away, sighing. "I'm thinking I should be a grownup and go back to the hotel."

She didn't trust herself to answer. It had been an anxious day. In twenty-minute increments she was flung between reckless surrender and prudent cautiousness. Overwhelmed with wanting to touch him, grab him hard and never let go. Circumspect with guarding her heart to avoid being shattered again. Now, nearing eleven-thirty at night, the tank was empty.

I can't take the temperature of this situation, she thought. *Let him go back. We should both sleep on it.*

She wanted to sleep with him.

"Do you trust I won't run away in the night?" he said, smiling.

She picked up her tea. "Maybe you should leave your wallet here or something."

"How about..." He reached behind his head as if to unclasp his necklace.

"No," she said, a little too sharply, even though she knew he was joking. "No, that stays on your neck."

He laughed, and then dug careful hands under Bastet and scooped her up. "Sorry, dude."

Basted yowled in her sleep, limbs and claws extending, then went limp as she was passed into Daisy's hands.

With the cat slung on her shoulder like a stole, Daisy walked Erik to the door.

"I had a good time tonight," she said. "Even with the nausea."

He smiled as he shrugged into his coat, pulled on gloves and his hat. "When will I see you tomorrow?"

"Whenever you want. Call me in the morning and we'll make plans."

Bastet gave another low yowl as they hugged. Erik kissed Daisy's face, seemed to hesitate a moment, then pressed his mouth between her eyebrows.

"I'm going to be a grownup," he whispered, his voice tight like a nail through the yearning space between their bodies. "But I don't want to."

"I know." She ran her free hand down the length of his arm, curled it around his gloved fingers. Squeezed once and forced herself to let go.

He felt his pockets, looking for his keys. Drew out two sets and regarded them a moment, then handed one over to her.

"My house keys," he said. "I'll pick them up in the morning."

"I trust you," she said, laughing.

"Then trust me and keep them."

He kissed her on the mouth, fast, then staggered out onto the porch, clutching his chest.

"Can you die of longing?" he cried to the night sky.

Daisy kept laughing from the door. "It's a chronic, wasting condition. No known cure."

The night was bitter, but she stayed in the doorway and waved until his car was out of sight, then turned off the light and locked up.

She took cups and plates to the sink. Banked the fire and closed the hearth doors, turned off lamps and Christmas lights. Heading upstairs, she paused by the bookcase where she displayed Joe's netsuke on a shelf.

Her netsuke now.

The day after Thansgiving, before she left La Tarasque for the airport, Joe had taken the carvings from their place in his study and put them into the bowl of her cupped hands.

"Dad, no," she said, even as a child's greedy delight splashed her heart.

"Yes," he said. "They're yours now. It's time."

"Why?" she said, her fingers curling around soft wood and ivory. "Why is it time?"

He put a hand on her cheek and kissed her brow. "Because your war is over, Dézi."

Now Daisy picked up one of the carvings, a little fish perched on its tail, the wood grain blending with the intricately carved scales and fins.

"And we come back from war changed," she said.

She kissed the little fish, put it on the shelf again. Then changed her mind and took it upstairs with her, to set on her bedside table.

COME BACK

"I WANTED TO SAY goodnight," she said.

Erik sighed. "Night, Dais."

Holding the phone carefully, she wiggled her shoulders further down under the covers. "Are you in bed?" she asked.

"I am. With the pillows up against my back so I can pretend they're you."

"Shut up."

"I do it all the time."

"Well, if it makes you feel better, I have your keys under my pillow."

"You do not."

She drew them out and jingled them against the phone so he could hear. Him going back to the hotel tonight was the right choice. The smart choice. And every atom in her body was throwing itself on the floor in protest, beating fists and toes and yelling. *Me. Want. Now.*

"Tired?" she asked, curling up against the receiver.

"I'm tired but I can't sleep. I'm not done talking to you."

"I don't think I'll ever be done now."

"Good. Because I want you to tell me everything." His voice slid around her like arms. She imagined him curled on his side, facing her. Her hand reached out, feeling his body beneath it. The hard rolling hills of his chest and shoulder. His face under her palm. A little beard growth rasping against her skin. His lower lip soft and trembling beneath her thumb.

I want to touch you.

"Can I ask you something?" he said.

"Ask me everything." She closed her hungry fingers around the dark. *I want to hold you again so bad...*

"Even if you hadn't been moving in with John, would you still have sent my stuff back?"

"I'm not sure," she said. "Living with him was the catalyst, of course. But also one of the biggest breakthroughs I reached in therapy was taking what I'd done to you, and how I felt about it, and allowing it to be important without letting it define everything I was. It would always matter to me. I would always love you, I would always be sorry for what happened. Up until then, those statements were always followed by a big *but*. My therapist showed me how to change the *but* to *and*."

"What do you mean?"

"I'm sorry," she said. "I will always be sorry, I will always regret what I did, I will always love you. *And* I am moving on now."

He drew in a slow, sharp breath. "And," he said.

"I changed one word and changed my life. *But* is a restriction. *But* is either-or. *And* means you can do both things at the same time. I can give back the physical things that belong to you *and* keep the things I feel about you."

"And," he said again. "That's huge."

A long moment passed, quiet except for them breathing.

"Feels like I'm staring in your eyes," Erik said. "It works over the phone, who knew?"

She put her forearm over her face, feeling her heart was breaking.

His breath formed a sigh in her ear. "I miss you."

"I miss you too."

"I can't wait to see you tomorrow."

She took her arm away and looked at the clock. Almost twelve-thirty. "It is tomorrow," she said, touching the fish netsuke.

"Happy birthday."

"Best present ever," she said. "Well. Second best."

Now the silence stretched, taut and trembling.

"I was never the same," he said. "Being your lover, it changed me. Or rather, I became me. Became myself."

"You said it was the best thing you ever did."

"It was. And leaving you was the worst thing I ever did. I changed again. Became someone I barely recognized."

She rubbed her wet eyes with a corner of the pillowcase. "I lost myself, too. For so many years."

"But I have to tell you, when you picked up the phone on Thanksgiving? I swear, within minutes, I started feeling it turn around. Like a compass. I could feel myself pointing in the right direction again. Something about you brings out the best in me. It always has."

An aching bit of time clutched at the electric air. Daisy closed her eyes, her soul rabid, howling at the moon, gripped in a desperation she thought might kill her.

"I'm so sorry about what happened," she said. "All I had to do was walk out. Stand up and walk out of David's house and everything would've been different."

"You were so broken. I don't know how I didn't see it."

"I didn't even see it."

"But when you screwed up, I couldn't see past it. If things weren't perfect, they were useless. And I bailed out because something in my soul equated the end of a love affair with desertion. If you think about it, honey, neither of us knew any better."

Her smile unfolded. "Been so long since I heard you call me honey," she said.

"Please don't beat yourself up anymore," he said. "We both screwed up. And I want to let go of it. I really do."

She clutched at it. "But I broke your heart."

"Didn't I break yours, too?"

"Yes," she said, relaxing her fingers, turning her palm up to receive whatever the night brought next.

"I never stopped loving you, Dais," he said. "I know my behavior said the complete opposite, but I see the truth now. And I've got to live it. I can't throw any more time away pretending I don't feel what I feel."

She swallowed hard. "Erik, come back."

"I'm right here."

"No, I mean come back."

His voice rose a little. "To your house? Right now?"

"Yes, now."

"You want me to?" And his voice cracked open.

"I want nothing more. Come back, please, I need you."

"Dais." She heard him pull in a long breath. "If I come back, then I'm staying." He was crying. His words shook through the phone. She gathered them up, clutching them tight to her chest.

"Erik," she said. "Come back. For twelve years, I've been talking to you out loud. Saying 'come back.' Calling out to you, reaching out to you. Begging you to come back. You can hear me now and I'm asking, please, come back"

"Oh my God," he said. "This is happening."

"Come back to me." She was crying now. "I swear I only let you leave tonight so I could ask you. Please come back. I can't breathe."

"I'll be right there."

A click and then empty silence in her ear. She swung her legs out of bed and stuffed feet into slippers. Her heart was pounding fast and thick and she cried out in punchy alarm as the phone rang again.

"I'm coming back," Erik said. "But I just wanted to say that was the last time I am *ever* hanging up on you."

A laughing sob poured out of her throat. "Hurry," she cried.

"I'm on the way." A clumsy pause. "Bye."

"Bye."

Her feet pattered down the stairs. She unlocked the door and turned on the porch light. Pulled the throw blanket around her shoulders and sat on the middle tread of the stairs to wait. Her heart pounded against her eardrums. Her mind reached feelers across the miles to track him. She had him in her sights. Pulling on his clothes and jacket, seizing his keys, running down to the car park and turning out onto the highway.

Coming to find her.

He had come like this once before. After she had breathed herself onto a bit of paper, laid bare her heart and asked him to be kind if he didn't feel the same.

But if you're thinking right now, "Me too," then please come find me.

"God, I can't breathe," she said. She closed her eyes and stretched her hands out, willing him along.

"Come back," she called to the headlight beams sweeping the road.

I never stopped loving you.

I can't throw any more time away pretending I don't feel what I feel...

"You're what I want," she said, curling up against her kneecaps. "You're everything I want, you're all I feel. Come back. I'm waiting for you. I'll wait for you..."

The clock ticked. The house settled. Daisy waited. A spray of gravel in her driveway followed by the slam of a car door. Footsteps crunching, then thumping up the stairs.

He didn't ring or knock, just came in, as if he were home. As he shut the door behind him she stood up, came down two steps and jumped the rest into his arms.

They both cried out as their hearts collided. He caught her like a partner, sure and strong, his embrace snapping shut. He heaved her up high on his chest and her hands slid to his face. She was in his arms, up in his mouth and his breath filling her lungs. A bright clean wind blowing the lost years away and bringing the life back into her. He was warm like lime. Cool like mint.

Her feet touched the floor, arms still around his neck. Her throat unleashing a single sob before she was kissing him once more, running her fingertips on his shaking lips.

"Dais," he said under her touch. "I don't believe it."

"You came back," she said over and over, between kisses, between their trembling limbs, under their eyelids and over their heads. "You came back. You came back to me."

"I'm here." His hands held her head, moving her around his kiss as he slid his kiss around the words. "God, I missed you so much. You have no idea."

"I do," she said. "Every day I wanted you. I never stopped thinking about it. Not one day."

He was shaking all over, his knees knocking hers. He pressed his forehead hard to her brow. "I don't ever want to miss you again."

"You won't," she said. "I know where you are now."

"You will always know where I am," he said. "I promise, Dais. No matter what happens from here, I'll never disappear like that again."

She held him tight, her wet cheek pressed up against his, crying all over his collar. "You came back."

"I want to stay," he said.

"I want us. The new us."

"A different us. And everything that goes with it." He kissed her. "I'm letting go of the past but I'm not going to pretend it never happened. Because it all belongs to us. The years together and the years apart. It's our story and I want it. I want all of it back."

"And me?"

"You." His fingers dug hard into her hair. Not pulling but holding her still. "I want you back."

They kissed again. She opened her mouth to him, filled herself. Felt him take back all the bits and pieces of himself she carefully collected and preserved and saved. Her arms went around his shoulders and she drew on the jacket of his simplest self. Felt it meld to her back and arms and still fit her perfectly.

"I have so much to tell you," he whispered against her face. "And not enough time."

"We have nothing but time now," she said. "Come lie down with me. Tell me everything. We'll talk forever."

As she led him up to her room, she sensed two wolves following, the dim light shining on their sugar-white ruffs. Golden eyes glowing wise and warm in the dark.

A pair of souls manifested.

And mated for life.

ACKNOWLEDGMENTS

IT SEEMS ODD TO THANK a fictional character, but I do thank Daisy for persuading me to tell her story.

Writing a second book was a vastly different experience, if for no other reason than I have triple the support network I did the first time around. I have met so many wonderful authors, bloggers, designers, promoters and readers in the past year and I treasure every one of these new friendships. As well as the cadre of Yodas who continue to have my back.

Ami Harju, who read it first, as usual, and as usual helped me find what was and wasn't a thing. #YMF.

Ellen Harger, who is always there when I need her and an irreplacable partner on the path of this insane thing called being an author. I'll see you in the steam bath, dear.

My street team, whom I prefer to think of as my Army, deserves to be called out by name, for they do more than just help me promote. They read everything I throw at them, and relentlessly point out the truth, always pushing me to be a better writer: Stacie, Tina, Krista, the Melissas, Heather, Francesca, Mireille, Caryn, James, Bianca, Kathy, Rosie, Linda, John, Felicia, Mary, Mike and Kylie. I cannot do this without you.

Becky Tsaros-Dickson, my editor, who ruthlessly trims, shapes, chisels and chops but *never* loses my voice. I don't know how you do it. Don't tell me. And don't stop.

Tracy Kopsachilis, my cover designer, my treasure, you always know what I want. Colleen Sheehan, formatting guru, for taking that sh*t out of my hands and making it beautiful.

The professionals who generously and patiently gave their expertise on the little details which make a book gritty and real: Dr. Jennifer Powell-Lunder, who helped me get Daisy admitted; Fran Curry, Broadway dresser extraordinaire, who described life on the road; and Michelle Joy of the Metropolitan Opera Ballet, who shared anecdotes and regularly sent pictures from backstage.

My parents, who continue to grow and evolve and inspire me. And show me it's never too late to reinvent yourself.

My children, who make me feel so important: Julie, my artist, who fights her battles bravely yet has the courage to be a mess. And AJ, my storyteller, who always looks back to wave at me.

And my husband, JP, who partners me seamlessly in this dance of life. I breathe easiest when I'm with you.

ABOUT THE AUTHOR

A FORMER PROFESSIONAL DANCER and teacher, Suanne Laqueur has gone from choreographing music to choreographing words. Her goal is to create a new kind of emotionally-intelligent romance that appeals to the passions of all readers, crossing gender, age and genre.

Laqueur's debut novel *The Man I Love* won a gold medal in the 2015 Readers' Favorite Book Awards and was named Best Debut in the Feathered Quill Book Awards. Her follow-up novel, *Give Me Your Answer True,* was also a gold medal winner at the 2016 RFBA.

Laqueur graduated from Alfred University with a double major in dance and theater. She taught at the Carol Bierman School of Ballet Arts in Croton-on-Hudson for ten years. An avid reader, cook and gardener, she started her blog EatsReadsThinks in 2010.

Suanne lives in Westchester County, New York with her husband and two children.

Visit her at suannelaqueurwrites.com

CPSIA information can be obtained
at www.ICGtesting.com
Printed in the USA
LVHW02s2046150518
577262LV00016B/1545/P